THE PURE LAND

ALAN SPENCE

ISIS
LARGE PRINT
Oxford

Copyright © Alan Spence, 2006

First published in Great Britain 2006
by
Canongate Books Ltd.

Published in Large Print 2007 by ISIS Publishing Ltd.,
7 Centremead, Osney Mead, Oxford OX2 0ES
by arrangement with
Canongate Books Ltd.

British Library Cataloguing in Publication Data
Spence, Alan
    The pure land. – Large print ed.
    1. Glover, Thomas Blake, 1838–1911 – Fiction
    2. Glover, Thomas Blake, 1838–1911 – Relations
    with women – Fiction
    3. Merchants – Scotland – Fiction
    4. Merchants – Japan – Fiction
    5. Japan – History – Meiji period, 1868–1912
    – Fiction
    6. Japan – History – 1912–1945 – Fiction
    7. Biographical fiction
    8. Large type books
    I. Title
    823.9'14[F]

ISBN 978–0–7531–7776–1 (hb)
ISBN 978–0–7531–7777–8 (pb)

Printed and bound in Great Britain by
T. J. International Ltd., Padstow, Cornwall

To Janani

CONTENTS

1. **The Gateless Gate**
   Nagasaki, 1945 1

2. **The Known World**
   Aberdeen, 1858 11

3. **Guraba-San**
   Nagasaki, 1859 40

4. **Silk and Tea**
   Nagasaki, 1859–60 64

5. **Alchemy**
   Nagasaki, 1860 94

6. **Ronin**
   Nagasaki – Edo, 1861...135

7. **Night Journey**
   Nagasaki, 1862...168

8. **Flower of Kagoshima**
   Nagasaki – Kagoshima, 1863...191

9. **Burning Bright**
   Nagasaki, 1864...230

10. **Brig o' Balgownie**
   Aberdeen, 1865–66 285

11. **Daimyo**
    Nagasaki, 1867–68.................................312

12. **Meiji**
    Nagasaki – Edo, 1868–69 348

13. **Maki**
    Nagasaki, 1869–70................................377

14. **Hot Ginger and Dynamite**
    Tokyo, 1911.....................................419

15. **Form is Emptiness**
    Nagasaki, 1945..................................450

16. **One Fine Day**
    Nagasaki, 2005..................................454

17. **The Pure Land**
    Nagasaki, 1912..................................460

    Acknowledgements 487

CHAPTER
ONE

The Gateless Gate

Nagasaki, 1945

If Tomisaburo hadn't seen for himself, he would not have believed. This was the terrible end of everything; annihilation, nothingness. One single blast had laid waste half the city, destroyed it in an instant, reduced it to rubble and dust. His house was on *Minami Yamate*, the southern hillside, overlooking the bay. It was far from the epicentre, lay sheltered in the lee of the hill. That simple fact had saved it from destruction.

He'd been seated at his desk, looking out at the pine tree in the garden, the tree that had given the house its name, *Ipponmatsu*, Lone Pine. The tree pre-dated the house, had been there before his father chose the site, laid the foundations. The first western house on the hill, stone built. If it had been made of wood and paper, would it have burned to ashes in that searing wind?

He'd been looking at the pine tree, that was all, trying to empty his mind. Not think. Or think of nothing. *Mu*. The pine tree in the garden. The week before, he had opened the Diamond Sutra, turned the pages, looking for meaning. *Awaken the mind without fixing it anywhere*. The poet Basho had written, *Learn of the pine from the pine*. Learn how to pine. Everything these days was a meditation on transience, impermanence. He was an old man. It had been cruel of the *kenpeitai*, the not so secret police, to interrogate him. Because of his background they'd thought he was a spy. This was his fate, his *karma*, to be caught between two worlds. Neither one thing nor another. Neither fish nor fowl. Now the Americans were coming. They had wrought this horror. There was no hope.

The flash had lit the sky, white light, momentarily brighter than noon. He'd closed his eyes, an afterimage of the pine tree burned on his retina. Then the noise had filled the heavens, huge and thunderous, so loud it hurt. He'd covered his ears as the whole house shook and every window shattered and the hot dry wind rushed in, ripped through everything.

Not thinking, a man in a dream of himself, he'd stood up, shaken shards and particles of glass from his clothes. Not thinking, he'd brushed his sleeve with his hand, felt the sting as the blood welled up in each tiny cut on his fingers, his open palm. Not thinking, he'd stumbled outside, tried to take in the enormity of what had happened. It had suddenly grown dark, like a winter afternoon, but the wind that blew was still warm. Smoke from a burning building cleared and he looked towards the city, but it was gone. Everything to the north was obliterated, every landmark razed. Nothing vertical still stood, except here and there a factory chimney, the skeleton frame of a warehouse.

Everywhere small fires burned and flared, adding their smoke to the grey pall overhead.

Not thinking, a man in a dream, he walked towards the devastation, one foot after another, laboured and slow, over uneven ground, scattered detritus. His teeth ached, and his back, and his knee joints. Some of the particles of glass had landed in his thin hair, cut his scalp. But all of this might just as well be happening to somebody else, was as nothing compared to what he saw around and before him. This was beyond imagining. It could not be. But it was.

A Shinto temple had disappeared but its red wooden *torii* gate stood miraculously intact. A gate to nowhere. He walked through.

Awaken the mind without fixing it anywhere. He looked out at everything, numbed.

A horse crushed under the cart it had been pulling.

Two young men on their knees, dead where they had fallen, their legs tangled in electrical wires.

Three charred corpses, seated on an iron bench where a bus stop had been.

The post office, gone. A shop that sold incense, gone. The pleasure quarter, gone. His favourite teahouse, gone.

The further he went, the worse it became.

Bodies and bits of bodies strewn on the road, trapped in burned-out cars, floating in the harbour, the water a murky rust-red.

A man's shadow, burned on a white wall; the man gone, incinerated in an instant. A young mother, alive, with a baby to her breast; her face and arms, the baby's

3

head, all burned; only the breast unmarked, white. The desperate need to hold on, to go on living, even in hell.

People crawling over wreckage, scorched and blinded, their clothes in shreds, crying crying for water, and as if to mock them, a grimy rain starting to drizzle down.

A statue, in the middle of an open space. No, not a statue, the body of a monk, burned black, seated in meditation, accepting this too, this too, even to the last. Awaken the mind.

Tomisaburo's own mind was empty, his heart dead. Perhaps he himself had been killed in the blast, was now a disembodied spirit, doomed to wander this place of the dead, the realm of the *gaki*, the hungry ghosts. He tried to remember a prayer, but the words wouldn't come.

Then he realised his own face was burned, and stinging from a trickle of tears. He watched, detached, a few of the drops fall, make tiny grey beads in the dust at his feet. He turned and started the wretched trek back.

All this was how long ago? Days that felt like years. With the windows blown in, the house lay open. He had swept up the broken glass, gathered up the books and papers scattered on the floor. More than that was beyond him.

There was nowhere to buy food, no food to be bought. He survived, day to day, on a handful of cooked rice, a few pickles. It was enough. He had little appetite. He allowed himself an occasional sip of

Scotch whisky from the last bottle he'd kept aside, for use in case of emergency. In case of emergency! The irony of that was galling.

It was hard to get reliable news about the situation. Reception on his radio was almost non-existent, drowned out by crackling static. Neighbours would pass by his gate, respond tersely to his questions. He was half-western; that made him partly to blame. Hadn't the kenpeitai taken him in for questioning?

No smoke without fire.

In any case, the news had been unreliable for so long. All they'd been fed was propaganda and rumour. Now it was worse. The Nagasaki bomb had followed the one on Hiroshima. Now there would be more.

The Americans would bomb Kyoto, then Tokyo, unless the Emperor surrendered. And that was impossible, for the Emperor was infallible, divine. The nation was prepared for a speech from the Imperial Palace, calling for The Honourable Death of The Hundred Million, mass suicide. It was magnificently insane. He felt tears well up again, blurring his vision. The pine tree wavered. The scorching wind, the toxic rain, had shrivelled it, stripped it bare. It stood stark against the grey of the sky. He had gone out one more time, headed towards the city, but once again had turned back, hopeless. Thousands had been taken, or had dragged themselves, to *Michino-o* station, to the makeshift medical centre. Only a few hundred had been treated and had any hope of survival. The rest had died, would die.

I would never have believed death had undone so many.

He had read that long ago, in another life. Dante's *Inferno.*

So many.

He turned again to his copy of the Diamond Sutra, seeking guidance, light in the darkness, trying to understand. The verse read, *Shiki soku ze ku.*

Form is Emptiness.

The signal wasn't clear, but there must have been a surge in the power supply, just enough for the message to come through. The Emperor himself was addressing the nation, his voice formal and frail. Surrender was total and unconditional. He was no longer to be regarded as a god but remained the symbol of the state and of the unity of the people. He would no longer command political power. Henceforth government was to be by an elected House of Representatives. The armed forces, and the people as a whole, were to lay down their arms. Japan herewith renounced war and the maintenance of military forces forever.

The announcement was followed by a sombre recording of the national anthem, then the airwaves fell silent. Tomisaburo slumped to his knees, his face in his hands, stayed like that a long time.

Eventually he hauled himself up, sat in front of his desk. He felt sick in his stomach, his joints creaked, his bones ached. But his mind was clear. Sooner or later they would come for him. It might be the kenpeitai, intent on retribution; or it could be the Americans, to make him collaborate, help them take over. It mattered little.

Civilisation was at an end. The barbarians were at the gate.

On the desk in front of him he had laid a short *wakizashi* samurai sword in its sheath, something his father had treasured. In the desk drawer was his father's revolver, loaded.

He had shaken the broken glass from the framed portraits of his father, his dear wife Waka. He was glad she had not lived to see this. He had placed the portraits on the desk, facing him, his father's gaze stern, Waka's gentle and sad. Already it was more than two years since she'd died, seemed like no time, though the days without her were slow to pass. How could that be? Life was short, the days long.

Beside the portraits were a few small things he'd kept since he was a child, things his father had given him for good luck; a bamboo token that had once been used as currency, a Mexican silver dollar, an *origami* butterfly of folded white paper. His father had achieved so much, had kept these little things to remind him how it had begun, had passed them on as mementos.

Tomisaburo's desk had a roll-top compartment, locked with a tiny brass key. He opened it and took out a package, wrapped in cloth. Carefully he unwrapped it, held in his hands the book that was his own life's work, twenty years in the making, an illustrated guide to Nagasaki's marine life. He had commissioned local artists to paint every species of fish and whale and shell in minute and intricate detail. At first the artists hadn't understood. They were Japanese, trained in depicting the *movement* of fish or bird, capturing some essence, the quick flick of life, in a few strokes of the brush. Painstakingly he had explained, had shown them drawings from America, anatomically exact, right to the number of scales on each fish. And finally they had produced the paintings, more than 800 in all, meticulously accurate but vibrant and alive. The book was a thing of precision and beauty. Not much to set beside his father's achievements, but he'd thought it important in its way.

As he turned the pages, felt the handmade paper, he realised he had never been happier than when he was working on this, inscribing each title in his own careful calligraphy. He peered at the illustrations till the light in the window started to fade. Then he closed the book, wrapped it again and locked it away, put the brass key in his waistcoat pocket.

He opened the drawer, took out the pistol, felt the weight of it in his hand, put it down again. He picked up the sword, started to ease it from its sheath, tensed as he heard a noise outside, the crunch of broken glass underfoot, heavy footsteps on the path to his door.

The two GIs picked their way through the ruined garden, the wreckage and debris, their guns at the ready. They'd been told they couldn't be too careful, they might still meet pockets of resistance, buildings might be booby-trapped. But it wasn't possible to move quietly, scuffing through rubble, the scatter of broken glass, shattered roof-tiles.

The house didn't seem too badly damaged. A decent size, solid built. Good location overlooking the bay. They might commandeer it as a base. There was no sound from inside. The occupants might have fled, or they might have been in the wrong place when the bomb fell, been obliterated. That would make things easier.

The sergeant motioned to the corporal to try the door. It was closed, didn't give. They could go in through one of the gaping windows, but why bother? On a count of one-two-three they booted in the door, smashed the lock and splintered the wood, kicked it open and stepped inside, guns raised.

Tomisaburo turned from his desk to face them.

"Take it easy, old fella," said the corporal. "Don't piss your pants!"

"And put down the bowie knife!" said the sergeant.

Tomisaburo sheathed the sword, placed it back on the desk. Then he bowed to the two men, spoke to them in his clipped, cultivated accent.

"Good evening, gentlemen. I apologise for not being able to offer you hospitality."

"Jeez!" said the corporal. "Where'd you learn to talk like that?"

"My father," said Tomisaburo, nodding towards the framed portrait.

"No kidding! You're a halfbreed?"

Tomisaburo flinched, nodded. "My father was Scottish."

The sergeant lowered his gun, picked up the portrait. "Handsome looking man," he said.

9

"Indeed," said Tomisaburo. "And that was taken when he was very old. As old as I am now."

His father in the portrait looked powerful and impressive. His white hair and whiskers were well groomed. He was formally dressed with a white tie and wing collar, a medal pinned to the chest of his black frock coat.

"Must have been somebody," said the sergeant.

"Yes," said Tomisaburo. "He was."

He indicated another photograph on the mantelpiece. "That was taken when he was young, perhaps nineteen or twenty."

The picture was tinted, sepia fading out at the edges. The background was indeterminate, a low building, the sea. The figure was full-length, the young man posing, cocky, hands on hips, seaman's cap jaunty on his head as he stared out so sure of himself at another world, another time, almost a century ago.

CHAPTER
TWO

The Known World

Aberdeen, 1858

The grey permeated everything. Even on a summer day, like this, the cold haar off the North Sea closed in, damped everything down. Glover stood, braced, on the sea wall, stared hard into the mist — no sea no sky just gradations of grey. He minded the old minister's voice, ranting in the dark kirk. *And the earth was without form and void.* That was the way of it right enough. The haar soaked into him like fine rain, made the nap of his jacket damp to the touch. Drops of moisture gathered on his hair, on his eyelashes. He blinked, his sight momentarily blurred. He rubbed his face with his hands, licked his lips, tasted salt. A ship's horn moaned low, close. Invisible seagulls called and called. There were worlds out there. The church bell started to clang the four quarters before striking the hour.

"Christ!"

He jumped down off the wall, skidded on the wet cobbles.

"Shite!"

But he kept his balance and righted himself, ran as hard as he could past the docks and up the road, wheeled at the corner of Marischal Street on the second stroke, almost crashed into two young women, on their way to work gutting fish down at Footdee. Fittie. Their faces and arms were red. Warm flush of blood. They smelled of the fish, of their work. But he felt himself respond as they flashed quick smiles at him, flirted. They laughed as he made to raise his hat to them though he wasn't wearing one.

On the fourth stroke his path was blocked by two scrawny wee boys, schoolbooks dropped at their feet, hacking at each other with sticks for swords, a fight to the death.

"Ha!"

They put up their swords, startled, as he cut between them, mimed stabbing the pair of them with hardly a break in his stride.

On the seventh stroke of the bell he bounded up the worn stone steps to the door of the office. *James George. Shipbroker.* He got to his desk on the stroke of eight, bringing the outside in with him, a rush. The office clock, half a beat behind, finished chiming the hour as he sat down at his desk.

Robertson, the other junior clerk, looked up from his papers.

"Cutting it fine, Tom."

"Timed it to the second!" said Glover.

He caught his breath, stretched, clasped his hands behind his head.

"Call this a summer?" he said, peering out the high window into the grey.

Robertson followed his gaze.

"Call it Aberdeen!"

Glover cracked his knuckles, dipped the nib of his pen in the inkwell, settled to work through the pile of papers on his desk.

By mid-morning the sun had started to burn off the haar. He stood up from his work and crossed to the window, looked out. Great granite buildings took shape, crenellated bulk rising out of the mist.

This city. Its solidity.

In the other direction, down the street, he could see the masts of the ships at anchor, gulls circling overhead.

"Have you dealt with those bills of lading, Mister Glover?"

He hadn't heard old George come in to the room. The voice was quiet, dry. Rustle of parchment.

Glover turned.

"Aye, sir. They're on my desk."

"Well, Mister Glover. I would appreciate it if they were on *my* desk."

George swished out the door again. Glover picked up the documents, caught Robertson's eye and mimicked the old man's soor prune face to perfection.

The air of the pub was a yellowing haze, a sepia fug, nicotine tinted, thick with the reek of tobacco.

Glover shouldered his way from the bar, through the hard drinkers crowded into the smoky den, made it back to his table holding steady the two mugs of beer.

13

Robertson shouted to him above the noise.

"I'd appreciate it if that pint was on *my* table, Mister Glover!"

"It'll be over your fucking head in a minute, *Mister* Robertson!"

He set down the mugs, licked the spillage from his fingers, shoved his way along the bench.

"Your health!" Robertson took a sip.

"Aye." Glover swigged, wiped the froth from his mouth with the back of his hand.

"Dour old bugger," said Robertson. "Old George, I mean."

"Tornfaced," said Glover. "And prim. Mouth on him like a cat's arse."

Robertson spluttered and sprayed, almost choked on his pint. When he'd recovered, he said, "Makes you wonder how he could have fathered a divine creature like young Annie."

"I would imagine," said Glover, "in the usual way. Mind you, there are some things I would rather *not* imagine!"

He swilled down more of his beer, for the first time all week began to relax, unclench.

"Thank God for Saturday night, man."

"You think it's God's work?"

"Isn't it all?" said Glover. "Six days shalt thou labour, and on the Saturday night thou shalt be half seas over."

"Amen to that!"

By the fourth pint, Glover could feel the surge of it through him, euphoric. It was glorious, bathed

14

everything in a warm benign glow. Yes. Aye. Life was good. He threw back his head and laughed a great roar of a laugh.

"What?" said Robertson.

"Nothing," said Glover. "Everything!"

When Robertson had taken a drink or two, he liked to quote Burns. Tonight it was Tam o' Shanter.

"*We sit boozing at the nappy, getting fou and unco happy.*"

The place sweated and stank, dripped condensation from the low ceiling. It swayed and heaved, ship in a heavy swell. At closing time it pitched them out into the street. They surfaced, gulped in air. The cool was a sudden rush, delicious shock of exhilaration.

"Yes!"

The sky was cobalt, the nearest it would get to full dark. Simmerdim. The light nights.

They fell in with a few others they knew, young clerks like themselves. Now they made a company, and they roistered and swaggered, their boots clattering on the cobblestones down a dark lane by the docks.

Glover stopped. He had an important announcement to make. He articulated his words with great care.

"I need," he said. "To pish."

He heard himself and laughed at the pompous sonority of it. The others moved ahead and he unbuttoned himself, released a steaming stream against a dank wall. The relief was exquisite. Yes.

He turned, shaking off the drips, and caught his breath as he realised someone was watching him.

She had stepped out of the shadows, stood half-lit in the faint erratic flicker of the gaslight, its mantle damaged, the light an eerie sputtering flare. Her red hair was piled up on top of her head, but tousled, coming undone, and her blouse was part unfastened, pulled back, her throat and shoulders bare. She leered at him, the only word for it, part mockery part invitation. He felt exposed and vulnerable, open to her gaze, a wee boy pale and naked. But she kept looking at him, that way, and her look made him hard, a man. It was all right to feel like this, it was fine, no shame in it at all.

The woman stood with her hands on her hips, tossed back her head.

"Looking for business, big fella?"

But before he could reply, another figure came out of the dark behind her, a gaunt, hardfaced man who put his thin arms round the woman's waist, pulled her to him, nuzzled her neck and whispered something in her ear.

She let out a harsh screech of a laugh. The man glared at Glover, the look pure spite, dismissal. He spat.

The woman threw Glover a look of regret that said Maybe another time. They faded back into the darkness, left him yearning and foolish and limp.

"For God's sake, man!" a voice shouted. "Put that away! You'll catch your death!"

Robertson had come back to see what was keeping him.

"Consorting with the ladies of the night, Tom?"

"Not quite consorting," said Glover. "A mere flirtation. A dalliance." He buttoned himself up again. "She did give me the eye, though."

"Dog!" said Robertson.

They hurried to catch up with the others. The night was full of possibilities and demons.

Robertson chanted. "*The night drave on wi sangs and clatter!*"

Now they were scuffing along King Street, bawling out music-hall songs. Now they were stumbling along the beach, laughing as they sank in the sand, feet splayed at every step. Now they were passing St Machar's Cathedral, its twin squat steeples like granite minarets, silhouetted against the deeper dark of the sky. And in spite of themselves they shooshed and hushed each other, affected sobriety, walked upright and respectful past the graveyard, the dead in their long sleep. Now they had reached Brig o' Balgownie, the old stone bridge over the Don, and Glover was climbing up on the parapet for no good reason other than the sheer doing of it, because he could. And he made his way, step by slow step, on and up to the crest, arms out for balance, the river slithering fifteen feet below. He'd done this as a boy, heedless, padded quick and barefoot along the wall, dived off head-first to splash down into the chill waters. He felt some of that fearlessness now, but had to move steady, tightrope walker in a circus, feet in his muckle boots feeling for purchase. Robertson was full of himself, shouted out, "*And win the key-stane of the brig!*"

17

One more step and Glover was there, stretched his arms out wide. "Yes!"

One of the others threw him up a bottle of ale and he caught it, slugged it down. Then he jumped back down onto the cobbled pathway of the bridge, bowed as they cheered and clapped. Robertson joined in, then drew himself up, rolled his shoulders.

"I could do that. Easy." The drink talking.

The others howled, started a rhythmic handclap.

"Yes! Yes! Yes! Yes! . . ."

He heaved himself onto the wall, arms shaky, not as easy as it looked, stood carefully up and swayed there till he found some centre of balance. For a moment he didn't dare move, for fear of falling.

Then he lurched forward . . .

"Yes!"

one step, then stood there rigid, hunched over, wanting to crouch down and kneel, inch forward like that, but no, he would swing the other foot, take one more step . . .

"Yes!"

Arms flung back he almost toppled . . .

"Yes!"

edged inch by inch, rigid and sweating, then rushed it three-steps-in-a-row and made it to the top, stood unsteady but triumphant.

"Yes!"

Glover handed him the bottle and he raised it to his lips, suddenly flailed his arms, gaped one frozen startled moment, keeled over backwards and was gone.

"YES!"

Then the reality of it hit them and they lurched to the parapet, peered down at the river. Only Glover was alert, quickwitted, scrambled down the bank and under the bridge to where Robertson had bobbed downstream, thrashing. Glover waded in, grabbed him by the scruff and hauled him to the side where he lay coughing, grabbing breath. He managed to stand up, soaked through and shivering, water squelching in his boots.

Glover laughed. "Better get you home, Mister Robertson, or *you'll* catch your death!"

Sunday morning in the grim grey kirk, Glover sat upright on the hard wooden pew. His neck felt clamped, but he knew if he moved too abruptly he would set the blood thudding in his head. He turned slowly and carefully, squinted along the row. His sister Martha darted a wee glance at him, half smiled. His mother shifted her bulk in the unforgiving seat, nudged his father whose head kept nodding forward, jerking back.

Christ!

He remembered rolling home at God-knows-what time, wet clothes dripping, telling Martha he'd been swimming, and could swim like a fish, and she'd said Aye, and drink like one. She'd brought him a dry towel and a mug of hot tea. He realised now she had probably stayed up waiting for him, and the thought moved him unexpectedly, the goodness of it, the simple loving kindness. His mother and father had been tightlipped at breakfast.

The minister, old Naysmith, was a long thin streak of misery, his voice a grinding whine, insistent and numbing.

The very air felt oppressive, felt stale, cold with the dankness of old stone. He looked round the congregation, saw them as a gallery of grotesques: hard gargoyle faces carved from granite, features exaggerated like caricatures — gaunt thrawn men, hewn and weathered, women grown too quickly old, their pale skin scoured, hands and arms red-raw, gormless loons, gawky and glaikit, expressions that registered nothing.

Glover felt something akin to panic. He saw their sheer physicality in minute unsettling detail: white sidewhiskers growing on florid cheeks, a great wet mouth, skewed broken teeth, tufts of hair sprouting from ears, from the mole on the end of a hook nose, wee ferret eyes, a slaver of spittle dribbled down a chin.

The minister's voice droned on. *Now let us pray.* Glover closed his eyes. Dear God, please let there be more to life than this. As a child he'd been scared to open his eyes during prayers, feared God would be watching, would strike him down dead. Now he eased them open, looked round. Across the aisle he saw Robertson, face grey, eyes clenched shut. He was shivering, barked out a cough. Glover wanted to laugh but stifled it. In the row behind Robertson sat young Annie George with her father. He willed her to open her eyes and look at him, sweet seventeen, Dear God, tight blonde curls under her bonnet, framing her face, just open her eyes and look, that was all, and she did. She did. She looked right at him, and her mouth opened in a little O of perfect astonishment, matching his own amazement at the moment. The Lord be praised. A quick shy smile then she turned away, closed her eyes again, a slight flush rising to her face.

Glover turned and found himself grinning at the minister, brows gathered in righteous implacable wrath. *Lead us not into temptation, but deliver us from evil.* Glover bent his head, but his heart was light. He had been vouchsafed a vision of saving grace.

Outside, Annie lagged a little way behind her father, left a gap. Glover caught up.

"Tonight at seven?" he said, quiet. "Brig o' Balgownie?"

She blushed, flustered. "I'll try and get away."

Her father, a few yards ahead, stopped and turned.

"Annie! Come on, lass!"

She glanced back over her shoulder, smiled again. Her father met Glover's eye, gave a curt nod that contrived to be a greeting and a warning, both at once. Glover nodded back. Understood. Then he saw Robertson, leaning against a gravestone, and he couldn't help it, he laughed out loud.

"You look like death warmed up!"

The minister had just come out into the churchyard, fixed him again with that hard admonishing gaze.

"Remember the Sabbath Day, Mister Glover, to keep it holy."

"Oh aye, sir," he said. "I will that."

The moment would stay with him — young Annie on a summer's night, simply herself, her elbows leaning on the parapet of the bridge, up on tiptoe as she stared, intent, at something downstream. It looked for all the world like a painting. *Young girl at evening, Brig o' Balgownie.* She wore a simple white dress and the sun touched her fair hair.

She hadn't seen him, was unselfconscious, lost in whatever she saw. Then she must have sensed him, heard his footstep on the cobbles, and she turned to him, eyes wide, shooshed him with a finger to her lips. He moved to her side and she pointed down at the river, showed him what she was watching — a heron standing, angular, on a rock midstream, poised and absolutely still.

"Isn't it bonnie?" she said.

"It is that," he said, touching her arm.

The bird unfurled, spread its grey wings and took off, settled further away at the water's edge.

"I don't have long," said Annie. "I said I was just away out for a walk. He gave me one of his looks."

Glover nodded. "The kind he gives me every morning!"

He furrowed his forehead, put on her father's disapproving glower. She laughed, said it was just like the thing. He took her face in his hands and kissed her, tasted her soft warm mouth, the sweetness sheer intoxication. They walked arm in arm down from the bridge and along by the river. The heron flew on again, kept its distance, stayed always just ahead.

Monday morning, the stroke of eight, cutting it fine again, or timing it to perfection, he flung open the outside door, rushed in, nodded briskly at Robertson, headed straight for his desk. But before he could sit down, the door to the inner office opened and George stood there, the look on his face grimmer than ever.

"Mister Glover. A moment, please." He disappeared back inside, left the door open. A summons.

Robertson raised his eyebrows, mimed cutting his throat.

Glover shrugged, affected a casualness, a bravado he didn't feel. "Sounds serious!"

He entered the room, closed the heavy door behind him. George stood with his back to him, framed in the window, looking out at the harbour, at the cargo ships and fishing boats, the hulks under construction in the Hall Russell yard.

"Sit down," said George, turning to face him.

The room smelled of wax polish and tobacco, George's pipesmoke gone stale, and behind that the mustiness of old ledgers, dusty paper. Glover felt his throat dry, a sudden anxiety clenching at his innards. There couldn't be a problem with the job — he worked hard, got on fine with the other clerks. He feared then it might be about Annie.

George's face was stone, gave nothing away. On the desk in front of him was a long buff-coloured envelope. He pushed it towards Glover.

"This is addressed to you. It's from Jardine Mathieson."

Glover took in air, a quick sharp gasp. He observed himself maintaining formality, reaching forward to pick up the envelope. He read his name, the address of the

23

firm, written in fluid clerical script, the letters even, the lines perfectly spaced. He stared at it, astonished to see the envelope shake in his hand to the thud of his heartbeat, the pulse of the blood in his veins.

"You'll have been expecting this," said George.

"Aye, sir." He turned the envelope over, read the firm's name on the back.

Jardine, Mathieson & Co.

"I just didn't . . ."

The interview had been months ago, in Edinburgh. He thought he'd done well enough, just hadn't dared hope.

"For what it's worth," said George, "you received a good reference from here."

"Aye, sir. Thank you."

He heard his voice, strange to him. A character in a play. The moment felt ponderous, imbued with a gravity, serious and real. But at the same time he felt distanced from it, watching. The clock ticked on the mantelpiece. Outside, a horsedrawn cart clattered by. A boy shouted and laughed. The seagulls cried. Life went on, living itself.

"Well?" said George, impatient.

"Sir?"

"For God's sake, man! Are you going to open it?"

"Right." He gathered himself. "Aye."

George reached across, offering him a bonehandled paperknife, but he'd already worked his thumb under the flap, ripped the envelope open.

The letter was on headed notepaper, gave the address of their head office in Hong Kong. *Dear Mister*

Glover. He raced ahead. The tone was clipped and fastidious, businesslike, precise. *Further to your interview, we have pleasure in offering you a position.*

"Dear God."

"What?" said George.

"They've offered me the job, sir. In Japan!"

George's mouth twitched in approximation of a smile, then righted itself again.

"You'll have a great deal to think about."

"Aye," said Glover. But this place, this time, were receding. He was already moving on.

"Japan!" said Robertson.

Glover waved the letter. "I told you I'd applied for a posting."

"But Japan! It's the ends of the earth!"

"Folk say that about Aberdeen!"

"I know, but . . ."

"Off the map! Ultima bloody Thule!"

"But *Japan!* I mean, the folk aren't like us. They're barbarians. Lop off your head as quick as look at you."

"There's folk here could turn you to stone wi a look!"

Robertson laughed. "Christ, don't I know it! But you know what I'm saying, Tom."

"I know fine."

Pinned to the main office wall was a faded map of the world, with shipping routes marked on it. Glover took in India and China, and at the furthest edge, Japan.

"Are ye no feared?" said Robertson.

Glover still looked at the map, felt a moment the vastness, the distance.

"Here be dragons!" he said, then turned to look at Robertson, said more quietly, "Of course I'm feared. But that's no reason not to go."

"Sounds a good enough reason to me!" said Robertson.

"If I stay here," said Glover, "my life's mapped out. Maybe in a few years, if I work really hard, I'll get George's job, be running the office, end up as dry and dusty as himself. Christ, man, I want more!"

Robertson nodded, but there was something in his eyes, something unspoken.

"What about Annie?" he said at last, and Glover felt it in his guts.

Annie.

His mother had to sit down when he told them about the letter. She tugged the hanky from the cuff of her blouse, dabbed her face with it, wafted the familiar scent of lavender.

"Japan?" she said, staring at him, unable to make sense, the word strange in her mouth, like a bad taste.

Martha put a hand on her arm, said nothing.

"It's a bit far, is it no?" said his father, then he took the letter, snapped the paper taut, perused it at arm's length so he could focus. When he'd read it through, and through again, he cleared his throat, preparatory, intoned with Presbyterian gravitas, "Jardine Mathieson."

He gave the names weight, due deference, like books of the Old Testament.

"They're likely the biggest company in the world," said Glover.

His father nodded. "They'd be paying you good money."

This was what mattered. Hard currency of the workplace. Prospects. Advancement. A job for life. His father had come as far as he could, worked his way up to his present position, Lieutenant in charge of the Coastguard Station.

"With a start like this," said Glover, "there's no limit."

"See the world," said his father, unconsciously glancing at the window, the sea beyond.

"Make my fortune."

"Come back a man of substance. Settle down."

"But what if he doesn't?" said his mother, quiet and grim. "What if we never see him again?"

There was silence a moment, a beat, the heavy tick of the clock in the room, *memento mori*, time passing.

"Ach!" said Glover, breaking it. "You'll not be rid of me as easy as that!"

"It's no joke, Tom!" said his mother. "They're savages out there. They're not civilised. Not Christian."

"The Lord takes care of His own," said his father, and he left another silence. "Perhaps the best thing might be to ask Him for His guidance."

He handed back the letter. The discussion was ended, for now. Glover nodded, said simply, "Aye."

Out in the back garden he breathed deep the night air, tried to clear his head. This place was home, was all he knew. The solid stone house was tied to his father's job. It was all achingly familiar but now, suddenly, strange. The garden sloped down, overlooked the mouth of the Don, where the river met the North Sea. The waves crashed in, rolled back, endless. The full moon hung in the sky still pale with that halflight, that never quite dark. Above the roar and hush of the sea the cry of an oystercatcher came sharp and clear, pierced him to the core. He heard a step on the gravel behind him, and Martha was standing there, taking it all in. They stood and watched the sea a while.

"How soon would you be going?" she said at last. "If you go."

"I'm not sure," he said. "A few weeks. Maybe a month."

"That's awful soon," she said.

"I know." He looked back at the house. The lamp was lit upstairs in his parents' room.

"Faither was funny," he said, and he copied his father's gruff voice, his terse Northeast understatement. "It's a bit far, is it no?"

She laughed but it was halfhearted, in spite of herself. He could hear it, the catch in her voice. She didn't feel like laughing.

He looked up at the window, the lamplight wee and yellow in the gathering dim. "They'll be talking about it maybe."

"Or not talking."

"Praying for my soul, more like."

"They mean well," she said. "They want what's best for you. Och, we've always known we wouldn't be able to keep you here, keep you *here*." She looked from the house, north along the grey coast, the harsh grudging landscape. "But to go so far, so very far away. That's hard. And God, Tom, they'll miss you. We all will. More than you know."

There was nothing he could say to that. The depth of emotion behind it was too great. Glib reassurance would be empty. An easy joke would be crass. There were no words adequate.

No words. The screech of the seabirds. Relentlessness of the waves.

She turned away, wrapped her shawl tighter about her. The moon had disappeared behind a bulk of cloud, turned the night a little darker, colder. She shivered, breathed hard. He heard her sniffle, try to stifle it, saw her wipe her face with her hand.

"Something in my eye," she said.

He took a white handkerchief from his pocket, handed it to her. "It's clean, mind!"

She sobbed out a laugh, through the tears. "I should hope so!"

He waited, let her take her time. Her voice was calmer when she asked him, "Have you told Annie?" And he felt it again, that twist in the pit of his stomach, gutting him.

"Not yet," he said. "I will."

"When?"

"When I've made up my mind."

"I thought you already had?"

In her tone, in the way she asked, he heard the half hope that he might not go, even yet.

"Almost," he said. "But there's always the doubt, the not knowing."

"Aye," she said, quiet again, resigned. Then she looked full at him, her dark eyes wide. "The lassie cares for you."

For a moment he thought she was going to cry again, but she gathered herself. "Be kind, Tom. That's all." She gave him back the handkerchief, held his hand a moment in both of hers. "I'll away inside now. I'll see you in the morning."

He watched her go, closed his fist round the hanky, still damp. Now he was the one dealing with the welter of emotion. Far out at sea a ship's light flickered. The mass of cloud silvered at the edges and the moon slid out again, shone pure and clear and cold.

Back in the house, Martha had left the gas lamp lit for him, turned down low. The front room reeked of his father's last pipe of the day, the thick black Bogie Roll he liked to smoke. The family Bible had been left out, conspicuous, on the scoured oak table in the middle of the room. Glover smiled. That was like the old man. Ask the Lord for His guidance.

The book was old and worn, its cover boards warped, its pages musty from the damp. The page edges were gilt, beginning to fade with years of turning. He'd been amazed at that as a child. Holding a single thin page between finger and thumb, it was hard to see the sheen at all. But flick the pages, let them cascade, and they shimmered, glistered. Closed, the book was a solid block of gold, encased.

He stood in front of it now, said quietly, "Lord, guide my hand." And he closed his eyes and opened the book, or let it fall open where it would. And he read. Deuteronomy Chapter 26.

And it shall be, when thou art come in unto the land which the Lord thy God giveth thee for an inheritance, and possessest it, and dwellest therein . . .

Dear God, he knew this passage, read further down the page.

And he hath brought us into this place, and hath given us this land, even a land that floweth with milk and honey.

In spite of himself, he was shaken, took the words as a sign.

"A land of milk and honey?" said Robertson next morning, looking up from behind his desk.

"Well," said Glover, pacing the room, restless with the excitement of it all, "silk and tea!"

On a bookcase in the corner was a globe of the world. He rotated it on its axis, found Japan. "There's a fortune to be made, a whole world opening up."

Robertson shook his head. "Sometimes you worry me, Tom. Looking for signs and wonders."

"You don't think we're guided sometimes, led the way we're meant to go?"

"Maybe," said Robertson. "But we can just as easily be misguided, misled."

"And for fear of that we'd do nothing? Christ, Andrew, sometimes *you* worry *me*! I mean, do you want to be still sitting here, polishing that chair with your arse when you're thirty? Or forty?"

"There are worse jobs." Robertson's tone was clipped, his top lip tight.

"I just think sometimes you have to take a chance, grab your life by the scruff, say to hell with it!" Glover spun the globe, blurred continents and oceans. Robertson gave him a thin, wan smile, across a great distance.

It was raining, a thin drizzle, a smirr. Like the haar it rendered everything grey. It wet the cobblestones, gave the streets a dull sheen. It deadened sounds, the rumble of cartwheels, the clop of hooves, a voice raised, the cry of a gull. Glover was walking home at the end of his day's work, bareheaded, his jacket collar up, his mind empty, or so full it was numb.

The summer, such as it was, was passing. Any day now his father, or some old wifie in the kirk, or one of the senior clerks at work, would grimly pronounce that the nights were fair drawing in, and take a miserable satisfaction in it.

He walked by the docks and the shoreporter's warehouse, stopped for a moment to watch the stevedores unload cargo in the rain, heaving crates, stacking them on the quay. A gaffer, a thickset terrier of a man with steam rising from his shoulders, shouted up at him, said he should get his arse down there, get his jacket off and do some real work instead of fucking gawping. One or two of the other workmen laughed, hard and humourless.

Glover said nothing, turned away. He cut up the narrow lanes and wynds, the backstreets where the pubs and grogshops were just opening, where the whores like the one he'd met would be out after dark, working a night shift in the unlit doorways and vennels.

He kept his head down, walked on to Old Aberdeen, past the university to Bridge of Don. The bells of St Machar's struck the hour, six o'clock, and for no good reason he was overcome by melancholy. He looked back towards the city. He had just walked the length of what was, for him, the known world. The rain fell harder. In the cold kirkyard an open grave awaited him; a granite tombstone was carved with his name.

He decided, once and for all; no more uncertainty, the matter was settled. He would go; he would sail to the East, make his way in the world. And the act of deciding, the fact of it, freed him. He was stepping into his life.

His father nodded, said simply, "Aye." Then he filled his pipe, added, "What's for you will not go by you."

His mother took in a quick sharp breath. Her eyes widened in momentary panic, then settled to the bleakness of acceptance. What would be would be.

Martha looked at him with a calm, resigned sadness, her eyes deep dark pools he wouldn't forget.

Robertson's look flickered between a kind of envy and a sly, relieved gladness, his thin mouth twitching in a nervy smile. He told him he was a mad bugger and wished him good luck, said he would need it.

George peered at him over his spectacles, shook his hand firmly in his own bony claw, said he was sure he'd go far, be a credit to the firm. Then he looked out the window, said the nights would soon be drawing in.

Annie was waiting for him at their trysting-place, Brig o' Balgownie, where they'd met that evening, when they'd seen the heron and walked by the river, arm in arm to a quiet place he knew. Was it really only a few weeks ago? A couple of months? That was no time, no time at all. And yet. He couldn't believe he felt so discomfited, so raw.

She already knew, she said, her father had told her, and she'd wondered when he would be man enough to tell her himself.

He'd only just decided, he said, that very day, and hadn't wanted to trouble her until he was sure.

That was most considerate of him, she said. It was good to know he was so sensitive of other people's feelings.

At that she turned away, stood with her back to him, and he saw her shoulders shake with the sobs she'd held in.

"Aw Christ," he said. "Annie."

And he went to her, held her to him, kissed her neck, her hair, her mouth, and she kissed him back with a fierce need that made him want to die into her soft warmth. They walked to the quiet place, the long grass above the dunes, and lay down there, breathing hard, and he lifted her skirts and she undid his buttons, he pushed, clumsy, and with a shock, a sudden give, was in her, she gasped and he thrust till he felt it coursing through him and he pulled out and spurted, spent.

He had done this before, in this same place, with a lassie from the docks, with another from Fittie; it had been quick and brisk and driven by drink; houghmagandie, a ride, a bit of a laugh. But this was Annie, somebody he knew and cared for. This was different.

They lay a long time, clinging to each other, shaken by what had happened. It had been her first time; he knew that. He stroked her hair, tried to speak but had no words. Above them the sky was starting to darken. A peewit cried clear and shrill in the emptiness.

"Ach, lass," he said. "I'm sorry."

"I let you," she said. "I wanted to. You're going. We might never."

It was as if she were saying the words to herself, matter-of-fact, making sense, ticking off her reasons on a list. But when she sat up, straightened her clothes, she started to cry again, and he felt useless. He fumbled in his pocket for a hanky, handed it to her as he'd handed it to Martha; the same gesture but charged with so much more intensity. Annie took it from him, dabbed at her eyes. Then she reached down under her dress, wiped herself between the legs. He felt he shouldn't be watching this, but couldn't turn away.

She looked him in the eye, held out the hanky to him, smeared with his seed, her blood.

"Will you be wanting this back," she said, "or should I keep it to mind me of you?"

She dropped the hanky between them on the sand, turned and made her way through the coarse grass.

He caught up with her and they walked in silence to the end of her street where the gas lamps had just been lit. She said she'd walk the rest of the way by herself.

The preparations were made. He would sail to Southampton, then out via Cape Town to Calcutta and Hong Kong, spend time in Shanghai, cross from there to Nagasaki. The very names were a charm, an incantation, filled him with excitement and awe. Southampton, Cape Town, Calcutta. Jardine's would pay for his passage, by steamship and schooner and clipper. The journey would take months, was further than most folk would travel in a lifetime. Hong Kong, Shanghai, Nagasaki.

In the kirk, on the Sunday before his departure, the minister offered up a special prayer for his safety, asked the Almighty to keep him from harm on his long and hazardous journey, bade the congregation stand and sing, *Will your anchor hold in the storms of life?* His father cleared his throat, launched into the hymn. His mother blew her nose, dabbed at her eyes. Martha sang out, her voice clear with only the slightest tremor on the high notes.

He glanced round, confirmed what he'd thought: Annie wasn't there. The pew beside her father was empty. Old George fixed his gaze ahead, grumbled out chorus and verse.

Outside, they fell into step, along the path through the churchyard. Glover took a deep breath, affected calm, and asked after Annie. George said she was fine, she'd just caught a chill somewhere, would be right as rain in a few days.

He stopped and looked Glover in the eye. "I know you two have been walking out together. And to be honest, I would rather you'd seen fit to tell me and ask my permission."

Glover said nothing, couldn't keep out the memory; Annie lying back in the dunes, himself moving on top of her, inside her. "Be that as it may," George was continuing, "there's no harm done, and maybe this posting of yours is the best thing that could happen. I don't think you're of a mind to get married and settle down."

"Not just yet, sir, no."

"And she's ower young. So this will be an end of it before it even begins."

Annie bucking under him, gasping.

"Aye."

"Of course," said George, "when you come back from the East in a year or two, the story may be different."

Annie crying out. His seed spilled in the sand.

"Aye, sir. I'll mind that."

A peewit's call. The grey North. That empty grave waiting for him.

He went one last time to Brig o' Balgownie, stood watching the river flow by. He turned to go and there was Annie, just looking at him.

"I thought you'd be here," she said. "No, I knew you'd be here. I kenned it. Don't ask me how, I just did."

"And here was me," he said, "just coming by on the off chance."

"Chance?" she said, as if holding up the word to the light, examining it. "Is that all there is? Is that all it was?"

"I wanted to see you," he said. "Before I go."

"Well, here I am."

"I wanted to say goodbye."

"It sounds awful final."

"I have to do this, Annie. I can't not go."

He put his hand to her face, stroked her cheek. He kissed her forehead, her sweet mouth, the kiss not fierce like before, but gentle and sad.

"I have to."

"Then go," she said.

They kissed once more, then she pushed him away and he walked on across the bridge. He looked back and she was still standing there, watching him. He waved but she didn't wave back. Further on he looked again and she was gone.

Annie didn't come to see him off at the quay, and neither did her father, or Robertson, or anyone else from the office. It was during the week, a working day, and nobody could take the time. His mother couldn't bear the parting, had said her goodbyes and stayed at home. His father and Martha had come with him, stood awkward and tonguetied till the last moment, when his father shook his hand, gripped it tight, and Martha threw her arms round him, hugged him as she'd done when they were children.

Then he was on deck, the gangplank hauled aboard, hawsers untied, sails set, the ship moving out of the harbour. His father raised his cap to him, a salute. Martha waved a white hanky. And he watched as quickly, so quickly, they receded, were far away, too small in the distance to discern. And the harbour itself, the seafront, the whole town, his entire world, dwindled and faded. He looked back at the wake, saw two dark shapes breaking the surface, dolphins rippling out of the water, and he felt his own heart soar, felt a huge expansiveness, an infinite sense of possibility, as the sleek creatures leapt the waves, followed the ship, out to the open sea.

CHAPTER
THREE

Guraba-San

Nagasaki, 1859

He concentrated on his feet, negotiated his way down the shaky gangplank. The ground steadied itself beneath him. He took one tentative step, another. He breathed deep, took in the scents and smells. There were fragrances he didn't know, heady and sweet, a spicy wood-smoke, something fermented, something bitter and dark, acrid, and in behind it all the stink of fish that reminded him of home, made him laugh. He felt lightheaded. The air was warm, the colours bright. The hillside opposite was a swathe of deep red, as if it had been painted crimson. Everything felt dreamlike, unreal.

All around, cargo and baggage were being unloaded, exotic boxes, bales of silk, a bright-coloured bird in a cage. The labourers were stocky and compact, naked except for loincloths, moved swiftly and efficiently. He found his own luggage, a battered old trunk, and that too made him laugh. It sat there, familiar, solidly itself, but incongruous, transposed to this far strange place.

He caught a flicker of movement out the corner of his eye, something tiny and white. He focused, saw it clear, a butterfly hovering and dipping in the air. But the wings didn't flutter — it was made of paper, and what kept it dancing there was the updraught from a paper fan. And the fan was being wielded by a young girl with a deftness and lightness of movement the like of which he had never seen. He stared at her, enchanted. She looked up and the shock of seeing him, looming there, made her stop, hold the fan to her face and peer at him over it. The butterfly fell.

He bent and picked it up, held it between finger and thumb, amazed at the simple intricacy of it, the paper almost translucent.

A voice boomed out behind him, loud and male, the accent Scottish.

"Mister Glover?"

He turned, saw a middle-aged man striding towards him.

"Aye."

"I thought you looked the only one likely to be an Aberdonian!"

The man held out his hand, but Glover, still holding the butterfly, was suddenly awkward. He turned again, meaning to give the butterfly back to the girl, but she was gone, faded into the crowd. He took the butterfly in his left hand, held out his right.

"Ken Mackenzie from Jardine Mathieson."

The handshake was firm, the grip Masonic, pressing with the thumb.

"Pleased to meet you," said Glover.

The set of the man's features was hard, dour, a certain tightlipped northern grimness to the line of the mouth, the face weathered. The eyes were sharp, missed nothing, but were not without a dry humour. He registered Glover's discomfiture over the handshake, let his gaze drop to the butterfly. Glover closed his hand round it, put it away in his jacket pocket.

"Aye," said Mackenzie, laconic.

A sternfaced official came over, backed by two armed guards. He gestured towards Glover, spoke at him rapidly in Japanese, the voice gruff but with a kind of singsong tonality to it.

"I'm sorry," said Glover, "I don't . . ."

"He could speak to you in Dutch," said Mackenzie. "But I doubt you'd find that any easier!"

Then Mackenzie spoke to the man in Japanese, his manner brisk, assured. They seemed to argue, haggle. Glover looked on as if from far away, the ebb and flow of their voices, the background noise, all washing over him. He understood none of it, but one word recurred again and again. *Dejima*. Eventually they reached some kind of agreement. The man bowed stiffly to Mackenzie, gave a little grunt. Mackenzie bowed in return, but less deeply. The man bowed to Glover, the merest inclination of the head. Glover nodded in response, said "Fine."

"Welcome to Nagasaki!" said Mackenzie, as the guards stood back to let them pass.

Glover moved to pick up his trunk, but Mackenzie said he would have it brought to Dejima.

"Where's that?"

"I'm afraid that's where you'll have to stay in the meantime," said Mackenzie. "But don't worry. As prisons go, it's not too bad."

"Prison?"

"Only in a manner of speaking. And it shouldn't be for long."

He strode off through the crowds and Glover followed.

The area next to the dock was a marketplace, lined with makeshift stalls fashioned from straw matting and bamboo poles. Live fish flopped in wooden tubs. Creatures he'd never seen writhed, twitched tentacles. Tiny turtles seemed to float in mid-air, but each was suspended from a thread and spun there, legs paddling. An artist drew sketches with a brush, another stall sold carvings and lacquerwork, and in the open spaces jugglers and acrobats performed. One old man, face a bland mask, balanced a plate, on its rim, on the edge of a swordblade. The butterfly girl must have strayed from here to the dock. Glover thought he might see her again, looked around, but she was nowhere. Mackenzie threw a look back at him, made sure he was keeping up. Along the waterfront they were the focus of astonished curiosity.

"Barbarians are still something of a novelty," said Mackenzie. "Especially tall blond barbarians like yourself."

A gang of workmen stopped what they were doing and stared, stonefaced. Glover nodded to them, but they didn't respond, kept staring. Young women, passing, whispered to each other and giggled behind their hands. Glover smiled at them, bowed politely, made them laugh even more. A gaggle of children walked alongside, shouting, making round-eye signs with their fingers in front of their own eyes. Glover stopped abruptly, turned, mock-ferocious, and roared. They shrieked and ran, tumbling over each other to get away and hide. Glover laughed and they tentatively re-emerged, started following him again.

Once more he played the game, turned and roared, and again they scattered. This time they were bolder about regrouping, skipping along in his wake.

A third time he turned, but this time they looked truly, genuinely, terrified, before he had even made a sound. They hid behind barrels or bales of cloth. Some of them threw themselves to the ground, pressed their foreheads in the dust. He was confused. Then he noticed some of the adults were behaving in the same way, stepping back and bowing deeply, getting down on their knees, grovelling in obeisance and real fear. He didn't understand, then realised one or two of the adults were looking beyond him, at something else.

He looked over his shoulder, saw a dark figure moving towards him, out of the sun. He shielded his eyes, to see more clearly. The man was short but powerfully built, walked with a slow, exaggerated swagger, an arrogance in his bearing. He wore a grey robe, a sash tied round his waist, and tucked into the sash were two swords, one long, one short. His hair was caught up in a topknot. The look on his face was truly ferocious, and the ferocity was directed at Glover. It wasn't just the unfamiliar set of the features. The look was pure hatred.

The man kept walking, straight towards him, barked out something that sounded like a command, the voice rough and guttural. Glover stood his ground. Then he felt a strong hand grab the collar of his coat, drag him back out of the way.

"There's a good lad," said Mackenzie, now gripping the back of his neck. "Just do as I do, if you please."

He bowed to the man, respectfully, bending from the waist, pushed Glover's head forward till he did the same.

The man seemed reluctantly appeased, glared at Glover long and hard, grunted something and moved on.

Mackenzie breathed out, relieved. "Not worth losing the head, son. And I do mean literally." He made a cut-throat motion. "That bruiser goes by the name of Takashi. He's what they call *ronin*, a disaffected samurai. They're the warrior class. They're used to being obeyed, and they don't like us being here." He started walking again. "Three things to remember and you'll get on just fine." He counted them off on his fingers. "Don't cross the samurai. Keep out of the politics. And mind where ye dip yer wick!"

Further along he stopped by a stone bridge that led to a small island in the harbour. Two Japanese guards, armed with barbed pikes, barred the way across.

"Right," said Mackenzie. "Here we are."

"Where?" asked Glover, looking at the guards.

"Dejima," said Mackenzie. "Your home for the next few days." He indicated the row of two-storey buildings, behind a sea wall. "The whole thing's man-made, you know. Ingenious buggers, the Japs. They built it so they could contain the Dutch, keep an eye on them."

Glover was still staring, suddenly exhausted, numbed. He was here, the dead end of his journey.

Mackenzie must have seen it in his face. "Don't look so crestfallen, man. I stayed here myself when I first arrived. It's fine. And the guards are there for your protection as much as anything else."

"Protection from what?"

"Oh, cut-throats, brigands, ronin like our friend Takashi."

He addressed the guards, again spoke his brisk Japanese. The guards bowed, perfunctory, and let them cross over, go through an iron gate onto the island. There was one main street, dusty and rutted, running the whole length, a hundred yards. Along one side were the two-storey buildings visible from shore, European-style, built of wood, with green-shuttered windows, the paintwork weathered and fading. Along the other side were warehouses, a store. Mackenzie showed Glover to his lodgings, a sparse second-floor room. One small window looked out over the bridge they'd just crossed, back to the mainland.

Mackenzie said he would take his leave, said Glover would be needing to rest. He would call for him in the morning, take him to the workplace, show him the ropes.

"I'll be ready," said Glover.

"There's a club across the way," said Mackenzie. "A glorified barroom selling warm Dutch beer. They serve food too, of a sort. We'll arrange an advance on your wages tomorrow. In the meantime just sign for what you have."

"Thanks."

Mackenzie stopped in the doorway. "Oh, and there's usually some entertainment provided by *ladies* from the town. So, look out for yourself, keep your wits about you, and mind what I told you before."

"I will, sir. Right. Aye."

He listened to Mackenzie's footsteps, clumping down the wooden stairs. And he felt it again, closing in on him. He was alone, in this drab cramped room that smelled of mildew and tobacco and damp. He took it all in: the single bed against one wall; above it, hung squint, a framed painting of a merchant ship; a small table and a kitchen chair; resting on the table an earthenware basin, a ewer full of water.

He pushed open the shutters and looked out the window, saw Mackenzie cross the bridge, nod to the guards, disappear into the crowds without looking back. Now Glover was overcome with weariness, kicked off his boots and lay down on the bed. The bed creaked, the mattress was hard, stuffed with straw. He would rest for a few minutes.

He was woken, dragged up out of sleep, by a sudden banging. He got to his feet with a kind of confused urgency. The room came into focus, unfamiliar, a place in a dream. Then he remembered. The journey. Where he was. The ends of the earth.

The banging came again, a knocking at the door, and for no good reason he braced himself, ready for confrontation. But it was only a young Japanese man, a porter delivering his luggage.

The man bowed. "*Guraba-san?*"

"I'm sorry," said Glover, "I don't understand. But that's my luggage, if that's what you're asking." He nodded and smiled, pointed at his old trunk.

"*Hai,*" said the man, bowing, and he dragged the box into the room, bowed again.

Glover mimed patting his trouser pockets, pulling them inside out to show they were empty. He shrugged his shoulders, turned down the corners of his mouth in a clown-mask, a grimace of regret. The young man laughed, waved his hand, bowed one last time and was gone, light and barefoot down the stairs.

Glover lay down again. Just a few minutes more. He plunged into a deep heavy sleep, and when he half-woke the room had grown dark. He hung in a kind of limbo, trying to surface, treading water, then with a huge effort willed himself awake, sat up. His dreams had been vivid but incoherent, were already starting to fade. Fragments came back to him, a sense of himself in a huge empty house, wandering from room to room, something small and white flitting ahead of him, just out of reach, and behind every door a vague nameless threat.

He poured cold water into the basin, splashed his face. He would wash properly in the morning, shave, put on clean clothes. For the moment he just wanted to wake himself sufficiently, wipe the bleariness from his eyes. He would stretch his legs, go outside, see what his prison had to offer.

The night air was mild, the scents and smells that heady mix of familiar and strange, the sea tang a constant, just the same. Across the way was the building Mackenzie had mentioned, faint light shining from the windows, the dull muffled rise and swell of male voices from the bar. He pushed open the door, went inside. The accommodation was simple and basic, a counter of dark wood along the back wall, a few tables scattered about the room, an old upright piano in the corner. There was a momentary lull in the conversations as he entered. A few men turned to look in his direction, but there was no acknowledgement, no word of greeting. The conversations picked up again. At the counter he ordered a beer from the surly barman he guessed was Dutch. The man took a bottle from the shelf behind him, put it down on the bar, put beside it a halfpint glass he'd wiped on his apron.

"Chit?" said the man.

"Sorry?" said Glover.

"You work for Jardine's?"

"That's right, aye."

The man pushed a piece of paper towards him, handed him a pen, an inkwell.

"You sign."

"Fine," said Glover, and he signed his name in full, with a flourish. *Thomas Blake Glover*. He sat by the wall, raised his glass to two men at the next table.

"Your health, gentlemen!"

"A new arrival!" said the man nearest, darkhaired and thin-faced, the accent unmistakeably English.

"Another Englishman?" said the other, a sallow, balding man with a wisp of moustache. His inflection was European, most likely French.

"A Scot," said Glover.

"Oh, well," said the Englishman. "Next best thing, eh?"

"I'm Tom Glover."

"Charles Richardson."

"Montblanc," said the Frenchman.

"Cheers!"

"Down the hatch!"

"*A la vôtre!*"

Perhaps it was his tiredness, the strangeness of the place, but he didn't feel at ease with these men. They maintained an amused detachment, as if they were assessing him, weighing him up with an air of condescension, ready to find him wanting. The tiredness had also rendered him particularly susceptible to the beer, even this insipid brew he was drinking. Three bottles and he was drifting. The faces of his companions began to look demonic. He had to take his leave, get back to his room and sleep. He stood up to go and the room tilted, spun. The faces leered as music started up, a thin tinkling jingle from the out-of-tune piano in the corner. It was played by a huge Japanese woman; no, a man dressed as a woman, a corpulent Dutchman in a silk robe, a black wig on his head, face powdered white, lips painted a bright red pout.

The effect was clownish, grotesque, a pantomime mask.

"Ah!" said Richardson. "The entertainment!"

Montblanc had suddenly become animated, laughing shrilly and waving at the pianist who grinned back at him, teeth yellow against the make-up.

Glover sat down again, steadied himself, let the room settle. The piano continued to tinkle and from a back room came three young Japanese women, yes, this time they really were women, gliding forward with tiny, shuffling steps. They were greeted with a spatter of applause, a few ironic, desultory calls of approval, as they moved into a dance, flicked open the fans they were carrying, bowed to their cackling, braying audience.

Glover imagined the dance must be a parody, rendered crude by the music-hall accompaniment. But even at that, there was something inherently graceful in the way the women moved, a lightness that touched him, in spite of how he was feeling.

One of the dancers came towards their table and he found himself captivated by the way she cocked her head, the coy, knowing look she gave him over the top of the fan that she fluttered in front of her face. When the music stopped, she bowed to their table, kept her eyes on Glover.

Richardson laughed. "I certainly have no intention of going native! As for Montblanc, I think his predilections are quite other." He made a grand gesture, a wave of the hand towards Glover. "That leaves you."

The girl was still looking at him, still fluttering. She gave a little giggle, said, "I come you?"

"Now there's an offer!" said Richardson, slapping the table.

And what else could this day become? And could it really have been only a day? The dreamlike quality had deepened, intensified. He had gone beyond exhaustion into another state entirely, a strange clear-eyed detachment, mind and body separate as he watched himself, watched events unfold, play out. He had stumbled out of the bar, the girl following him. The sudden change of air had gone to his head and the girl had taken him by the arm, steadied him. He'd felt the warmth of her body through the thin cotton robe she wore, smelled her perfume, been suddenly roused. He'd indicated the door to his lodgings, let her guide him up the stairs and into this room, the room that had been his for only a few hours.

Now she sat on the edge of the bed, *his* bed, and slipped the robe off her thin shoulders. He remembered a shrieking redhaired harridan, laughing at him in a back wynd by the Aberdeen docks. This young girl, here with him now, was so different. Her black black hair was gathered up, exposed the delicate nape of her neck. Something in the vulnerability of it filled him with a kind of tenderness, made him want to kiss her just there. He thought of Annie.

"*Atsuka*," said the girl, with a little nod of the head.

"Sorry?"

She repeated it. "*Atsuka*." And she mimed fanning herself, dabbing her brow with her hand.

"Hot?" he said, and he tugged at his collar, blew out air in a big exaggerated sigh.

"*Hai!*" she said. "Yes. Hotu!"

He put on a deep, gravelly voice, growled the word back at her. "*Atsuka!*"

She let out a highpitched laugh that suddenly became a scream as something, a rock, crashed through the window, shattered the glass.

His first instinct, in the moment it took to make sense of what had happened, was to shield the girl, put a protective arm round her bare shoulders. She was shaken, trembling, clung to him as he made soothing sounds, stroked her hair. There was noise from outside, angry shouting. Tentatively he disentangled himself and she pulled on her robe, held it tight around her. He stood up, went carefully to the window and looked out. A gang of Japanese men had gathered on the mainland, on the other side of the bridge. In the flicker of light from torches and lanterns he could make out some of them, chanting, brandishing sticks, hurling stones across at the settlement.

What else could the day become? He pulled on his trousers, his jacket, his boots, told the girl it was all right, everything would be fine, and he rushed headlong down the stairs and out into the street. A few others had gathered at the bridge, looking across at the mob on the other side. There were still two guards on duty, pikes at the ready. But they stood with their backs to the mainland, facing the island.

"Christ!" said Glover. "They're keeping us penned in instead of driving them away!"

Richardson's voice was languid, unconcerned. "I think they're trying to prevent an incident. If anyone did manage to get across there, they'd be hacked to pieces."

"So we just stand here and take it?" said Glover.

"The Jap rabble are just making mischief, trying to provoke us. If they really wanted to cross the bridge, it would take more than those two to stop them."

A stone landed at Glover's feet and he picked it up, hurled it back across the bridge into the crowd. The two guards took a step forward, threatening. On the other side, a powerful figure looked ready to lead the mob onto the island. In a flare of torchlight, Glover saw him clear, the samurai Takashi he'd encountered that day, his features suddenly, sharply visible as if in limelight, held in that same intense grimace of pure hate, contained rage. His right hand reached for the hilt of his sword, but another man, by his side, placed a hand on his arm, restrained him. They exchanged words, the other man bowed and Takashi turned on his heel, moved off through the crowd, which parted to let him pass. The other seemed to give a command and the crowd broke up, moved away. The guards stood at ease again, motioned to the foreigners on the island to disperse.

Richardson lit a cigar, blew its fragrant smoke into the night air. "Whatever next?" he said.

Aye. What else?

The girl was waiting for Glover, back in his room, and they sweated and slid together in his cramped bunk, and he lost himself in her, sank at last into oblivion.

He woke alone, thought himself in Bridge of Don and his journey a dream. But no, he was here, in Dejima. The girl had gone in the night, and now the morning light streaked in through his broken window. The fragments of glass had been swept into one corner. She must have done that before she left. He hoped she hadn't cut those fine white hands. He'd had no money to pay her and a chit wouldn't do. He remembered saying, Next time. And she'd laughed and said, I come you again! He could still smell her, taste her. Welcome to Nagasaki.

Christ! He had to start work today, this morning. Mackenzie would be coming to collect him.

He hauled himself upright, pulled on his clothes. Even he could recognise that he smelled choice now, stale and sour from the travelling, from wearing the same sweatstained suit for weeks on end. He opened up his old trunk, took out a rough cotton towel, a cracked lump of carbolic soap that smelled of home, laid out his only other suit of clothes. Downstairs in the bathroom was a wooden tub that could be filled from a handpump. He cranked the handle till the tub was half full. The water was cold, but there was nothing else for it. He stripped and stepped into the tub, gasped as he sat right down in it, immersed himself completely, let it shock him awake.

Back in his room he shaved, peering at a little hand mirror propped on the windowledge. Looking out through the broken window he saw Mackenzie crossing from the mainland. He wiped the last of the lather from his face, hurried down the stairs to meet him.

"Keen," said Mackenzie, nodding to him. "And presentable. That's a good start. Now, some facts and figures, Mister Glover. It has cost Jardine Mathieson almost three hundred pounds to send you out here. I imagine that is in the region of three times your father's annual salary. They see you as someone with a future. So, let's prove them right, shall we?"

Glover nodded, eager. "Aye, sir."

"I know you'll be anxious to get to work straight away." Again there was that hint of humour, dry and ironic, about the eyes. "But first things first. Big lump of a lad like you, you'll be needing your breakfast."

He hadn't wanted to mention it, but his stomach was rumbling. "That would be grand."

"We can talk as we walk," said Mackenzie. "I understand there was a bit of excitement here last night."

"I thought maybe it was always like that," said Glover.

"Not at all," said Mackenzie. "Sometimes it gets dangerous!"

He strode across the bridge, off the island, Glover hurrying to keep up.

"But to be serious," Mackenzie continued, "the situation is volatile, and the violence can get out of hand. Just last week, down that very street." He nodded

56

to his right down a narrow lane. "Two American sailors were run through and beheaded."

"Dear God!"

"No doubt they were drunk, and loud, and aggressive, probably stumbled towards the red light district, blundered into one of the ronin feeling more disaffected than usual."

"That's all it would take?"

"They are rather quick to take offence!"

Glover remembered the face in the torchlight, on the other side of the bridge.

"I'm sure I saw our friend Takashi last night, leading the mob."

"That doesn't surprise me," said Mackenzie. He stopped by a low open doorway, lifted back a flap of fabric that hung across the top, white Japanese writing painted on dark blue. "In here," he said, and he stooped and entered.

Glover followed him in, to a dim room filled with the dark smoky smells of cooking. A few Japanese squatted on the floor, scooping up food from bowls. They seemed to eat with thin wooden sticks, a pair held between finger and thumb. Mackenzie exchanged greetings with the owner of the shop, placed an order and sat on a low stool by the one table tucked in the corner. The owner bowed, pulled up another stool for Glover.

"I'm afraid bacon and eggs are in short supply," said Mackenzie. "And oatmeal, for that matter. I hope you won't find fish disagreeable at this hour of the day."

57

"I'm quite partial to kippers for breakfast, as it happens."

"Arbroath smokies!" Mackenzie chuckled. "No, what they have is a wee bit different."

"I could eat a scabby horse," said Glover. "Scabs and all!"

"Aye, well," said Mackenzie. "We'll see how you get on with the local cuisine!"

The owner of the shop brought each of them a bowl, a pair of the eating-sticks, a scoop-shaped bone spoon.

"*Arigato*," said Mackenzie to the man, and to Glover, "That means thank you."

"*Arigato*?" said Glover, and the man laughed and bowed.

"Good!" said Mackenzie. Then he picked up the sticks. "These are called *hashi*. In China we called them chopsticks."

"*Hashi*."

"But I wouldn't try eating the soup with them just yet!" Mackenzie picked up the spoon. "*Bon appétit*. Or *Itadakimasu*, as they say here."

"*Itadakimasu*," repeated Glover.

The bowl was brim-full of steaming broth. Glover prodded and poked beneath the surface, saw a glut of slimy vegetables, what looked like tiny inch-long eels, a chunk of what might be a chopped-up tentacle with suckers. "Smells like Torry foreshore at low tide."

"You did mention scabs and a horse," said Mackenzie.

"I have eaten tripe," said Glover. "And potted hough." He took a deep breath, slurped a mouthful of the soup, found it chewy and slippery once the liquid had slipped down. The taste was pungent but not unpleasant. "It's fine," he said, spooning up more. He waved to the owner, mimed rubbing his own stomach. The man laughed, and so did Mackenzie. Glover felt as if he had passed a test, an initiation. When they'd eaten, they sipped some bitter green tea from rough unglazed cups.

"A history lesson," said Mackenzie. "The Japanese have been working in splendid isolation for centuries. They described themselves as *sakoku*, the closed country. They had no desire to open their doors to us at all. But they were persuaded."

"American gunboats."

"Commodore Perry's black ships, to be precise. They dropped anchor in Edo bay. The threat was sufficient. The Shogun agreed to limited trade with the West. We had a foot in the door. Mind you, that was five years ago, and it's taken till this very summer for the treaty to be fully effective. As you'll discover for yourself, the wheels grind slowly here. The Shogun and his administration, the Bakufu, make damn sure of that."

"The Shogun is the ruler?"

"The Emperor, the Mikado, is effectively exiled in Kyoto. He's a figurehead, nothing more. The Shogun rules in his stead. He was not at all happy about signing the treaty, but the Commodore gave him no choice. All the Shogun can do, to save face and placate the traditionalists, is make things as difficult as possible for us. For example . . ." Mackenzie handed Glover a small piece of bamboo, a Japanese symbol painted on one side. "This is what passes for currency around here. And of course, they're bloody difficult to get hold of."

"You can't just buy them?" Glover knew the question must be naïve, even as he asked it.

"Not even for pure Mexican silver dollars. Like this."

He produced a shining silver coin, flicked it spinning in the air towards Glover, who caught it.

"Try," said Mackenzie, nodding towards the owner of the shop. "See if he'll sell you any."

Another test. Glover held out the bamboo token in his left hand, the silver dollar in his right, tried to indicate that he wanted to exchange quantities of the one for the other. "You sell?"

When the man realised what he was asking, he was suddenly frightened, looked around at the door, waved his hand in front of his face, mimed cutting his own throat.

"He's not exaggerating," said Mackenzie. "It's more than his life's worth."

"So how do you get anything done?"

"Sheer bloody-mindedness! And finding out which officials have their price." Glover handed back the dollar and the bamboo token, but Mackenzie waved him away.

"Take them as payment on account."

"Thank you," said Glover, and he put them in his jacket pocket, felt in there the paper butterfly. He'd transferred it from his other coat, kept it with him for good luck. He knew it was foolishness, superstition. But still.

Outside he walked with Mackenzie along the waterfront.

"This is the Bund," said Mackenzie. "It's the main thoroughfare. All these warehouses are owned by western companies; British, American, Dutch, French. They're all investing heavily, and there's more than enough to go round."

"Can I ask you something?" said Glover.

"Of course."

"You said the treaty had only just come into effect."

"That's right. A few months ago."

"But you've been trading here for over a year."

Mackenzie grinned. "Ways and means, laddie. I said it before, sheer bloody-mindedness. And a willingness to take risks."

He stopped outside a two-storey building, set back from the harbour. "Here we are, the furthest outpost of the Jardine Mathieson empire!"

The office, on the ground floor, was simple, the furnishing sparse: basic hardwood tables and chairs, bookcases laden with ledgers. Mackenzie's accommodation was upstairs. Through to the back of the building was the warehouse, stacked with bales and boxes, crates and sacks. Two young Japanese men in shirtsleeves were checking a consignment of silk. They stopped what they were doing, bowed deeply to Mackenzie, less so to Glover.

"Mister Shibata and Mister Nakajimo," said Mackenzie. "Mister Glover. Guraba-san."

Glover nodded to the young men. "Guraba-san?" he said to Mackenzie. "That's what the lad said to me last night, the one that delivered my luggage."

"It's your name in Japanese," said Mackenzie. "They find it hard to get round some of our consonants. You'll get used to it."

"Guraba-san," said the two young men, simultaneously.

It was warm in the warehouse, close in the confined space, the air thick with the scents of spices and tea. Glover fanned his face with his hand, said "*Atsuka!*"

He was proud of himself for remembering the word, but the two young men couldn't help themselves, they laughed out loud. One of them said something to Mackenzie and laughed again.

"They are very impressed that you're learning the language already," said Mackenzie, that look of wry amusement again in the eyes, at the corners of the mouth. "But they point out that in polite society they use the word *atsui*. The word you used is generally to be heard spoken by young ladies of a certain class, and they are intrigued as to where you may have heard it."

"Aye, well," said Glover, uncomfortable.

"If I may paraphrase," Mackenzie went on, broadening his accent a little, "you've been in Nagasaki five minutes and you're picking up the speak o tinkers and hoors!"

Now Glover felt overheated. *Atsuka* or *atsui*, it didn't matter, it was stuffy in the room.

"Never mind," said Mackenzie. "As long as that's all you pick up from them!" He indicated the two

Japanese, maintaining composure, stifling the laughter. "They'll be telling that story for a month."

Back through in the office, Mackenzie showed Glover to a desk in the corner of the room. This was where he would be working. Mackenzie had to go out for the rest of the morning, told Glover to start sorting through the pile of papers on his desk. Glover looked at the top sheet, recognised the familiar layout, the delineation of the words and figures on the page. Bills of lading. Mackenzie left him to it and he settled to work, first taking out the three small objects from his jacket pocket — the bamboo token, the silver dollar, the paper butterfly — and placing them together on the desk, a little shrine to good fortune.

CHAPTER
FOUR

Silk and Tea

Nagasaki, 1859–60

A land flowing with milk and honey. Or at least, he'd said, silk and tea. He'd spun the globe on its axis, stopped the world with his finger on Japan. Here be dragons, and a fortune to be made. He wanted it all.

He threw himself into the work, hurled himself at it fulltilt. He wanted to learn everything Mackenzie had to teach, was hellbent on finding out more.

Within months he had made himself indispensable. He took charge of documentation and paperwork, the dull, repetitive, essential grind, gradually delegated most of it to Shibata and Nakajimo. That freed him to get out, away from the desk, watch Mackenzie in action as he haggled, argued, bargained with merchants, fought for the best deal. They tramped the muddy lanes and backstreets of the city, visited storerooms and warehouses, back-shops and flimsy godowns, checked merchandise, sifted samples.

"You have to watch," said Mackenzie, delving into a crate of tea, rubbing the leaves between fingers and thumb, sniffing. "Some of the bastards are up to every trick under the sun. They'll sell you the best quality leaf then substitute half of it with floor-sweepings as soon as your back's turned. Or you'll buy the finest raw silk and they'll adulterate it with sand."

Glover watched and learned. Soon he was signing documents in his own right on behalf of Jardine's. Mackenzie, from referring to him in letters to head office as his *able young assistant*, started calling him, only half jocular, *the chief*. His reputation in the small community began to grow.

Mackenzie introduced him to a Chinaman by the name of Wang-Li, a trader, he said, a dealer in anything and everything under the sun. Glover was surprised, said he thought the Chinese were barred from trading, by law.

"They are," said Mackenzie. "But again, there are ways and means. There's many a European or American who can't thole a bland diet of fish, rice and noodles, and they've been allowed to employ Chinamen as cooks. Mister Wang-Li can rustle up a creditable beef stew and has a repertoire of French dishes in addition to Chinese cuisine."

Wang-Li grinned, bowed.

Mackenzie continued. "Officially he's a chef and manservant in the pay of an American trader by the name of Jack Walsh — and that's somebody else you'll be meeting before long. But there's more to Wang-Li's accomplishments than cooking. He has many strings to his bow. He's a veritable magician when it comes to procuring whatever you might need."

Again Wang-Li smiled. "You want, I get."

"He's not joking," said Mackenzie. "Last week he acquired for me a whole crate of Lea and Perrins Worcester Sauce!"

"Impressive."

"You keep in mind," said Wang-Li.

"I will."

Mackenzie had met Wang-Li during his time in Shanghai, before he'd come to Nagasaki.

"I was never so grateful to get out of a place in my life," said Mackenzie. "Think yourself lucky you didn't get posted there."

"I saw enough of it just passing through," said Glover.

He'd walked the streets by the Shanghai waterfront, overwhelmed by the crush of the crowds, the heat, the noise, the stench of the river, the underlying sense of threat, armed guards posted on the walls round the foreign settlement.

"A cesspit," said Mackenzie. "A sewer. I think I was here a month before the smell of it cleared from my nostrils. It stinks to high Heaven. They call it the Whore of the Orient. There's a street called Blood Alley where the price of a pint includes a twelve-year-old girl behind a grubby curtain."

"You want, I get!" said Wang-Li, laughing.

"I believe he's making a joke," said Mackenzie to Glover, "though I'm never entirely sure."

"Shanghai my home town," said Wang-Li.

"That would explain a great deal," said Mackenzie.

★ ★ ★

Mackenzie continued Glover's education by telling him which customs officials were bribable, which local merchants would break a contract before the ink on it had dried. He warned him too that some of the foreign traders were equally unscrupulous and ruthless, regarded all Japanese as corrupt beyond redemption. The same traders regarded their own diplomats as soft, excessively reasonable, lily-livered, and the diplomats in their turn described the traders as the scum of Europe.

"All in all," he said, "an interesting environment in which to conduct legitimate business!"

The heart of the trade was straightforward import and export. Jardine's clippers sailed to the China coast, six days away, laden with silk and with seaweed, a local delicacy. To make the journey worthwhile, the ships had to return with other cargoes, commodities that could be sold in Japan: sugar, cotton, Chinese medicines. It was Mackenzie's job, and now Glover's, to find a market for these goods.

Learning the Japanese language was essential, at least a smattering. Mackenzie had mastered the basics and Glover had made a start, undaunted by the embarrassment of his early efforts. Mackenzie still had only to growl "*Atsuka!*" for Shibata and Nakajimo to laugh.

At the Foreigners' Club Glover had picked up a cheaply produced phrasebook purporting to give a newcomer to Japan a few rudimentary expressions, conversational gambits.

I, it said, was *waterkoosh*.

"*Watakashi*," said Mackenzie.

You was *O my*.

"*Omai.*"

Tea was *otcher*.

"*Hocha.*"

Silk was *kinoo*.

"*Kinu.*"

"It ventures into entire sentences," said Glover, "most of them peremptory commands."

"First thing your foreigner needs to learn!" said Mackenzie.

"Here's some sound advice," said Glover. "If you want to tell a native to make less noise driving nails into the wall or else you shall be obliged to punish him, you should shout, *O my pompon bobbery waterkoosh pumguts!*"

"First-class gibberish," said Mackenzie. "Pidgin. A bastard mongrel hybrid. They half-hear and misunderstand, stir bits of mangled French into the mix along with scraps of Dutch and Chinese, even Malay — that's where *piggy* comes from."

"I've heard that, at the docks."

"A rough translation would be *Get a move on!* or perhaps *Bugger off!*"

"That'll be useful if I meet the compiler of this book," said Glover, and he shouted, "*Piggy! Bobbery waterkoosh pumguts!*"

Mackenzie chuckled. "Oh, another piece of advice about learning the language — I'd advise you to mimic the way the menfolk speak, rather than copying your lady friends. The difference is quite noticeable, the men have a much rougher, harsher tone, and if you speak like the women then the Japanese merchants may get entirely the wrong impression, if you take my meaning."

"That's all I'd need."

"And you a muckle great hairy Aberdonian! They'd be really confused!"

"Thanks for the advice. I'll get Shibata and Nakajimo to keep me right."

Shibata and Nakajimo had already helped him further his education. They led him one Saturday night, their work over for the week, along the Bund, towards the entertainment district, the floating world.

"*Maruyama*," said Shibata. "Flower quarter."

The air was warm, mild. They came to a low wooden footbridge across a stream. "This is called *shian-bashi*," said Shibata. "Means hesitation-bridge. Still time to turn back."

Glover smiled, followed him across.

Further on they reached another bridge, this one smaller, narrower.

"This one is *omoikiri-bashi*," said Nakajimo. "That's made-your-mind-up-bridge. No turning back."

Glover laughed. "Lead on!"

Time was short. The cargo had to be unloaded before the tide turned, and already it was close to high water, would soon start to ebb. Crates packed with bales of cotton were stacked high, precarious, on the flotilla of small boats that ferried them from the ship, at anchor out in the bay. Mackenzie was overseeing the operation, yelling instructions as the boats bobbed and jostled at the quay.

"Come on!" he shouted. "We have to do this *now!*"

A red-faced young Englishman, a foreman from the warehouse, took his cue from Mackenzie, started screaming at the coolies.

"Shift, you lazy bastards! Get a move on! *Piggy! Piggy!* For God's sake, put some beef into it!" He cuffed one of the workmen, shoved another. "Fucking useless!"

Glover was lending a hand. He grabbed a line thrown from one of the boats, strained to hold it steady, arms and shoulders aching with the effort, hands starting to chafe with ropeburn. Another boat came in alongside. It was overloaded, started to tilt as the crates shifted, finally keeled over and capsized, tipped cargo and workmen overboard into the harbour.

For a moment it was chaos, the water churned up, the men yelling as they kept afloat, tried to right the boat, save the cargo. But one man was in trouble, thrashed and floundered as if he couldn't swim. He was panicking, gulping in water, gasping for air.

Glover didn't think, shoved the foreman aside and jumped in, grabbed the man who was still struggling and kicking. With great difficulty he managed to get an arm round the man's neck, drag him to the quay where other workmen hauled him out.

Glover pitched in again, helped lug crates onto the dockside. When it was over he slumped, exhausted, dripping, clothes sodden and sticking to him.

The Japanese he'd pulled from the water came over and bowed low, then kowtowed, kneeled and pressed

Acknowledgements

This is a work of fiction, obviously, a work of the imagination, but I've tried to make the historical background as accurate as possible, while not letting the facts get in the way of the story! There are a number of people who have helped the book along and I want to give them my thanks. To Alex McKay, not only for his fine biography of Thomas Glover, *The Scottish Samurai*, but for his generosity and kindness in sharing his vast knowledge and his research materials with me. To Sachiko McKay for adding her own advice on matters linguistic and cultural. To Brian Burke-Gaffney, author of *Starcrossed, A Biography of Madame Butterfly*, for his help on my visit to Nagasaki and for his *Crossroads* magazine and website, the fount of all knowledge on Nagasaki and its history. To Mari Imamura for translating some passages into Japanese. To Richard Scott Thomson for believing in the film version of this story, which one day *will* be made! To Steve McIntyre and Scottish Screen for development funding and to Bob Last for his input. To Isobel Murray and the late Giles Gordon for suggesting the material might make a good novel! To Liam

McIlvanney, David Mitchell, Sian Preece and Amanda Booth for putting material my way. To Judy Moir for her initial response to the opening chapters. To my agent Camilla Hornby for encouragement and support through the writing process. To all at Canongate, especially Jamie Byng for Thinking Big, Francis Bickmore for being a courteous, meticulous and creative editor, Jo Hardacre for pitching the book and Jessica Craig for selling it worldwide. To Janani for living with this. To Sri Chinmoy for his constant inspiration and for showing me how much I could push myself.

Domo arigato gosaimasu!

his head to the ground, stood up and turned away with as much dignity as he could muster.

"That was well done, Tom," said Mackenzie. "And politic too."

Another westerner stood behind him, puffing at a cigar, a wry grin crinkling his face.

"Impressive," said the man, his accent American. "I'd heard you were throwing yourself into the business!"

Mackenzie made the introductions. "Tom, Jack Walsh. Jack, Tom Glover."

Walsh held out his hand, but Glover was awkward about shaking it, dripping wet as he was.

"Pleased to meet you, Tom," said Walsh, taking his hand anyway, shaking it vigorously. "When you've dried off, I'd like to take you for a drink."

They crossed the two bridges, hesitation, mind-made-up, entered the other world of *Maruyama*. Walsh was expansive, initiating him into the mysteries of the place, a garden of earthly delights. "The Russians have their own whorehouse," he said, "at Inasa, on the other side of the bay. They call it a rest house, but there's not much rest to be had! It's on a level with what you no doubt saw in Shanghai, a row of cubicles, girls laid out like so much meat, sailors lining up for a quick fuck. Brutal in the extreme. Of course, if you like that sort of thing . . ." He tailed off, laughed at Glover's expression. "The Russian authorities have taken the trouble to have a doctor on hand, examine the girls. A sensible precaution." Again he laughed. "Don't look so alarmed! Where we're going is the other extreme."

"I just . . ."

"I can see you still have something of the Presbyterian about you after all!"

"Maybe I do," he said. He was used to the whole business being furtive. It was the openness of it all that was strange to him, the matter-of-factness.

"Never mind," said Walsh, "*Maruyama* will set that to rights!" He gestured back down the hill, the way they had just walked. "Even at the lowest level, down there, it's a cut above what you'll find anywhere else. That's where the little *nami-joro* operate, simple working girls. Further up the hill, and further up the ladder, are the *mise joro*, a little more cultivated, a little more refined. I expect that's the section you visited with Shibata-san and Nakajimo-san."

To his own ridiculous irritation, Glover felt himself blush. "Christ!" he said. "Are there no secrets here?"

"It is a small community," said Walsh. "Word gets around."

"Clearly," said Glover.

Walsh led him on and up, higher still.

"Now," said Walsh, coming to a stop at the crest of the hill, in front of a bamboo gate. "This is the highest level of all, Heaven itself! The women here are another species altogether. They're called *tayu*, the absolute epitome of refinement."

"*Tayu*," said Glover, savouring the word.

"They're also known as *keisei*, which means *castle-topplers*. They've driven many a rich man to ruin."

"Same the whole world over!"

"And of course it's only rich men who can afford to spend time in their company. They don't come cheap, as it were."

Glover stopped. "I don't know if I can afford this yet. When you invited me for a drink . . ."

"Exactly," said Walsh. "*I* invited *you*. So, this one's on me. And by the way, I like that *yet*! Shows the right attitude. You'll be able to pay me back in no time."

"Thanks," said Glover. "I appreciate your faith in me."

"Let's just say I know a good bet when I see one." He led Glover through the gate. "Welcome to the *Sakura*."

"Cherry blossom."

"Very good!"

The garden was exquisite, an actual cherry tree beside an ornamental pond, stone lanterns, a statue of a goddess, one hand raised in benediction. From the pond a small stream flowed, and over it, leading to the porch, the discreet shoji screen doors, was yet another bridge. They crossed over, walked the last few steps, feet crunching on raked white gravel. The door slid open. From inside came the scented smoke of incense, a waft of music, plucked strings, almost discordant. He recognised it, the bittersweet twang, an instrument called the samisen.

"First things first," said Walsh. "We have to bathe."

★ ★ ★

For the second time that day, Glover was immersed in water. But now instead of thrashing in the cold depth of the harbour, he was soaking in the hot tub at the teahouse. One of the young girls had been assigned to him, another to Walsh. They'd been soaped and scrubbed — the girls giggling at the thickets of hair on chest and legs; they'd been rinsed clean with buckets of warm water, and only then had they eased down into the tub. The heat of it had gone straight to Glover's head, a sudden rush, made him feel almost dizzy. But that had passed, and now he lay back enjoying it.

"The trick is not to move," said Walsh, "or it feels even hotter."

"I had noticed!" said Glover.

Their voices boomed as they spoke. Walsh had lit another cigar, its fragrant smoke curled, mingled with the steam from the tub.

"Mackenzie says you're doing good work, Tom."

"Does he now?"

"Of course, he'd never tell you to your face."

"No. Of course not!"

"Have you thought about setting up in business for yourself?"

"I've thought about it, aye, eventually, when I'm ready."

"Why wait?" said Walsh. "I think you're a natural: smart, hard-working. You have the gift of the gab too, by all accounts. Add that to your height and build and you can't go wrong. You'll charm the pants off the women and scare the shit out of the men!" He laughed

74

again. "I'd be happy to put work your way. Mackenzie could get you a loan from Jardine's. You can still do work for them and trade on your own account. That's what Ken does. And let's face it, there's plenty to go round!"

They stepped, dripping, from the tub. The two girls, giggling again, brought towels to wrap round them, helped to dry them off. The one attending to Glover led him to a small room where a futon was laid out on tatami mats. He mimed roaring, beating his chest. She laughed and motioned to him to lie facedown. She removed the towel and sat astride him, started massaging his back, working down the spine with her tiny hands, the strokes even and firm. By the time she turned him over onto his back, he was ready, gave himself over entirely to her ministrations.

He was kneeling on the floor, blindfold. He knew the room was in semi-darkness, lit only by a flickering candle he could sense rather than see through the cotton bandana tied tight over his eyes, knotted at the back of his head. He could smell the smoke, the dripped wax, like the cold smell of an old chapel, could smell too the damp mustiness of the room, the thick fusty male-smell of tobacco-reek from much-worn coats. He was in his shirtsleeves, his shirt open at the front, baring his chest against which something hard and sharp was pressed, something he knew was the tip of a sword-blade.

A voice came out of the darkness. "Do you feel anything?"

75

And he made the correct response. "I do."

There was a knocking, three times on the wooden floor, then he was taken by the arm, helped to his feet and led forward a few steps.

Now he could smell incense, and paraffin.

The voice spoke again. "Having been kept in a state of darkness, what now is the predominant wish of your heart?"

Again he responded, as he had been instructed to do. "Light."

The blindfold was removed and he blinked as he looked round him, the room now lit by lamps.

"Do you promise to hold fast and never repeat the secrets of initiation into this mystery?"

"Hele, conceal and never reveal."

"If you break this oath, your throat shall be cut, your tongue torn out and you shall be cast out, branded as void of all moral worth."

For the first time the urge to laugh rose in him, the thought of responding, *Is that all?* But he quelled it, responded with due formality. "I understand."

The man who had spoken, middle-aged, bearded, held out a Bible, leather-bound, gold-embossed.

"Kiss the Volume of the Sacred Law."

Glover pressed his lips to the book.

The man spoke again. "Let the candidate be entered as an apprentice in the First Degree."

Behind him he heard Mackenzie's voice. "So mote it be."

The man held out to him a pure white apron, folded. "This emblem is a badge more ancient than the Roman

Eagle, the Golden Fleece. It is a symbol of purity and the bond of friendship. I urge you never to disgrace it."

"I shall honour it," said Glover, and he heard his own voice, strange to him, and he felt for a moment absurdly moved, thought of his father, the old Bible on the kitchen table.

He looked round the room, these people, this place, saw it dreamlike but intensely clear, in the midst of it came to himself here, came to *himself* here. This was his life and this was him living it.

Then the bearded man was shaking him by the hand, pressing with the thumb in the secret Masonic grip, and Mackenzie was doing the same, and the others, welcoming him into the brotherhood.

When the ceremony was over and they'd adjourned to the Foreigners' Club, he ordered a round of drinks.

The bearded man, the Master of the Lodge, was Barstow, a Captain in the Royal Navy. There were three young Englishmen, a year or two older than Glover, and they introduced themselves, Frederick Ringer, Edward Harrison, Francis Groom. Like Glover, each of them had come to Japan to make his mark, find his own grail, seek wealth and adventure far from home.

Harrison speculated in property, real estate. Groom gambled on the fluctuations of foreign exchange. Ringer dealt in tea, knew the business inside out. Glover could learn from all of them.

"To friendship and brotherhood!" he said, and they clinked glasses.

Walsh had come in to the Club, waved to him from the bar.

Glover beckoned him over. "Come and join us!"

"I'll join you," said Walsh, "but not join you, if you know what I mean." He touched his finger to the side of his nose, winked.

"You could do worse, Jack," said Mackenzie.

"I'm all in favour of oiling the wheels of commerce," said Walsh, "but I draw the line at rolling up my trouser-leg and giving a funny handshake."

"There's more to it than that," said Barstow, "and you know it."

"It amazes me," said Walsh. "The settlement here is barely established and you fellows have already formed a Lodge. You're as keen as the Catholic Church to spread your influence."

"There is no comparison, sir," said Barstow, irritated.

"Just as well," said Walsh. "I'd hate to see you meet the fate of the early missionaries and end up disembowelled, flayed alive or boiled in oil!" He raised his glass. "Your health."

The same night, the night of Glover's initiation into the Lodge, the community was once more shaken to its core. Hunt, the young English foreman from Jardine's warehouse, had taken a drink or two, gone wandering off on his own towards Maruyama. He was seen by an American sailor, crossing the first bridge, and the second. He was heard roaring out, drunk, that he wanted to buy a Japanese woman, that he had a few shillings in his pocket and that was all they were worth.

What happened next was sudden and vicious. Two black-robed figures appeared out of the dark, one in front of him, carrying a lantern, another moving up behind him. The one in front shoved the lantern in his face. As he stepped back the one behind ran him clean through with the blade of his sword, drew it out again pushing him forward, cut him down with two more swift strokes as he fell. The lantern was doused, the two men disappeared into the night.

The American had run across, sobered in an instant, looked down at the man's remains. One stroke had filleted him, another had severed his head. The American had thrown up on the spot.

"He should be grateful for his own squeamishness," said Walsh. "If he'd given chase, he'd have ended up in pieces too. Or in two pieces!"

"Hunt was rather brutal with the natives," said Glover. "Maybe this was by way of reprisal."

One wit from another firm had said Hunt's name was obviously rhyming slang. Glover would tell that to Walsh, but not now.

"I guess he was in the wrong place at the wrong time," said Walsh. "Sounds like he should have been heading for the Russian rest house instead of Maruyama!"

"It's a vile business," said Mackenzie, serious, changing the tone. "It smacks of Takashi and his crew."

"That bugger!" said Glover. "I'm sure I saw him a week ago, glaring at me out the shadows, down by the warehouse. Then I looked again and he was gone."

Mackenzie sounded even more serious, looked at Glover intently. "You want to be careful of that one,

Tom, mind your back. He's a fanatic, and if he's got you in his sights, it's a matter for concern."

"I don't understand," said Glover. "What has he got against me personally?"

"I'm sure just the sight of you was enough," said Mackenzie, "that first time he saw you, the day you arrived."

"Hate at first sight," said Walsh.

"More or less," said Mackenzie. "He's a member of a group called *sonno-joi*, hardline traditionalists, resolutely opposed to any interaction with the West."

"And pledged to rid Japan of all foreign scum," said Walsh.

"Or die in the attempt," said Mackenzie. "They take a fearful blood-oath, promise to end their own lives if they go back on it."

"Sounds a bit like your Freemasons!" said Walsh, laughing.

"With one difference," said Mackenzie, tightlipped. "For these men it's more than symbolic. They really will kill, and die, for their beliefs."

"And the Masons won't?" said Walsh. "You disappoint me."

Mackenzie ignored him, wouldn't be deflected by his levity, spoke again directly to Glover.

"It is serious, Tom. Don't be in any doubt about it. They'll often pursue an individual. It's like what the Italians call a *vendetta*, and it's a matter of honour."

"Isn't it always?" asked Walsh.

"So it is personal?" said Glover.

"Randomly so," said Mackenzie. "As I said, the very sight of you that first day would be an affront to him, a threat to everything he believes in."

"You do loom large," said Walsh, "stand out in a crowd. Especially here."

"And for Takashi it would be a matter of pride to cut you down to size," said Mackenzie.

"With two strokes of that sword," said Walsh.

"Bloody hell!" said Glover.

"Well," said Mackenzie, "there's folk would say, Hell mend you for leaving Bridge of Don! I'm not saying you should go around in fear and trepidation every minute of the day."

"Just keep your wits about you," said Walsh.

"Did you ever learn to use a pistol?" asked Mackenzie.

"As a boy, aye. My father taught me. Just in case."

"Aye, well, we keep a few on the premises, for security. It might be no bad idea for you to have one."

"Just in case!" said Walsh.

The rapidity of Glover's rise to prominence was breathtaking. He seemed to hit his stride early on, grow in confidence with every step. In spite of his youthfulness, or perhaps because of it, he had a swagger about him, an assurance. That, allied to sheer physical presence, rendered him formidable, but it was tempered by an innate affability and graciousness, an easy charm.

Mackenzie entrusted him with ever more responsibility until he was effectively running the Nagasaki operation, freeing Mackenzie himself to make trips to Shanghai for meetings at Jardine's offices there, the hub of their empire.

With Mackenzie's help, and on his recommendation, Glover negotiated his first loan from the company, invested it immediately, on Harrison's advice, in a warehouse property in Oura, right on the waterfront. There was living accommodation to the rear, and he moved in there himself. He still worked five or six hours a day for Jardine's, but the rest of the time he was building his own business, tramping the streets and the back alleys, purchasing for himself some of the commodities he would export, the silk and tea, seaweed and dried fish, anything that would turn a profit. In his warehouse he stored the goods he imported, to sell in Nagasaki and its hinterland, herbs and medicines, quantities of cotton. He took advantage of Groom's financial expertise, made quick gains on a few swift currency exchanges, cashing in on the time it took to transfer funds from Yokohama, or Shanghai. He made money, but not on the scale to which he aspired. He wanted to make a killing.

He spoke to Ringer, took his advice on the tea trade.

"There's definitely money to be made," said Ringer. "Japan exports 4,000 tons of tea in the season, and half of that goes through Nagasaki. There's definitely money to be made."

"Is there any way we could steal a march on the competition?" he asked. "Make the business more efficient?"

Ringer looked thoughtful. "The tea is picked in the interior," he said, "on hillsides that won't support rice. It's part-time work for the farm women. The leaves have to be dried before being shipped out, otherwise it's damp and it just rots in the cargo hold on the long haul to Europe or America. The women do the drying out after the crop's been picked, just heat the leaves over open-air fires."

"I'd imagine that's slow," said Glover.

"And not entirely effective. I've often thought if we established a factory where the tea could be thoroughly dried in large quantities, it would transform the industry."

"Well then," said Glover, "we shall do exactly that."

He registered the company in his own name, had a sign painted and mounted on the front of the warehouse. *Glover & Co.* Groom and Harrison would be junior partners, Ringer his adviser on the tea trade. Shibata and Nakajimo would work for him part-time while continuing to hold down their jobs with Jardine's. Mackenzie would continue to steer him clear of troubled waters, and Walsh would continue to head him right back into them, urge him to take risks.

They all stood outside the new premises, drinking a toast to the company as the sign was unveiled. Walsh had provided champagne, courtesy of Wang-Li. Their glasses sparkled and fizzed, overflowed.

"Glover and Co!" said Walsh.

"Glover and Co!"

A week later Glover was woken in the middle of the night by alarm bells ringing, shouting in the street. A hammering at his door had him reaching for his pistol, but it was Nakajimo telling him there was a fire and it was spreading and he should get out quick. He could smell burning, taste it, acrid, at the back of his throat. He threw on his clothes, ran through to the warehouse, swept the contents of his desk into a canvas bag and rushed out into the street.

Mackenzie was hurrying towards him, wide-eyed and manic, his grey hair dishevelled.

"Thank God, Tom!" he said. "I thought you might have been incinerated!"

They stood back, saw the flames lick the roof of the warehouse, sparks spiralling into the night air.

"The bastards!" shouted Mackenzie. "It started two buildings away, in Arnold's office." Arnold's were another British trading house, like Glover recently established. "Bloody firemen stood back and watched, waited to see what would happen. As soon as the sparks started flying they were on the alert, and the first flicker of flame on Japanese property was doused double-quick. But when it reached your warehouse they stood back again, let it burn." He screamed at the firemen lolling back, indolent, taking in the scene. "Bastards!"

They stared back at him, moved with desultory slowness, cranked a trickle of water from a hand-operated pump, prodded at the collapsing walls with hooks attached to long bamboo poles, watched the building cave in on itself in clouds of smoke, flares of flame.

"Dancing Horse," said Nakajimo, watching the conflagration. "Is what we call fire."

They watched it leap, dance the building down.

Next morning they stood in the gap where the warehouse had been, smoke still rising from the blackened site, nothing left but charred beams, ash.

"I blame the fucking Shogun," said Mackenzie, "and his fucking Bakufu advisers."

"I hardly think they came skulking down here in person," said Glover, "mobhanded, torched the place in the middle of the night!"

"They might as well have done!" said Mackenzie. "God knows I'm fond of this damned country, but they have to wake up. They can't do anything about the fact that we're here, so they should fling the doors wide open, allow complete freedom of trade instead of this shilly-shallying, welcoming us in and trying to drive us away, allowing us to do business then making it impossible to function."

"It's early days," said Glover. "It'll come right in time." He looked around him. "You know, in this instance I think they've done me a favour. The warehouse was ramshackle, falling to bits. Ideally I'd have liked to tear it down and build something more substantial. Well, now they've forced the issue."

Mackenzie shook his head, laughed. "You really are quite something, Tom. I doubt if this place is ready for you just yet!"

There were lulls, longueurs, long lazy days between consignments when the pace of life slowed down and nothing much was happening. Glover was restless at such times, would walk along the waterfront, taking everything in, supervise the work on his new building. It amazed him to see the workmen, barefoot, go shinning up thin bamboo poles tied together to make flimsy scaffolding, leap and step across it with a breathtaking agility. He would wave to them, call out. "Good work! *Ganbatte*." And one or two might catch his eye, nod to him, but never faltering or breaking stride.

He had purchased another warehouse, again on Harrison's advice, in the street behind the Bund. This would replace the building destroyed by the fire, had the same basic construction, clapboard, with simple living quarters at the back. He moved in, settled, set up once more his little shrine. He had rescued his good luck tokens, the paper butterfly and the rest, when he'd swept up the contents of his desk as the fire approached. Not that he was superstitious, but it did no harm to placate the gods of fortune.

During one quiet spell, the days long and time hanging heavy, he prepared to ride into the interior, visit some of the hillside villages where they harvested and dried the tea, packed it for shipping.

Mackenzie was wary. "You'll be at risk," he said. "Outside the city you'll stand out even more."

But Glover was determined, said he could look after himself. He would carry his pistol, be accompanied by Nakajimo who would translate for him, had an ear also for the rough guttural dialect of the country folk.

"Otherwise," said Mackenzie, "you'd be like an Englishman trying to talk to a Glaswegian, or, for that matter, an Aberdonian!"

"Aye," said Glover. "Fit like!"

Mackenzie also insisted a bodyguard travel with him, a young samurai by the name of Matsuo. He was from the Choshu clan, spoke no English, maintained a stonefaced reticence, spoke only when directly addressed. But Mackenzie said he was alert, conscious of his duty and adept in the use of the two swords he carried at all times.

"Isn't it beneath his dignity," said Glover, "to be minding out for the likes of us?"

"You would think so," said Mackenzie. "He had some dealings with Nakajimo here, and seems to have been impressed. Nakajimo asked if we might employ him from time to time in situations where his samurai demeanour would be a distinct advantage."

"As a deterrent?"

"Exactly."

"And he agreed?"

"After consultation with his clan leadership. I think they felt it might be to their advantage to have one of their number observe us at close quarters."

"Intriguing."

Glover, Nakajimo and Matsuo saddled up, a packhorse in tow, laden with supplies.

"Well shod," said Mackenzie. "You know, it's no time at all since the Japanese shod their horses with straw. Then the westerners arrived, and their horses had iron shoes. One bold Japanese blacksmith asked if he could borrow one of the shoes, have a look. He copied it, passed on his expertise, and in a matter of months iron horseshoes were in use right across the country."

"Impressive."

"It's the nature of their genius," said Mackenzie. "Learn quickly, copy, adapt."

"We can work with that," said Glover.

Walsh had turned up to bid Glover a safe journey up country, into the interior.

"I hear it's a different world," he said. "Oh, but one thing will be to your liking. I hear the women work near naked!" He cupped his hands in front of his chest, laughed.

"I see plenty of that in Nagasaki," said Glover.

"There was a letter in today's *Advertiser*," said Mackenzie, "bemoaning that very phenomenon. It wondered that there could be *any* market here for Manchester cotton. And referring to the bathhouses, he said he never saw a place where the cleanliness of the fair sex was established on such unimpeachable ocular evidence."

"Stuffed shirt," said Walsh.

"Fashioned from Manchester cotton!" said Glover. "I say, Long live unimpeachable ocular evidence!"

He had never seen such countryside. The landscape back home had a harsh beauty of its own, a ruggedness, a craggy grandeur. This was lush, green, fragrant, mile after mile of wide open paddyfields, soft-contoured hills rising behind, covered with vegetation right to the top, and tucked away here and there, in the folds of the hills, castles that might be from the Middle Ages, stockaded and fortified, overlooking the domain of some *daimyo*, the local feudal lord.

Matsuo rode ahead, watchful, Glover behind him, Nakajimo following, the packhorse at the rear. The heat beat down. Glover sweated, rode in his shirtsleeves, a battered, widebrimmed straw hat jammed on his head to shield him from the sun.

From time to time they would pass through a village of low, thatched huts, and every man, woman, child, dog, cat, chicken would stop, gawp at him. The old folks, withered, leathery-faced scarecrows, looked stricken at the sight of him, confused. The young and middle-aged looked apprehensive, and perhaps fearful of Matsuo's twin swords, the mark of the samurai, bowed their heads. The children, the animals, the poultry yelped and squawked, turned tail and ran, the children peeking out at him from a safe distance, behind a wall, on the other side of a ditch. Glover doffed his hat, waved to them, expansive, laughed, rode on.

They reached their destination towards evening. Ringer had said the tea produced here was finest quality, he had been here himself to check the supply. So the villagers had encountered the *ketojin*, barbarians, before. But that didn't stop them staring at Glover.

"I think is because you are *so* different," said Nakajimo. "Opposite."

The elder of the village welcomed them, showed them to a *ryokan*, a tiny wayside inn where they could spend the night, then invited them to his own home to eat. It was basic fare, rice porridge, fish broth, a few vegetables, but Glover ate it hungrily, greedily, smacked his lips and made the appropriate noises of appreciation. The old man grinned, his wife twinkled.

Glover explained, through Nakajimo, what he had in mind, the quantities of tea he would require, the fact that the drying would no longer have to be done here, but in huge batches at the firing plant being built in Nagasaki. In fact some of the workforce from the village might want to come to the city to work for him, would earn more in a season than they did now in two or three years.

The old man listened, nodded, occasionally grinned. He haggled over the price, and Glover allowed him to beat him down a little, so honour and dignity could be maintained. They bowed, Glover held out his hand and the old man shook it, then threw back his head and laughed. He brought out a flask of sake, poured generous measures for all of them.

Glover woke in the night, his bones one long ache, stretched out on the tatami mat on the hard floor, a harsh noise rasping, setting him on edge. The day's travel, the sun on his head, the too much sake had all left him dazed, stupefied. The room smelled fetid, stale. He had a drouth on him he needed to slake, struggled to his feet. His eyes got used to the dark, the huddle in the other corner was Nakajimo, the noise was him snoring. Matsuo had said he would rest in the corridor, outside the room, would need only a little sleep. Glover slid open the shoji screen, saw Matsuo sitting there, cross-legged, head nodding forward. But startled by the noise, he reached for the sword at his feet, in one quick reflex movement unsheathed it and held the blade to Glover's throat.

"Matsuo-san!" he shouted. "It's me! Guraba *desu!*"

Matsuo stood up, lowered the sword, apologised, bowed deep.

In the morning neither of them mentioned the incident. Matsuo continued as before, contained, watchful, stonefaced.

At the elder's home the old man's wife brought them rice and broth, gave Glover a piece of fruit, a persimmon.

"*Itadakimasu!*" he said, and bit into the fruit. Its juices brimmed in his mouth, slavered down his chin.

"*Oishi desu!*" he said, laughing. "Delicious!"

The old woman cackled, handed him a cloth to wipe his face.

Outside, a few small wood fires had been lit, the flames disappearing in the already bright sunlight. The women brought baskets of picked leaves, spread them out on trays and shook them over the fires. The women kept up a chatter and banter as they worked. As Walsh had said, some of them were bare-breasted, and comfortable with that, unashamed. Nakajimo caught Glover's eye, gave him a sly half-smile. Matsuo stared straight ahead, concentrated. One of the women said something to Glover he didn't understand and the others laughed out loud.

"What did she say?" he asked Nakajimo. But even he didn't know. "Local accent," he said. "You say *argot*?"

"I'll bet we can be sure it was crude!" said Glover.

"Yes," said Nakajimo. "Very sure!"

Glover doffed his hat to the women and they laughed again.

He took samples of the tea to show to Ringer, make sure the quality was as good as he'd expected. He thanked the elder and his wife, gave them gifts, a length of cotton, a sack of sugar. They walked with him and his companions to the edge of the village, waved to them as they rode off on the long trek back to Nagasaki.

All along the road, at intersections where paths and tracks ran off towards the castle of the local daimyo, the clan banner had been stretched across, barring entry, obscuring their view.

Nakajimo explained. "Word has spread you travel on this road. Daimyo want to shut you out, tell you westerners are not welcome."

It made him irritated and uneasy in equal measure. The last few miles in to town he had the distinct feeling they were being followed and watched, and he noticed Matsuo looking over his shoulder, tense and even more alert.

Mackenzie had been to Shanghai again, had brought back a letter for Glover. As well as investing Jardine's money, he had overdrawn on his loan from them, diverted funds from their account to his own, temporarily, to cover outlay on his tea business. The letter was a reprimand.

Your draft for $2000 has been presented and honoured. We should, however, beg you to note that we wish to be advised beforehand when you are in want of funds, for we make it a rule not to accept drafts unless permission to draw on us has been granted.

"So you've had your knuckles rapped," said Walsh. "The important thing is, you got away with it!"

Mackenzie had been terse, telling him to mind out, be careful. "Ca canny!" But Glover could hear the grudging admiration in it.

The scale of his operation was the talk of Nagasaki. Nobody had seen anything like it. The tea was transported by cart and wagon, from the village he'd visited and others like it, by boat from further up the coast. In the warehouse the tea was sorted and sifted, pressed and fired — heated over huge copper pans. The workforce numbered over a hundred, women doing the deft finicky work, the sorting, but also the firing to dry out the tea. The men packed the dried tea in great wooden crates, lugged it out the side door directly onto barges for transport. The heat was intense, and the noise of the place was enormous, cacophonous, the clanging of the pans, the dragging of the crates, the voices raised, shouting, singing.

He had made this happen. It was just a beginning. The smell of roasting tea filled the air, exhilarating incense. He breathed it in. It smelled sweet.

CHAPTER
FIVE

Alchemy

Nagasaki, 1860

Coils of smoke curled around him, took on fantastic shapes. The background shimmered, broke up into intricate filigree patterns, picked out in gold leaf. He lost himself in it, lay back and floated downstream through fabulous landscapes, temples and pagodas, mountains rising through clouds, dragons moving in swirls of mist.

He drifted into oblivion, woke to drab reality, himself sprawled on a grubby couch in a shabby room, the windows curtained over, the air rank and stale.

On another couch lay Walsh, in the same state, returning to consciousness, or returning *from* consciousness to this grey half-world.

A third figure crouched on the floor, back against the wall: Wang-Li, watching them, waiting for them to come round.

Glover sat up, groaned at the thud in his head, the numb ache. "God Almighty!"

Walsh grinned over at him, eyes puffy. "Back to the land of the living!"

"Strong stuff," said Glover.

"Big business," said Walsh.

Wang-Li brought them their coats, led them through to a warehouse stacked with wooden crates. He prised one of them open, lifted out a compact red-brown ball, like a small rust-coloured cannonball, handed it to Walsh.

"This is what we just had?"

Wang-Li nodded. "Best Patna."

"I'm used to dealing in Turkish," said Walsh, handing the ball to Glover. "But there's a glut of this on the market. Jardine's make a tidy sum shipping it into China. Our friend here has merely diverted some of the supply. If you want to trade in it on your own account, he's your man."

Glover weighed the ball of opium in his hand, gave it back to the Chinaman who nodded, said "Good deal!"

Outside, Glover took his leave of Walsh, headed past the docks. He was edgy, his skin prickly, the night's euphoria just a dream. He turned, scared by a noise from the shadows, a scratching and rustling; but it was just a rat, scuttling into a warehouse, intent on survival, like himself and every other creature. He shivered though it wasn't cold, walked home in the first grey light of dawn.

He asked Mackenzie what he thought.

"Jardine's make no secret of it, Tom. It's perfectly legitimate. Medicinal use. I mean, where would our own physicians be without it? I've taken it myself, in tincture. Best cure I know for diarrhoea, fever, aches and pains . . . you name it."

There was something unsettled in the way Mackenzie spoke; a hesitancy, a defensiveness.

"But this was different, Ken. It's so bloody powerful!"

"That's why it's such a valuable commodity." He paused, again that uncharacteristic note of uncertainty in his voice. "And why so much blood was shed over it in China."

"Legitimate business?"

"It was the forcing of China's door. It had to be done, for the sake of free trade."

"But you never traded in opium yourself?"

"I was years in Shanghai, Tom. I saw what this stuff can do. I suppose I didn't want to dirty my hands." He looked at his big gnarled hands, as if actually checking to make sure. "I just did my job for Jardine's. That was all." He stood up from behind his desk, looked out the window, his face set. "You know, the Jardine family own this country estate in Dumfries. I went there once, just before I shipped out to Shanghai. And I never forgot this — do you know what they've got carved on the gateposts?"

"What?"

"Poppies. A tacit acknowledgement of how they've made their fortune."

"*Pleasures are like poppies spread.*"

"Burns, eh?"

"*You seize the flower, its bloom is shed.*"

"Aye."

★ ★ ★

Glover decided he would import the opium in comparatively small amounts, through Wang-Li, simply add it to his consignments of Chinese medicine. He sensed that trading in the drug too openly and on too grand a scale would be messy, and besides, Jardine's already ruled that particular roost and he wasn't ready to challenge them just yet.

He also resolved not to indulge in the drug too often himself; he could imagine all too clearly where that might lead. Just now and then, if the mood was on him, he might go again with Walsh to Wang-Li's den, smoke a pipe, have another wee taste of paradise.

More often, more regularly, he crossed the two bridges, returned to the teahouse, the Sakura.

Again he was soaking in the hot tub, Walsh lolling back on the other side. They were both smoking cigars, sipping whisky, and Walsh was celebrating some particularly astute investment he'd made.

He was vague about the details, said simply, "To the fast buck!"

"The faster the better!" said Glover.

Walsh laughed, narrowed his eyes from the smoke curling into them, looked even more cunning.

"There is another way to make good money," he said. "High risk, quick return."

"And what might that be?" said Glover.

"Arms."

Glover stared at him. "Gunrunning?"

"That makes it sound romantic," said Walsh. "Not to mention criminal! I prefer to think of it as a simple business proposition."

"But not strictly legal."

"That depends whose laws you want to obey. Personally, I believe in the law of the marketplace. Supply and demand."

"So where's the supply?"

"Believe me, that's not a problem. In the wake of your country's little bloodbath in the Crimea, there was a flood of weapons across Europe. And with my own dear country — Sweet land of Liberty, to Thee we sing! — on the verge of tearing itself apart, the munitions factories worldwide are gearing themselves up. There's no shortage of armaments. It's just a matter of diverting them to these shores via China."

Glover took it all in, lightheaded from the heat, the steam and smoke drifting about them, but shaken too by the reality of what Walsh was suggesting.

"And the demand?" he said at last.

"There are factions here who want change," said Walsh. "The southern clans in particular, the Choshu and Satsuma."

"They want rid of the Shogun."

"Who has no intention of being removed."

"Understandably."

"It's moving towards a stand-off," said Walsh, "and both sides are ready to arm themselves to the teeth."

"So which side do you choose? Which of them do you supply?"

"One criterion," said Walsh. "Can they pay?" He grinned. "Hell, I'd arm them both! Let them slug it out!"

"Jesus!" said Glover, and he must have looked so serious, so dumbfounded, Walsh laughed out loud.

"Welcome to the big bad world, Tom. Oh, and there is one other law we abide by. Don't get caught!"

Walsh arranged a meeting for him with an agent of the Shogun. They sat round a table in the smoky back room of an inn down by the docks. The agent had brought his own translator, and two guards, armed with swords and pikes, who stood with their backs to the door.

Walsh spoke quietly with the translator, explained to Glover. "He says the Shogun wants rifles and ammunition which the suppliers may not be willing to sell to him directly. He says we are in a position to arrange it, and it would be very much in our interests to comply with the Shogun's request."

"Could that be construed as a threat?" asked Glover. He was suddenly acutely aware that the armed men, as well as guarding the entrance, were blocking the exit.

"You're learning," said Walsh.

He stood up and moved away from the table, beckoned Glover to the far side of the room where they could confer.

"I'm in two minds about this," said Glover, under his breath. "I mean, it is the bloody Shogun who's been making life so difficult for us."

"So we get on his good side. That's what this fellow's saying. Should lead to a few more concessions."

"And if it doesn't?"

"Well then, we can make sure his enemies are better armed than he is!"

They shook hands on it, returned to the table and indicated to the agent they were ready to do business.

Walsh would take a cut for brokering the deal. Glover's job was to make the crossing to Shanghai, hand over payment, pick up the merchandise. Wang-Li would accompany him, act as translator, hire bodyguards.

Shanghai was even worse than he remembered it, perhaps because he was used to Nagasaki. There were even more armed guards round the foreign settlement. Rumours of uprising were always rife; according to Walsh, the latest threat was from a warlord who regarded himself as a reincarnation of Jesus Christ, determined this time to establish the Kingdom of Heaven by force. Glover had laughed at that, but here, now, as he walked these backstreets, the hellish reality of the place assailed him. Blood Alley. The Whore of the Orient. Stinking to high Heaven.

The meeting place was near the waterfront, and Wang-Li led him through a warren of crowded back streets, narrow alleyways, the two Chinese bodyguards following close behind, circumspect, alert. As they approached one doorway, the entrance to some drinking den, Wang-Li raised a hand, stopping them, just before a brawl came spilling out; two drunk sailors, tangled up in each other, punched, kicked, butted, gouged, tumbled to the ground, grappling. By the sound of them one was Irish, the other Russian. They fought on with ferocious animal intensity, grunted and

100

snarled. Wang-Li stepped round them, led on, down an even darker, narrower alley. He leered at Glover as they passed one doorway after another, in each one a grotesque tableau, a grim coupling; a sailor ramming a scrawny young woman hard against a dank wall, another holding one by the hair as she kneeled in front of him, took him in her mouth.

"Fucking hell!" said Glover, the images searing into him.

Wang-Li laughed, led on further till they came to an archway leading into a courtyard. Two armed guards stood outside a warehouse; Wang-Li spoke to them, led the way in, through the warehouse stacked with boxes and crates, to a half-lit back room where a fat Chinese merchant sat at a table, welcomed them, grinned, motioned them to sit. His name was Chan. He called out and a young woman brought through a deep lacquer tray, on it a kettle and teapot, little unglazed ceramic cups. Wang-Li and Chan began their dialogue straight away, in their own language, and Glover understood none of it, had simply to trust. His ear had grown attuned to the sounds and rhythms of Japanese, but this was entirely other, had a strange music all of its own, nasal and singsong with utterly unfamiliar vowels, some of it half-swallowed and all delivered rapid-fire. He watched the young woman pour the tea, go through a whole brisk ritual; pouring hot water into the teapot and into each cup, swilling round, slopping out into the tray where it drained away underneath; then stuffing a handful of green leaves into the pot, scalding them with more hot water. She looked up and caught Glover's eye, held his gaze, gave a flick of a smile just as Chan and Wang-Li seemed to come to some kind of agreement, gave a gruff little laugh.

One of Chan's guards dragged a crate through from the warehouse, levered it open, showed it was packed full with rifles, wrapped around with wadding. The lamplight glinted on a metal barrel, a polished wooden stock. Chan lifted out one of the guns, passed it to Glover, who felt the weight of it, squinted along the sights, handed it back.

"We agree price," said Wang-Li. "We pay and take."

"No haggling?" said Glover.

"Hag-ling?" said Wang-Li.

"No arguing over the price? No trying to beat him down?"

"Not this time," said Wang-Li, a wee shrewd glimmer in his eyes. "Good price. Not good to argue. Maybe next time when we buy more, make bigger business."

"Right," said Glover. "Next time."

He raised his cup of fragrant tea to Chan, took a sip.

"Next time!" said Chan, grinning, carefully shaping the English words. Then he called out to the girl again and she brought through three pipes.

"Best Patna?" said Glover.

"Turkish," said Wang-Li.

Glover smiled at Chan. "A pleasure doing business!"

It was only when his head was clear, a full day into the return voyage, that Glover realised perhaps it hadn't exactly been prudent to share the pipe with Chan, might have left him vulnerable. But he'd trusted in

102

Wang-Li, followed his lead. Clearly too it had been a signal to Chan, a way of sealing the deal.

The clipper slipped into Nagasaki harbour towards evening after six days at sea. The tides had been favourable and they'd made good time. The Shogun's agent was waiting at the quayside, this time accompanied by a whole troop of armed soldiers.

With the same brusqueness, verging on hostility, that he'd demonstrated at their previous meeting, the agent came on board, checked every crate of merchandise, every rifle and pistol, every box of ammunition. Grudgingly satisfied, he nodded at Glover, supervised the transfer of the consignment directly onto one of the Shogun's ships, an antiquated junk riding at anchor. It would sail directly to Osaka, through the Inland Sea.

Through the agent's translator, Glover said if the Shogun was ever of a mind to import modern ships to replace his worn-out fleet, Glover could arrange it through his contacts in Scotland. The agent's only response was to take umbrage at the implied slight to Japan, and he said if the Shogun ever did want to engage in such an undertaking then he would be the one to initiate negotiations.

The money was paid into Glover's account at the Hong Kong and Shanghai Bank. He had more of a swagger than usual as he walked into his office after checking that the payment had gone through. But he'd no sooner settled at his desk than Mackenzie came barging in. He'd heard rumours of the deal; now they were confirmed and he was raging.

"This is madness, Tom!" He banged the desk.

"I know what I'm doing, Ken," said Glover, keeping calm though the attack unsettled him.

"You're going against Jardine's restrictions. You're defying the British Government. You're messing in local politics. That's what you're doing!"

"Do you think I want to sit on my arse selling silk and tea the rest of my life! There's real money to be made here, Ken, and you know it."

"And I also know if you sup with the Devil you need a long spoon."

"What's that supposed to mean?"

"The Shogun's a powerful man, Tom."

"That's why I'm doing business with him."

"He has enemies."

"Hell, I'll trade with them too!"

"You're dealing with forces beyond your control!"

Glover stood his ground. "I know fine what I'm dealing with, and I'm not afraid to take risks."

"Ach, Tom," said Mackenzie, shaking his head. "Tom."

Glover was undeterred, took another order from the Shogun's agent, made a return trip to Shanghai, exhilarated. Again the delivery was made at night, the consignment transferred directly to the Shogun's own ships. Once more Glover was disparaging about the state of the vessels, and this time the agent indicated the Shogun might indeed be interested in the purchase of Scottish-built ships. The agent also asked about bigger and better weaponry, specifically cannon. Glover remained businesslike, said he would make discreet enquiries, but his heart was thudding in his chest.

The combined profits on his two previous deals amounted to $10,000. The order under discussion would be worth ten times as much. He discussed it with Walsh, who let out a rush of air through his teeth. "Serious money, Tom."

It would take time, an order on this scale would probably have to go to Europe. Glover set things in motion right away. He contacted Armstrong & Co., the munitions manufacturers in Newcastle, worked out costs. He met the Shogun's agent again, discussed specifics, drew up a detailed order, for delivery to "The Japanese Government". It was for some 15 muzzle-loaders, 70-pounders with carriages and slides, 20 breech-loaders and, in total, 700 tons of shot and shell.

Walsh was impressed. "Christ, Tom, you really are learning fast!"

A down payment on the consignment, in the sum of $40,000, was paid into Glover's account.

Glover had still been living in the clapboard house behind the warehouse. Now he wanted something more in keeping with his ambitions. His credit was good; he took advice and employed a master craftsman, the architect Hidenoshin Koyama, to design and build a bungalow. No half measures, he wanted the best.

The site was spectacular, on Minami Yamate, the southern hillside. Koyama had chosen it for its outlook, down to the waterfront, north to Dejima, across the bay to the hills beyond. Koyama spoke no English, had no intention of learning. Glover's Japanese, though improving, was still basic: the sweet-talk of the teahouse, the formalised evasiveness of the business gambit. They communicated in signs and gestures, where necessary used an interpreter. Koyama made sketches and diagrams, full-blown plans, showed them to Glover, pacing out dimensions and layout. Glover took a liking to him, his energy, his straightforward workmanlike manner. There was a sense of strength contained, disciplined and held in check, nothing wasted.

There was one thing that was not negotiable. Koyama insisted on it. In the centre of the open space which would be the garden was a pine tree. Koyama was adamant it should stay, not be uprooted. The language he used did not readily translate. One word in particular seemed to recur. *Wabi*. The translator had difficulty, came up with *emptiness*.

"*Wabi*," said Koyama again, and he pointed at the tree. "*Ipponmatsu*."

"Lone pine," said the translator.

"Fine," said Glover. "Ipponmatsu it is."

At the next meeting, though, he had to set his mind at rest about this *wabi*, this emptiness.

"I mean," he said, "I'm not wanting tatami mats and cushions. I want room inside, proper tables and chairs."

The translator explained. Koyama chuckled, twinkled. "*Hai. So desu!*"

Glover needn't have worried. Even from the finished drawings he could see it would be something special.

★ ★ ★

The building had a character all of its own, its three sections honeycomb-shaped, interlinked. It was a marriage of East and West: solid foundations, spacious, airy rooms, meticulous attention to the detail, the craftwork — ceramic roof-tiles, a hardwood porch, a rising sun design in the windowframes. When it was complete, Glover held a reception for his colleagues and friends — Mackenzie and Walsh, Groom and Harrison, Shibata and Nakajimo, Ringer and a few others.

They stood sipping drinks on the lawn, looking out across the bay as the evening light touched the hills opposite.

"You've done well for yourself, Tom," said Mackenzie.

"Success!" said Walsh, raising his glass.

"To all of us," said Glover.

Koyama had arrived and Glover hurried across to him, bowed respectfully. He bowed in return, just a little less deeply.

"Koyama-san," said Glover. "Thank you once more. The house is magnificent."

"*Do-itashimashite*," said Koyama, accepting, acknowledging and disregarding the compliment all at once. It was nothing.

His assistant, the translator, was carrying something, heavy by the look of it, elaborately wrapped in thick ricepaper.

"*Dozo*," said Koyama, taking the package and handing it ceremoniously to Glover.

He mimed being weighed down by it, out of breath at the effort. Koyama smiled, indicated he should open it.

It was a piece of rough stone, two ideograms carved into it, the lines graceful and fluid.

"Is Koyama-sensei's own calligraphy," said the translator, pointing to the symbols. "*Ippon. Matsu.*"

"*Arigato gozaimasu,*" said Glover, bowing to Koyama more deeply than before.

Again Koyama nodded, accepting the thanks as his due, but happy nonetheless at Glover's response. He supervised the placing of the stone, just so, inside the gateway.

"I guess that's your house named," said Walsh.

"I like it fine," said Glover.

Before Koyama left, he stood in front of the tree, intensely silent. Then he bowed to it, placed his hands a moment on the trunk, nodded once more to Glover and was gone.

Walsh lingered after the others had left; he savoured a last drink, one more cigar.

"It's a wonderful house," he said. "But you know what it needs now? A woman's touch."

"I can get somebody to come in and clean," said Glover. "Keep it tidy."

"You want more than that," said Walsh. "You should get a *musume*, a little mistress to move in."

"I'm not sure."

"Conveniently meets *all* your needs," said Walsh. "And no strings. Simple business arrangement. There's hardly a westerner living here who doesn't have his little musume tucked away. Hell, I've had three of 'em!"

"Aye," said Glover. "I know."

"What else is a fellow to do?" said Walsh. "There are no western women, apart from the occasional trader's wife or horsefaced daughter. And we're not exactly welcome in the upper echelons of Japanese society, so any romantic liaison there is out of the question. And hell, let's face it, marriage is just legalised prostitution anyway, except you're paying for life! So what do you say?"

He felt big and out-of-place in the small room; his legs ached from kneeling on the floor; the incense was starting to cloy, the koto music grate. This was foolishness. He should never have listened to Walsh.

The madame of the teahouse, the *okama*, herself an ageing courtesan, sat in front of the shoji screen. The screen was decorated with paintings of a garden, birds and blossoms, a bridge leading to a pavilion, a lovers' meeting. Each time the screen opened, a different young girl was kneeling there, bowing to him, making eye contact then looking away, all coy and shy.

It was one thing to come here, visit the girls, pay for their services. But to have one move in with him, effectively buy a wife, felt unnatural. He would end the business now, thank the *okami* and go home. His knees creaked as he stood painfully up. The screen opened one more time and he stopped, stood there gaping. The madame made to close the screen again but he told her to wait.

This was the one, unbelievably beautiful, with the same easy grace as all the rest, but something more besides, a spark in the eyes; in behind the worldliness, an innocence.

He went forward, held out his hand. She took it in hers, such a lightness in her touch, stepped in to the room.

"Your name?" he asked her. "*O namae wa?*"

She bowed. "Sono *desu.*"

"Sono," he said, enjoying the sound of it. He smiled, pointed to himself. "Thomas Blake Glover."

She looked confused, covered her mouth with her hand.

"Thomas," he said, pronouncing it carefully.

She repeated it. "Tomasu."

"Blake."

"Bureku."

"Glover."

"Guraba. *Hai.* Guraba-san."

"Tom," he said.

"Tomu."

She nodded, very serious. He laughed and so did she, again putting her hand to her mouth. Her black black hair was held up by a silver clasp shaped like a butterfly. The line of her neck was exquisite, exposed by the curve of her kimono collar. The silk of the garment swished as she moved. He caught her scent and he was lost, undone.

Later, back at his house, he led her into the bedroom. She looked round, giggled in delight at the western furniture, the carved armchairs, the heavy iron bedstead. She laughed too at his eagerness — he was pulling off his own clothes, hurried and clumsy, leading her to the bed, not even waiting for her to undress, groping in the folds of her clothes for the moist warmth, and she was reaching up to unclasp her hair, let the blackness of it shimmer free, engulf him as she straddled, mounted him, guided him in, and he bucked and bucked and came into her quick.

Sono moved in the next day, brought a small bundle of her few belongings. Glover had to work, but when he came home at the end of the day, she was already settled, at home. She had made tea, poured it for him.

On the table was a little doll, rounded at the bottom. "Is yours?" he asked.

For a moment she looked alarmed. "Is all right?"

"Of course it is." He tipped the doll over, let it rock back upright.

"*Hai*," she said, doing the same. "Is Daruma. Bodhidharma."

The doll had the painted face of a fierce-looking patriarch, staring eyes, bristling whiskers.

"Bring good luck," she said, struggling with the words. Again she pushed it over. "Down." She let it go. "Up."

"Bounces back," he said. "Every time. I like it!"

She clapped her hands, laughed. He leaned forward and kissed her sweet mouth.

He was settled, ensconced, in his favourite leather armchair in the lounge of the Foreigners' Club, by an open window that looked out over the Bund. He'd been turning the pages of the *Nagasaki Advertiser*, glancing at the news reports tucked away among the shipping lists.

Walsh came in, flicked the paper to get his attention.

"Good evening, Guraba-san!" he said, and made an exaggerated bow.

"Bugger off!" said Glover. "I'm trying to read."

"Keeping your finger on the pulse."

"This eminent journal reliably informs me that Her Majesty the Queen is suffering from a nervous depression, that her time of life is a very critical period for ladies, that there is a certain excitability inherent in the Royal Family, and that all of this, taken together, is giving rise to great anxiety with respect to Her Majesty's health."

"I can see the anxiety writ large on your face!" said Walsh.

"There are reports from your own neck of the woods," said Glover. "President Lincoln has issued a proclamation calling for the recruitment of 75,000 troops."

"A good time to be in Nagasaki," said Walsh.

"The hub of the universe," said Glover. "There is an account of last week's performances here by Baron von Hohenlohe and Signor Spectacolini. They sang duets then took part in a comic opera entitled *Little Toddlekins*."

"I was heartbroken at being unable to attend," said Walsh.

"Aye," said Glover. "Me too. The report praises their performance, then continues, *Both men were excellent. But what shall we say of Miss Belle Chimer as Mrs Whiffleton?*"

"What indeed?" said Walsh. "But if I can drag your attention away from such riveting accounts, I have something for you."

He took from his waistcoat pocket a small, shining, silver coin, held it up so it glinted in the light. He flipped it through the air to Glover, who caught it.

"It's called *itzibu*," said Walsh.

"Pretty," said Glover, turning the coin, a Japanese symbol imprinted on either side.

"Of course," said Walsh.

"Trust them to go for silver instead of gold."

"More subtle, right? But there's a problem."

"Why am I not surprised?"

"They were introduced in Yokohama," said Walsh. "American traders threw their dollars in the scales at the Customs House, got these in exchange."

"But not enough?"

"Exactly. The rate is distinctly unfavourable. There was practically a riot!"

"Christ!" said Glover. "They'll have to sort this out."

"Oh, they will," said Walsh. "In their own good time."

Glover turned the coin between finger and thumb, spun it and plucked it from the air, pocketed it.

He sat facing Sono across the dining-room table, took the silver coin from his pocket with a flourish.

"Itzibu," he said, and placed it on the table beside three inverted sake cups. "Silver."

"*Hai!*" she said, nodding and smiling at him. "Siruba."

"Now watch."

He put one of the cups over the coin, did the old conjurer's trick of switching the cups around rapidly. He'd learned this as a boy, so long ago, from a tattered pamphlet he'd bought for a penny at Inverurie fair. Secrets of Magic. Prestidigitation. Sleight of hand. Sono looked on, bamboozled. He motioned to her to guess where the coin was. She focused all her attention, a wee pucker of concentration between her perfectly arched eyebrows; she swithered a moment then pointed decisively at the middle cup.

"*Kore wa!*" she said.

This one.

He lifted the cup.

No coin.

She shrieked and held her hands up. Glover chuckled, straightened his cuffs, did the trick again. Now she pointed at the right-hand cup.

"*Kore wa!*" This time she was definite.

Again he lifted the cup; again there was no coin.

She let out a little gasp. He lifted the left-hand cup and there it was, shining.

"*Voilà!*"

She gave a startled *Oh!* that made him laugh out loud.

"Magic!" he said.

★　★　★

Mackenzie was raging, dumped a moneybag full of coins onto his desk, the silver itzibu spilling out.

"Bloody Shogun! Bloody Bakufu! Bloody country! Why can't they stick to gold like everybody else?"

"Ah!" said Glover. "There you have it. They're not like everybody else. They're not like *anybody* else."

"It's wilful," said Mackenzie. "It's obstructive."

"It's Japanese!"

Glover sifted the coins, let them shimmer through his fingers, the gesture enormously satisfying, theatrical, the miser with his hoard. Silver and gold.

He stopped, suddenly jolted by a thought so preposterous he didn't dare trust it.

"Jesus Christ!" he said.

"What is it?" asked Mackenzie, still tetchy.

"A daft idea," said Glover.

"Another one?"

Glover checked the *Advertiser*, commodity prices, the going rate for gold bullion.

"God Almighty!"

He threw down the paper, rushed out, left Mackenzie shaking his head.

He shouldered his way into the Customs House, Shibata and Nakajimo following in his wake. The place was jampacked with traders — Americans, Europeans, Chinese, all haggling and angry, the noise a raucous babble. He saw Montblanc looking petulant, piqued, as only a Frenchman could. Behind the counter sat a customs official, face bland, expressionless, weighing out coins on a set of scales, his movements practised and unhurried as if he were performing some ancient religious ritual, refusing to be ruffled or flustered by the racket and hubbub around him.

Shibata bowed low to the official. Glover had primed him on what to ask. The official grunted out a reply. Shibata gave Glover a nod, and he turned and shoved his way back out, the two clerks hurrying to keep up.

He was back in half an hour. With the help of the two clerks he had emptied his own safe of the silver coins, filled six bags, loaded them on a handcart. He had also taken the precaution of bringing his pistol, tucked into his belt. They carried the bags straight up to the counter, thudded them down. Then they waited, patient, while the high priest of commerce, in his own time, set their offerings on the scales, wrote a set of figures on a paper scroll with a brisk flourish of a bamboo brush. Glover checked with Nakajimo that the figure was what he expected.

A second time he led the way out and down the street, stopped at the heavily guarded Hong Kong and Shanghai Bank. Inside he handed over the document from the Customs House, received a quantity of gold bars from the strongroom. Nakajimo and Shibata loaded them onto the handcart, covered them with a length of rough cloth, trundled the precious load back to Glover's office. Glover walked ahead, alert, one hand on the pistol at his belt.

When the gold was securely locked away, he hurried out again in search of Mackenzie and Walsh, found them at the Club.

"You're not going to believe this!" he said, trying not to speak too loudly, but unable to keep the eagerness from his voice. He held up an itzibu coin. "These are worth their weight in gold. In fact they're worth three times their weight!"

"You have my full undivided attention," said Walsh.

"Explain," said Mackenzie.

"It's simple!" said Glover. "Four of these — that's about six shillings at the present rate — buys a cobang of gold. But ship that gold out and a cobang sells for eighteen shillings. Two hundred percent profit!"

"Good God!" said Mackenzie.

Walsh was already on his feet, heading towards the door.

"We'll have to move fast," he said, "before every freebooter in Nagasaki has the same idea."

"Every *other* freebooter!" said Mackenzie.

For weeks it was chaos, a goldrush, as word spread and traders cashed in. Ship after ship left for China, laden with Japanese gold. Fortunes were made before the customs officials imposed restrictions on the number of itzibu issued to any one trader. But they simply bought under assumed names. Glover, Mackenzie and Walsh became Messrs Hook, Line and Sinker respectively. Finally the Shogun's government intervened, reluctantly returned to the gold standard, closed the door on further profiteering.

The three of them were back in the Foreigners' Club, drinking a toast to their success.

"To alchemy!" said Mackenzie.

"Magic!" said Glover.

"The fast buck!" said Walsh.

"Mister Hook!"

"Mister Line!

"Mister Sinker!

They drained their glasses.

"Of course, the Shogun's none too pleased about the whole business," said Mackenzie. "It could have destabilised their entire economy."

"They've nobody to blame but themselves," said Walsh. "They were the ones trying to cheat, undervaluing the dollar. It just backfired on them, that's all."

"Hell mend them," said Glover. "And if it undermines the Shogun, well and good."

He was seated again at the table, facing Sono, the little sake cups once more between them. Again he placed a silver coin beneath one of the cups, performed his *legerdemain*, worked the magic. She chose the middle cup. He lifted it, revealed a gleaming gold coin. Then he lifted the left-hand cup, and there was a second gold coin; he lifted the right and there was a third. She scooped up all three coins, jingled them together, laughed in sheer delight.

Sono was expecting a child. She had been hesitant about telling him, tentative, unsure how he would react.

He was overwhelmed — thrilled, excited, intoxicated, terrified. A child! Himself a father! He laughed, thumped the desk, said they'd get married straight away.

"You don't strictly have to," said Walsh when he told him the news. "I mean, there are ways and means. The girl can be farmed out, paid off. The child can be adopted."

Glover was stung. "Christ!" he said, "I knew you were callous, but this is bloody coldhearted. It's beyond belief!"

"Sorry," said Walsh, realising he'd misjudged. "I'd forgotten you were a man in love!"

The word discomfited Glover. "Aye, well."

But when he stood with Sono at the temple on the hill behind Ipponmatsu, he was moved by a huge tenderness towards her.

His wife.

His wife. And she was carrying his child, a son perhaps, to continue the line, bear the family name; and if a daughter, then that was good too, it was all good, and a son would come later.

The ceremony was simple. The Buddhist monk from the temple chanted a mantra, bestowed a blessing. A Christian minister read the vows, and as Glover repeated each one, Sono nodded in agreement.

Till death us do part.

"*Hai, so desu.*"

Mackenzie and Walsh were there as witnesses, the madame from the teahouse smiling her own benediction.

Back at Ipponmatsu Glover and Sono stood on the lawn, watching the evening light on the far hills, the ships at anchor out in the bay. They had talked about going to Kagoshima, to visit Sono's father. Now it seemed essential.

"He's going to be a grandfather," said Glover. "*Oji-san*."

She laughed, clapped her hands. "*Oji-san!*"

"You think he'll be happy about that?"

"I hope so," she said. "He very strong man. Like you."

She had already spoken of her father, a samurai from Satsuma clan. Kagoshima, in the far south, was their strong-hold. Now she said her father, and the clan, might want to do business with him.

"Well," he said. "Now that he's family . . ."

She smiled.

"Isn't that right, Mrs Glover? *Guraba-fujin*."

She laughed and covered her mouth. He hugged her, made her shriek, lifted her and carried her, so light, into the house.

Sono had gone on ahead, travelled to Kagoshima a few days earlier, prepared her father, Shimada-san, for the meeting. She was waiting at the quay to greet Glover as his ship docked. She clapped her hands with a childlike eagerness when she saw him, then consciously regained her composure, her poise, bowed formally. Glover laughed, bowed ridiculously low, then took her hand and kissed it.

Kagoshima was not one of the treaty ports. The Satsuma were hostile to change, resented the western invasion and the Shogun who had allowed it. As he walked with Sono along the narrow street to the ryokan, the inn where they would be staying, Glover sensed it in the air. People stared at him, not with curiosity but with open hostility, with hatred and fear; the women turned away, the men spat out curses, the children ran and hid.

He had read accounts of the American Wild West, by traders who had ventured into Indian settlements, and he imagined it must feel like this, the atmosphere predatory, himself as prey. Some of the men were armed, swords tucked in their waistbands. More than once he saw a hand rest on a hilt, in readiness, and was glad he had brought his pistol. He was grateful too that he was with Sono. Then the unease he felt, the nervousness in his gut, even made him suspicious of her. She might be under her father's sway, be leading him into a trap. They had only been together a few months, and if he knew anything about the Japanese, it was that he knew nothing. The sense of apprehension grew, the unease deepened. This woman, his wife, was a stranger to him. Then she stopped at the entrance to the inn, turned and looked at him with such openness that he felt ashamed.

The meeting with Shimada-san was set for later in the day. Glover gave himself over to Sono, to show him her town.

"Kagoshima beautiful," she said.

"So I see."

She laughed, mimicked what he'd said, singsong. "So I see!"

In the distance, on an island offshore, was a volcano, its sheer sides blue-green, a plume of smoke above its peak.

Sono saw him looking. "*Sakurajima*," she said, naming it.

She showed him gardens and temples, a pottery with exquisite bowls and vases, some black some white, tastefully displayed. Past it ran a small stream, and placed in the flow was a length of bamboo. It was open at one end and fastened, mid-length, to a cross-piece, a fulcrum. It faced upstream, so it gradually filled with water, and the weight tipped it so it hit a rock with a satisfying thunk. Then the bamboo emptied and the whole process started again. He stood watching it, fascinated, as it filled and emptied, filled and emptied.

Thunk.

"*Shishi-odoshi*," said Sono.

"That's what it's called?"

"*Hai.*"

"But what's it *for*?"

She shrugged, didn't understand the question. *Shishi-odoshi.*

At a shrine she stopped and bowed to a little stone statue, one of their gods, its face benign and compassionate, one hand raised in benediction. Round its shoulders was a tiny piece of silk, wrapped like a shawl, and in front of it someone had placed offerings, a single chrysanthemum flower, a ricecake, a sake flask.

"Jizo," she said, and patted her belly. "We pray to him for baby."

She faced the statue again, seemed to be uttering a prayer. She folded her hands and bowed once more. He smiled and did the same.

Shimada sat, cross-legged, at a low table. Glover had removed his shoes, kneeled on the tatami mat, facing the old man; Sono was between them, even more deferential and self-effacing than usual, the dutiful daughter, meekness incarnate. She introduced Glover, formally, and the old man grunted.

"Shimada-san," said Glover, bowing low enough to show respect, but still maintain his own dignity. "*Hajimemashite. Yoroshiku onegai shimasu.*"

Shimada seemed pleased at being greeted in his own language by the gaijin. This time his grunt was a little more expressive, more accepting. He gave a barely perceptible incline of the head, indicated Sono should pour them drinks, sake in small black ceramic cups.

"*Kanpai!*" said Glover, and they drank.

Sono refilled the cups and Glover raised his again. It was time to try his party-piece, a toast he had prepared, rehearsed with Sono's help.

He looked straight at the old man. "*Shogun!*" he said, and the old man paused, cup raised halfway to his lips, before Glover continued, "*Nanka kuso kurae!*"

The old man looked startled, weighed up what Glover had said, let it sink in. The Shogun! To hell with him!

Shimada's face seemed to crumple, fold in on itself. A choking sound gurgled in his throat. Then he spluttered and roared with laughter, thumped the table.

"*Nanka kuso kurae!*"

This was good! It was a story to tell: the gaijin, his son-in-law, cursing the Shogun!

Now they could talk business.

It was slow and laboured, the language a problem, but with Sono's help and the sake flowing, they found common ground. At one point Shimada saw the pistol in Glover's belt, under his coat, and he pointed at it. Glover thought he was angry at him for bringing a weapon into the house, and he started to apologise, but the old man simply wanted to see the gun, take a closer look.

Glover made sure the safety catch was in place, locked, and he handed over the gun, handle-first. Shimada made a great play of weighing it in his hand, observing it was heavy.

Then time stopped.

The old man levelled the pistol straight at him, drew a bead on him, cocked the hammer. Glover was instantly hard stone-cold sober, looking down the barrel. The old man's eyes were ice, gave nothing away. Then he laughed, handed the pistol back, indicated his approval. This was what he wanted to buy, and more. He mimed firing a rifle. Glover mimed clutching his heart, as if he'd been shot. Again the old man roared.

They talked on into the night, drank more, haggled over prices and quantities, delivery dates. Finally, in the wee small hours, as far as Glover could understand, they reached agreement. The deal was done.

Outside in the cool air, Shimada, in fine humour, said goodbye. Glover and Sono walked the short distance to the ryokan. In the distance the tip of the volcano was a red glow in the dark.

In the morning they set out for the harbour, Shimada escorting them. As they made their way along the main street, they heard the low thud of a drum, saw a procession coming the other way, towards them, banners catching the breeze, emblazoned with the clan crest, a cross inside a circle. The procession was led by half a dozen fully armed samurai, in helmets and breast-plates, behind them a *norimon*, a palanquin carried by four more men, and behind that another column of armed guards, twenty in all. The street cleared as folk scattered.

"Daimyo," said Shimada, and he gave Glover an anxious look, but he was wise enough now to step well back, bow his head. Shimada did the same, Sono kneeled in the dust.

The Daimyo was the clan leader, ruler of the territory. Glover thought it prudent not to look up, just kept his head down, felt his neck tense. But as the norimon passed him there was a shouted order, a sharp bark of command from inside, and it stopped right in front of him. Shimada got down on one knee, spoke rapidly in response to questioning from behind the curtain. To Glover it was a garble, gruff, slurred and hurried, but he recognised his own name, mention of the Shogun, reference to doing business. The curtain opened a moment and Glover looked up, neck still

125

tensed, into the face of the Daimyo, glaring at him, that now-familiar grimace of distaste contorting the tight grim mouth. He was almost sorry to disappoint by being merely human, wished he could breathe fire, sprout a second head; then perhaps he might meet the intensity of expectation. But whatever was going on, he seemed to have passed muster. The Daimyo gave another guttural grunt, like clearing the throat of some unpleasant blockage. The curtain was closed. The procession moved on.

Mackenzie explained the situation to him. The daimyo were powerful men, many of them hardline traditional-ists, opposed to the Shogun. But he had ways of keeping them in check.

"Such as?"

"For a start," said Mackenzie, "he insists that their wives and families stay in Edo right under his nose. The daimyo are allowed to visit only at the Shogun's express invitation. If they step out of line, their families are under threat."

"So they're effectively held hostage"

"Exactly."

"Ruthless," said Glover.

"Aye," said Mackenzie. "So mind your step."

But a week later Glover was once more in Shanghai, buying more crates of rifles, this time for the Satsuma. On the journey back he was aware of a ship in the distance that seemed to be following, tailing them. He raised a spyglass to his eye, saw it was one of the

Shogun's fleet, the Tokugawa banner flying at the masthead.

"One of the Shogun's clapped-out old junks!" he called out to the pilot. "They'll never catch us!"

And he was right. The junk was no match for the Jardine's clipper he'd commandeered for the run. They tacked and veered, picked up speed, left the Shogun's vessel far behind.

Shimada was waiting to meet him when he docked at Nagasaki. Once more the cargo was unloaded at night, transferred this time to one of the Satsuma's own merchant ships for the journey on to Kagoshima. He suggested to Shimada that the Satsuma also might think about buying better ships, that he could use his contacts in Scotland, get them a good price. A second-hand steamer, reconditioned and in excellent working order, should cost about $30,000. With Glover's good offices he could reduce that to $25,000. Shimada laughed, said it was good to have a businessman in the family, and he would discuss the matter with the Daimyo. In the meantime, he would arrange payment for the consignment of rifles, partly in gold, partly in Mexican silver dollars, another substantial sum, in the region of $3,000.

Shimada and Glover bowed to each other, the deal done.

He was walking on his own, lost in thought. He turned down a narrow back street, to no particular purpose, was suddenly jolted, startled, by a dark figure emerging from an alleyway, standing right in front of him, blocking his way. The man was a samurai, young, probably no older than Glover himself. He cursed his stupidity in letting his attention drift, being off-guard. He tensed and braced, ready to fight or flee.

The man stared right at him, right into him, intent. "Guraba-san?"

"*Hai*," he said. "*So desu.*" He spoke with a kind of guarded truculence, might have added *Who's asking? Why do you want to know?*

"I am Ito Hirobumi," said the samurai, bowing, "from Choshu clan."

"You speak English?" said Glover, genuinely surprised, again caught off-guard.

"I need to understand my enemy," said the man, with almost a smile.

"Interesting way to open a conversation," said Glover.

"May we talk more?" asked the man.

Glover was unsure, and Ito nodded towards another figure, standing just inside the alley, alert and on guard.

"You know Matsuo-san?"

Glover saw, recognised the young man who had travelled with him up country. He greeted him with a wave of the hand. Matsuo bowed, stiff.

Matsuo's presence was some reassurance, and somehow Glover felt he could trust this Ito, followed the man back down the alley, through a low doorway into a smoky inn. Glover had to duck his head to enter, and when he straightened up he was looking at three other samurai, one of them Takashi.

For the second time Glover cursed his own stupidity. He had been led into a trap, would end his short life here in this miserable den, be hacked to pieces, scattered as carrion. The three samurai had got to their feet. But Ito stepped forward, challenged Takashi, their grunted exchange a guttural cadenza of low growl and bark, hackles raised. It ended when Takashi slammed the table with his fist, shouted "*Ie!*" He pushed past Glover, confronted Matsuo, who had just come in the door. Takashi spat some challenge at him, voice hissing with disdain. Then he threw a last murderous look at Glover and strode out, followed by the other two.

"I hope he hasn't gone for reinforcements," said Glover.

"You are safe," said Ito. "For now."

Matsuo stood on guard by the door. The barman cowered, rigid, behind the counter. Ito called out to him, ordered drinks. The man scurried to fetch them. The other few customers in the room seemed to relax again, breathe easier, pick up where they had left off. At a table in the far corner, an old man sat watching them. Laid out in front of him were brushes and an inkstone, a few sheets of paper rolled up. Two other old men muttered to each other, laughed, resumed some age-old conversation.

The barman brought a tray with a flask of sake, two cups.

"Please," said Ito, motioning Glover to sit down.

"So," said Glover, "you don't mind drinking with your enemy?"

"I hope you don't have to be enemy," said Ito. "From what I have heard, maybe you are different from the other gaijin. I think maybe we can even do business."

"I'm flattered," said Glover.

"Ito does not flatter."

"Well then, I'm honoured." Glover raised his cup. "*Kanpai!*"

"Cheers!" said Ito, and they drank.

The old man in the corner unrolled one of his pieces of paper, started drawing with a quick flourish of the brush. The other two old fellows cackled.

"All right," said Glover, giving Ito his full attention. "What is it you want from me?"

"You have sold guns to the Shogun," said Ito.

"Your spies have been doing their job."

"I keep my own eyes open. You have also sold to Satsuma, clan of your wife."

"I'm impressed!" said Glover.

"So," said Ito. "This makes Choshu clan weak. You should sell to us also. All Shogun's enemies should be strong."

"Straight to the point!" said Glover. "But how do I know you won't turn your guns on the foreigners?"

"You have Ito's word of honour."

Ito's face was clenched in a grimace, an exaggerated *bunraku* mask of determination, integrity, the corners of the mouth turned down. It could have been ludicrous, but it wasn't. He meant what he said, truly felt his word was guarantee enough, and Glover, for no good reason other than the feeling in his gut, believed him.

130

They talked, over more sake, tentatively sounded each other out, haggled.

"I have to give the matter some thought," said Glover, "make enquiries. Perhaps we can meet again to discuss things further."

They stood up to go. Glover bowed, Ito reached out and shook hands. Ito glanced across at the old man in the corner, the artist. The old man beckoned him to come over, see what he'd been doing. Ito looked at the piece of paper, laughed. He gave the old man a few coins, picked up the paper and showed it to Glover. It was a drawing, recognisably Glover, but a vicious caricature — the westerner as seen by the Japanese. The eyes were bulging and demonic, facial hair sprouting grotesquely.

"How the Japanese see you!" said Ito. "The barbarian!"

Glover laughed. "Devil, more like!"

He rolled up the drawing, put it in his coat pocket, nodded to the old man, who threw back his head and laughed, his ancient face crinkled.

Mackenzie was uneasy about Glover's dealings with Ito, told him so.

"It's not so long since this man was shoulder-to-shoulder with Takashi," he said, "pledging to rid the country of all barbarian scum. You'll mind your first night in Dejima?"

"How could I forget it?"

"That was only two years ago, Tom. And rumour has it Ito orchestrated the attack."

Glover minded the night, the powerful figure he'd seen restraining Takashi, telling the mob to fall back. That could have been Ito right enough. In fact the more he thought about it, tried to visualize it, the more certain he was.

"Was that really just two years ago?" he said. "It seems longer."

"No time at all," said Mackenzie.

"Time enough for folk to change."

"There was more than just a bit of rabble-rousing, Tom. Ito was involved in a damn sight worse. I'm sure of it."

"And I'm sure he's a man of his word, Ken. I trust him."

"Aye, well," said Mackenzie. "That's as may be. But keep your wits about you."

He arranged another meeting with Ito, at Ipponmatsu, by night. Matsuo, armed with his two swords, stood guard outside the door.

"Can not be too careful," said Ito. "May be watched by *ometsuke*, Shogun's men. Or Takashi may take interest. Even your own government have spies."

"The place is probably surrounded!" said Glover. But he took Ito's point, respected the need for caution, especially as he knew his own movements were under the same scrutiny.

Once again he was impressed by Ito, his strength of character, a resolute hardheadedness that didn't preclude a wry humour. He could see that in his eyes, a readiness to laugh. He was close to Glover's age, and right from the beginning they were at ease in each other's company. The respect was mutual.

Ito spoke passionately about the need for change. The Tokugawa clan had ruled for two hundred years and would be happy to keep things just as they were for two hundred more.

"Japan, you say, backwater? But should not be. Japan is great nation, ancient nation. But must be modern nation also. Can be powerful, like your country."

"I see that," said Glover. "I feel it."

"We make it happen," said Ito. "First step, Shogun must go."

They drank to it, first in sake, then in the finest malt whisky that Glover opened specially.

Glover agreed to supply an initial consignment of rifles, brought in through the same source in Shanghai. This time he didn't go in person, let Wang-Li negotiate the deal. Another night delivery, another payment lodged in Glover's account, this time from the Choshu clan and their representative Prince Ito Hirobumi.

"A prince among men!" said Glover. "It's an honour doing business with you!"

"Honour is good," said Ito.

The next consignment was larger, and Glover decided to make the run to Shanghai himself. Ito asked if he could accompany him.

"You want to meet my contact?" said Glover. "Next time cut out the middle man!"

Ito worked out what he was saying, looked offended. "Not so. Just want . . ." He struggled to find the word. "Adventure."

Glover laughed. "Yes!"

CHAPTER
SIX

Ronin

Nagasaki–Edo, 1861

The baby was born too soon, while Glover was away on another run to Shanghai. He was told when he disembarked and he ran up the hill to the house. He entered the bedroom, quietly. The windows had been opened to let in air, but the atmosphere still cloyed with the heavy metallic tang of blood and struggle. Sono, pale and drained, sat up in bed, nursing the baby. She looked up at Glover from very far away, her forehead furrowed in concentration. Then as if suddenly recognising, remembering him, she managed a sad, tired smile and held the baby up towards him. This ragged scrap of life was his son, red face puckered and angry, eyes gummed shut, tiny hands clenched, hanging on to existence. His son. He felt the emotion surge in his chest, choked it back as a sob rasped out of him. As gently as he could, he took the child from Sono, was overcome by the lightness of this wee creature, fragile, barely there, twitching and floundering in this new element, a fish out of water. He smiled at Sono, saw it all in her eyes, the exhaustion and pain, the desperate hopeless hope.

The coffin was so small, so light, a simple white pine box. Glover cradled it in his arms. It weighed nothing at all, might as easily have been empty. But what a weight was in that *nothing*, that *empty*. He walked ahead of Sono, carried it up the path to the tiny grave. They had given the baby a name, Umekichi. Weeks premature, he had only survived a few days.

The day was mild, the air smelled of newness and spring, the damp of the clay, the turned earth. It was a small gathering. Mackenzie was there, all sober gravitas, and Ito with that rigid samurai dignity.

Even Walsh looked sombre and subdued, gave Glover a nod, put a consoling hand on his arm.

The Minister read a prayer. The monk from the temple burned incense, chanted a mantra, invoking the Buddha of the Pure Land.

Ashes to ashes, dust to dust.

Namu Amida Butsu.

Glover stepped forward, kneeled by the edge of the grave and eased the box in, straining as he leaned forward with it, felt the shake in his arms. For all its lightness, that almost-nothing took work to hold steady, to lay down gently in its resting place with only the slightest bump at the last, a wee dunt.

Almost nothing. Dust to dust. The Pure Land. In sure and certain hope.

Namu Amida Butsu.

Glover stood up, took a handful of soil from the little heaped-up mound by the grave, threw it down on the lid of the box. Even the sound was small, a patter, a hollowness. He nodded to Sono and she did the same, threw a handful of dirt, watched it scatter. Then she turned away, kneeled in front of a statue of Jizo. She bowed and placed a single white flower at the foot of the statue, wrapped a child's woven shawl around its shoulders. Then she placed a few pebbles in a line on the ground, bowed again and clapped her hands once in front of her face.

"Is to help make pathway for our baby," she said. "To cross *Sai no Kawara*. River of Hell."

He put his arm round her thin shoulders, and only then did she break and cry, the sobs shaken out of her.

She left the next day, said she was sorry but she had to go, back to her family in Kagoshima, she was sure he would understand. Her face was composed when she spoke to him, a mask, all feeling held in check. There was nothing he could say. Even if he'd had the language, there were no words for this. He walked with her to the harbour, carried the small sad bundle of her few belongings. At the jetty he made to embrace her but she turned away. He thought he understood; if she gave way to the emotion it would swamp her completely, so she had to stay composed, not cave in on herself. He thought he understood, but still it pained him, that turning away, the swish of her kimono, waft of her perfume. At the top of the gangplank she stopped and turned back towards him. He waved and she bent her head, bowed to him one last time and was gone.

He walked back slowly, along the waterfront, past *shian bashi*, hesitation-bridge, up the hill to the empty house. He poured himself a whisky, sat a long time in his armchair, staring out, not seeing, at the pine tree in the garden. He didn't light the lamps, just let the room darken as the evening passed, his mind empty, numb.

When at last he stood up to go to bed, the dark had settled on everything, and he'd sat so long without moving he was stiff and cold. He fumbled to the sideboard, lit a candle, saw his sudden, troubled reflection in the glass of the window-pane. Back where he came from, that was supposed to be bad luck, seeing your reflection by candlelight. Back where he came from, in another life.

Through in the bedroom, the flame glinted on something that flashed a moment, bright. He bent and picked it up. Sono's hair-clasp with its silver inlay. He pressed it to his lips, kissed it.

Mackenzie had told Glover there was increasing disquiet at the highest level over his links with Ito, with the rebel clans. Official directives had been sent out from the British Consul at the Legation in Edo, not mentioning Glover by name, but warning against any action which might undermine the Shogun and the official government of Japan. The baby's death, Sono's departure, had left an emptiness in him, rendered him numb, sullen. He would have to jolt himself awake, move on. He made up his mind. He would go to Edo, to the Legation.

138

"I have to speak to these people," he said to Ito, "make them see sense."

They stood in the garden at Ipponmatsu, looking out across the harbour, the trading ships at anchor, the blue hills beyond.

Ito nodded. "Is good. But the journey will be dangerous. Matsuo will go with you."

Matsuo was standing respectfully in the background, knowing his place. He stood to attention, bowed from the waist.

"So, you still think I need protection?" said Glover.

"Is still hostile territory," said Ito. "There are many ronin like Takashi who would prize the head of a barbarian."

Glover laughed, but the image chilled him, and he knew Ito was right.

"Besides," Ito continued. "We need you for the work. I can't do it alone."

"So your concern for my welfare is utterly selfish?"

"Of course!"

This time they both laughed. But it was agreed. Matsuo would travel with him as his bodyguard and guide. They would sail as far as Yokohama, continue on horseback to Edo.

Yokohama was busier than Nagasaki, messier, given over entirely to servicing foreign trade. Its growth had been rapid and largely unplanned; it was a sprawl, a clutter, thrown up along a half-mile stretch between a creek and a swampy marsh, between a river estuary and the vast Pacific. Part of the intention, according to

Mackenzie, had been to contain the foreign invasion, limit expansion through the sheer inhospitable nature of the place. "A prison settlement," he'd said. "Dejima on a grand scale."

But some things refused to be contained. The ratification of the treaty had seen to that.

Glover and Matsuo disembarked at the granite jetty, shouldered their baggage and set out on foot. They passed by the solid stone-built Custom House, made their way along Main Street, past ramshackle godowns and sturdier bungalows, a mishmash of stores and warehouses, flimsy wooden homes. In one clear space, charred by a recent fire, a family sat down to a picnic of rice and fish, a flask of sake, while carpenters started rebuilding the house round about them.

Mackenzie had told Glover to head for the Bluff, the cliff-top area at the far end of town where most of the incomers had settled, looking down on the overcrowded waterfront. At the foot of the Bluff, by the entrance to a guarded causeway, an Englishman in a grubby frockcoat, a clerical dog collar, stood on a wooden crate, a Bible in his hand, ranting at passersby. He caught Glover's eye, started haranguing him directly.

"Take care, young sir, lest you fall into evil ways! This place is a cesspit, a sink of iniquity, awash with vermin in human form. They all gravitate here — disorderly Californian adventurers, Portuguese desperadoes, the refuse and scum of the earth. I have made it my business to count the number of grog-shops, and believe me, sir, it is excessive in the extreme. And out there at the edge of the swamp . . ." He pointed over

Glover's head, the rage making his hand shake. ". . . is a vile establishment known as the Gankiro Teahouse where two hundred women are employed to provide every facility for profligacy and vice."

"Have you made it your business to count them also?" asked Glover.

"I have heard reports," said the man, fixing him even more intently with his gaze, "and I have no reason to doubt their veracity. It has become common practice for a young man simply to *buy* a woman for the purpose of living in sin, in *unholy* matrimony."

He thought of Sono, saw her face clear, remembered what they'd had, what it had become. And he knew this man would never ever understand, and he felt a sudden anger, felt his hand clench, make a fist, as if he might actually strike the man down in the dust. Instead he asked him, "Could you maybe show me the way to yon teahouse — Gankiro is it? I may be of a mind to pay it a visit."

He walked on, Matsuo following, and the man called after him, outrage choking his voice. "The wages of sin is death!"

They stayed the night at a ryokan, built in the narrow gap between a warehouse and a temple. Glover's room was small, the size of six tatami mats, and the futon mattress rolled out on the floor took up almost the whole space. Matsuo paced the corridor, settled himself outside the shoji screen door, indicating that he would take rest, but that he slept light, would be alert to any intrusion. Glover thought the precaution excessive but he was learning not to argue with Matsuo's ferocious sense of duty. He understood it, respected it.

He lay down, let the background noise of the settlement wash over him — voices calling out, scatter of laughter, the bittersweet twang of a koto. He drifted off, breathing in the smells of fish and incense.

The Right Reverend Robert James, Episcopalian preacher, was done ranting for the day. He climbed down from his fishbox pulpit, kicked it irritably to the side of the road. That young Scotsman had put him in a foul humour, blackened his mood. The arrogance of it, paying no heed. Well then, let him rot in hell.

He was so caught up in his anger that at first he didn't notice the figures coming towards him, four men walking with that samurai swagger, lords of the dung-heap, kings of the midden. By the time he did notice, they were almost upon him, not slowing their pace but expecting him to scramble out of the way.

With the righteousness still strong in him, he raised his right hand, brandishing the Bible at them. For the second time that day he began quoting. "The wages of sin . . ."

But the verse was cut, punctuated, by a slash of the sword, a single, eviscerating swipe across his belly. He felt his entrails shift, managed to complete the quotation — "is death" — before another stroke took off his head.

Takashi looked down at the slumped form, wiped his blade on the man's coat and re-sheathed his sword. With his foot he rolled the body into the drainage ditch

142

by the roadside and, with his three companions, walked on.

Glover slept deep, woke at first light. Matsuo had already been out, negotiated the hire of two horses — iron-shod — and stocked up on provisions for the journey: a batch of cooked rice, pickles, dried fish. They rode out through streets already bustling with commerce and haggle, all manner of trade and marketeering, headed out towards the Tokkaido, the Edo road.

Through a gap between two buildings, Matsuo pointed into the far distance. The low cloud cover had cleared and there, suddenly revealed, stood a mountain the like of which Glover had never seen. Its singularity lay, in part, in its symmetry. Its sides sloped up to form a perfect cone, but truncated at the apex, a volcano, its colour a deep, dense blue.

"*Fuji-san,*" said Matsuo, bowing his head.

Glover had no idea how far away it was, or how high, but the look of it was impressive. Matsuo spoke of it with reverence, as if it were a living being. Fuji-san. They rode on and Glover turned to take another look, but the mountain had disappeared, was lost again in cloud and mist.

Throughout the day they caught glimpses of it, always different. It rose above the clouds again, or poked through a thicket of trees. It stood framed by bamboo scaffolding on a building site, or planks of timber in a woodcutter's yard. They saw it in the window of a teahouse where they stopped along the way, through the massive red gateway of a temple, reflected in a puddle by the roadside.

At one point, where the curve of the road brought them into open country, it loomed suddenly large, dominated the horizon, and Matsuo stopped his horse and dismounted, prostrated on the ground. Then without saying a word, he remounted, nudged the horse forward again.

Glover had a sense they had changed direction, were going the wrong way. He mentioned it to Matsuo, who grunted, said, "*Kamakura. Daibutsu.*"

That seemed to constitute a full and adequate explanation, and Glover decided to trust. It must be a necessary detour.

They reached a small town an hour later, a settlement surrounded by hills and facing out across a bay.

"*Kamakura*," said Matsuo.

This time it was Glover who grunted.

Yokohama had been so thronged with foreigners that nobody had given him a second look. Here it was different, and everyone stared at him the way folk had on his arrival in Nagasaki, on his visit to Kagoshima, with that mix of curiosity and open hostility, trepidation, dread of the barbarian. The children played the same old round-eye game. He half-expected to see Takashi come striding along the narrow street.

They rode out of town, toward the hills, stopped at the entrance to a temple, tethered their horses. Matsuo led the way in, past a few outbuildings, through an

144

arch, stopped and bowed his head. There in front of them, in an open courtyard, stood a massive statue of the Buddha, forty feet high, cast in bronze.

"*Daibutsu*," said Matsuo. "*Amida Buddha*."

For the second time that day, Glover felt a sense of awe. As with the mountain, it was the sheer scale of the thing, but again there was something more, a presence.

They moved closer and once more Matsuo threw himself prostrate on the ground, then he stood up and bowed, clapped his hands three times. Next to the statue was an ornate incense burner, also in bronze, shaped like the leaves and petals of a lotus. Matsuo wafted the fragrant smoke towards himself, a purification, then he clapped his hands again, walked clockwise round the statue, chanting his devotions.

Namu Amida Butsu.

Glover looked up at the huge bulk of the statue looming above him, tried to take it in. In part his appreciation was detached, analytical; the technical expertise necessary to build such a thing was massively impressive. Like Matsuo he walked round it, but his was the stroll of the observer, not the tread of the devotee. He saw where the bronze had been cast in huge sections, fused or bolted together.

"Quite a feat of engineering," he said to Matsuo, realising he wouldn't understand, but hoping he would at least hear the respect in his tone.

But even as he heard himself say the words, they sounded small and empty, as if spoken by someone else. He knew his admiration was for more than the technicalities of its construction, that this was art rather than artefact. More than that, it had been imbued with a power that was quite overwhelming. No matter how much he resisted, he was affected by it, in spite of himself. Everything conspired together — his tiredness from the journey, the peacefulness of the setting with its backdrop of tree-covered hills, the scent of the incense wafting in the air, the low drone of Matsuo's chanting — to create an atmosphere rarefied but suffused with a kind of intensity. Objects stood clear, sharply outlined, resolutely themselves, none more so than this gigantic figure. The sculptor had caught something entirely other, imbued it with life. The surface had weathered to a patchy patina, a pale green that almost glowed.

Thou shalt not worship any graven image.

And yet.

The face that looked down at him was at once austere and benign. The eyes were half open, the mouth turned up in a faint half-smile. He felt boundaries, distinctions, dissolve, as if he were losing himself, falling up into it.

Matsuo clapped his hands once more. An iron bell clanged. Glover was definably himself again, incongruously here, alien, in this far-off place. He shook his head, rubbed his face with his hands.

Matsuo walked back round behind the statue, nodded to Glover to follow.

"What now?" asked Glover, suddenly impatient, anxious to be moving on, to get to Edo.

"In," said Matsuo, indicating a little door in the statue's base. "Up."

146

A few steps and they were inside the statue, a dimly lit cavern in the shape of the Buddha's body. Matsuo set off climbing a flight of rickety wooden steps, right to the top, and again Glover followed, stood on a flimsy platform, inside the Buddha's head, looking out through the Buddha's eyes at the temple grounds, the town beyond.

Matsuo laughed, his voice echoing, and led the way back down again. Glover felt strangely unsettled as they remounted their horses, continued their journey.

It was evening when they arrived in Edo, rode into the compound housing the British Legation. The Consulate was set in the grounds of a secluded temple — Tozenji — a pleasant sprawl of outbuildings and courtyards, linked by winding pathways, wooden bridges over sleepy lotus ponds, a placid lake. The perimeter was heavily guarded by Japanese militia, but Glover noticed a certain lazy indolence in their manner as he and Matsuo rode unchallenged through a moss-covered gateway, along a shady avenue of pine and bamboo.

The building itself was low, wood-framed, the rooms divided by sliding pine-and-paper doors. It seemed too flimsy for the heavy western furniture that had been dragged in, filled up the space — the solid oak tables and dining-room chairs, the leather armchairs, the bookcases and desks. Beyond those would be wardrobes and cupboards and kitchen stoves, dressing tables and iron-framed beds. The effect was claustrophobic, cluttered, especially in this late summer heat.

In the entranceway, hung precariously on one of the thin walls, was a gilt-framed portrait of Queen Victoria, and beneath it, lolling in an armchair, was a familiar figure, the Englishman Richardson whose acquaintance Glover had made on his very arrival in Nagasaki. It seemed a lifetime ago.

"Glover!" said Richardson, standing up, offering his hand. "Charles Richardson. We met in Dejima."

Glover shook the dry, bony hand, said, "Aye, I mind you fine. This is Matsuo-san."

"*Hai.*" Matsuo bowed.

Richardson nodded, addressed Glover again. "Your bodyguard, I presume. A wise precaution these days. We can't be too careful. News just came in this afternoon from Yokohama. Apparently some itinerant English preacher was casually disembowelled in the street."

"We were just there," said Glover, remembering the clergyman they'd encountered, choleric, spitting hellfire and damnation. The wages of sin.

"Well, there we are," said Richardson. "There but for the grace of God."

"Aye."

"But what business brings you to Edo?" asked Richardson. "Are you moving here from Nagasaki?"

"Nagasaki suits me fine," said Glover. "I'm here to speak to the Consul."

"I'm sure Sir Rutherford will be delighted to see you," said Richardson. "We've been hearing all about your . . . activities!"

At that a stocky, greyhaired Englishman came along the corridor, stopped and fixed Glover with his gaze. The eyes held a weariness, long-suffering, but still intense, quizzical.

"Thomas Glover," said Richardson, making the introduction. "Sir Rutherford Alcock."

"I'm pleased to meet you at last," said Alcock. "We've heard a great deal about you."

"So I've just been told."

"Not *all* of it bad!" said the Consul. "In any case, I'm sure you'll add spice to the mix at dinner. What with Richardson here, and yourself, and young Mister Oliphant also among us, I shall be experiencing surfeit after famine. In this wilderness the foreigner is entirely a stranger and absolutely repudiated by the natives. I look forward to your company, sir. We dine at eight."

Matsuo fed and watered the horses, stabled them at the edge of the compound, was himself billeted with the Japanese guards. Glover's accommodation was cramped but adequate, a small guest room off the main corridor. He washed and shaved, did his best to brush the dust of travel from his clothes, and presented himself at dinner.

They were four round the table, Glover and Richardson, Alcock and the young man he'd mentioned, Laurence Oliphant. Glover had heard of Oliphant. He had come out to Japan as secretary to Lord Elgin, been part of the first British delegation to Japanese shores. Oliphant was in full flow, responding to Glover's simple enquiry as to how he had come to apply for the posting.

"I find myself fired by the constant need," said Oliphant, "to go to some out-of-the-way place, do something nobody else has done."

Glover nodded, eagerly. "I can understand that."

"I have already been to Kathmandu, across Crimea in a farm cart, to Ubooch in the Western Caucasus, and from Lake Superior to the headwaters of the Mississippi in a bark canoe. I was in Calcutta during the Indian mutiny and observed the bombardment of Canton from the deck of HMS *Furious*."

The litany was clearly well rehearsed, had no doubt been delivered at many a dinner table. But Glover found the young man engaging, his enthusiasm a breath of air.

"There cannot be much of the world left for you explore," said Richardson.

"Japan was a logical next step," agreed Oliphant.

"And what a foetid backwater it is," said Alcock.

"Ah," said Richardson. "Sir Rutherford is mounting his hobbyhorse!"

"Oh, I am comfortable enough here," said Alcock. "I have my library, my work . . ."

Again Richardson interjected. "Sir Rutherford is preparing an English–Japanese grammar."

"And a thankless task it is," said Alcock, "Herculean in scale. The language has no genders for nouns, no definite articles, a multiplicity of forms for addressing people, depending on rank, and a perplexing plethora of verbs. I almost despair of seeing the undertaking to any useful end, much in the same way as I despair of our bringing about any real friendship or conciliation

150

with the Japanese. In short, I cannot escape the feeling of exile and banishment from all that is familiar and civilised."

"There is much still to be explored here," said Oliphant. "It is a beautiful country. Mister Glover, did you observe Fujiyama on your way here?"

"The mountain," said Glover. "It is indeed spectacular."

Oliphant nodded agreement. "The very embodiment of grandeur and mystery."

"From a distance," said Alcock.

"Sir Rutherford had the gumption to climb the wretched mountain not long after his arrival," said Richardson.

"It was no picturesque stroll," said Alcock. "The ascent was a grinding slog of a climb, an ever steeper clamber over rough harsh terrain, trees and vegetation ever more sparse, till we were scrambling over sliding scree, stumbling on boulders, gasping in the thin rarefied air." He was warming to his tale, no doubt much refined by many a telling. "At last we reached the crude shelters where we could rest through the night, flimsy wooden huts where we huddled in the freezing cold, niggled and bitten by fleas. At first light, aching and stiff, we hauled ourselves on and up, over bare rock, three more hours to the very rim of the crater."

"Now that is impressive," said Glover.

"And what did I see for my trouble?" asked Alcock. "A glorious panoramic view of this wonderful land? A suddenly altered perspective? No. I peered over the rim of the crater into its grim depths as into the abyss. I

151

looked outward and saw no distance at all, the whole place obscured once more in mist and cloud, hidden from our gaze."

"Typical," said Richardson. "It's as if the damn country wants to remain hidden!"

"It's not an easy place to understand," said Oliphant, "but the effort is worthwhile."

"Tell Glover about your own efforts," said Richardson, and he laughed. "Your collection of bugs!"

"I am," said Oliphant patiently, "preparing an entomological collection for the British Museum, and have already found a number of rare beetles."

"My excitement knows no bounds!" said Richardson.

"What is your opinion, Mister Glover?" asked Alcock.

"About collecting insects?" Glover smiled, but was on guard, alerted by something steely in the tone of the question.

"About the possibility of understanding this place. Or indeed the wisdom of trying to co-operate with the Japanese."

"I believe Mister Glover has already been co-operating with them quite extensively," said Richardson, drawing on his cigar.

"And what do you mean by that, sir?" asked Glover.

"We heard you had gone native, had a Japanese wife and child."

"As of last week," said Glover, "I have neither. My son died. My wife left."

"Bad luck," said Oliphant into the awkward silence.

"Perhaps less messy in the long term," said Richardson.

Glover could not believe what the man had just said, and for the second time in as many days found himself clenching his fists in the face of an arrogant ignorance, forcibly restraining himself from striking a blow.

"Mister Richardson's pragmatism is extreme," said Oliphant, "and carries with it a certain callousness."

Richardson said nothing, simply narrowed his eyes in the curl of cigar smoke as Glover held his gaze.

"The co-operation to which I refer is a different matter entirely," said Alcock.

"This may be the very matter I have come here to discuss with you."

"It is my understanding that you have been working hand-in-glove with Mister Ito Hirobumi of the Choshu clan."

"Ito is a business associate, and a friend."

Richardson laughed out loud. "Ah, the *naïveté* of it!"

"Such men are dangerous," said Alcock.

"I fear Sir Rutherford may be right," said Oliphant, quietly.

"Your business dealings are your own affair," said Alcock. "Unless they become illegal, or politically reprehensible. And I fear, Mister Glover, you are sailing close to the wind."

"Don't you *want* to be rid of the Shogun?" asked Glover.

"I am entirely indifferent to his fate," said Alcock. "What matters is that Her Majesty's Government does *not* want rid of him. The Shogun is the officially recognised de facto ruler of the country, and we have to recognise his authority."

"Ito and the others have their own authority," said Glover. "It's our duty to recognise that, and convince our Government to do the same."

"We can't take sides," said Alcock.

"By backing the Shogun, we're doing just that!"

"Nevertheless," said Alcock, "by doing anything else, you are breaking the laws of this country . . ."

"The Shogun's laws!"

"The laws of this country! You are also defying the stated policy of your own Government. Now let that be an end of it!"

The silence round the table was ponderous, then Oliphant broke it, addressing Glover. "Of course, Sir Rutherford carries no torch for the Shogun, or, for that matter, for the Emperor. Nor does he make any distinction between the two, though I feel the distinction may yet prove important."

"A pox on both their houses!" said Alcock.

"His favoured policy," continued Oliphant, "would be to bring back Commodore Perry's black ships, reinforced by a few of our own gunboats, and simply bombard the Japanese into submission."

"Mister Oliphant knows I deplore violence," said Alcock, "but I confess there are times when I yearn for the simplicity of such a solution!"

It was a clear warm night and it had been predicted that a comet would be clearly visible, flashing across the sky around midnight. Oliphant was keen to view it from the lawn, and had persuaded Glover to accompany him. Richardson and Sir Rutherford showed no interest in the spectacle and retired early to their rooms.

The air was heavy with the scent of pine. Oliphant breathed it in, turned to Glover. "When the Consul said he deplored violence, he was understating the case. In fact his fear of violence is pathological, almost hysterical, and he lives in constant terror of the samurai blade at his throat."

"It's understandable," said Glover, "in the present climate."

Oliphant pointed out a glow in the distance, rising from the outskirts of the city.

"Fire," he said. "They call it the Flower of Edo that blooms all year round. These wooden buildings catch like tinder, and it spreads rapidly. I fully expect one day to see the whole city ablaze."

There was a movement in the bushes and both men tensed, then the form of a small dog scuttled across the grass towards them and wrapped itself around Oliphant's ankles.

"Useless mutt!" he said, laughing and ruffling the dog's fur. "This is Mister Thomas Glover," he said to the animal with exaggerated formality. "Mister Glover, this is Inu-san. A rather unimaginative name, I'm afraid. It simply means Mister Dog!"

"Delighted," said Glover.

"On my first visit here," said Oliphant, "it seemed that every member of the delegation bought one of these creatures. I resolutely resisted, mindful of the fact that they tore their paper kennels to shreds, whined and howled dismally the whole night through, and invariably fell sick and died. However, this shabby cur appeared one day, begged a few scraps from my lunch and made himself quite at home. He has an official post now, guarding my collection of beetles from his station outside my door!"

Glover chuckled, but then something else moved in the shadows, this time unmistakeably a human figure. Oliphant tensed, the dog growled, raised its hackles, but the man who stepped forward was Matsuo, and he silenced the dog with a gruff word of command.

At that, Oliphant looked up, pointed. A sudden flare of light, the comet, flashed briefly in the night sky.

Glover couldn't sleep, swiped at the mosquito zinging in his ear. It bit him again, again. Raging, he got up, lit the lamp in the room, sat sentinel, waited for the insect to come to rest. At length it did, sat twitching on the shoji screen above his bed. He moved closer, swatted it with his rolled-up necker-chief, splattered it against the screen. He peered at it, realised what he was looking at was a smudge of his own blood.

He lay down again and slept, woke in the small hours, a sense of threat grabbing at his throat, quickening his breath. He took his bearings. Edo. The Legation. Here. Matsuo was guarding outside the door, would stretch out in the corridor between spells of wakefulness, alert to any danger. That should be enough to allay any fears, but something had intruded into Glover's sleep, some irritant had awakened him.

156

He heard a scratching, a high sharp whine, smiled as he realised it was Oliphant's dog. So the creature was going to be as fretful and troublesome as the rest. He only hoped it wouldn't start tearing at the paper screens with its claws and teeth.

He lay down again, but the dog became more agitated, started barking.

"Fucking animal!" he said out loud, tetchy and tired, irritated.

He got up, pulled on his clothes, stubbed his toe against the table beside his bed, cursed again, pulled on his boots. Now the dog's bark seemed more insistent, a yelp, and in behind it there was some kind of commotion, outside in the compound, then he was aware of Matsuo yelling out, and the noise of a struggle, and the paper screen burst inwards as two figures, one of them Matsuo, came crashing through into the room.

Glover wondered for a moment if he might actually still be asleep and dreaming, the whole scene a nightmare, so unreal did it seem, as Matsuo was struck to the ground, his attacker towering over him, an assassin dressed in black, head covered, a scarf over his face, turning now towards Glover and raising his sword in the air, swinging it forward, delivering what would surely be a terminal blow. In that instant, time seemed to slow, and Glover observed it all unfolding, felt a curious detachment, himself watching, a player in some exotic melodrama. On instinct, he stepped back, raised his arms to ward off the blow; but the blow never fell, the sword stopped in mid-arc.

Again the sword swung, again Glover tensed, his scalp tingling in anticipation of the blade cleaving his skull. But again the sword stopped short. A third time the sword was raised, and once more the blow did not fall, was blocked. Then Matsuo picked himself up, threw himself at the assailant and barged him to the ground, held him there and dispatched him with the quick brutal slash of a knife-blade across the throat. The man gurgled and twitched and lay still. Matsuo slumped then, crumpled to the floor. Glover went to tend to him but he motioned him away, indicated he was all right. Glover found his pistol, checked it was cocked and loaded, stepped out into the corridor.

Now the noise from the compound was a cacophony, the din of a full-scale battle, shouting men, the crack of gunfire, harsh clash of swords. The building itself shook from the onslaught. Lanterns flared, were doused again, gunshots flashed, the whole thing an infernal flickering shadow-play. In one burst of light, Glover saw Oliphant's dog, teeth bared, chasing itself in circles, whimpering. Then from Oliphant's room came an almighty crash, the shattering of wood and glass, followed by an all too human cry of pain. Glover pulled open the screen, stepped in, pistol at the ready. In the dimness, he made out Oliphant, back against the wall, and another black-clad figure, staggering in the centre of the room, choking out little gasps at every lurch and stumble. Then the figure straightened up, steadied, swiftly raised a sword and let out a battle-cry. Glover levelled his pistol and fired straight at the intruder, felled him, but not before the man could hack at Oliphant, take him down.

There was sudden light from a lantern in the doorway — Alcock was shining it into the room and, like Glover, carrying a pistol.

"Good God!" said Alcock when he saw the mess. The ronin had clearly launched himself into the room, through the window from outside. But he'd landed on the glass case housing Oliphant's insect specimens, shattered it and cut his bare feet on the shards. The accident had given Glover time to get into the room. But had he been too late? Oliphant lay on the floor, drenched in his own blood pouring from a gash in his arm.

Alcock set down the lantern and his pistol, looked at the wound while Glover stood guard. Oliphant's arm was sliced to the bone, laid open, a cut of meat on a butcher's slab. Hands shaking, the Consul tore a kerchief into ragged strips, tied it tight round Oliphant's arm as a makeshift tourniquet.

Outside, the fighting grew even louder, a volley of gunshots ripped the air, men screamed. Glover and Alcock did their best to barricade themselves into a corner of the room, overturned a table and hunkered down behind it, propping up Oliphant with a bolster behind his back. He flinched as they moved him, his face in the lamplight eerily white, all colour drained. Glover blew out the lamp and they waited.

Time passed, God knew how long. The noise subsided, rose again in surges and waves then faded again to a strange calm. Oliphant was moaning, drifting in and out of consciousness. Alcock spoke to Glover in not much more than a whisper. "I wonder if the bastards will torture us before they kill us."

"For God's sake, man!" said Glover. "We'll get out of this!"

But he felt his heart thud in his ribcage, the chill of sweat trickle down his back as he stood up, tentative, made his way across to the doorway, broken glass crunching under his feet. He stepped over the inert bulk, the body of the man he'd shot.

Out in the corridor the darkness was deeper. From his left came a voice he recognised, Matsuo. "Guraba-san?"

"*Hai*, Matsuo, *so desu*."

Matsuo lit a lantern, held it up. The light flickered, and there, to the right, just two yards away, his face suddenly lit, stood Takashi, motionless, sword in hand, ready to strike. Again there was the sense of unreality, of vivid, waking dream, as Glover raised his pistol, suddenly heavy in his hand. Then Takashi raised his sword, Glover levelled his pistol, then there was chaos, dark-clad figures crashing in from every direction, no way of telling who were ronin, who were militia, and the lantern was suddenly extinguished, knocked to the floor. Glover braced himself once more for a blow that would split him in two, and again it never came. Another light appeared in the doorway and Takashi was gone, had leapt through the open window and made his escape. The guards were crowding the corridor, checking the rooms, terrified of what they might find.

★   ★   ★

The scene was one of horror, utter carnage, Alcock's worst imaginings made real. The corridors and the compound were strewn with dead bodies, some dismembered, beheaded, disembowelled. One severed head lay where it had rolled, in the entrance to the building, the face a startled grimace, the headless body yards away, bloated and grotesque.

The Consul's first concern was for his guests. Glover he knew was fine. Oliphant needed urgent medical attention. Nobody had seen Richardson.

There was a British frigate, HMS *Ringdove*, anchored in Edo bay. They would transport Oliphant on board, let the ship's surgeon do his best.

Richardson appeared towards morning, dressed in a Japanese robe and covered in mud. He had initially gone out to the compound, drawn by the first sounds of commotion, and been horrified to see battle joined, hand-to-hand fighting, medieval in its brutality. One of the guards, concerned for his safety, had thrown him the robe to disguise himself for fear of attack.

"Not much of a disguise," he said, his arms protruding from the short sleeves. "So I threw myself to the ground, crawled under the building into the gap below the foundations, and there I stayed till I deemed it safe to come out of my hiding-place."

Glover stared at the man, knew he was prattling with a kind of nervous agitation out of sheer relief at being alive, not skewered or hacked to pieces. Glover's immediate response was to retreat into silence, try to tap into some core of strength at the centre of himself.

But he too had been shaken, knew how close they had all come to a brutal, bloody death.

The full story began to emerge. Some fifteen ronin had banded together and mounted the attack, and through sheer determination, allied to the general torpor and ineptitude of the guards, had quickly wrought havoc before being beaten by sheer weight of numbers. There were scores of dead, and the building itself had been ravaged — doors and windows, screens, walls, floorboards, furnishing, smashed asunder with intense one-pointed ferocity.

Alcock turned to Glover. "And these are the rebels you want us to arm to the teeth?"

"On the contrary," said Glover. "These are the very people who want to keep Japan in the Dark Ages. The progressives want an end to this. They want to work with us."

"As long as it suits their purpose. When it doesn't, it's the knife-blade at your throat. They're all the bloody same, including your friend Ito."

"Ito is a man of honour."

"Oh yes," said Alcock. "They are all honourable men!"

"He's an idealist, a reformer."

"He is a fanatic. We can't support him."

"He's the future of Japan. We must support him."

Glover bowed curtly, aggressively, took his leave, went back to the wreckage of his room. Matsuo was once again stationed in the corridor, on guard. The side of his face was bruised, he moved stiffly as if aching in the neck and shoulder, but he was otherwise unhurt.

162

The shoji screen wall was destroyed. The body of Glover's ronin attacker had been dragged out, dumped in the compound with the rest. The bloodstains on the tatami had turned black, smelled sickly and rank.

Just inside the room, where the ronin had raised his sword, was a low beam, not much above head-height. It was gashed and hacked by the cuts of the sword. The man hadn't seen the beam in the dark and that was what had impeded the blade, saved Glover's life. That close. There but for the grace.

Glover was packed and saddled up, ready to depart. He went to bid farewell to Alcock, who looked defeated, a ghost of himself.

"The Minister of Foreign Affairs," he said, "has sent a basket of ducks and a jar of sugar as a gesture of amity! You see what I mean about this place, sir? It is a lunatic asylum!"

"As a gesture," said Glover, "it does seem a wee bit . . . inadequate."

Alcock looked at him, managed a wry half-smile.

"Godspeed on your journey, Mister Glover. I would offer you a contingent of the Legation guards to protect you on your way, at least as far as Yokohama. But you have seen how effective they are. I wish you well in your endeavours, and pray you have a speedy escape from this hell-hole."

On his way across the compound, Glover heard Alcock's voice raised, yelling at some unfortunate messenger. "I want justice and redress, not ducks and bloody sugar!"

As they rode back out along the Tokkaido, Glover subdued, Matsuo even more wary than before, they saw Mount Fuji again, above the pine trees, above the clouds. Then the mist closed over it, hid it once more from view.

There was extensive coverage of the incident in the *Nagasaki Shipping List and Advertiser*. It seemed one of the dead ronin had been carrying a paper scroll, a declaration signed by all fifteen of the attackers. They called themselves *Shishi* — men of high principle. A translation of the document was appended to the newspaper article.

We have not the patience to stand by and see the Sacred Empire defiled by foreigners. With faith and the power of warriors we will drive the barbarians from our shore.

For a moment, Glover was back at the Legation, in the dark, waiting for the sword to fall. He showed the article to Ito, explained what it was saying.

Ito had been grim since Glover's return. The attack on the Legation had stung him, particularly Takashi's involvement.

"Long way to Edo," he said.

"I am beginning to take it rather personally!" said Glover.

"Definitely," said Ito. "He want to kill you. He made promise."

They were seated in the front room at Ipponmatsu, Matsuo on guard outside on the lawn. Glover was suddenly serious. "Ito-san, there is something I want to ask you."

"*Hai.*" Ito nodded, braced himself.

"After the attack on the Legation, I was defending you. They were talking about other attacks." He was finding this difficult, looked hard at Ito. "They said you were involved."

Ito set down the copy of the newspaper, met Glover's gaze. "One time I was like Takashi-san. I hate all foreigners. But you have to know it was a matter of honour. I love my country. I don't want Japan to be colonised, like India, like China."

"*So desu,*" said Glover.

"When I was very young man," said Ito, "I knew great teacher called Yoshida Shoin. He taught at academy when I was there. Not only great teacher, but great man, great hero. He taught importance of old ways, love of Japan, loyalty to the Emperor."

"He also hated all foreigners?" asked Glover.

"Saw them as threat," said Ito

"So what became of him?"

"Bakufu arrested him. He was executed."

"So."

"Now past is dust. I still love Emperor, love Japan, want rid of Bakufu and Shogun. But I want Japan to become strong, like your country, like America. We have to open to the West. Take what we need and learn."

Glover nodded. "*Hai.*"

A few weeks later, Glover received a letter from Oliphant.

Dear Glover,

I was happy to meet you in Edo, though in the end the circumstances could not have been less fortunate. I hear you escaped from the whole vile business unscathed and am glad to hear it. I owe you a debt of gratitude for discharging your pistol when you did, and fear that otherwise my own fate would have been even worse. As it is, I have endured torment these past weeks.

On board the *Ringdove*, I was given a berth in the Captain's own cabin, but there was no comfort to me there, rather unremitting agony. My wounds were severe and the ship's doctor had to strap my arms to my sides, necessitating my being fed like a baby. I lost such a quantity of blood that I broke out in boils all over my body. Then, my defences being down, I fell prey to an eye infection — *ophthalmia* — which was rife among the crew. The doctor bandaged my eyes and poured in silver nitrate which stung like daggers. All of this I endured in ninety-five degree heat in a cabin swarming with flies and mosquitoes, my body all the time swelling and aching.

It is for such emergencies that a beneficent providence has especially provided the consolation of tobacco! By some miracle, I survived, and just yesterday, with some assistance, I was able to climb on deck and breathe the fresh evening air. I am, however, in need of further medical treatment, followed by a lengthy period of convalescence. Sir

Rutherford has informed me that, as soon as I am well enough, I shall be returning to England.

I trust this letter finds you well, and wish you every success in your own endeavours to come to terms with this glorious infuriating country.

Yours most sincerely,
Laurence Oliphant.

For a moment Glover was back at the Legation, cowering in the dark, waiting for the blow to fall. He shook himself, put the letter aside. The ronin had achieved some small part of their aim. One barbarian invader had been driven out. But Glover had no intention of being beaten back, steeled himself all the more.

CHAPTER
SEVEN

Night Journey

Nagasaki, 1862

For months after the attack on the Legation, the settlement in Nagasaki, like the enclave in Yokohama, was on the alert, fearful of an uprising. The Shogun announced that the perpetrators of the attack would be tracked down and punished. But nothing more was heard. There were no further incidents. Trade and commerce continued as before.

Glover and Ito had another consignment to pick up, from Shanghai. Again Wang-Li would accompany them. Walsh came to the dock to see them off, wish them *bon voyage*.

Glover called out to him, from the deck.

"You're sure you don't want to come with us this time?"

"Not my style, Tom. You know me. I prefer to delegate."

"Keep your hands clean!"

"Exactly! Wang-Li's going to pick up a few things for me. I hope you don't mind."

"As long as it doesn't stink to high heaven. Or blow up in our faces!"

Walsh laughed. "Them's the chances you take, partner!" He waved. "*Adios!*"

Glover waved back. Ito stared at Walsh, impassive. The ship cast off, headed out of the harbour.

Everything, it appeared, was proceeding according to plan. The arrangements were exactly as they had been on every previous trip; they disembarked from the clipper, went straight to the warehouse, led by Wang-Li; they passed the same disreputable establishments where the same young girls plied their trade behind ragged curtains; they sidestepped what looked like a continuation of the same street brawl; they followed Wang-Li into the same narrow lane, across the same courtyard, through the same warehouse to the same back room, and only then did they feel something was different. There was a change, not for the better, in the atmosphere. Glover felt it, a tension in the air, and glancing across, he saw Ito sensed it too. Wang-Li looked particularly agitated, fanned himself, dabbed sweat from his brow.

Behind the desk was not Chan, the affable businessman who had overseen their previous dealings, but a younger man, altogether tougher-looking, his whole demeanour actively hostile. Behind him stood two guards, massive and implacable.

Wang-Li explained, Chan had been replaced. This was the new boss.

There was no tea on offer, no invitation to share a pipe. It was straight to business. The consignment was already being loaded onto the wagons; they could hear the boxes being quickly, briskly stacked. Ito heaved a battered leather bag onto the desk, set it down with a thud. It was bulging with gold, a mix of dollars and bullion, to the exact amount agreed.

The new man did not waste time. Glover produced the list of what they had ordered, ten cases of breech-load rifles, as many again of ammunition. The man glanced at the list, nodded, handed over a list of his own. Wang-Li read it, looked even more alarmed.

"Is there a problem?" asked Glover.

Wang-Li cleared his throat. "He say money not enough. Price go up."

"How much?"

"Two times," said Wang-Li. "He want twice as much."

Glover snorted, laughed, but kept his eyes, hard and cold, on the trader. "Impossible." He jabbed at the list, the paper scroll. "That's what we agreed. Now, I'll bid you good day."

He stood up, the discussion over.

The trader banged the table, shouted at Wang-Li, who was stammering now.

"He say you pay more."

"More!" said the trader.

"I brought the amount we agreed," said Glover.

Wang-Li translated again. The trader yelled at him.

"He say you pay this amount, you only take half the guns."

"We made a deal," said Glover. "He has to stick to it."

He nodded to Ito, moved towards the door.

The trader stood up, screamed, "No!"

As if the moves had been choreographed, several things happened in the same instant: one of the guards blocked the exit, drew a pistol and pointed it at Glover, who raised his hands in the air; the second guard grabbed Wang-Li by the scruff and slammed him against the wall; Ito moved swiftly, light on his feet, across the room and behind the trader, in one movement held his unsheathed sword to the man's throat; the second guard also drew a pistol and pointed it at Ito. They stood frozen in a tableau, a stalemate.

Glover nodded to Ito, shrugged at the guard in front of him. Then everything seemed to slow down, and he saw the guard reach forward to take Glover's own pistol from his belt; as the man leaned forward, Glover butted him in the face with his head, and the other guard half-turned, was caught broadside by the trader, shoved across the room by Ito. Glover's guard dropped his pistol and Glover hit him again, this time with a classic straight left that felled him, dropped him to the floor. Once again Ito was across the room, held his sword to the throat of the second guard, its point piercing the skin.

For a moment there was a silence, a stillness, their breathing loud, the sounds from the courtyard far away.

"Now," said Glover. "We'll be going."

Almost as an afterthought, he reached into the leather bag, took out two gold bars and tucked them into the pockets of his coat.

"For the inconvenience," he said, and raised his hat.

The trader could barely contain his rage, looked like a caricature, eyes bulging, neck sinews stretched and taut.

Wang-Li was shaking as he led the way out the door, Glover following, Ito covering their retreat. As Ito turned his head a moment, the second guard made one last effort to stop them, threw himself at Ito. Not flinching, Ito cut him down calmly with a single stroke, stepped over him, hurried down the stairs.

In the courtyard, they moved quickly, took over from the labourers loading the carts. There were three carts and they took the reins of one apiece, nudged the horses out of the yard.

At the dock they moved quickly. Wang-Li haggled with another Chinese over the crate he was picking up for Walsh. Glover organised the crew to load the consignment of arms on board. Ito stood on guard, sword at the ready.

By the time the trader arrived in pursuit, an entourage of armed men at his back, the clipper was already heading for the open sea.

On deck, Ito sat cross-legged, his sword, in its scabbard, laid in front of him.

"You were very useful with that," said Glover.

"Sorry?" said Ito, not understanding.

"The sword," said Glover, and he mimed cutting with it, swiping the air. "Very good."

"Ha!" said Ito, and he smiled, nodded.

"You could teach me," said Glover, miming again.

Ito laughed. "You want to be samurai?"

"A Scottish samurai!" said Glover.

The Japanese sense of humour still took Glover by surprise. Ito threw his head back and roared with laughter. When he'd recovered, Glover continued. "I could teach you how to box."

Ito looked confused. "Box?" He pointed at a wooden crate.

"Boxing!" said Glover, jabbing with his fists.

Ito understood, laughed again. "And this!" He mimed butting with his head.

"Ha!" said Glover. "It's an old Scottish move!"

Ito butted again, mimicked Glover's expression, made him laugh just as loud.

As they began the run in to Nagasaki harbour, Wang-Li called out, handed Glover a telescope. He peered through it, brought a ship into focus.

"Damn!" he said. "It's not one of the Shogun's junks this time. It's the bloody Royal Navy. There's no way we can outrun them."

"So," said Ito, picking up his sword. "We fight them."

"Let's hope it doesn't come to that," said Glover, raising the telescope again.

The frigate ran them down easily. A boarding party clambered on deck, held Glover and Ito at gunpoint.

"This is an outrage!" said Glover. "I'm a respectable merchant on legitimate business!"

The cargo was dragged from the hold. An officer jemmied open a crate, took out a rifle, a box of ammunition. "Respectable?" He held up the rifle. "Legitimate?"

Glover stayed calm, but raised his voice. "I insist on speaking to your Captain."

Another voice, authoritative, spoke behind him. "Mister Glover."

Glover turned, recognised the man, thank God. It was Mackenzie's friend Barstow, the one who had presided over Glover's initiation in the First Degree. Hele, conceal never reveal.

"Captain Barstow," said Glover. "You know me. You know my intentions are honourable."

"Indeed?" said the Captain with a slight raise of the eyebrow, a faint smile behind the bristling full-set beard.

"This consignment of guns is for the protection of the foreign settlement in Nagasaki. You know the situation as well as anyone. It is unpredictable, volatile. The place is a powder-keg, especially since last year's attack on the Legation in Edo."

"I understand you experienced that first-hand," said the Captain.

"I was lucky to escape with my life, sir."

The Captain nodded. "Quite."

"The need for security is paramount. We have to be ready to defend ourselves."

"And the danger lies with these rebel clans, the Satsuma, the Choshu?"

He stared directly at Ito, who stood rigid, met his gaze.

"There are certain elements within those clans," said Glover, "who pose a serious threat to our very presence here."

The Captain nodded to the boarding party, who lowered their guns. "Very well, Mister Glover. I shall accept your explanation. A report will be entered in the log and no further action will be taken, on this occasion. But take heed. Some of my fellow officers may not be so accommodating."

He turned away, prepared to descend the rope ladder back to his own vessel. "We shall escort you safely into the harbour. As you are no doubt aware, these waters are infested with pirates, and it would be unfortunate if your cargo were to fall into the wrong hands." He saluted. "I bid you good day."

Back on shore, in their favourite drinking den, Glover proposed a toast.

"To British fair play."

Ito remained sullen, grunted.

"He insulted Choshu clan, and you agreed with him."

"I said elements of both clans were dangerous. Your friend and mine, Takashi — remind me to which clan he belongs. Ah, yes, Choshu!"

"He say we are same as Satsuma. But Satsuma are much worse. Cause all this trouble."

"God, give me strength!"

"Now Satsuma buy a ship from your country."

"A very smart piece of business, which I was happy to broker."

"Ship is called the *England*."

"So," said Glover. "Japan is buying England!"

Ito let the words sink in, caught the joke, threw back his head and roared again his great throaty laugh.

"One day!" he said.

"To Japan!" said Glover, proposing another toast.

"*Nippon!*"

Together they said, "*Kanpai!*", knocked back their drinks, banged their cups down on the table, ordered more.

They were on the lawn at Ipponmatsu, Glover in shirtsleeves, Ito in his usual loose-fitting Japanese clothes. Matsuo was in attendance, carrying two full-size wooden swords. He bowed, handed them both to Ito, who passed one to Glover.

"*Hai!*"

He showed Glover how to stand, weight evenly balanced, light on his feet, demonstrated how to hold the sword, the grip firm but light.

Glover tried to copy, felt cumbersome and awkward.

Ito showed him again, emphasised the importance of the stance, the readiness, told him to breathe deep, feel his own strength, the fire in his belly an energy he could tap.

"So." He demonstrated a few cuts and sweeps with the sword, his movements graceful and dynamic, fierce but controlled. "Now, you."

176

Once more Glover tried, mimicked the moves with great gusto but a certain lack of finesse.

"It's harder than it looks," he said, laughing. "Still. A bit of work and I'll get the hang of it."

"Much work," said Ito, straightfaced. "Again."

Again Glover swiped and hacked the air. The evening was warm. He was working up a sweat.

"Again."

Stand firm but relaxed, feel the grip, raise the sword. Strike and step forward. Again. Again.

"Again."

"Christ!"

"Again."

"Bloody taskmaster!"

"Again!"

Glover was ready to crack the wooden blade down on Ito's skull. He was breathing heavily; the sweat prickled his scalp, the back of his neck; his shirt stuck to him.

"Now," said Ito. "You get your breath back, you attack. Hit me."

"Gladly!" said Glover.

"Remember," said Ito. "Breathe deep." He patted his stomach. "Feel it here."

Glover tried to calm himself, concentrate.

"Good," said Ito. "Now."

He stood, balanced, poised, the sword held out in front of him, nodded to Glover to come at him.

Glover raised his own sword, charged, brought the blade down with real force.

Casually, almost disdainfully, Ito deflected the blow, sent Glover staggering.

"You see?" he said. "I use your own strength against you."

"Aye," said Glover. The impact had jarred his arms, his wrists. "I see!"

"Now," said Ito. "Again."

It was late afternoon, a faint coolness in the breeze. Matsuo had helped them lace up their gloves. Glover had bought them on a whim — two pairs — from a market stall at the docks, part of a job-lot that included a cricket bat and a leather football, probably brought out by some missionary full of zeal to convert the natives to the way of sport.

Now it was Ito's turn to look uncomfortable.

"A return bout," said Glover. "The noble art!"

Ito looked, flummoxed, at cumbersome wads of padding on his hands. "Noble art," he repeated.

"Fisticuffs," said Glover. "Queensberry Rules."

Ito looked even more confused.

"Seconds out!" said Glover, and he took up position, left foot forward, hands in front of his face. Ito did the same, but with his right foot forward.

"A southpaw," said Glover. "Makes it interesting."

Ito gave up even trying to comprehend, did his best to follow Glover's movements, ducking and weaving, weight on the balls of his feet. Glover showed him how to keep his guard up, jabbed once or twice, let the blows land on Ito's gloves.

"Straight left," said Glover, and he motioned to Ito to hit back, parried each jab.

"Good!" said Glover. "Now." And he feinted with the left, cut under Ito's guard with a right to the solar plexus, knocked the wind out of him.

Ito straightened up, bowed, resumed his position, guard up. He managed to block the next uppercut, after two or three attempts succeeded in retaliating, landing a punch to Glover's head.

"Grand!" said Glover. "You have the makings of a pugilist! Maybe some day we'll fight with the gloves off, bareknuckle."

Ito nodded, understood the challenge. "Maybe some day we fight with real swords, cold steel."

And Glover saw in an instant the coldness, the steeliness, in Ito's gaze, knew if it ever did come to such a fight, Ito would fillet him. For all the apparent depth of their friendship and trust, it was still there, that otherness, that distance. Ito lived by a code that was absolute, overrode everything, and Glover, like the rest of the barbarians, would always have to keep up his guard.

The incident, as it happened, featured two of Glover's acquaintances as its principal players. The sheer brutality of it, the sudden barbarism, ensured the tale was told and retold.

Glover heard it first as a rumour, then as a newspaper report, later by word-of-mouth from an eyewitness to its initiation.

Charles Richardson, whom Glover had met on his arrival in Dejima, and again at the Legation, had gone out riding along the Tokkaido from Yokohama with two companions, a young diplomat named Dawes, and his fiancée Miss Clemence, recently arrived from England. By their account, Richardson had been in a boisterous mood, revelling in his role as their guide to this land of savages.

Unfortunately, as fate would have it, they encountered, coming in the opposite direction, the Satsuma Daimyo with his entourage. Glover remembered vividly his brief meeting with the Daimyo, the power of the man, the intensity and ferocity of his gaze from inside the norimon. The Daimyo was on his way from Edo where he had been summoned for an audience with the Shogun. Glover could imagine the scenario all too vividly, a drama shaping itself with a kind of implacable inevitability, given the characters involved.

Richardson was ahead of his two companions, nudging his horse along the narrow roadway. The Daimyo's advance guard, two formidable warriors, fully armed, ran ahead of the norimon, ordered Richardson and his party to get out of the way.

Richardson, foolhardy, shouted back at them, refusing to budge, told them to stop yabbering their bloody gibberish, he was a British citizen and refused to kowtow.

Dawes realised the danger, called out to him to back down. But it was too late. Four more guards rushed forward, drawing their swords, followed by four more on horseback. A single cut sliced Richardson's arm and

180

he was dragged from his horse, shouting at the others to save themselves for God's sake. Dawes felt a blow to his shoulder as he managed to turn his horse. Miss Clemence screamed as a sword was swung at her head and she somehow, miraculously, turned away, the blade taking off her hat and cutting through her hair.

The young couple managed to spur their horses clear, ride at a gallop back to Yokohama and raise the alarm before collapsing, exhausted and bloodstained.

Word spread and the reaction was outrage. That westerners should be attacked in this way was bad enough, but that a woman should be involved was unforgivable. Fifty men armed themselves, saddled up and rode along the Tokkaido — British sailors, French troopers, Dutch and American merchants, all ready to do battle.

The precise scene of the attack was not hard to find; there were dark bloodstains on the road, flies buzzing around it, a few scavenging dogs. Some distance away they found the remains of Richardson, dragged under a tree and left there, covered by straw mats, disembowelled, the throat cut, the head and face hacked and slashed, the right hand severed where he'd tried to ward off a blow.

Glover learned these gruesome details from Dawes himself some months later. Dawes was passing through Nagasaki, en route to Shanghai and thence to England. His fiancée had already gone home, much shaken by her experience. Dawes would follow her, take up a posting in London. He had recovered from his wounds, apart from a continuing ache to the shoulder where the swordblade had struck.

"I fear that'll be with me the rest of my days," he said, seated in an armchair at the Foreigners' Club, peering into his glass of whisky as if reading his future there. "That and the deeper scars."

"Console yourself," said Mackenzie, "that it could have been much worse, for yourself and your fiancée. The fate of Mr Richardson could have been your own."

"Indeed," said Dawes.

"What in the name of God possessed him?" asked Mackenzie.

"Bravado," said Dawes, "pure and simple."

"And entirely inappropriate," said Glover. "The man was a fool."

"Well then," said Dawes, bristling slightly, "he certainly paid for it."

"My fear," said Glover, "is that many more may yet have to pay the price. The consequences may yet be far-reaching."

"It was only by the grace of sweet reason," said Dawes, "that there were no further consequences on the night of the attack. The band of men who rode out of Yokohama that night quickly became a mob."

"The urge to revenge is strong," said Mackenzie.

"There was a faction eager to pursue the Daimyo and his party, settle the matter there and then."

"It would have been a bloodbath," said Glover.

"The Consul preached restraint," said Dawes. "He argued that it was a diplomatic affair and must be settled through the proper channels."

"I bet the mob loved that!" said Glover.

"There were indeed rumblings, about lily-livered appeasement. But sanity prevailed. The pursuit was called off, thank God."

"Amen," said Mackenzie.

"Aye," said Glover. "But it's not over yet. Not by a long way."

In the drawing room of Ipponmatsu the atmosphere was solemn and formal. Five young samurai, Ito and four others, sat straightbacked round the table. Matsuo came into the room, bowed to Glover and to Ito, took his short *wakizashi* sword from its sheath. He stood behind Ito, who braced himself, sat upright, breathed deep. Matsuo took Ito's topknot of hair, symbol of his status as a samurai, tugged and held it in his left hand, cut through it with the sword, let the clump of hair drop to the floor. Ito bowed, and Matsuo went to each of the young men in turn, repeated the action, ritually and ceremonially, cut off the topknot, and each of them bowed.

When it was done, Ito looked at the others, shorn and slightly bedraggled. He ruffled his own hair, threw back his head and laughed, and the others did the same. Glover produced a pair of scissors.

"Right," he said. "They just need tidied up a bit and they'll pass for perfect English gentlemen!"

Initially it had been Ito's idea, and Glover had dismissed it as a pipe dream, thought it impossible, too dangerous by far. Now he saw it as the only way

183

forward, for Ito, for all of them, for Japan itself. Ito had to go to the West.

He would take with him four companions, young samurai from his own Choshu clan. Glover would make the arrangements, smuggle them out.

Mackenzie had been appalled. "It's madness, Tom! Think of the risks!"

"We have. We know what we're taking on."

"What if it all goes wrong? You'll be expelled from the country. Your assets will be forfeit. You'll be ruined."

"Then so be it. Ito and the others are risking so much more."

"If they're caught they'll be summarily executed."

"They know that. They accept it. It would be cowardly not to help them."

Mackenzie had shaken his head. "It's a step too far, Tom. Even for you."

"So you won't help?"

"I can't."

Glover had nodded. "Fine."

He had to admit there was something comical in their appearance, their hair still ragged, roughly trimmed. They had discarded their samurai robes, put on western suits that Glover had acquired for them, and even the smallest suit was long in the sleeves, the trouser-legs, lent an aspect that was almost clownish.

But then Ito lined them up, a general inspecting his troops. They stood in front of Glover, looking for his approval, stiff and selfconscious, like a family group in a photographer's studio, posing for a formal portrait. And something in the sheer dignity of their bearing, an inherent pride, shone through. Glover found himself quite moved by it, bowed low to them.

He fetched a bottle of his best whisky, poured each of them a dram in a small sake cup, proposed a toast.

"To the Choshu Five!"

They raised their cups, drank.

Ito cleared his throat. "Is tradition, when we go on journey like this, to make haiku poem. May be last journey. I make for all of us."

He drew himself up, recited in Japanese, the words slow and incantatory. The others made noises of approval, bowed.

Then he turned to Glover. "I make translation.

> Night journey —
> How far is it
> to the other shore?"

"Good," said Glover, and they all bowed once more. "Now, it's time."

The night was warm and close. Glover led them down a narrow lane towards the harbour, their collars turned up, hat-brims pulled down, Matsuo following behind, alert to any threat. Their bags had been loaded, earlier in the day, onto a company clipper, at anchor out in the bay. A long-boat waited at the harbour, ready to ferry them out. The hope was that in the dark, from a distance, the five might pass for a group of young

Europeans. If challenged they were to keep silent, turn their faces away, let Glover do the talking.

It was all going well till they reached the quay and a lantern suddenly flared at them out of the dark and a voice roared at them to stop, stay where they were.

"Christ!" said Glover, under his breath.

The guard was one of the Shogun's men, patrolling the docks. The fear was that there were more of them, that they'd been alerted, were ready to attack.

Glover stepped forward, said these men were English traders. "*Igirisu no shounin desu.*" They were leaving for Shanghai. "*Shanhai e iku tokoro desu.*"

The guard held up the lantern, shone it in their faces. His own face in the harsh light was hard, unconvinced. He said they would have to wait, barked it out. "*Koko de matte ore!*"

Ito and the others tensed, braced themselves. Matsuo positioned himself between Glover and the guard, right hand resting easy on the handle of his sword. Then from behind them came another voice, booming out, authoritative, taking the guard to task.

It was Mackenzie, saying the men were his responsibility, they were on Jardine's business. "*Jardine to akinai o shite oru no desu.*"

The guard looked reluctantly placated, turned to go.

"Good timing, Ken!" said Glover.

Mackenzie nodded, laconic. "Aye."

"Now we go to England!" said Ito.

Relief spread through the group, and one of the younger samurai laughed, said "Hello. Good morning.

186

Good afternoon. Good evening. How are you? I am very well, thank you."

Another of them shoved him, playful, but a little too hard and he stumbled and fell, his hat coming off and rolling some distance.

The guard stopped and turned, shone his lantern again, lit up the figure lying on the ground, the young man clearly Japanese. He drew his sword, opened his mouth to call the alarm, but Matsuo was already on him, had drawn his own sword, sliced the man's throat and he pitched forward, dead.

"Dear God!" said Mackenzie.

"Go!" said Glover, urging Ito and the others into the boat.

Matsuo lugged the guard's body to the quayside, shoved it into the water with a deep dull hollow splash, the water imploding then closing over it. The boat moved off and there were shouts in the distance, voices raised, more guards running from the other side of the docks.

"*Hayaku!*" said Matsuo. "Quick!" And he set off running down a sidestreet, Mackenzie and Glover following.

"Christ Almighty!" said Mackenzie, wheezing, out of breath. "I can't keep this up!"

There were guards coming after them; they could hear them getting nearer. They turned off down a narrow lane, into an alleyway. As they passed a doorway, Matsuo stopped, pushed both of them inside, put a finger to his mouth to indicate they keep silent, and carried on running.

They waited, tense and strained, nerves taut, conscious of the sound of their own breathing. There were more footsteps along the alley but they kept on going, past the doorway, on out of their hearing. Then it was quiet again, and Glover was aware of the thud of his own heartbeat, heard it gradually slow down, back to its normal rate.

It was dark, but he could just make out they were in the courtyard of a small temple, a wayside shrine. The thick woody scent of incense hung in the air, faintly musty. Mackenzie had slumped, was sitting on the ground, his back to the wall, his face in his hands.

"What in the name of God are we doing?"

Glover motioned him to be silent again. He had heard something, the low drone of a voice. Carefully, slowly, placing one foot, the other, he made his way across the courtyard, trying to move quietly, but crunching gravel underfoot with every step. He was stopped dead by another sound, the clang of a gong, a struck iron bell. Then he realised the voice was of a monk, chanting, inside the shrine. He took two more steps and peered in. By the faintest glow of a lamp burned almost out, he could see the silhouette of the monk, an old man, sitting cross-legged at his night-watch, his devotions. The monk turned and looked at Glover, looked through him and beyond him to some other place, as if his presence or absence were a matter of supreme indifference. His concentration fierce, he resumed his chanting. *Namu Amida Butsu.* And he struck the iron bell once more, and the sound reverberated, rang in Glover's skull, drove everything else out.

The next morning Mackenzie, still shaken, paced in front of Glover's desk.

"That was absolute madness, Tom! We could have been killed!"

Glover was maintaining a surface calm, but the excitement churned in him, surged in waves. "But we did it, Ken. We got them out!"

"That's not the point . . ."

Glover thumped the desk. "That's exactly the point! Can you imagine what it'll do to these men?"

"If they survive the journey."

"Of course they'll survive. They're samurai, for God's sake!"

"Aye, don't I know it!"

"And Jardine's will look after them when they get to London, I'll make sure of that."

"It'll be one hell of a journey."

"Can you imagine what it'll be like for them?" said Glover. "Even Singapore will shake them to the core, when they sail in past the British warships. Then when they dock at Southampton, get on a train to London, they'll be overwhelmed! And the first thing they'll realise is they can't fight that power. It's impossible. Ito already knows this in his bones. I just want him to realise it fully, put it beyond all doubt."

"And then?"

"He'll be more determined than ever to work with us, build from the ground up, turn Japan itself into a great power."

Mackenzie looked at him, held his gaze.

"And then?"

CHAPTER
EIGHT

Flower of Kagoshima

Nagasaki–Kagoshima, 1863

The wheels of diplomacy had ground with inordinate slowness, so far from London, the hub of the known universe. But the announcement, when it came, was chilling in its businesslike simplicity, couched in the language of commerce and the law, not quite masking the massive threat implied.

For allowing a civilian Englishman, Charles Richardson, to be murdered, and for failing to arrest his assassins, the Shogun shall pay Her Majesty's Government the sum of one hundred thousand pounds, in Mexican silver dollars. A further twenty-five thousand pounds shall be payable by the Satsuma Daimyo to be distributed to the relatives of the murdered man. The assassins shall be apprehended, and executed in the presence of British officers. If these conditions are not met within 20 days of this proclamation, there shall be a revenge attack on the Satsuma clan.

It was what Glover had feared most. It was likely, though by no means certain, that the Shogun would pay up. He would hesitate, prevaricate, bluster, delay. But in the end he would pay, at the very last moment possible. He had no alternative, no answer to the power of the British gunboats which were already, it was rumoured, heading for Kagoshima. The Daimyo, however, was unlikely to back down, whatever the consequences.

Alcock, the British Consul, had finally given up his post, retired to a quiet life in China, a country he regarded as infinitely more civilised than Japan. His successor was an altogether harder man, Sir Harry Parkes. He had been alerted to the fact that Glover had links with the Satsuma, had traded with them, even married into the clan. He wrote Glover a formal letter, asking if he would use his good offices to intercede with the clan leadership, attempt to make them see reason.

"Reason?" said Glover, reading the letter. "The man obviously hasn't been in this country for long!"

"They'll see reason all right," said Walsh. "When hell freezes over."

Glover replied to Parkes that he would give the matter some thought. Parkes replied that time was short and there was some need of urgency.

On the twentieth day after the proclamation, the very deadline specified, the Shogun handed over payment of the hundred thousand pounds. A gang of labourers lugged the money, in heavy wooden crates filled with Mexican silver dollars, from the treasury to the British Legation in Edo, now rebuilt and fortified, heavily guarded. The coinage was counted and weighed by a crew of Chinese *shroffs*, money-changers skilled in the detection of forgery, the substitution of base metal for silver. They painstakingly sifted through the piles of shining coins, set them in their scales, nodded their approval.

An illustration depicting the scene appeared in the *Nagasaki Advertiser*, an artist's impression by one Charles Wirgman who was in attendance. It showed in the foreground the pigtailed Chinese, huddled over the heaps of coins like misers in some stage melodrama or pantomime. Behind sat three Japanese dignitaries, representatives of the Shogun, stiff and formal in their robes, faces set, stern. On either side stood the British delegates, each of them affecting a judgemental righteousness, but unable to conceal an avaricious smugness at the sight of the fortune shimmering at their feet.

"They really put the Shogun in his place," said Walsh, passing the newspaper back to Glover. "Showed him who's boss."

And the picture should have delighted Glover, showing as it did a moment of triumph over the Shogun and all his works. But somehow the scene made him uneasy, the money-changers mercenary, parasitic, the British observers gloating, casually powerful, the Japanese maintaining a stoical dignity in the face of ignominy and humiliation. He was unsettled, folded the newspaper and threw it down.

It was later, when he received another, more urgent communication from Parkes, renewing his request for

Glover to intercede with the Satsuma, that he realised why the picture had affected him so much. It gave absolute confirmation of the power wielded by the West, and it epitomised the spirit of Japanese defiance which would now be expressed in extreme form by the Satsuma Daimyo. Now more than ever he would refuse to back down, lose face. Now he could make his stand, be seen to be braver, more honourable than the Shogun who had so feebly capitulated. The bombardment of Kagoshima was inevitable.

Ito had returned from his sojourn, full of tales to tell. He sat in the front room at Ipponmatsu, recounting his adventures, and Glover listened, hung on every word.

The journey out now seemed like a distant dream. Initially there had been apprehension, the danger of being caught and executed.

"But *Hagakure* tells us to have firm resolution, be ready for death. So we were ready, had right mind."

When they had reached open seas, bound for Shanghai, they knew they were safe. But the journey ahead was fraught and perilous, endlessly long, fully tested that samurai resolve.

The size and scale of the western ships in Shanghai harbour was overwhelming. Ito at least had seen the like on his gunrunning expeditions with Glover. But to board one of these ships, to set foot on its deck, was salutary. The ship carrying them was the 300-ton *Pegasus*, owned by Jardine's. Their quarters below deck were cramped and dank; they were worked hard, expected to pitch in along with the apprentice seamen;

the rations were meagre, the food itself inedible, leathery salt beef and hardtack. Their health suffered, they were racked by vomiting and diarrhoea, had to remain on deck even in the roughest of seas; at one time Ito, in the throes of sickness, had to be tied to the rail so he wouldn't be swept overboard.

Ito laughed as he told the story against himself, not to admit his weakness, but showing pride at what he had endured.

"Firm resolution. Readiness for death."

The journey took four months, and did indeed almost kill them. Then, docking at Southampton, they looked in awe at the massive British warships anchored there.

"I wanted you to see the possibilities," said Glover.

"We see," said Ito, leaving much unspoken.

They had travelled to London by train, another salutary experience, hurtled through the English countryside at unimaginable speed down mile after mile of iron track. It had shaken them, not just physically, but deep in their being, inspired sheer wonder and awe. Japan, by comparison, was crawling out of the Middle Ages.

In London the travellers had been received and welcomed by representatives of Jardine's. In contrast to their long and arduous sea-crossing, stowed away like chattels, less than steerage class, they found themselves suddenly fêted, treated like heroes, like honoured guests. Their itinerary was mapped out and they embarked on a grand tour of industrialised Britain, visited factories and shipyards, universities and museums. They spent time in Glasgow, saw the extent of shipbuilding on the Clyde; they made it as far north as Aberdeen.

Ito shivered, mimed being extremely cold, blowing on his hands, rubbing the warmth back into his arms.

"Now I know why you so tough!"

Glover laughed, could picture Ito's discomfort, head down into a dreich grey drizzle off the North Sea.

"I bring you this," said Ito, and he carefully, formally, with both hands, handed Glover a letter.

Glover took it, moved by the sight of the handwriting. It was from Martha, even smelled faintly of scent, something with lilies. She must have doused the paper, the envelope.

He put it down on his desk, would read it when Ito was gone.

Ito's return journey had been much less difficult than the outward voyage; Jardine's had paid for their passage on an American-built clipper; he and his companions had travelled in cabins like the other passengers, and arrived, exhausted but unscathed, in Yokohama, disembarked without incident, and Ito had made his way directly to Nagasaki, to give Glover his full report.

Glover took it all in, nodded.

"Now you have returned to a situation even more volatile than it was before you left."

Ito pronounced the word, queried it. "*Volatile?*"

"More dangerous," said Glover. "Like gunpowder." He mimed lighting a fuse. "Boom!"

"*Hai,*" said Ito. "*So desu.*"

"The Satsuma Daimyo is making life difficult."

"Satsuma always difficult," said Ito. "No good sense."

Glover told him about the letter from Parkes, asking him to intervene. Ito thought on no account should Glover go to Kagoshima.

"Daimyo not change," he said. "He is like Takashi, but more."

"I understand," said Glover. "But I feel I *have* to go."

"Is matter of honour?"

"Something like that, aye."

Ito nodded, but looked perturbed. "Not good for me to come with you. I not be welcome. Choshu and Satsuma not friends."

"Don't I know it!"

"Same reason, Matsuo not go."

"So I'll go alone," he said. "Maybe it's best."

Ito looked as if was going to say something else, changed his mind.

When he'd gone, Glover read the letter from Martha.

Dear Tom,

I am sending this dispatch in the care of your Japanese friend, Mister Ito. It was wonderful to have news of you, directly from him. (He seems to hold you in high regard.)

He impressed us as a charming fellow, in spite of his unusual appearance, and his English, though heavily accented, is remarkably good. You can imagine the stir he caused in Bridge of Don! Of course, Father had not two words to say to him, and the little he did say, he shouted as if the poor man were deaf! Mister Ito for his part was happy to sit in silence, balancing a teacup in his lap. I don't know which of them was the more taciturn. Mother, on the other hand, and as you would expect, talked nineteen-to-the-dozen! She wanted to know if you were well, and how he came to know you, and whether you would soon be returning home. He in turn was the soul of politeness and said you had made a great success of yourself, but that you had not forgotten your home and family. He thought, however, that your work in Japan might yet keep you there for a few more years. I hope and pray that is not the case.I'm minded of that old song, "Will ye no come back again?", and if I'm not careful I'll be blubbering like a bairn!

Mother and Father are both well, though not getting any younger. In fact, Father will be retiring soon, and that will necessitate some upheaval in that we will have to find a new house in the neighbourhood, our tenancy of this one being tied to Father's position. So, unless you hurry up and pay us a visit, we'll likely have moved from your childhood home by the time you get back!

I hadn't intended this to be a long letter, Tom — I sent you one of those not so long ago, full of news and gossip! But I couldn't miss the opportunity of sending you a message by special delivery, directly via the hand of Mister Ito, or *Prince* Ito as he styles himself! (Is he really a

Prince? Does the word mean something else in his part of the world? I didn't like to inquire too closely, for fear of appearing rude.) In fact the gentleman in question departs tomorrow morning, and he is downstairs at this very moment, awaiting delivery of this missive.

I shall therefore end forthwith.

Your loving sister,

Martha

He read the letter, re-read it, read it again, smelled the fading perfume, redolent of home. She had written it in April; he could picture her sitting at the window looking out towards the sea; the air would still be chilly but with that first faint promise of spring.

He went outside to the garden. The night was heavy and warm, humid. The task ahead weighed down on him, oppressive. He went back inside, read the letter one more time, folded it carefully and put it away in his desk drawer.

As he disembarked at Kagoshima, he felt it wrench at his guts, the sense, all at once, of familiarity and strangeness, a waking dream. There was the volcano, *Sakurajima*, with its plume of smoke, casting its pale grey pall, leaving a faint trace in the air, the acridness of ash. There was the road through town, past the gardens and temples, the pottery. He had come here with Sono; it seemed so very long ago. They had walked by a stream, looked at the bamboo in the water, filling and emptying itself. *Shishi-odoshi*. Sono had bowed to a statue of Jizo, prayed for their baby. He had drunk sake with his father-in-law, Shimada, come face to face with Shimazu Saburo, the Daimyo, seen at close quarters that ferocious intransigence that would yet bring destruction on the whole town. He felt suddenly, profoundly, wearied, saw himself useless and helpless in the face of events. He had replied to Parkes, begged him to use his influence to call off the attack, or at least delay it. Parkes had replied that it was impossible, matters had gone too far and were beyond his control. Unless the Daimyo could be persuaded to change his mind, retribution would be stayed no longer.

Did he really think he could deflect a warlord from his grand gesture of defiance? The Daimyo would probably refuse to see him at all; or worse, he might have him taken prisoner, executed for his insolence, for the crime of being western, alien, a barbarian invader plundering his country. It was madness. And yet.

He steadied himself, felt a sudden sense of purpose. Like an actor in a drama, he had to play his part, see this through. And he knew that even if he were not to succeed with this larger plan, this impossible task, he might at least speak to Sono, persuade her to leave with him. He might save one life, and hers was worth the saving.

He knew Shimada-san would be putting his own life at risk by bringing him to the Daimyo's residence, and he was grateful. He had brought a gift for the Daimyo, a fob-watch, elaborately wrapped. Shimada had taken the gift, given it to one of the Daimyo's attendants.

Glover's pistol was confiscated; he was instructed to remove his shoes, wait in an anteroom. He waited an hour that felt like a day. The room was bare, austere; no chairs, no cushions; dark wood, a hard polished floor. He sat upright, his legs crossed, till his back and knees ached, his calf muscles cramped. Then he kneeled, till that too became intolerable and he crouched, at last had to stand up, pace the floor in his stockinged soles.

When he had gone beyond boredom, through agitation, to contained rage, then beyond even that to a kind of numb acceptance, the screen to the inner apartments opened and Shimada stepped out. He was carrying Glover's gift, not even unwrapped. Shimada gave him a look that said there was no hope. Behind him came the attendant who told him the Daimyo had no time to speak to him and he should go.

Glover held himself in check, from somewhere found a form of words that indicated the utmost obeisance, humility and respect. But his voice was firm, commanding, as he suggested the Daimyo would demonstrate his wisdom by agreeing to pay the recompense. By delaying longer than the Shogun, he had already shown himself stronger. By forcing the West into this show of strength, he had further demonstrated his power. And now he could avoid destruction and loss of life by his tactical awareness in making an honourable retreat.

There was a silence. Shimada stood with his head bowed. Then the Daimyo himself emerged from his chambers, stood glaring at Glover, and Glover knew this man would never, ever back down. His face was a fierce mask, mouth set, eyebrows gathered, nostrils flared. He muttered something to the attendant, who bent almost double, relayed the message to Glover.

"The Daimyo does not accept your gift, or your advice. Instead he gives *you* a gift. He allows you to keep your head."

The screen was closed.

The attendant motioned to Glover. "Now you go."

Shimada shuffled out backwards, kowtowing. Glover followed him, pulled on his shoes. His pistol was returned to him. Shimada led him out of the compound, watched all the way by armed guards.

In Shimada's home, the atmosphere was heavy, tense. Glover had offered the old man the watch, he had refused. They drank sake, as they had so long ago, and Glover repeated the toast that had made Shimada laugh. *Shogun nanka kuso kurae!* The Shogun. To hell with him. But this time he didn't even smile.

Glover tried replacing *Shogun* with *Daimyo*.

"*Daimyo nanka kuso kurae!*"

The old man slammed the floor.

"*Ie!*"

No! This was a breach of protocol, disloyalty to the clan, and could not be countenanced.

Glover apologised, humbly.

The silence lay even heavier between them.

After a while, Glover tentatively broached the subject of Sono, asked how she was. The old man grunted, said something he didn't understand, got up and left the room.

Glover held his head in his hands. What in God's name was he doing here? Probably making matters worse, blundering around. A Scottish bull in a Japanese china shop. He heard the shoji screen open, stood up ready to make a final apology, take his leave. But it was not Shimada standing there, it was Sono.

Although he had hoped to meet her, seek her out, he was completely taken aback at seeing her, suddenly there.

Shaken, he blurted out her name, all he could say. "Sono!"

She stepped into the room, kneeled in front of him, bowed her head to the floor. "Guraba-san."

"Tom!" he said, taking her arm and raising her to her feet. "For God's sake, *Tom!*"

"*Hai*," she said, a sad little smile flicking briefly across her face. "*Tomu.*"

"Look at you!" he said, stroking her face, her hair. She looked thinner, more haggard, dressed in simple, almost dowdy robes. That sadness in the eyes had deepened, taken hold. But she was still beautiful; it shone through.

She turned away a moment, fetched a tray she had set down outside the room, placed it on a low table in the corner of the room, motioned him to sit.

"*Dozo.*"

Please.

She had made food for him, laid it out. He was moved, choked back the emotion, sat down cross-legged.

Only when he started to eat did he realise he was hungry, and he wolfed it down, slurped the noodles noisily, munched through the rest, the stewed terrapin, the boiled rockfish, tough and chewy, the bitter pickled radish; plain fare but good.

"*Oishi-desu!*" he said, and he meant it. It was delicious.

Again he saw that faint half-smile, fleeting, a memory of better times.

"*Arigato,*" she said, bowing.

The moment of simple domesticity, something shared, touched him again. This woman had been, was, his wife. He had to make her understand the danger of her situation, the necessity of leaving this place. But he found himself suddenly dumbstruck, tonguetied. The language deserted him. And she, in all likelihood, had spoken no English since she'd left him. She'd had little enough anyway, and now even that little would have atrophied, dried up. They had no words.

He spent the night in the same ryokan where they'd stayed on that first visit, but this time alone. The old innkeeper was gruff, grudging, reluctant to rent him the room; but he payed in advance, a little extra, slammed the money down on the counter; the man relented, let him in. He kicked off his boots, carried them with him up the wooden stairs.

He was weary, unrolled the futon in the middle of the floor, slumped down on it fully clothed except for his jacket which he pulled off, threw in the corner. But for all his exhaustion, he couldn't sleep. The night was warm, his mind was agitated, the sense of impending disaster like lead in his belly. When he did sleep it was fitful and riven by dreams. Faces loomed at him, Shimada looking grim, Sono melancholy, the Daimyo ferocious. They were here in the room with him and the whole place was on fire; it was going up in flames and he couldn't stop it, lay paralysed, unable to move.

He woke in terror and panic, drenched in sweat, sat up, his breathing shallow and quick. The dream faded but left him with a sense of threat, alert to any sound. He reached for his pistol, tensed, but the noises he heard were only the wind in the pines, the harsh rasping cry of cicada. He lay down again and he was in Bridge of Don, trying to get back to the house, to alert his family, warn them of some nameless danger, evacuate them to safety; but he couldn't run, sank knee-deep in mud.

Again he woke, took his bearings, sat up. The night-watch, the wee small hours, time of demons. He lay back, eyes wide open, staring into the dark. Not quite awake, not quite asleep, he felt himself strapped into some vast mechanism, knew that if he even flinched, moved one muscle, he would set off a conflagration that would engulf everything around him. But in order to stop this he had to move. He couldn't move, he must move. He prayed, Dear God, wrenched himself upright and sat, waiting. But nothing happened. The world did not end. He was alive, and alone, in this shabby inn, in a small town in the far south of Japan, in a life far stranger than any dream; but it was real, it was actual; he was here.

This time he resolved to stay awake. He sat up, his back against a wooden pillar. His head nodded once, twice, and the first grey light of day was filtering in to the room.

He walked down to the docks, felt even more the hostility directed at him, the threat. It was there in every glance in his direction, every muttered malediction. He had come early to check on the times the boats might be departing for Nagasaki, but everything was in disarray; nothing was entering or leaving the harbour, the invading fleet had dropped anchor out in the bay.

So events were moving swiftly at last, after the long months of delay. He had seen a dispatch before leaving for Kagoshima, listing the ships that would make up the squadron; the flagship HMS *Euryalus*, a pair of corvettes, the *Perseus* and the *Pearl*, a paddle sloop, the *Argus*, a dispatch vessel and two gunboats, the *Racehorse* and the appropriately named *Havoc*. He could see the shapes out there, sinister in the mist just starting to disperse. If he were to borrow a telescope he would be able to make out the figures on deck, moving about their predatory business.

He hurried back to Shimada's home. The old man received him dressed as for battle, his swords at his waist, a pistol in his belt, his samurai helmet under his arm. Glover asked if he could see Sono again, Shimada indicated she had gone to the temple, to pray.

He made his way through the crowded streets, past the shrine to Jizo, the gardens, through a red Shinto *torii* gate, but she was nowhere to be seen. Further out

206

there was another temple, Buddhist, and he thought she might have gone there, might be praying to anyone who would listen. But no, there was still no sign of her; he had the feeling he was just missing her at every turn, sensed she was always just a little way ahead of him, just out of reach.

He looked back across the town, towards the harbour, shielded his eyes, saw there was a longboat approaching from the flagship riding at anchor. He hurried back, had to shove his way through the crowds near the dock. A deputation was disembarking, a naval captain, a civilian who looked English, an armed guard of four blue-jackets. Shimada was there to meet them, and the civilian greeted him in Japanese more fluent than Glover's. He relayed the Captain's commands to Shimada, insisted on being taken to the Daimyo to deliver one final ultimatum. Shimada refused, stood resolute, explained that the Daimyo did not deign to see them, but that the message would be passed on and a reply might, or might not, be forthcoming.

"That's as good an answer as you'll get," said Glover.

"I'd feared as much," said the Englishman. "You must be Tom Glover."

"Aye," said Glover, surprised.

"Sir Harry told us you might be here, making one last effort at diplomacy. I'm Ernest Satow, and this is Captain Josling."

Glover nodded. He had heard of Satow, a linguist based at the Legation, who had made himself indispensable as a translator.

"A rum do, this," said Satow.

He was thin, and to Glover's eye looked weak, effete, had lank dark hair and a wispy moustache.

"That's one way of putting it," said Glover.

"Not exactly the way I imagined it when I first came here," said Satow. "I'd pictured a land of perpetual sunshine and endless blue skies, where the whole duty of a man might consist in reclining on a matted floor, looking out through an open window at an exquisite miniature garden in the company of attentive red-lipped black-eyed damsels!"

Glover stared at him; the man's tone, his languidness, seemed inappropriate in the present situation.

"And of course," said Satow, continuing, "the place undoubtedly has its charms, its enchantments. Unfortunately, the reality is complex."

"Aye," said Glover.

"It can be harsh to the point of being brutal."

"We can match them in terms of brutality," said Glover. "As we seem hell-bent on demonstrating."

"If I may quote you," said Satow. "That is one way of putting it."

The naval officer spoke up. "I take it our business here is done?"

"Indeed," said Satow. "Insofar as it can be."

"Then let us return to the ship forthwith."

Satow turned to Glover. "Will you dine with us on board the *Euryalus*? I am sure the Admiral would be delighted to welcome you as his guest, and under the circumstances you might be safer offshore."

"Under the circumstances," said Glover, "I have to decline. The food would stick in my craw."

Satow looked at him with something like admiration. "I understand," he said. "I really do."

"Come, sir!" said the Captain, anxious to be away.

Satow bowed to Shimada, took his leave graciously with just the right degree of formality; then he turned to Glover, said, "Perhaps sweet reason will prevail."

"I fear it has gone beyond reason," said Glover, "on both sides."

Satow nodded, followed the Captain and the four guards down the gangplank onto the longboat. Shimada grunted to Glover that he should have gone with them, then turned away, strode off with his own contingent of guards in the direction of the Daimyo's residence.

Early next morning, tired after another restless night at the ryokan, more troubled dreams of desolation and panic and loss, Glover headed for Shimada's home. This time he was stopped at the gate by two of the guards, armed with pikes. He explained his business and one of them went inside, the other kept Glover at bay with his barbed blade. After some time, Shimada came out, and Glover asked once more about Sono.

At first Glover thought the old man was speaking to him in Japanese, saying something he didn't understand. *Shisei yugo.* Then he realised he was making the effort, speaking in English.

"She say you go."

"It's not safe," said Glover, struggling for the words. "*Anzen de wa nai.*"

"She say, her place here, you go."

The old man bowed, the look in his eyes regret, resolve. No more to be said.

An hour later, Glover was at the dock again and the British delegation had returned to receive their reply. Captain Josling looked on, his expression one of disdain, as Satow repeated the British Government's demands and Shimada read the Daimyo's reply, refusing to pay the indemnity, in fact insisting that the barbarian invaders depart from Kagoshima and from Japan forthwith.

Satow expressed his regrets, bowed, then turned to Glover and suggested it might not be a good time to be stranded here, and he should perhaps accompany them back to the ship.

"You may join me on the deck of the *Argus,*" he said, "a suitable vantage point from which we can observe the proceedings."

"The *proceedings?*" said Glover. "I find myself unable to contemplate the bombardment of a town and consequent loss of life with such a degree of equanimity and detachment."

Satow bristled. "The offer was made in good faith, sir, and with your own safety in mind."

The Captain was already moving towards the longboat, spoke to Satow. "We must leave before the tide turns. Mister Glover has clearly made his mind up and is impervious to reason. On his own head be it."

Satow pleaded with Glover one last time. "If you change your mind, I'm sure you can negotiate with one of these bargees to ferry you on board."

"I won't change my mind," said Glover.

"No," said Satow, and he shook Glover's hand; the exchange was at an end.

Whether it was bravado, or recklessness, or plain foolhardiness, he had no sense of imminent danger to himself, in spite of what Satow had said. It was true his situation was precarious, and he might have been safer if Matsuo had been accompanying him, but he was surrendered to fate, or history, or whatever other forces were at play. If anything, he was more concerned about Sono. If he could not persuade her to leave altogether, perhaps he could at least ensure she moved further from the docks, up to higher ground.

Shimada's home was now barricaded; there was no sign of Shimada himself, who would be marshalling defences, commanding the gun emplacements, nor was there any sign of Sono. He prayed she had gone out of town, headed inland, or was at least taking refuge in the Buddhist temple; there at least she should be out of range of the ships' cannon.

The area near the docks was alive with folk scurrying to move their possessions, get out of the way. One old man was scrambling to pack up his stall, struggling to cram his goods into crates. Much of it was junk, old kitchen equipment, a set of scales, odd bits of pottery. But in amongst it, Glover saw something he wanted, a spyglass.

He asked how much. "*Ikura?*"

The old man, in a panic, quoted more than it was worth. Glover paid him double, shoved the spyglass in his coat pocket, headed out of town.

By noon the heat was intense. At the temple he was thorough, searched the grounds, disturbed an old monk in the meditation hall, startled a group of young nuns raking a gravel garden. They must have thought him a demonic visitation. He apologised, ascertained Sono was nowhere in the precincts.

He found a spot, in the shelter of a tree, where he could command a view of the harbour. He sat down on a rock and was suddenly overcome with a kind of dizziness. The intensity of the past few days' events, the lack of sleep, the turmoil, all combined, now that he had finally stopped and was still, to wash over him like a tide. For a moment he was quite shaken, then he gathered himself again. But he could not throw off the sense of strangeness and distance; it was all dreamlike, yet vividly real.

A sudden memory came to him, of a moment from his childhood. He had been playing on the beach at Bridge of Don, run pellmell along the sand in pursuit of some childish game, and he'd stopped and turned around, seen his companions as if very far away, their voices, the cries of seagulls, thin and empty against the crash of the waves. And it was as if he had awakened to the absolute reality of his own existence; this was his life and this was him living it; he was here, the centre of his own story. And now it was happening again, in this alien land; the life flowed through him, his story unfolded as it must.

He felt his breath come and go of itself, he looked out at the expanse before him, the town spread below, the harbour and the bay beyond, the volcano sitting ageless on its island, clouds and mist at its summit. Insects buzzed in the air and from somewhere behind him came the sonorous clang of the temple bell.

He brought his gaze to rest on the ships in the bay, was jolted into full awareness of the present, the precise situation; this too was real, was actually happening. There was movement among the ships, the gunboats manoeuvring into position.

Time had slowed, but now seemed to accelerate. The weather suddenly turned, clouds gathered, high winds whipped up. Three Japanese steamers had moved towards the harbour, were surrounded by the British warships. Glover raised the telescope to his eye, adjusted the focal length, managed to home in on one of the steamers. Blue-coated figures were moving on deck, a boarding party; shifting the spyglass, he focused on the other two steamers, saw that they too had been boarded, their crews forced to abandon ship and head for shore in lifeboats. Now the blue-coats seemed to be ransacking the steamers, carrying off plunder, heading back to their own ships. Then there was a sudden flare high in the rigging of the first steamer, and the second, and the third, and all three were ablaze, in no time scuttled, sunk.

The winds rose even higher, the sky turned darker grey, the threat of a storm. Glover braced himself

213

against the gusts. Now there was a response from the Satsuma, the boom of cannon-fire from the batteries on shore. Glover watched in amazement, the puff of smoke from each shot, the shells exploding in the air above the ships, sudden bursts against the darkening grey of the sky, the ships rolling in the gale, the waves turbulent. Again he was visited by that sense of dreamlike vividness; he was here, watching a battle commence. And these were his people, out there with their squadron of ships; the guns firing back at them were cannon he had sold the Satsuma, the clan of his wife; he was caught between the two worlds, could do nothing but watch the events unfold.

There was another barrage from the batteries, and this time there was a hit, directly on the flagship. Glover held the telescope to his eye, tried to hold it steady, saw a confusion of water and sky as the lens veered, then he settled on the *Euryalus*, saw the commotion on deck, smoke and flames, crew rushing to douse the fire, drag bodies clear. This was no dream. The cannon fired again, and again, and one of the gunboats was hit, the other seemed to be struggling in the gale, driven towards shore.

Then the inevitable, the inexorable, happened. The ships steadied themselves, regrouped and opened fire, bombarded the shore. There was one explosion after another around the gun emplacements, black smoke curling into the air. Buildings caught fire and the fire spread in the high winds, the whole dock area suddenly ablaze. Glover didn't think, didn't hesitate, took off running towards the conflagration.

The scene by the docks was infernal, folk falling over themselves, trying to escape, one building after another going up in flames. He remembered Oliphant, talking about fire, *the flower of Edo, that blossoms all year round.* Now it was the flower of Kagoshima, and its blossoms flared, orange and red.

A troop of firemen marched into action along the main street, ludicrous and courageous, a banner at their head, a ladder and a handpump borne along behind. A family dragged their precious possessions, wrapped in quilts, from their burning home, just before it collapsed. The firemen ushered them away from the site, used barbed poles to tear down what was left of the building before setting up the pump, cranking a trickle of water towards the blaze.

Glover tried to help the family, but they turned on him, the father threatening him with a bamboo pole. All they would see would be a barbarian; they probably thought him part of a landing party, the invading force. He backed off, shoved his way through the crowds, face scorched with the heat of the burning.

The gun emplacements had taken a pounding; direct hits had left craters where men and guns had been. Through the smoke he saw the figure of Shimada, marshalling the remaining gun crews. At one position the guns were being loaded and fired by young boys, no more than twelve or thirteen years old. A shell whistled overhead, exploded in the air above their heads. They ducked, took cover, got up again and recommenced firing. Glover caught Shimada's eye, gave him a kind of salute. Shimada nodded, carried on barking orders.

Stumbling over rubble, he made his way to Shimada's home, or what was left of it. The roof had been ripped off, two walls blown out, the rest was on fire. Christ, Sono. Desperate, he shielded his face with his arm, looked in the burning wreckage, saw no one. She must have made her escape, surely to God. He staggered away, stumbled through the town, hoping by some miracle to find her in the midst of the chaos.

He had never seen destruction on this kind of scale, would not have believed it possible. The bombardment had gone on for hours, far longer than it took to batter the defences into submission. It had become an act of vengeance, of wrath, a demonstration that might would always prevail. Hundreds had been killed, the whole settlement flattened, laid waste. A rumour had spread that Josling, the Captain of the flagship, had been mortally wounded when that first shell hit its mark. The retribution had been vicious and fierce, pounding the town to rubble and dust; the destruction was indiscriminate, wantonly random. When sufficient damage had been wrought, the squadron had weighed anchor, set sail for Yokohama, secure that justice had been done.

Glover walked through the ruins, through what had been a beautiful town, looking for landmarks, trying to find his way. The pottery had been blown to smithereens, the gardens scarred by great craters, churned to quagmire, the little shrine to Jizo blasted to nothing.

The fires had burned long, fanned by the rising winds, the edge of a typhoon, then the rains had come, doused the flames, left only the odd pocket still smouldering. Glover walked in a waking nightmare of utter desolation, drenched by the downpour, past families returning to their burned-out homes, past the injured, the dead and the dying. He came at last to where Shimada's home had been, found him standing, staring at the wreckage, or through it, beyond it, at nothing.

Glover waited till he sensed him there, turned to face him.

"Bad," said Glover, the only word adequate.

The old man nodded. "Many dead."

Glover waited, left the silence there between them, left his one question unspoken till he couldn't any longer.

"Sono?"

The old man nodded, a choke in his voice as he spoke. "*Hai*."

There was nothing, not one word more, to be said.

Weary, Glover made his way back through the ravaged town, went one last time to the ryokan.

Desultory, mechanical, distanced from himself, he packed his bag, sat staring at the walls of the room.

The next day he negotiated a passage on the first ship out, a Dutch clipper bound for Nagasaki. Repair work had already begun on the docks. As the ship moved out he looked back, thought for a moment he saw Sono standing there, dressed in white, but looking again he saw only a wisp of smoke, blown by the wind.

★ ★ ★

Nothing had any meaning. He kept to himself, kept his own counsel, shunned company. He delegated work to his clerks. When Walsh and Mackenzie expressed concern, he told them to go and bugger themselves; he told Ito the same in Japanese. Days, weeks, passed by. He received a letter from Satow, in Edo.

Dear Glover,

Word has come to me that you have returned to Nagasaki safe and well. I am relieved to hear it, and take the liberty of sending you this communication. The Kagoshima incident is much in my thoughts. I believe I suggested to you at the time that it was "a rum do". In retrospect, that seems a woefully inadequate description.

When the skirmishes commenced, when we boarded and scuttled the Japanese steamers blocking our way, I confess I was rather caught up in the excitement of it. I myself was allowed to board one of the vessels and I carried off trophies, a Japanese matchlock, a conical war-hat, which I bore in triumph back to the Euryalus. The whole affair felt like quite an adventure, and seeing the boats fired and sunk was rather thrilling. Even when the batteries on shore began firing at us, the spectacle was exhilarating, the shells bursting in the air above us, exploding against the backdrop of gathering clouds.

Our delay in returning fire was due entirely to one rather singular circumstance, the irony of which, I feel, will not be lost on you. When the Shogun had finally handed over his payment of indemnity for the Richardson affair (which gave rise to this whole sorry business in the first place), the sum of £100,000, in Mexican silver, was delivered to the Legation in Edo and transferred thence, in huge reinforced boxes, to the deck of the Euryalus. In fact, the boxes were stacked in front of the door to the ammunition magazine — an error of judgement on the part of the ship's officers, one might have thought, and so it proved to be. It took almost an hour to gain access to the ammunition, by which time the weather conditions had deteriorated, and the accuracy of the enemy gunners had increased. To our alarm and dismay, there were two direct hits on the flagship with ten-inch shells; one landed on the main deck, the other hit the bridge and killed both Captain Josling and another officer, Commander Wilmot.

When we did engage, it was with a vengeance, and eventually the day was won, though not without cost: some 63 British personnel were killed or seriously wounded in the engagement. Admiral Kuyper, the expedition's commander, deemed it, notwithstanding, a great success insofar as the Satsuma clan were taught a salutary lesson and some £100,000 worth of damage was done to Kagoshima.

I know that you will take a rather more circumspect view of the matter, as indeed do I. The circumstances of our meeting were somewhat strained, and I hope there is no bad blood between us. Like you, I have faith that we can work towards ever greater cooperation with the Japanese, and I hope we can leave this sorry incident behind us and do just that. Here in Edo, and in Yokohama, the community is no longer on a war footing. Things have settled down again, calm has been restored and trade continues very much as usual. I trust it is the same in Nagasaki, and that your own business goes from strength to strength.

I remain, yours sincerely,
Ernest Satow

Glover read the letter through again, crumpled it up and threw it across the room. He poured himself a drink, knocked it back, threw on his jacket and headed out of the house. He had to do something to discharge this rage inside him. The evening was beginning its quick descent to night as he crossed *Shian Bashi* and *Omoikiri Bashi*.

He had drunk too much, or not enough. The madame had insisted on introducing him to a new courtesan, Maki Kaga. He'd been brusque with the girl, perfunctory, done the business, taken more drink. At some point he had sworn at her, told her to go; then he'd drunk more, passed out. When he woke from his stupor he was alone, the tiny room dimly lit. He stood up, unsteady, stark naked, felt trapped. He had to get out, but every wall was a shoji screen, closed over; he was shut in, and his head hurt and his bladder was full to bursting. Fuck it. He pished on the floor, spattered the tatami. He stood swaying, disorientated. The first time he'd seen Sono, the shoji had opened and she'd sat there, bowed to him. He let out a roar of anguish and blundered at the screen, crashed right through it, smashing and tearing it as he fell on the other side. He heard screaming, female voices, and hands were on him, turning him over, trying to help him up. He saw Maki's face a moment, anxious, then she was gone and the voices were male, familiar. Walsh and Ito had come out of other rooms, had pulled on *yukata* robes to cover themselves.

Walsh looked at the damage, screwed up his face. "Jesus Christ, Tom, you've pissed on the goddamn floor!"

"Pish tosh!" said Glover. "Pish fucking tosh!"

"We get him home," said Ito.

"Right," said Walsh.

Everything blurred even more, but he had a sense of Maki helping him on with his clothes, then Walsh and Ito taking over again, themselves fully dressed, taking an arm each, supporting his weight, half carrying half dragging him out into the night where the cool air hit him and he retched, threw up. The others let him go and he turned on them, brought them into focus.

"Bastards! What's the point? What is the point in anything? It's all fucking mad!" He pointed an accusing finger at Walsh. "You! Bloody Americans. Fuck you and your fast buck!"

He rounded on Ito. "And you! Bloody Japanese. Cut my throat as quick as look at me."

He staggered a few steps, threw up again, wiped the vomit and spit from his face. "Fuck the lot of you!" His legs buckled and he pitched forward, dead to the world.

He woke, dragged up aching out of some hellish nether world where the light seared his eyes and just to breathe was pain. Bombs and rockets had rained on Ipponmatsu, the lone pine was a tree of fire, the house itself was ablaze, but he knew if he moved quickly, fought his way back inside, he might still save Sono. The heat was intense, his throat was raw, black smoke choking him.

He sat up, was here on his bed fully clothed, stinking of piss and sick. He retched, his throat still on fire, acrid with heartburn. He was still half in the dream, wondered how the blaze had been put out, how the room was intact. Then he came back to this, remembered. The night before was a muddled blur, but he minded some of it, groaned. And behind all that, in at the back of it, was the darkness that was Kagoshima, and all of it had really happened, he had really been there, and Sono was really dead.

He got to his feet, the sick dull pain thudthudding in his head. The need for water was uppermost, it was absolute, Godalmighty, he had to drink. He lurched, unsteady, through to the front room, and she was there, in a white kimono, kneeling with her back to him. Shimada had got it wrong, she had somehow survived, had come to him here.

"Sono!"

She turned, alarmed, not her, not Sono, another young woman. She put her hand to her throat, bowed.

"*Ie*. No." She pointed to herself. "Tsuru *desu*."

"Right," he said. "Tsuru. Pleased to meet you. *Yoroshiku onegai shimasu*. Now what the hell are you doing here?"

She bowed again, more deeply. "Ito-san tell me to come here, help you."

"Oh, did he now?" The pain in his head thudded again, nausea swamped him.

The girl stood up, brisk and efficient, attentive. "I make you *hocha*, tea. Get hot water for wash."

"Fine," he said, sitting down. "But water first, to drink." He mimed swigging from a cup.

"*Hai*," she said, "*so desu*." And she bowed again, shuffled into the kitchen.

He held his head in his hands. He smelled vile and that made him gag again, his mouth parched, rank.

The girl came back, a jug of water in one hand, a cup in the other. She filled the cup, handed it to him. He slugged the water down, drank it in one, held out the cup for a refill, glugged cup after cup till the jug was empty, then handed the cup back to her.

"More."

She came back with the jug, full to the brim. This time he took it from her, waved away the cup, drank straight from the jug, slopping water over himself, drained it, gave back the empty, said, "Fine. Enough. *Arigato*."

She smiled, glided out, little stockinged feet sliding on the wooden floor. He lay back in the chair, wishing he could disappear, be nothing.

He woke with a jolt, and the girl was indicating he should come to the bathroom. The tub was full; he peeled off his stinking clothes, sank into the water that was almost too hot to bear, felt the heat of it ease his bones, the steam make him lightheaded.

After it, he dried off, threw a yukata round him. The girl had turned his mattress, replaced the stained bedding with clean sheets, a fresh pillow. He fell into it, slept again, woke once more unsure of who he was, and where.

A change of clothes had been laid out for him, the filthy clothes he'd been wearing spirited away. Dressing, he still felt fragile. The girl was in the kitchen, cooking something, a broth flavoured with ginger. The smell made him gag again, retch. She took the pot from the stove, covered it with a lid, bowed and backed out.

"Thank you," he said, struggling to remember her name. "Tsuru-san?"

"*Hai*," she said, "*so desu*."

"Fine. You go now."

She looked confused.

"*Sagare*," he said, remembering the word.

She understood, went immediately, closing the door quietly, leaving him to himself.

He needed a drink, went to the Foreigners' Club, sat in the furthest darkest corner, away from the bar.

Mackenzie sought him out, asked how he was faring.

"Oh, fine and dandy," he said. "I watched our navy flatten a whole town, kill women and children and innocent old folk, kill my *wife*, for God's sake! And for what? To avenge the life of one stupid Englishman! It's madness on a grand scale!"

Mackenzie looked morose, stared into his drink. "I know, Tom. I know. It's gunboat diplomacy at its worst."

"And I just had a letter from that idiot Satow, talking as if the whole thing was a prank, a jape, as if it only hit home when that arsehole of a captain was blown to bits by cannonfire. Then he has the fucking gall to say, Oh well, toodlepip, old boy, let's put it all behind us, get back to trading as usual!"

"Aye, well."

"I mean, Jesus Christ, Ken, what the hell are we doing here?"

"Just making a living, Tom. That's all."

"We don't belong here. We should get the hell out!"

Mackenzie stared into his glass, swirled his drink. "It'll come good, Tom, in time."

"But at what cost? How many more towns do we flatten? How many folk do we kill? Just so their leaders get the fucking point?"

He was shouting, caused conversations at the bar to stop, heads turn in his direction.

He stood up to go. "Now, if you'll excuse me . . ."

Walsh had just arrived, made to speak to him. "Tom . . ."

Glover was venomous, spat the words at him. "And what the hell do you want? Got another idea for a fast buck? Faster the better. One law. Supply and demand. One criterion. Can they pay?" He pushed Walsh aside, shoved past him, headed out into the night.

Back home, at Ipponmatsu, he drank again, slumped into numbness and stupor, another uneasy sleep.

The next day passed in another dwalm, a vague haze. At the end of the afternoon he went to his warehouse, didn't look through the paperwork accumulating on his desk; made a desultory pass by the docks, didn't oversee the unloading of a cargo. Then something caught his eye, a workman supervising the operation. He couldn't place it, but there was something awkward, furtive, in the way the man looked about him. He clearly hadn't seen Glover, who was half hidden from view behind a stack of crates. The workman quickly, surreptitiously, bundled a box onto a handcart wheeled by another workman, who covered it with a cloth, wheeled it away.

Glover saw what was happening; his business was bedevilled by this kind of pilfering. It was on the increase, was eating into his profits. The anger rose in him, and he roared at the two men.

"You thieving bastards!"

He picked up a length of bamboo, rushed at the men and laid into them, beat them. The barrowboy managed to break clear, jumped into the harbour to escape. The other stumbled and fell and Glover continued to batter him with the stick, lashed down on him with all the pent-up unreasoning rage that had suddenly welled up.

Then as he raised the stick once more, a hand was catching it, holding him back, restraining him. He wrested back the stick, saw that it was Matsuo who had blocked him.

"So you're part of it too?"

"You kill him, not good," said Matsuo. "I stop you." And he bowed.

Glover glared at him, enraged, but knowing he was right.

"Ach!" he said. "Bugger off! Leave me alone!"

Matsuo stepped back but didn't move away.

"Go!" shouted Glover. "*Ike!*"

He threw down the stick, turned away.

The thief had dragged himself to his feet. Matsuo yelled at him, then followed Glover, keeping his distance.

He couldn't face going home, didn't want to talk to Walsh or Mackenzie at the club, couldn't go back to the teahouse after the damage he'd caused. He sat at his desk, aware of the evening darkening. With one movement of his arm he swept the pile of papers onto the floor, sat staring at the little collection of objects he'd gathered, kept for good luck: the paper butterfly, bamboo token, silver coin. A sake cup sat, inverted; he lifted it, looked at the gold coin underneath.

A sudden noise at the door made him turn. A figure stepped out of the shadows, moved into the room. He braced himself, ready for trouble, but it was Ito. The apprehension turned to irritation.

"What do you want?"

"This no good," said Ito. It was a challenge. *This* was Glover's mood, his demeanour.

227

"Oh, really?" said Glover, aggressive.

"You must get over this," said Ito.

This.

"Is that right?"

"Existence is suffering," said Ito. "Have to continue. Important thing is what you do next."

Glover snorted. "What I do next is get out of this damn country. I've had a bellyful of it."

Now it was Ito's turn to be angry. "You have belly full all right! You get fat on our country then you go. You just like all the rest."

"Now wait a minute!" Glover was scraping back his chair, standing up.

Ito was in full flow. "You sell your opium, you sell your guns, you take our gold. You don't care who suffer, as long as you make money!"

Glover shouted at him, outraged. "Enough!"

"I thought you were a man. I thought you were a warrior, like samurai. But you are a coward."

This was too much to take, an insult too far. He swung a punch, caught Ito on the side of the head, sent him staggering. But Ito was tough, steadied himself, hit back with a blow to the stomach, knocked the wind out of him. They squared up to each other, slugged it out, punch for punch. Glover was tiring, grabbed at Ito and held him in a bearhug. Ito managed to break the grip, shove him clear, connect with a perfect left to the jaw that felled him, knocked him to the floor.

Glover sat up, dazed, tasted blood. Ito helped him to his feet, bowed.

"Jesus!" said Glover, holding his jaw. "If I've taught you nothing else, I've taught you how to throw a left hook!"

Ito's expression remained serious. "You owe this country something."

Glover spat blood. "Aye."

CHAPTER
NINE

Burning Bright

Nagasaki, 1864

Kagoshima had changed Glover for good. Or for ill. Only time would tell which. He felt something of Ito's *firm resolution*, that *readiness for death* at the heart of the samurai code. In Kagoshima he had seen so much death at first-hand, knew himself and everyone else already dead. He knew the imminence of his own death, not just as an idea, but in his very bones. Very well. He was already dead, so let him live.

His actions had consequences and he was answerable for them. This also he knew, irrevocably.

He aligned himself completely with Ito and the other rebels. To hell with the Shogun! To hell with the British Government! Damn them all!

He threw himself into his work with a fury, an unremitting energy, cranked everything up.

He beefed up his regular trade, in tea, silk, opium, Walsh's "blessed trinity". He bought and sold property, mortgaged from Jardine's. He dealt in anything that would turn a quick profit, exported vegetable wax and camphor oil, imported cotton goods and woollens from home. He heard of a quantity of sapanwood some merchant had bought in Malaya and been unable to sell. The knock-down price was a dollar a picul; he bought 8,000 piculs, had it shipped in, sold it in Yokohama for 35 dollars a picul. He invested the profits in shipping, bought a second-hand steamer, the SS *Sarah*, sold it to the Satsuma for 70,000 dollars. He argued that, in the long term, Japan had to build its own ships, in its own dry docks, mine its own coal, forge its own iron and steel. He was drunk on the dream of it.

He re-entered the floating world, spent time again in the teahouse — he had paid for repairs, made good the damage he'd done in his dark night; he'd recompensed the madame, handsomely, and was once more an honoured guest.

Tsuru came every day to Ipponmatsu; she cleaned and cooked for him, flirted a little with that fluttering lightness. But she didn't move in; he wasn't ready for that; and at the teahouse he enjoyed the favours of Maki Kaga, the young girl he'd met that same night. Her image had stayed with him, through his drunkenness and boorishness, and on his return he'd sought her out. There was something about her, a naturalness and ease, a lack of formality, a character he found engaging; she laughed easily; behind the mask of the courtesan she was alive, uninhibited, and that suited his mood. When she served him tea, turning the bowl, just so, or arranged a single spray of flowers, or played some haunting melody on the samisen, it was balm to his soul.

Ito had a favourite song he would sing when he was drunk. At first Glover couldn't make out the words — it was sung in some rough throaty argot — and when they were in their cups, Glover's Japanese deserted him and Ito's English became imaginative and improvised. But eventually they'd worked out a rough translation.

Drunk I lie, my head pillowed on some beauty's
    lap.
Sober and awake, I'll grab power and lead the
    nation.

Lying one night in Maki's arms, he heard Ito bawling out the song from another room. He tried to join in, mangled the words, heard Ito laugh out loud, pretend to howl like a dog. Maki laughed till the tears ran down her face, and he pulled her to him again.

Both Ito and Maki, in their own distinct ways, taught Glover something of Zen, through stories and poems, parables and riddles. Some of it was baffling, enigmatic, some of it outrageous, ferociously illogical. It was often funny, and much of it, to Glover, seemed grounded in a kind of enlightened common sense.

"Aye," he'd say, in response to some direct, clear-eyed observation. "That's very like the thing."

Maki had learned from one of her first clients, a young monk who would escape from time to time the rigours of monastic life, make his way to the Sakura. He would tell her the stories, make her smile, whether she understood them or not. She took them as a kind of part-payment for her services, treasured them, told them now to Glover.

There was one about two monks approaching a river where a beautiful young woman was waiting to cross. One monk ignored her, obeying the injunction of his master not even to look at a woman. The other, however, carried the woman on his shoulders, waded across the river, set her down on the other side, bowed and walked on. The first monk walked alongside him, clearly upset. A mile down the road he stopped, complained bitterly to the second monk about his behaviour. The second monk looked baffled, said, "The woman? I left her back at the river. Why are you still carrying her?"

That made Glover laugh.

As well as the stories, Maki had memorised poems she had read and loved, mainly haiku and tanka, little meditations, heartbreaking insights into the beauty and transience of the moment.

> The fallen leaf,
> returning to the branch?
> It was a butterfly.

"Very like the thing," said Glover.

Ito's Zen was altogether tougher, was rooted in *Bushido*, the way of the warrior. He would draw strength from *Hagakure*, the samurai code.

Meet a difficult situation with courage and joy. The more the water, the higher the boat.

At other times Ito would ask Glover unanswerable questions, riddles he couldn't fathom. Ito would call them out between drunken songs at the Sakura.

What is the sound of one hand clapping? Does a dog have Buddha nature? What was your face before you were born?

Glover asked what were the answers. Ito said he didn't know.

"Have to find answers, inside," said Ito.

"By thinking?" said Glover.

"By not thinking!" said Ito.

"Aye," said Glover. "Fine."

During Ito's absence, Takashi had grown more powerful, influenced the Choshu leadership to align more firmly against the West. In spite of Kagoshima, he still thought they could drive the invaders from their shores, or, perhaps even more glorious, they would die trying.

The Choshu had gun emplacements overlooking the straits of Shimonoseki, north of Nagasaki. The straits were strategically vital, a channel between the two islands of Kyushu and Honshu, leading to the Inland Sea, the main route to Osaka and beyond, to Yokohama and Edo. It was the principal passage for western ships; it was crucial that the lanes be kept open. The Choshu mounted a blockade, declared that no foreign ships would be allowed through, and began opening fire on any who made the attempt.

Ominously, a combined fleet of British, American, French and Dutch ships assembled in Yokohama harbour, a score of warships carrying two thousand troops.

As in the case of Richardson, an ultimatum was delivered to the Shogun, insisting that he take action against the Choshu or risk reprisals. The Shogun, playing on age-old enmities, ordered the Satsuma to send troops, attack the Choshu with a land-based force, diverting their attention from the Straits.

Still resistant to the Shogun and the West, the Satsuma were nevertheless circumspect about bringing another bombardment on their heads. But they could not resist the legitimate opportunity of doing harm to their rivals. They sent a contingent of infantry which docked at Nagasaki, marched north and took up position inland, cutting off the Choshu's retreat.

Ito came thundering in to Glover's office, raging. "I told you, Satsuma useless! Before, they very stupid but very brave, stand up to Shogun and fight West. Now they do what Shogun tell them, help West, attack Choshu!"

Glover said he was sorry to hear it, but it was the pot calling the kettle black.

"Why you talk like this?" said Ito, even angrier. "This English nonsense!"

"It seems to me it's the Choshu who are being headstrong and foolish."

"Takashi is a madman," said Ito. "*His* head too strong!"

"It's not so long since you agreed with him," said Glover.

"Not any more." Ito looked offended. "I change."

"I know," said Glover. "Now your whole clan has to change."

"Satsuma also," said Ito.

"Aye," said Glover. "Satsuma also!"

Parkes was attempting diplomacy again, had written, care of Glover, to *The Honourable Prince Ito Hirobumi of the Choshu Clan*. The letter briskly outlined the current situation, the aggressive actions of the Choshu leadership, the threat to peaceful trade. It then appealed to Ito as an honoured friend of the West, one who had so recently visited Britain under the good offices of Mister Glover and with the support and goodwill of Her Majesty's Government, one whose continued friendship would be valued, he hoped, in the years to come. It exhorted Ito to use his influence as a Prince of the Choshu Clan to dissuade the Daimyo and his advisers from their present aggressive course of action, and to persuade them to cease hostilities forthwith, or face the consequences.

Ito read the letter, looked at Glover. "He want me to make them stop?"

"That's the sum and substance of it."

"Sorry?"

"Yes," said Glover. "He wants you to make them stop."

"I don't think is possible," said Ito, quietly. "Daimyo listen to Takashi."

Glover remembered his own efforts in Kagoshima, the rock-hard intransigence of the Satsuma Daimyo.

For a moment he smelled gunpowder and burning, saw Sono's face.

"I know," he said. "It'll be difficult."

"But have to try," said Ito.

"Aye." Glover knew Ito was about to risk his life, knew also he had no choice.

Ito was set to leave the next day, with Matsuo and with Inoue Kaoru, another of the Choshu Five recently returned. Inoue was a serious-minded young man, less of a firebrand than Ito, but no less committed to change. He had come back from the West shaken and chastened by what he had seen. The three men were to sail to Yokohama, be given safe passage from there on a British warship, dropped off at Kasato island off Shimonoseki. There they would meet leaders of their own clan, present them with a document containing the demands of the British Government and their allies.

At the last moment, Glover decided to travel with them. On a Jardine's clipper, they sailed at night, under cover of dark, eased through the Straits without incident. At Yokohama they were met by a British delegation, including Ernest Satow, who handed Ito a scroll.

"It's the British ultimatum," said Satow, "translated into Japanese for the Daimyo." He nodded to Glover. "I'm afraid this all feels horribly familiar."

"Aye," said Glover. "It's Kagoshima, again."

They boarded the warship, HMS *Cormorant*. It would be accompanied by another, HMS *Barrosa*, in a show of strength designed to give the Choshu a foretaste of what was to come should they decide to continue being obdurate.

In charge of the *Cormorant* was Captain Barstow, the Master of the Lodge, who had once waylaid Glover and Ito returning from Shanghai with a cache of weapons. It seemed so long ago, so much had happened since.

"Mister Glover," said the Captain. "I see you are still defending British interests."

"Indeed," said Glover. "Perhaps more than you know."

"If I recall," said the Captain, "when we last met you had the foresight to warn me of the potential danger posed by these clans, particularly the Choshu."

"If I mind right," said Glover, "I also told you there were honourable exceptions."

"Mister Ito," said the Captain, recognising him, nodding in his direction.

Ito stared back at him, cold and hard, said nothing.

For the whole of the journey the three Japanese sat on deck, straightbacked, staring ahead. When the ship dropped anchor at Kasato, they stood up, bowed formally to each other then took their leave of Glover, each in turn bowing to him.

"Good luck," he said.

"Need more than luck," said Ito, and he smiled a tight, grim smile.

Before they disembarked onto the rowboat that would ferry them ashore, Matsuo stood in front of Glover, bowed once more with deep humility, bending almost double. Then he held out his hand, something he had never done before, shook Glover's hand, his grip quick and firm, said, "*Arigato gosaimasu*. Thank you, Guraba-san."

As they watched the boat head towards the island, Glover said, "God help them."

Satow, at his shoulder, said, "Let us hope He does."

"What do you think are their chances?"

"I'd say their chances of having their heads removed are perhaps seven out of ten."

"Christ!" said Glover.

"You might be better invoking *their* God," said Satow, "their Buddha."

Glover remembered that huge bronze statue at Kamakura, its presence, its benign detachment. And from somewhere the words came to him. *Namu Amida Butsu.* He'd heard them chanted, at his son's funeral, at the shrine where he'd hidden with Mackenzie, at the temple in Kagoshima; they came to him unbidden, and he said them in silence, to himself.

The arrangement was that they would wait, at anchor, for the whole of that day. If necessary, the three men would stay overnight, continue their negotiations the next morning, return to the ship by noon.

Glover was unable to sleep, paced the deck through the dogwatch hours, looked out across the dark stretch of water to the shore. Even peering through his spyglass he could see nothing, the odd flicker of light. Imperceptibly the sky began to lighten, the island took shape. At four bells, Satow joined him on deck.

"No sign?"

"Not a thing," said Glover.

"I would imagine," said Satow, "the longer it continues, the greater the hope."

Towards noon there was activity on the bridge. The launch had been sighted, returning from shore. It pulled alongside, bobbing in the swell, and Ito and Inoue swung onto the rope ladder, clambered aboard. Ito's face was grim. "No good. Takashi too powerful. They don't listen."

Glover had expected this. But at least Ito and Inoue were alive, safe. Then he realised something was amiss; he looked down at the launch, saw only the two crewmen.

"Where's Matsuo?" he asked.

Ito let out a long slow breath. "He stay. Is long story." He had two swords tucked in his waistband. He took out one of them, the shorter wakizashi, handed it reverently to Glover. "He give me this for you. He want you to have it."

Glover took the sword, bowed. "What happened?"

"He keep other sword. Tomorrow commit *seppuku*."

"In God's name why?"

This time Ito's sigh was pained. "I tell you, is long story. Very . . . complicated."

The gist of it was they had talked to a standstill. The clan leader's mind was already set; Takashi had seen to that. But they'd tried, they'd talked through the night, going over and over the same ground.

The British demand had been for an immediate cessation of firing on foreign ships, the dismantling of

240

the gun placements, the payment of recompense for damage already done. In elaborate and evasive language, the Choshu had refused on every point, citing the need to defend their territory with reference to "invaders".

Glover listened, heart sinking, a taste like metal in his mouth.

"And Matsuo, what happened to him?"

Ito tried to find the language. "I told you when I was young man, I was member of *sonno-joi*. We wanted to fight the West, throw out all invaders."

"You did," said Glover, glancing at Captain Barstow, who had flinched when Ito spoke.

"I was also part of that group," said Inoue. "So was Takashi."

"And so was Matsuo," said Ito. "Takashi get whole group to take oath, always to defend clan, drive out barbarian. Even sign in own blood. Matsuo do this."

"And you?" said the Captain.

"I was in Edo," said Ito, "doing business. So was Inoue-san. We don't sign."

"Very convenient," said the Captain.

"Perhaps Ito and Inoue were already seeing things more clearly," said Glover, rounding on him.

"Perhaps," said the Captain.

Ito ignored him, continued. "Last night Takashi say to Matsuo he is traitor, he break his oath. He sign in blood so he have to take own life."

"And he listened?" said Glover.

Ito nodded. "What make it worse, Matsuo's father there. He tell Matsuo he is dishonour to family and clan."

"God Almighty!" said Glover.

"Now Matsuo prepare himself for seppuku."

"No!" said Glover. "It's madness! We can't let him do it!"

"Is very sad," said Ito. "But is noble death. He will die well."

Glover held the sword in his hands, looked towards the island. There was nothing to be done.

"So," said the Captain. "We have our full complement? We can return to Yokohama?"

"*Hai*," said Ito. "We go."

On the way back to Yokohama, Ito delivered a rant against the Shogun. "He limit trade with West so he control it. He sit in his palace, get rich and fat, and nobody else get share. British should get rid of him, throw him overboard. Should go to Osaka and make treaty with young Emperor, restore him to power. This is what Japanese people want. Bring unity. All clans respect Emperor, come together, make Japan strong. Good for West also."

The Captain displayed his usual tired cynicism, dismissed Ito as a self-seeking troublemaker, wouldn't trust him an inch. Satow, however, was impressed by Ito's intensity, his clear-minded resolve. As the *Cormorant* steamed in to Yokohama harbour, he spoke about it to Glover.

"You really think Ito and the others offer hope for the future?"

"I'm convinced of it. They *are* the future."

"If he had his way, the *Cormorant* would steam towards Osaka straight away, carrying a delegation to the Emperor!"

"Unfortunately, it is rather more likely to return to Shimonoseki with the rest of the fleet, to pound the Choshu into submission."

"Indeed," said Satow. "I fear that the Consul, having amassed such a force, will feel the need to use it."

Satow was right. The events were well documented, reported the following week in the *Nagasaki Advertiser*. The seventeen-strong fleet entered the Straits and fanned out in formation. The bombardment of the Choshu batteries was relentless and decisive. Troops came ashore, splashed through paddyfields, drove on up the grassy hill to the fortifications and gun emplacements. After a last skirmish, some hand-to-hand fighting, the Choshu surrendered. The guns were dismantled, carriages smashed, shot and shell thrown into the sea, powder burned. The settlement was put to the torch; the inhabitants fled; the troops buried their dead on the hillside; the fleet weighed anchor and sailed back to Yokohama. The Straits were reopened to shipping forthwith, and the Choshu were forced to pay an indemnity, partly financing the expedition against them, an irony that would not be lost on the clan and its leadership.

Glover read the report with the now familiar feeling of dismay. The whole business was such a waste.

Satow had written to him, telling him that Parkes had received a letter from the Foreign Office, arriving some days after the bombardment. It advised him not to proceed with military action as it was not the policy of Her Majesty's Government in such circumstances. The Consul had drafted a reply, explaining about the delay in receiving their initial dispatch, and explaining that, regrettably, action had already been taken. But before this could be sent, a further communication came from London, saying that, in the light of further information received, the decision to use force had been the correct one after all.

Satow also made the point that sending a joint western force, including a French contingent, sent a clear signal to the Shogun and also undermined the possibility of a Japanese — French alliance, which had been brewing and which might prove troublesome.

Fine.

Glover re-read Satow's letter, tore it in half, in half again.

As long as Her Majesty's Government was satisfied that everything was proceeding satisfactorily, and their ships could come and go, then everything was as it should be, God was in his heaven, all was right with the world.

He threw the torn-up scraps of paper across his desk, picked up Matsuo's sword which he'd placed there with his other mementos. He eased the sword a little from its sheath. The keen blade glinted in the lamplight. He imagined, all too vividly, Matsuo with the other sword, face contorted as he leaned forward onto the blade, drove it into his entrails.

Waste.

He would never fully understand this country, these people. But he was committed to the work now, for better or worse, had to throw himself into it with everything he had.

He nicked the tip of his little finger with the blade, just enough to draw blood, satisfy samurai tradition. A tiny gob of red appeared, a jewel. He licked it, then he put the sword back in its sheath, touched it to his forehead, replaced it on the desk.

Market forces were constantly at play, demand for commodities shifting, changing. Glover was alert to the vagaries, looking for signs, straws in the wind. As if overnight, by some strange whim of fashion, there was a great demand for tea in America. Glover moved quickly to seize the moment, expand his operation, scale everything up. His firing shed was torn down and replaced by two huge godowns, great high-ceilinged ware-houses, effectively tea-processing factories. The tea business was suddenly an industry, employed a workforce of four hundred, men and women.

It was the start of the season; the raw crop was delivered in bulk from the countryside, had to be fired and dried as quickly as possible, packed in crates ready for dispatch, shipped out directly in clippers loaded to the gunwales with nothing but tea. The work went on, in shifts, day and night, and Glover would turn up at odd hours, himself fired up, exhilarated.

He stopped by one night with Walsh, on his way to the teahouse.

"Christ, Tom!" shouted Walsh above the noise of the work. "When you do something, you damn well *do* it!"

"No other way!" shouted Glover. "Otherwise what's the point?"

The heat in the place was intense, from hundreds of copper pans filled with red-hot charcoal. Over them the green leaves were dried in huge flat baskets, shaken from side to side, never still; the workers glistened with sweat, the men dressed only in loincloths, the women naked to the waist; flares threw a flickering light, cast shadows upwards, and steam from the leaves hung in the air. The noise too was overwhelming, great wooden crates violently shaken to settle the fired tea that poured into them in a constant unending flow.

"It's infernal!" shouted Walsh, loosening his shirt collar.

"Aye!" shouted Glover. "Isn't it?"

Walsh looked at him strangely, warily. "You look demonic!"

Glover laughed, recognised what Walsh meant, the mood that was on him. He felt the surge of it, indomitable. His blood was up.

Later, fired even more by a drink or two, he took exception to something Walsh said, about the workforce slaving away.

Glover glared at him, cold. "Those folk are glad of a job. I pay them well for what they do. And I don't think an American is in a position to lecture anyone about slavery!"

Now Walsh was angry. "I'll remind you, sir, that we're fighting a war to abolish it."

"And half of your countrymen are fighting a war to keep it!"

"Sometimes you go too far."

"Impossible!" said Glover, cuffing him a little too hard to the side of the head, then laughing again, grabbing Maki round the waist. She shrieked and clung to him. He breathed in her scent, intoxicated.

He exported his tea by the shipload; sold rice to China in contravention of the Shogun's law banning such trade. Investing his profits, he began to import gold bars from Europe, a hundred bars at a time, sold them to the Japanese Government at a price that undercut the Chinese, ending their monopoly on the supply of gold. He undertook to sell a steamer, *The Carthage*, for Jardine Mathieson, paid a Dutch engineer who attended the Nagasaki Lodge to oversee and approve repairs to the ship, sold it on to the Bakufu for $120,000. With the commission on that deal, he increased his imports of gold bars to a thousand at a time. He brokered further sales of ships to some of the smaller Japanese clans who could not pay cash but paid in huge quantities of rice, which he sold on to China. And so it continued, the spiral of his business success, onwards and upwards.

Mackenzie advised a modicum of caution, circumspection. "You're walking a tightrope, Tom."

"Aye," he said. "And I'm juggling and eating fire at the same time!"

He also knew the most lucrative dealings of all were in arms. But it was no longer good enough to sell to the highest bidder. He was happy to trade with the Shogun, the Bakufu, exploit them and take their money for gold, or merchant ships. But selling them weapons was no longer an option. Their time was over.

After Shimonoseki, there was a rapid change at the heart of the Choshu. The cursory, dismissive nature of the beating, followed by the humiliation of having to hand over an indemnity, left Takashi and his faction in disgrace. Ito and Inoue were finally heeded, held sway. They enlisted the backing and support of a powerful clan member, Kido Takayoshi, brought him late at night to Ipponmatsu for a preliminary meeting with Glover.

Initially Kido seemed hostile, ill at ease. He spoke little English, and communicated through Ito and Inoue as interpreters. Like them, he had initially been resistant to dealing with the West. He particularly resented the threat of Christian missionaries, and would still actively seek out Japanese *kakure*, hidden Christians, seeing them as violators of a centuries-old ban on that most hateful of religions. He argued that the sole purpose of Christianity was to undermine traditional Japanese values, convert and then conquer.

"However . . ." said Glover, wondering how they could conceivably find common ground.

Ito translated the word. "*Shikashi* . . ."

Kido was silent, staring hard at Glover. Then he continued, Ito again translating.

He had not meant to cause offence. He cared only about the future of Japan. He understood Glover was an honourable gaijin, who also cared about Japan, and who was willing to help them in their undertaking. The only way forward was to get rid of the Shogun and the other reactionary elements. Only then could Japan open up fully to the West, learn from the West and ultimately equal the West.

"*Hai,*" said Glover. "*So desu.*"

He poured sake into small whisky glasses for all four of them, repeated the toast he had once made in Kagoshima.

"*Shogun! Nanka kuso kurae!*"

They drained their glasses. Ito and Inoue grinned. Kido nodded but remained stern.

Glover opened a bottle of Scotch, refilled their glasses, proposed another toast.

"Japan," he said. "*Nihon.*"

Again they drank, repeated it, their eyes watering from the strength of the spirit.

"*Nihon!*"

He drove himself on, recognised no boundaries. His business interests, legitimate and otherwise, turned ever greater profits; more tea, more silk, more opium, more rice, more ships, more guns, more gold. Word spread he would take a chance on almost anything.

One evening a young man approached him in the Foreigners' Club.

"Mister Glover?"

The young man looked wild-eyed, haggard. By his appearance he had not slept much of late.

"Aye?" said Glover, cautious.

"I want to ask you, sir, if you would like to buy a tiger?"

Glover had heard aright. It was an odd twist on a familiar story: the young man, Mitchell, had recently arrived from Yokohama, had overreached himself, signing chits that were never honoured, running up debts that couldn't be paid. On one particularly excessive night of revelry in the pleasure quarter, he had found himself talked into a transaction guaranteed to earn him a profit. He had bought a tiger.

In spite of himself, Glover was intrigued.

"The gentleman who sold the beast to me," said Mitchell, "was a Chinaman."

"By the name of Wang-Li, perhaps?"

"You know him?"

"Indeed," said Glover. "Continue."

"He had acquired the animal in the Malay Straits. He was offering it to me at such a favourable price, he explained, that I could not fail to gain from the transaction. He was sure some travelling circus, making its way in these parts, would be eager to buy it. Mister Li would sell it himself, at a much higher price, if he had not been summoned to return to Shanghai on urgent family business."

"He is a man of rare commitment to his family," said Glover. "It is most touching."

"Mister Glover," said the young man, "it all seemed so reasonable at the time."

"Ah, yes," said Glover. "It always does."

"But in the cold light of day . . ."

"The taste of ashes in the mouth."

"Exactly so. And then when I saw the creature . . ."

Glover stopped him, suddenly alert. "You have seen it? It exists?"

"Oh, yes."

"It is here, in Nagasaki?"

"It is being kept in quarantine, in a shed down at the docks."

Glover was already up out of his seat, eager, moving towards the door. "Lead me to it, sir!"

On the way to the docks, Glover strode out, the young man struggling to keep up, explaining that the situation was complicated by the fact that the Japanese officials refused to issue a permit for the import of the creature. In the meantime, he had borrowed more money to pay Wang-Li in cash.

"Because he was in such a hurry," said Glover, "to get back to Shanghai, on account of his urgent family business."

"You know the man well!" said Mitchell.

"So you're out of pocket on the deal, and are unable to make good your investment."

"In a nutshell."

"You've bought a pig in a poke. A tiger in a box!"

In fact the tiger was in a bamboo cage that had been especially built to transport it, the thick solid lengths of bamboo bound firmly together with twine, the gate fastened shut with a bolt, an iron padlock. The whole thing was held to the ground by lengths of hawser tied to massive pegs hammered into the floor.

In the dim light they could make out the shape of the tiger where it lay, its huge bulk curled in the corner of the cage. The smell of it filled the air, rank and animal.

They had thrown the beast meat laced with laudanum, sedated him, rendered him numb. Now he was waking from his stupor, twitching, trying to stand up. He steadied himself, fixed his yellow eyes on Glover and young Mitchell, gave out a low threatening growl.

"Dear God!" said Glover. He had never seen the like, except in magazine illustrations, drawings on a circus handbill, and he'd always thought those fanciful, exaggerated. Now the reality stood before him, immense in its power, its menace, ferocity barely held in check.

"*Tyger tyger burning bright,*" said Mitchell.

"Is that from a rhyme?" asked Glover.

"William Blake," said Mitchell. "The English poet."

"Indeed?"

"*In the forest of the night.*"

"How does it continue?"

"*What immortal hand or eye . . .*"

"Yes?"

"*Could frame thy fearful symmetry.*"

"Ah," said Glover. "I'm not much of a man for poetry, except for Burns of course. But to my ear that sounds very like the thing."

"It is," said Mitchell.

Burning bright.

Glover stared the tiger in the face, looked right into those eyes now fixed on him, sensed their absolute otherness, saw the animal's nature, predatory and ruthless and unafraid. He turned to say something to

Mitchell and the tiger sprang, hurled itself straight at him, tail flicking, great paws battering the bars, shaking the whole cage, straining at the ropes.

On an instinct for survival, preservation, they stood back towards the door.

"Mister Mitchell," said Glover. "You have just sold your tiger!"

"Thank you!" said Mitchell.

"I shall give you what you paid for it, and add, say, ten per cent for your trouble."

"That is most generous," said Mitchell, "considering . . ."

"Considering I now have to deal with these recalcitrant customs officials and persuade them to issue a permit."

They shook hands on the deal. The tiger let out a great roar, and as if summoned, two of the customs officials appeared in the doorway.

Glover bowed to the men, told them he was anxious to complete the formalities speedily, remove his tiger from the premises. They replied that it was impossible, the regulations did not permit it, tigers were not an item on the agreed trade tariff.

Glover explained he had bought the animal from Mister Mitchell here (Mitchell bowed), who had in turn purchased it from Mister Wang-Li, a respected trader no doubt known to them.

The officials glanced at each other, the senior of them simply repeated his litany.

"*Muri o iuna!*" This is impossible.

Well then, asked Glover, what were they to do? Wang-Li had left the country and was not answerable. The original owner was somewhere in the Malay Straits. There was no one to whom the beast could be returned.

The officials said he would have to destroy it. Glover refused.

"I have just spent good money buying this magnificent animal. I have no intention of butchering it to be sold as dog meat!"

The senior official repeated again, "*Muri o iuna!*" And he added, "*Kyokashou nado dasen!*" I cannot give you a permit.

"Very well then," said Glover. "I cannot return the creature, I refuse to kill it, you will not let me bring it into the country. The only solution is to set it free, let it return to the wild."

He stepped up to the door of the cage. The tiger crouched, growled.

"Mister Mitchell!" He held out his hand. "If you would kindly furnish me with the key to this lock, we shall liberate this fine beast and relieve these gentlemen of any responsibility in the matter."

Mitchell looked alarmed, fighting down panic. But regardless, he handed over the key.

The officials hadn't understood what Glover was saying to Mitchell, but his intent was clear. They started screaming at him to stop, this was madness, the creature would eat them, each and every one.

The tiger threw itself again at the bars, rattled the cage. Glover twirled the key.

"Well?"

The senior official spoke in English for the first time, his voice shaking. "We give permit. You keep animal."

"Thank you," said Glover, and he turned again to Mitchell. "A pleasure doing business with you, sir."

The official muttered something, not quite under his breath. "*Yaban!*"

Glover heard. "Perhaps that's what I should call the tiger!" And he looked it in the eye again, raised a hand as if in benediction. "I name this beast Yaban, the Barbarian!"

The tiger opened its great jaws, roared.

The tiger was drugged again, the cage heaved by a system of ropes and pulleys onto the back of a horsedrawn cart, transported with much juddering and jolting up the hill to Ipponmatsu. The journey was made at night, to avoid spreading alarm among the locals, but even so, one or two startled workmen ran in fright when they saw the great beast asleep, torchlight flickering on his yellow and black flanks, and at least one drunken sailor looked ready to sign the pledge, forswear the opium pipe and the demon drink forever.

The cage was manoeuvred into place by the side of the house, made fast once more with thick ropes and iron pegs. The tiger slept.

The next morning Glover was awakened by a scream, a woman's voice, highpitched, shrieking in absolute terror. He threw on his cotton yukata, grabbed his pistol from the bedside drawer, ran out of the house.

The tiger was half awake, looked groggy, uncoiling, standing up, wobbling on his huge paws, a raw throaty growl forming in his throat, his eyes fixed on Tsuru. She had come up the path to the house as usual, carrying a wicker basket of provisions, clearly not expecting to encounter this great terrifying beast. She stood rigid, unable to move, the basket and its contents scattered at her feet.

Glover made soothing noises. "It's all right, Tsuru-san. It's fine."

She took a step back.

He spoke to the tiger. "Calm down, big fellow. You look like a man with a hangover! This is Tsuru-san, by the way." Tsuru took another step back. "I wouldn't go eyeing her up for breakfast. She'd barely make a mouthful!"

Tsuru was shaking.

"*Dozo,*" he said, motioning her to come inside. "Please."

In the house, he sat her down, made tea, brought it to her. The simple act seemed to shock her as much as seeing the tiger.

"I'm sorry," he said. "I didn't get a chance to warn you about Yaban."

She looked puzzled. "Yaban?"

"That's what I called him," said Glover. "The tiger, *tora.*"

"His name?" she said.

"*Hai.*"

"Is right name," she said. "Is like barbarian."

256

He laughed, glad to see her regaining her composure, even mustering a little defiance. But he had to go and pick up the basket, the provisions. When she left later, to go to the market for more meat to feed the beast, Glover had to walk with her to the gate, and she stayed close to him, her eyes downcast, not looking at the cage.

That night he brought Maki to Ipponmatsu for the first time. Her eyes widened when she saw the tiger; she clapped her hands and laughed, shrieked, terrified and excited all at once at the sight of it.

"Yaban!" she shouted. "Gaijin!" And she laughed again.

He led her inside, to the bedroom he had shared with Sono. Already aroused, she clung to him, pulled him to the bed; her back arched, feral, as she moved on top of him, cried out.

A month after he had bought the tiger, he read a notice in the *Advertiser*, announcing the arrival in Yokohama of a travelling circus, under the management of Professor Risley, late of the Strand Theatre in London where, as a talented acrobat, he had astonished audiences by his remarkable feats of strength and agility, including the propelling of his two young sons into the air from the soles of his feet.

Glover immediately wrote a letter to Professor Risley, entrusted it to the Captain of a clipper leaving next day for Yokohama. Within a week he received an enthusiastic reply, and three days after that the

Professor himself arrived at Ipponmatsu, anxious to see Yaban for himself.

He was not disappointed. "By God, sir, he's a handsome brute!"

Risley was compact and muscular, with a shining bald pate, a magnificent waxed handlebar moustache, every inch the showman, the very caricature of a circus performer. Glover refrained from asking him in what subject and from which university he had gained his professorship.

"I thought you'd be impressed," said Glover.

"I've never seen his like, and I've travelled from America to the Indies, from Australia to Russia."

He had lately arrived with his circus from San Francisco, had regrettably lost some of his animals to sickness on the voyage, among them a lion. The tiger would be a most welcome replacement, if they could agree on a mutually acceptable price. The hand of providence, he said, was indeed beneficent.

Glover took a liking to the man, his spirit, his indefatigable optimism. He had gone to Australia to join in the goldrush; the same quest had taken him to the Klondike.

"Never once saw the colour of the stuff," he said. "But nothing ventured, eh?"

Tsuru found him terrifying, cowered when he came into the house.

"Pretty little thing," said Risley.

"She is," said Glover, looking at her with affection. "Don't know what I'd do without her."

Tsuru was flustered, hurried out of the room.

258

"These Jap women," said Risley. "Damned appealing!"

"I'll take you to the teahouse," said Glover.

"If you don't mind," said Risley, "I'd prefer something stronger."

Glover laughed out loud. "The Sakura sells a lot more than tea!"

At the teahouse, the Professor took a shine to Maki, but Glover made it clear she was not available, was already, as it were, spoken for.

"By Christ, Glover," said Risley, "you're a dog and no mistake! That little wench back at the house, this one here. It's just plain greed!"

Glover steered him towards another girl, a friend of Maki's called Yumi.

"Yumi!" said Risley, delighted. He pointed at her. "You!" He pointed at himself. "Me!" He grabbed her by the waist. "You-me!"

Next morning they agreed on a price for the tiger. Glover didn't even haggle. He was happy to turn a substantial profit, find the beast a good home. Risley for his part was relieved that his circus had been saved; the creature would prove an irresistible attraction to audiences, would repay the outlay in ticket sales.

"The beneficent hand of providence," said Glover, clinching the deal with a handshake.

The tiger shook himself awake, stretched and yawned, flanks rippling.

"Now *there's* gold!" said Risley.

At the docks, the same customs officials were happy to be rid of the animal, see it go; they rushed through the paper-work, falling over themselves in their anxiety to speed the process along. The cage was hoisted on board a cargo ship, roped and battened down. The tiger lay groggy, drugged again for the journey. Glover felt a curious pang at seeing it go.

Risley called to him from the deck. "The circus will be visiting Yokohama and Edo, Osaka and Hyogo. You must come and see it!"

"I will!" said Glover, waving. "I will!" And he turned away feeling strangely bereft.

Back at the house, Tsuru said she was glad Yaban had gone.

"The tiger or the man?" he asked.

"Both," she said, so earnestly it made him laugh.

After the business with the tiger, there was a certain amount of anticipation, tinged with apprehension, as to what Glover would do next, what grand gesture he might make. His admirers, and his detractors, did not have long to wait.

"What we need to do," he told Mackenzie, "is put on a demonstration, let them see first-hand what we have achieved in the West, make them marvel!"

"What exactly did you have in mind?" asked Mackenzie, half afraid to ask.

"A railway line!" said Glover. "The first in Japan!"

"Fine," said Mackenzie, shaking his head. "Whatever takes your fancy."

There was a flat stretch of waterfront below his house, along the Oura coast road. He had the track laid there, two hundred yards of narrow-gauge rail. He imported the locomotive, the British-built *Iron Duke*, from Shanghai, stood watching, eager as a schoolboy, as the engine was swung ashore on the jib of a massive crane, chains creaking and straining. It was loaded on a specially built trolley, dragged slowly by a team of horses to the end of the rails, heaved and manoeuvred into place.

The engine would be fired by Japanese coal, mined locally at Takashima island. The Nagasaki Railway was set to make its maiden journey.

"All of two hundred yards!" said Mackenzie.

"It's a start!" said Glover.

"Your friend Professor Risley would be impressed."

And he was right; it was a carnival, a fair. Streamers and banners lined the route, crowds had come out to gawp. Glover himself rode in the driver's cabin, fired his pistol in the air, sounded the train's whistle. The furnace was stoked, the wheels cranked and turned, the train rolled forward, gained momentum, ground and clanked along the track in clouds of steam and smoke. Horses reared, children ran and hid, women covered their ears. Glover waved at Tsuru, who stood with her hand covering her mouth, at Maki, who stood giggling with the other butterflies from the teahouse, at Walsh, who gave him a congratulatory salute. When the train hit the buffers at the far end, it reversed, chugged and shunted back to the start. Glover jumped down, face blackened with soot, eyes shining.

"Yes!" he shouted to Mackenzie who laughed with him, caught up in it. "Yes!"

★　★　★

He lay beside Maki, her head on his shoulder, his face buried in her hair. He breathed in her fragrance, the scent of her perfume and behind it the actual smell of her, herself, her warm woman-smell. She nestled against him and he held her there, skin to skin, shared sweat and body heat. It was always like this afterwards. She had worked her magic, played him with her hands, her mouth; she'd teased and roused, awakened him, wrapped herself round him, taken him into her; with perfect timing like a dancer, she knew just when to ease back, when to let go, let it all build to that last thrust and surge, that burst of sheer joy, losing all sense of everything but this.

Then to lie a while quiet and sated and utterly content, the wellbeing spreading from his groin, the peacefulness radiating through him, narcotic. There was nothing better, nothing more important.

He must have drifted into sleep, woke in the night, saw Maki sitting at the edge of the mattress. Her hair was dishevelled from their lovemaking, she had pulled a cotton yukata round her shoulders, and she just sat looking at him in a way he hadn't seen before, just looking, her eyes faraway and sad.

"Maki," he said, overcome with a kind of tenderness. "What?"

"Is nothing," she said.

"Nothing?"

"Feeling," she said. "No English word for it. *Chotto monoganashii*."

"Chotto is little?"

"*Hai*," she said. "*Monoganashii* is . . . hard to say.
Mean a kind of sadness that time pass, things change."

"Everything's fleeting," he said.

"Don't know this word," she said. "But sound right."

"A sadness that everything's fleeting."

"Little bit sad feeling."

"*Chotto monoganashii?*"

"*Hai.*"

Chotto monoganashii.

Ito and Inoue approached him with a clear declaration
of intent. They had conferred once more with Kido,
now completely won round to their way of thinking,
had embarked on rebuilding Choshu as a strong
military power, capable of challenging the Shogun. To
this end they asked Glover to supply 1000 long Minie
rifles in the short term; their reconnaissance had
indicated this was the entire number available in the
Nagasaki area. In the longer term they ordered 7000 of
the rifles, in addition to a quantity of cannon and shells
— as many as he could obtain. To further underline the
scale of their ambition, they wanted a battleship to be
built for them in Europe and shipped to Nagasaki.
What they were planning was nothing less than
full-scale revolution, and Glover was eager to throw in
his lot with them.

All of this still had to be negotiated by stealth. In
spite of Ito's increasing influence, Choshu were still
regarded with hostility and suspicion, not only by the
Shogun and the Satsuma, but by the British
Government. Ito and Inoue came to Glover's house

after dark, fearful of their lives, disguised as Satsuma merchants. They talked through the night, drew up plans over a glass or three of sake, blessed the venture further by opening a bottle of Glover's special reserve of malt whisky. Ito sang his rebel songs; they dreamed of the new Japan.

The battleship would have to be built overseas, brought back. As yet there was no yard in Japan capable of building such a vessel, no workforce with the expertise. Glover had long argued that Japan had to mine its own coal, forge its own steel, build its own ships, bring in specialists to teach the skills.

A first step was to furnish the existing, small, Nagasaki yard with a dry dock, a slipdock, so the bigger ships could be built and launched.

By the time the sky began to lighten, Ito had pledged to gain support for the building of the dock, to raise the money and buy the land. In a moment of absolute clarity, lucidity, Glover saw that the dock, and the battleship, would be built in Aberdeen, at the Hall Russell yard, and that he himself would make a journey home to supervise the work. The thought had a rightness about it, a certainty. He could see himself there, breathing the air, bracing himself against the cold blast off the North Sea.

Ito came to the house again, a few days later, after dark as usual, not wanting to draw attention to himself. He also brought with him another young samurai Glover hadn't met, introduced him as Ryono Sakamoto.

"From Tosa clan," said Sakamoto, bowing.

Glover bowed deep in response. He sensed a strength about him, a clarity. Sakamoto said little, deferring to Ito; he had come to listen, observe.

Ito wanted to discuss the progress of the arms deal, make sure it was all going ahead.

"Kido very serious," he said. "Bring in military adviser, organise Choshu as powerful force."

There was a knock at the door, and Glover tensed, alert; unexpected visitors were rare. The knocking was repeated, three firm, hard raps. Glover nodded to Tsuru, who answered it, told him there were two young men who wanted to see him. He told her to show them in.

One of the men was Glover's age, the other was only a boy, looked no more than fourteen.

Ito stood up, looked uncomfortable, said he should go. Sakamoto made to follow him but looked regretful about it.

"Wait," said Glover. "Please."

Ito bowed. "They are from Satsuma clan. They don't want me here."

"Well, this is my home, and I want you here!" He couldn't conceal his impatience. "God, and I thought the Scots were bad. Bloody clans!"

The young man bowed to Glover. "I am Toamatsu Godai. This is Nagasawa Kanae. And yes, we are Satsuma."

"And do you object to Ito-san being here?"

Godai hesitated, but only for a moment. "No." He left a pause. "In fact, may be good thing."

Glover let this sink in. "Ito-san?"

Sakamoto said something quietly to Ito.

Ito nodded, made a gruff noise Glover recognised as reluctant agreement.

"Good!" said Glover. "*Dozo*. Please." He motioned to the visitors to sit down, asked Tsuru to bring tea. "Now."

The boy sat, straightbacked. Godai took a deep breath. "We are from Kagoshima."

The very name was like a punch to the stomach, the desolation, destruction; the dead. Sono. A wisp of smoke.

"Yes," he said, simply.

"What happened there," said Godai, "must not happen again. Not anywhere."

"No."

"Shimonoseki also was very bad." He shot a glance at Ito. "Choshu leaders, like Satsuma leaders, get things wrong. Stuck in old ways. Have to change."

Ito addressed Glover, but for Godai's benefit. "Satsuma attack Choshu. Do Shogun's dirty work."

"I know," said Godai. "This was very bad. Tell Ito-san I apologise on behalf of my clan."

He bowed deeply to Ito, who acknowledged the gesture with a nod of the head.

"Only way forward," continued Godai, "is to make strong Japan. Have much to learn."

"You're sounding like Ito-san!" said Glover.

Ito grunted.

"I know Ito and other Choshu go to the West," said Godai. "I know you help."

"I did my bit," said Glover.

"Now I want to go," said Godai, "with others from Satsuma."

Ito took a sharp in-breath, shifted in his seat.

"How many?" said Glover.

Godai looked thoughtful. "Maybe twenty."

Ito coughed, almost choked. Glover laughed.

"The Satsuma Twenty!" He turned to Ito. "Well, Ito-san. What do you think?"

Ito was silent; the matter was weighty, required thought.

Again Sakamoto spoke to him quietly.

Finally Ito breathed out, a long slow exhalation, said, "Maybe is time."

Glover had placed armed guards all around the house, by the gates, in the garden.

"If anyone asks," he said, "say you're a shooting party, hunting ducks."

"At night?" said Mackenzie.

"They'll just put it down to our strange western ways," said Glover. "And if not, a loaded rifle carries a certain eloquent authority, an invitation to mind your own business and leave well alone."

Inside the house, the contingent of Satsuma had assembled, crowding into the front room. Like the Choshu Five before them, they had cut their hair, wore ill-fitting western clothes, dark suits, shirts with over-large collars. The young boy Nagasawa in particular looked uncomfortable, like an overgrown ventriloquist's dummy in some music-hall routine. And yet, once more there was that dignity, the samurai bearing, so that Glover found himself absurdly moved.

The boy had already seen a bloody battle, stood beside Godai loading Satsuma cannon as Kagoshima was bombarded. And what motivated him, as well as the others, was not revenge, it was the need to emulate, to be as strong as the conqueror. Nagasawa's parents had visited Glover a few days before, travelled especially from Kagoshima. They were proud of their son but anxious for him, setting off into the unknown, beyond the edge of the world.

Using Godai as an interpreter, Glover had done his best to reassure them, said when the group arrived in Scotland, young Nagasawa would stay in Glover's family home in Aberdeen, and Glover's own mother would look after him.

The boy's mother was overwhelmed at this, sobbed. The father stood stern, taciturn, straightened his back even more, nodded a gruff, curt acknowledgement, the very picture of restraint. And because he had been talking about them, Glover was minded vividly of his own parents, his mother's blubbing, his father's few words. *Aye*, he would say, if the fiend himself were to stand in front of him at the Day of Judgement, *Aye, well.*

Nagasawa's father had thanked Glover, shaken his hand, entrusting him with his son's life.

Now the boy was here, with the rest of them, ready for their momentous journey. Glover did a headcount, ending with the boy, patting him on the shoulder.

"Nineteen?" said Glover, counting again. "I thought there were twenty?"

"One got sick," explained Godai.

"Sick at the thought?" said Glover. "Oh well." He poured drinks for all of them, in small sake cups, poured for himself and Mackenzie, and for Ito and Sakamoto, who had come along at Glover's specific request. Glover had the strong sense that Sakamoto's influence was good, and the fact that he was from the smaller Tosa clan meant he was not bedevilled by the Choshu — Satsuma feud.

"A toast," said Glover, raising his glass. "To the Satsuma Nineteen!"

They all drank.

Mackenzie looked ill-at-ease, half-expecting trouble, braced for a sudden invasion by the Shogun's guard. Ito was stonefaced, there under sufferance, but Glover thanked him, said his very presence argued commitment, a statesmanlike maturity, said he was an example to the others, a pathfinder, and many would follow in his footsteps. He grunted at that, pleased, and when Glover said there were no poets among the Satsuma Nineteen, asked him to compose a haiku for the occasion, he said he would see what he could do.

A few more cups of sake, a little more encouragement and he got to his feet, cleared his throat, said he had a poem.

"Is tanka," he said, "not haiku. Five lines, not three. But spirit is the same."

And he read his poem, intoned it, sonorous, translated for Glover and Mackenzie.

I led the way
into the dark night,
returned to the rising sun.
Now others awake
and follow.

Glover nodded, put down his glass. "Gentlemen," he said, "the West awaits!"

They left in groups of three or four to arouse less suspicion. Ito, giving truth to his poem, led out the first group. Godai and Nagasawa went last, accompanied by Glover and Mackenzie. This time there was no trouble, no encounters with the Shogun's militia. Their ship left at first light, at the turning of the tide.

Mackenzie had decided to retire, go home to Scotland.

"Christ, Ken!" said Glover. "Why?"

"Och," said Mackenzie. "I'm just getting too old for all this. I can't keep up wi' you young fellows any more! And I aye said I'd see out my days in Edinburgh."

"I owe you a hell of a lot," said Glover.

"Aye, well, a cheque paid into my bank account will do just fine!"

"You know," said Glover, "there is a job you could be doing for me back home."

"Oh aye?" Mackenzie's wariness was only half feigned.

"I need somebody to oversee this contract with Hall Russell, get the work started before I go there myself."

Mackenzie's brow furrowed. "So you're definitely going ahead with this?"

"I'm committed," said Glover. "I've given my word."

"There's folk would like to see you committed," said Mackenzie. "To a madhouse!"

"Ach!" said Glover. "The whole damn world is bedlam!" Then he looked at Mackenzie, quizzical. "Is there anyone in particular you had in mind?"

"Sir Harry Parkes is none too pleased with your latest capers. I'm thinking you'll be *persona non grata* at the Legation."

"If Sir Harry has anything to say to me, I'll meet him to his beard!"

"You may get the chance, sooner rather than later."

"How's that?"

"Folk here are planning a wee shindig to mark my retirement. It's rumoured Sir Harry may make an appearance."

"Good!" said Glover. "I look forward to setting him straight!"

Sir Harry Smythe Parkes, KCB, British Minister, Representative of Her Majesty's Government in Japan, expansive after supping brandy, was making a speech in honour of Mackenzie. Parkes gave an impression of compact strength, steadiness. There was an intensity in his gaze, in the steel-blue eyes that nevertheless twinkled from time to time with good humour, fuelled by the liquor. He concluded his speech, proposed a toast.

"We all owe a huge debt to Ken Mackenzie. He's been a true pioneer in these parts, a firm hand on the

tiller. I wish him *bon voyage* and a safe return home."
He raised his glass. "Ken Mackenzie!"

He drained the glass, replenished it. Mackenzie
approached the platform to cheers and applause, a
stamping of feet on the floor from the younger bucks.
When the noise died down he cleared his throat,
selfconscious, thanked Sir Harry for his tribute.

"A pioneer, eh? What is it they say about fools
rushing in? I have no regrets about my time here. And
of course a part of me is sorry to be leaving . . . Who
said *Which part?* But I have confidence in the younger
generation coming up to succeed me, hell, surpass me!
And not least of these is young Tom Glover. His too is
a firm hand on the tiller, even if he does sometimes sail
a bit close to the wind!"

There was more laughter, a spate of hooting in
Glover's direction, before Mackenzie continued.

"Och, bugger it! I was never much of a one for
making speeches, so I'll get my old arse out the road.
Arigato gosaimasu the lot of ye. Sayobloodynara once
and for all!"

The assembled company roared, cheered, stamped,
fell to drinking once more.

Mackenzie came straight across to Glover.

"Thanks, Ken. I appreciate the vote of confidence."

Mackenzie laughed. "Do you think I meant one word
of it?"

"Well, maybe *one* word!"

"D'ye mind when you first arrived here? I gave you
three pieces of advice. Don't cross the samurai. Keep
out of the politics."

272

"And mind where I dipped my wick."

"Did you pay any heed?"

"Not a great deal!"

"In fact, you set about systematically breaking all three injunctions."

"As you knew fine I would!"

"Aye, well."

Mackenzie glanced over as Parkes crossed the room towards them.

"Ken!" he said, holding out his hand.

"Thanks again for the eulogy!" said Mackenzie.

"All politicians are adept at lying through their teeth!" said Parkes, laughing.

"This is Tom Glover," said Mackenzie, introducing him.

"I thought as much," said Parkes. "So you're the young hothead I've heard so much about!"

The tone was still hectoring, bantering, but that steel was there again in the gaze.

"Pleased to meet you too, Sir Harry."

"Perhaps we could have a word," said Parkes. "In private."

"Maybe this isn't the time."

"I think the sooner the better."

Glover nodded, led the way to a club room behind the bar.

Walsh passed by, said, "Seconds out!"

In the room, all pretence was gone, the pleasantries dropped. Parkes rounded on him.

"What the hell do you think you're doing?"

"I thought I was saying goodbye to Ken Mackenzie."

"You know what I'm talking about! You've smuggled more of these rebels out of the country."

"They're from a different clan this time, to maintain some kind of balance."

"Balance!" Parkes spluttered, his face reddening from more than the brandy. "Balance! Have you any idea of the trouble you could cause?"

"Sometimes a wee bit trouble is what's needed."

"You're in contravention of the Shogun's laws. You're defying your own Government."

"The Shogun is on borrowed time, and his laws will soon be obsolete. And I'm sure Her Majesty's Government will be happy to deal with the new administration, under the Emperor."

"Even if that were so, we cannot be seen to side with the rebels."

"Sooner or later," said Glover, "you'll have to take account of these men."

"Men of violence, hotheaded young fools."

"They're intelligent men, visionaries. Today's revolutionaries are tomorrow's statesmen. Think of America."

"Always a good idea!" said Walsh, who had come into the room on some pretext or other.

"Think of France," said Glover.

"I am thinking of France!" said Parkes, fired up again. "They're solidly behind the Shogun. If we're seen to be helping overthrow him, we risk another colonial war with the French."

"I don't think it'll come to that."

"You don't think so?" Parkes was flummoxed. "You don't think so! On the basis of your vast experience of diplomacy and international affairs? Really, sir, your arrogance beggars belief!"

Mackenzie came into the room, looked anxious to mediate in the exchange. Walsh tapped on his brandy glass, as if ringing a bell.

"End of round one!" he said. "I think we're threatening to spoil Ken's party here. Perhaps we should postpone the rest of the bout to a later date!"

Glover nodded, and after a moment's hesitation Parkes did the same.

"In deference to the occasion," said Parkes. "But I remind Mister Glover that he risks losing his licence to trade, is effectively courting banishment and exile from Japan, while his would-be revolutionaries risk execution."

"Low blow," said Walsh, "after the bell!"

"Gentlemen," said Mackenzie. "Shall we go back through, to the body of the kirk?"

Parkes left the next day, returned to Edo without resuming his conversation with Glover. But his position had been made clear. Glover had to toe the line.

Mackenzie was also leaving, by clipper to Shanghai then by steamer to Southampton.

"It'll be a different place without you," said Glover, seeing him off at the dock.

"Oh aye," said Mackenzie. "Everybody will miss my crabbit face!"

"Well, I'll be seeing it again soon enough."

"It'll be gey strange for the both of us to be back there."

"Aye," said Glover. "It will."

"I'm sure Hall and Russell will have reservations about the contract."

"That's why I'm glad you'll be talking to them before I get there."

"Listen, Tom . . ."

"I've been listening to you for years!"

"And not taken a blind bit of notice!"

"Not true."

"Seriously . . ."

"I know."

"Ca canny, Tom. Mind how you go."

"I will."

"Now why don't I believe that?"

"Safe journey, Ken. I'll see you in three months."

Mackenzie shook his hand, the grip as firm as ever. He strode up the gangplank, waved once. Glover turned away, surprised at the choke of emotion in his throat, in his chest. He headed back to his office to start making preparations for his own departure.

Ken was right, it would be strange going back. So much had changed for him, yet he imagined everything at home being just the same. He knew Martha would have blossomed, there was a young man, talk of engagement. His father had retired and the family had moved out of the house by the coastguard station. Glover himself had sent money home for them to buy another place, further up the hill at Bridge of Don. He could imagine his father's response to the gift, a pride in his son, but discomfort at feeling beholden. He could see the old man's face, hear his voice, *Aye, well,* and it made him laugh. He could almost smell the place, its salt and reek, fish-tang in the stinging wind.

He had packed and was ready to go, had set his business dealings in order, insofar as that was possible. It was a wrench, leaving it to others, to Harrison and Groom, to the young Japanese Shibata and Nakajimo, now his senior clerks, with instructions to refer to Walsh if a tricky situation should arise. Walsh had been flattered, said he would never match Glover for deviousness and sheer cussedness, but he'd do his best.

Walsh tried to entice him to Sakura one last time, the night before his departure, but he wanted to keep his mind clear for the journey.

"And besides," he said, "Maki seems to have disappeared. I haven't seen her in weeks and the madame gives me the full weight of her silence whenever I ask."

"These butterflies," said Walsh. "They come and they go!"

He saw Maki's face a moment, could almost smell her perfume. Then he was taking a gruff goodbye of Walsh, heading home up Minami Yamate.

Tsuru had moved in to Ipponmatsu, stayed in one of the smaller rooms to the back. It made sense, especially with him going away, having someone to mind the place, look after it.

She had run him a hot bath, and he scrubbed himself clean, lay back and soaked in the tub, heard a light rain pattering on the roof, felt strangely content. When he'd dried himself off, he came through to his room mellow and rested, skin tingling. Tsuru had laid out his cotton yukata, now she brought him tea, poured it for him. Her movements were careful and unhurried, and he felt a kind of peacefulness in just watching her.

"I'll miss this when I'm back home," he said, touched by simple gratitude.

She bowed but he thought she seemed a little agitated, flustered. "You stay a long time in *Sukottorando?*"

"As long as it takes. A few months maybe, then with the journey there and back I'll likely be away a year."

"*A, so desu ka.*" She took in the information, poured him more tea. "I wish you not go."

"Och," he said. "I didn't know you cared!"

"Care," she said, nodding.

And he saw in the moment, clearly, she was moved, was struggling to stay composed. Then she was sniffling and there were tears in her eyes.

"Hey," he said, "what's this?"

"Is nothing. I be all right."

"Och, lassie," he said. "Tsuru."

Now her shoulders were shaking, her small frame wracked by real deep sobs. He put down his tea-bowl, went to her, held her to him, let her cry. He shooshed and murmured to her, like comforting a bairn. Her face was wet against the soft cotton of his yukata; he had tied the robe loosely and as he moved, it opened at the neck and he felt the warmth there, a trickle on his skin, in the hairs on his chest. He kissed her hair, the nape of her neck, felt his own nakedness under the yukata, stiffening, rousing towards her, and her responding, pressing against him, her breath quickening to sharp gasps, unfastening her sash, letting her kimono fall open and slide to the floor, and he was carrying her to the bed, amazed at the sheer unexpectedness of this, this, this.

Maki was certain; she had been for some weeks. The sickness and ache, the exhaustion, the missed periods. The madame had told her to go away and deal with the situation, one way or another, and she'd taken herself to a quiet place, outside town. Now it was time, she had to tell Tomu, Guraba-san. She had no idea what he would say. She had seen other gaijin who had fathered children grow angry, become redfaced devils, beat their women. She had heard of others who turned away from the mess, denied responsibility, headed home to their old life and left it all behind.

She could still get rid of it. It was not too late. There was a doctor in Naminohira, near the docks. She could take a chance, risk her miserable life, pray to Jizo, who cared for the unborn.

Or she could go to Tomu, tell him the child was his, she was sure of it, and not just from the dates, she knew, it was in her blood.

She had never minded the roughness of him, the barbarian smell, in fact she liked it, as he liked her craziness, the way she made him laugh. He had taken her to his home, showed him the tiger in its cage. Yaban! He had waved to her from that great roaring railway engine, his face black, like some wild-eyed demon.

She laughed at the memory, but was shaken by another spasm, cramped and gagged as the bile came back up her throat; she held her hair back from her face, retched and vomited into a basin beside the bed. A sudden shower of rain battered the roof, should have brought ease, but she ached, every nerve strained and taut. The window was wide open, to let in cooling air. She leaned out, held a cotton cloth to soak in the rain, not caring that it also soaked her sleeve. She wiped her face, dabbed the back of her neck to cool herself down. He had liked to kiss her there, holding up her hair.

From nowhere a poem came to her, a tanka written by Izumi Shikibu, almost a thousand years ago.

> My long black hair is as tangled
> as my tangled thoughts.
> I sleep alone and dream
> of one who has gone.
> He stroked my hair till it shone.

A thousand years. Izumi had been a famous beauty, had many lovers, been hated by the Lady Murasaki. What would she have written about this? Unkempt, dishevelled, sweating, assailed by the acrid stink of her own vomit. *This*.

Maki struggled to her feet, looked out the window again, gulped in the clear washed air. The shower had stopped as suddenly as it had started. The rising moon hung low in the sky, full and heavy, blood-red.

★ ★ ★

Glover stood on the deck of the clipper as it eased out through the long harbour, for all the world like a broad river, the hills sloping down on either side, and just for a moment he remembered arriving here for the first time, so long ago, himself so young and knowing nothing. Sometimes he thought he still knew nothing. The ship passed by the sugarloaf island of Pappenberg, tacked and headed out to sea. He took one last look back.

Tsuru moved around the house in a dream. It was bittersweet this feeling; the memory of the night still clung to her like his smell. It was like an old poem, a Noh drama, to be with the lover at last, only for him to go. But he would come back, she was sure of it. He had this house, his life here, his work. She picked up his yukata from the floor, held it to her face, breathed in its smell. She would tidy the house, clean it, but in her own good time, not yet. She would make the bed later; she folded back the sheets, lay down again; she would just lie there a few minutes more.

In the light of another day, Maki composed herself. She bathed, put up her hair with a silver comb, made up her face, put on a perfumed kimono — one he liked with a design of leaves and butterflies. She hired a norimon to transport her from the edge of town, carried by two men. They laughed and said she was so light she added little to the weight of it. As if a tiny bird had landed on the seat, said one. A butterfly, said the other, like the

281

ones on her kimono. She smiled, pulled down the blinds and closed her eyes, listened to the sounds she passed through, the strange, familiar music of it all, washing over her as she bumped along; vendors and hawkers haggling with their customers, the chop of an axe cutting bamboo, a child laughing, another crying, cartwheels turning, a nightingale, a cricket, the bark of a dog. She stopped at the foot of Minami Yamate, paid the two men. It won't feel any lighter going back, said the one. Might as well still be carrying her, said the other. And his words brought a story back to her, about two monks crossing a river. One of them carried a woman across, set her down. The other was still angry about it hours later, and his companion asked why he was still carrying her. Guraba-san loved her stories. They made him laugh.

She walked on up Minami Yamate, took short, slow, precise steps, placed one foot after the other, delicate in her woodensoled *geta*. She went in at the gate of Ipponmatsu, stood in front of Guraba-san's door, breathed deep, knocked.

Tsuru was dragged from a dream by the tap tapping. She had been with Guraba-san but knew that the tiger was outside; now it was tapping with its claws at the door and he had gone to answer it; she had to stop him. The tapping came again and now she was fully awake, sitting up. It wasn't the tiger, it had gone long ago. And Guraba-san had gone too, that very morning. And someone really was knocking at the door.

Maki had knocked twice, was about to turn away when she heard sounds from inside, movement. She would try one more time, rapped again, sharp and firm, waited.

Tsuru pulled her housecoat about her, tried to arrange her dishevelled hair as she hurried to answer the door. She eased it open, peeked out, saw the woman standing there, the other, his favourite from the Sakura, the one he had brought here to the house.

Maki looked at the woman staring out at her, the other, the one who cooked and cleaned for him, looked after him.

The women stared at each other, said nothing.

Glover, on deck, was thinking of Tsuru, remembering the unexpectedness of the night before. Then it was Maki he was picturing, her face a moment vivid to him, clear. She had told him stories, and one came back to him now. A man was crossing a field when he met a tiger. The tiger growled and chased him. The field ended in a precipice, and the man fell over it, grabbed a wild vine to stop himself plummeting to his death. The tiger stood above him, teeth bared. Far below, at the foot of the precipice, another tiger paced up and down, growling, looking up at him, waiting for him to fall. Two mice appeared and started nibbling at either side of the vine, little by little chewing their way through it. Just beside the vine hung a luscious strawberry. By holding on with one hand and reaching out with the other, the man could just reach the strawberry. He plucked it and popped it in his mouth. How sweet it tasted!

* * *

Maki bowed, asked if Guraba-san was at home.

Tsuru bowed, a strand of hair falling forward over her face, said she was sorry, Guraba-san had left, had gone home to Scotland, would be away for a very long time, maybe years.

The silence lay heavy. Tsuru excused herself and closed the door. Maki stood on the step, mind empty, a grey blank. She felt the sickness rise again in her throat. She would head back down the hill, go to Sakura and speak to the madame, ask for the address of the doctor in Naminohira.

CHAPTER
TEN

Brig o' Balgownie

Aberdeen, 1865–66

The train journey north, after the long sea voyage, was debilitating, took a day and a half. By the last stage, from Edinburgh, he was in a kind of limbo, a dead zone, neither asleep nor fully awake, drifting or jolting between the two. North of Montrose it all felt chillingly familiar, a dream of something he had once known, the harsh windswept landscape, grey rain falling out of a grey sky into the grey sea. So far. So far north. By Stonehaven he felt it clench in his guts, a sense that this was reality, and this was him waking to it, the last seven years just a dream. Then the train was gathering momentum, hurtling down the last sweep into Aberdeen, smoke and cinders billowing past, and they were passing the lighthouse, and the fishing village at Torrie, and trundling into the city itself, its grey granite heart.

He eased down the window, slipped its holding belt a notch or two, stuck out his head, took a deep breath of that unforgettable tang, in behind the smoke and oil of the station, the stink of fish that hung in the air. And there were the seagulls, swooping and diving inside the station, hovering under the iron girders, the massive overarching glass roof, filling the vaulted space with their cry. A specific fierce northern breed, tough and predatory, they swept over folk's heads, shouldered their way along the platform, scavenging for scraps.

Then he was out on the platform himself, stretching his limbs, negotiating with a porter to carry his luggage, the same old battered trunk that had served him all these years, and, in addition, a wooden crate laden with gifts; and all the time he was keeping an eye open, looking out, and through the hissing smoke and steam he saw something small and white, fluttering, a hanky waving at him; and the young woman waving it was Martha, his sister, the turn of her head, the way she stood, unmistakable, so dear and familiar it moved him, deeply and unexpectedly. It welled in his heart, choked in his throat. And there behind Martha stood an old couple, looking at him, unsure, and it took him a moment to recognise them as his mother, his father. Dear God. How could they have aged so quickly, shrunk in on themselves so much?

He went to them, hugged Martha, who laugh-cried. "Look at my big brother!"

"Look at you!" he said, holding her at arm's length, amazed.

He embraced his mother, felt her thin shoulderblades through her coat.

"Tom!" she said, reluctantly delighted. "You're . . . a man!"

286

"Ach, mother," he said. "You always were one for the sharp observation!"

He turned to his father. The old man cleared his throat, shook his hand, firmly, with dour restraint.

"Aye, Tom."

"Aye, faither."

Behind the family group, hanging back, stood another familiar figure, Mackenzie, grinning.

"Ken!" he shouted. "*O genki desuka?*"

"*O genki desu!*" said Mackenzie, and they bowed to each other formally, then laughed and shook hands.

"Just a wee exchange in Japanese," he explained to Martha.

"I'm guessing," she said, "a rough translation would be *Fit like? Aa right!*"

He laughed again, said, "Och, Martha! It's grand to see you, lass."

"You too," she said, beaming.

A sudden disturbance, a commotion at the other side of the station, made them all turn. The crowds in the concourse parted and there was a short, stocky figure, striding towards them with that rolling gait, that distinctive samurai swagger, so familiar, but incongruous here.

Young Nagasawa was dressed in full samurai garb, the dark wide-sleeved robes; in place of a full-length sword he carried a short dagger, tucked in at his waist, his right hand resting on the hilt.

"Christ!" said Glover. "Did he walk down Union Street like that? He must have turned a few heads!"

The boy's expression was all seriousness, composure, restraint. Folk in the crowd gawped at him, pointed, guffawed. One or two shouted out, jeered as he passed.

"Hey, daftie!"

"Chinkie boy!"

"Eezie peezie japaneezy!"

He stopped, turned to face them, gripped the handle of the dagger tighter.

Glover called out to him. "Nagasawa-san!"

The boy hurried the last few strides towards him, stood in front of him, bowed deeply.

"Guraba-san."

Glover also bowed, then laughed, took him by the shoulders, shook him till he grinned.

"You can take the boy out of Japan," said Mackenzie. "But you can't take Japan out of the boy!"

It was the first time he had seen the new house at Braehead. His father was trying to thank him for the money he had sent home, helping them buy the house.

"It was good of you," he said, top lip tight, keeping any unseemly emotion in check.

"Och," said Glover, ending the discussion.

The house was only half a mile from the coastguard station. Like Ipponmatsu, it stood on the brow of a hill, had a spacious garden and open views. Compared to their old home, it was a mansion.

Glover's crate was delivered by horsedrawn cart from the station. In the front room he prised it open with a crowbar from his father's toolshed, carefully unpacked his treasures. For his mother and Martha he had brought rolls of shimmering silk, to be made into dresses. For his father there was a set of samurai swords, sheathed and mounted, a carved hardwood pipe. For the house itself, for pure adornment, there was a little bronze Buddha, a suit of samurai armour, hanging silk scrolls delicately painted with birds and flowers, a trove of ornaments and knick-knacks, exquisite *netsuke* carvings, Satsuma pottery in black and white with its subtle dull glaze. His father handled a matt black vase, nodded his approval.

"There's so much!" said his mother. "You didn't have to."

"This is nothing," he said. "There's furniture on its way, and screens and rugs, and a whole crate of tea!"

"You'll be turning the place into a wee corner of Japan," said Martha.

"Nothing wrong with that," he said, and he produced from the crate a seedling, packed in earth, wrapped in muslin.

"*Kurumi*," he said. "Japanese walnut. I thought we could plant it in the garden."

For Mackenzie he had brought a book he'd had specially bound, full of bright woodblock prints of Nagasaki.

"A wee memento," he said.

"Och!" said Mackenzie, but he smiled, looked moved as he turned the pages.

For Nagasawa he had brought another, smaller, samurai sword. The boy looked stunned, unbelieving, as he took it, held it reverently. That Glover should bring him a gift, as if he were one of the family, and that the gift should be this. *This*. He was almost overcome, bowed and touched the sword with his forehead. Then he stood rigidly to attention, bowed again, turned on his heel and left the room.

Over dinner, warmed by a dram of malt his father saved for a special occasion, Glover regaled them with edited tales of his years away. He sang Mackenzie's praises, said Ken had taught him all he knew.

"I refuse to accept the blame!" said Mackenzie.

He told them of his business dealings, the fortune he'd managed to make, the rogue Walsh, the indomitable Ito. He made light of the dangers, the attack on the Legation, said it was a time of upheaval and change and he was glad to be a part of it. He completely excised all reference to the floating world, the pleasure quarter, once or twice caught Mackenzie's eye and saw there a knowing twinkle at the gaps he was leaving in his version of events.

When their talk started to veer towards work, the dealings with the Hall Russell yard, the progress being made, Martha interrupted, said they could discuss business tomorrow and there was something much more important, far more demanding of her brother's attention.

Chuckling, he let her lead him out to the garden. She had already chosen a spot, dug a little hole to plant the seedling, brought it out in readiness.

"I thought it was important that you plant it," she said, and he kneeled, eased the root into place, replaced the earth round about it, trowelled it flat.

"There!" he said, standing up.

She clapped her hands and he was once more amazed at her, this beautiful, poised young woman, his wee sister.

"This lad of yours is a lucky fellow," he said.

"John," she said. "You'll like him."

"I'm sure I will."

She looked at him, seemed to hesitate a moment, then came out with it.

"Was she bonny, Tom? Your wife, Sono?"

"Aye," he said, simply.

"And the wee lad, your son?"

"He barely lived."

"It must have been an awful hard time for you."

"Aye."

"You never said much in the letters."

"No."

"I had to read between the lines."

"Aye."

"But you're fine now?"

"It's been two years."

"Is that all?" she asked. "It feels longer."

"It does."

She took his arm and they walked to the end of the garden, looked down over Brig o' Balgownie.

"How's young Annie?" he asked, remembering a summer night, a heron skimming the river.

"Not quite so young," said Martha. "A bit like yourself!"

She laughed but seemed momentarily uncomfortable. "She's fine."

"I wrote when I first went out there," he said. "But she never replied."

"Och well," she said. "What's done is done. Sometimes it's best just to let things go."

"Aye," he said.

It was as if nothing had changed in all his years away. The same congregation, older, the same minister, greyer, more thrawn, the same grim oppressiveness and hard ardour, the same soberly resonant hymns, remembering the green hill far away, exhorting all people that on earth do dwell to sing to the Lord with cheerful voice. He felt again the mounting panic, the fear that life had caught up with him, returned him here to this dour place, his escape from it mere illusion.

He minded his younger self, casting about him in desperation, resting his eyes on young Annie, a vision of grace. Without thinking, he looked round now, and there she was, he was sure of it, the fair hair longer and a little darker, the bonnet covering part of her face. He couldn't see her clearly, but he knew her, remembered exactly the way she stood, the shape of her head. He willed her to turn round, look at him as she once had, but she didn't, stared straight ahead, singing the hymns of sober praise.

He left ahead of Martha, shook hands with the minister at the door.

"Aye, Mister Glover," the minister said. "We'd heard you were back." And he made it sound like a life sentence. You shall be taken from this place.

He waited in the kirkyard, saw Annie come out, stepped forward and doffed his cap to her. Older, her face thinner, but even more beautiful than he remembered, the beauty tempered by experience, a half-sad knowingness in the eyes.

"Annie."

"Tom."

She registered no surprise; word would have spread that he was back; she would be expecting to see him. But the recognition, the remembrance of him, came from deep. She knew him, as he knew her. He took her hand, held it. For a moment she seemed to respond with the tiniest pressure of her own, then she tensed, withdrew and turned away.

For the first time he noticed a man standing behind her, a little way off; Glover's own age or a year or two older, already corpulent, hair starting to thin.

Annie held out her hand, drew the man in, introduced him.

"You know my husband, Andrew."

Glover looked, saw the much younger man behind the flabbiness, the premature settling into middle age.

Andy Robertson, his fellow clerk from that old life, drinking companion from all those years ago, quoter of Burns, feared of adventure, wanting the quiet life.

"Andy!"

They shook hands, Robertson's grip limp, unwilling.

"Good to see you, Tom." The mouth smiled but the eyes flickered, said the opposite of the words.

Glover laughed at the memory of something. "D'ye still go diving off the Brig o' Balgownie?"

Robertson's smile was weak, the lips tight.

"Thon was a night!" said Glover. *"Gettin fou an unco happy!"*

"Aye," said Robertson, uncomfortable, not wanting reminded.

Out the corner of his eye, Glover caught a movement, a wee boy darting from behind a gravestone, rushing over, hiding himself among Annie's skirts.

She laughed, brought him forward. "This is our son, Jamie."

Fair hair, blue eyes. The boy darted a shy glance up at him, hid his face, peeked out.

Glover crouched down. "Pleased to meet you, Jamie."

"This is Mister Thomas Glover," said Annie.

"Tom," he said, and he hid his own face, keeked out between his fingers, made Jamie laugh.

"Come on," said Robertson, taking the boy's hand. "It's time we were going."

He looked at Annie, saw something in her eyes, unspoken, fleeting, a momentary yearning, regret.

"It really *is* good to see you, Tom," she said, then the door was closed, her face set.

"It was indeed," said Robertson. "I hope your visit home is a pleasant one."

Then they were heading out the gate, only the boy looking back, waving at him; Martha came out of the church, came up behind him, took him by the arm, said nothing.

★　★　★

He walked to the end of the garden, late afternoon, still a faint trace of warmth in the air, but tempered by that chill that was always there at the back of it, a sharpness in the breeze, turning to downright cold in the shadows. He smiled at the seedling Martha had planted; it was good to think of generations to come sitting under its branches, in its shade, Martha's children, maybe even grandchildren.

He looked down at Brig o' Balgownie. On a whim, a fancy, he decided to go down and take a look.

Like everything else it was smaller than he remembered. It sat there, quite the thing, in a wee stone dream of itself. But the drop to the river was still high enough, the parapet narrow and uneven. He thought of Robertson keeling over, laughed at the daft foolhardiness of it. How easily they might have cracked their skulls, drowned. But they hadn't. They had lived their lives, gone down different roads.

Annie.

He no sooner thought of her than he turned and she was there. They were here and this was happening, again; recurrence, a scene in a play, a dream in a dream. She too was amazed, but not completely surprised, had half expected it; he could see it in the way she looked, one hand reaching up to her throat.

Without thinking, he stepped forward, held her, kissed her hard on the mouth, felt her give, respond; then she disengaged, stepped back, coming to her senses as the boy ran towards her from the other side of the bridge.

"Jamie!" she cried out, too loud, flustered and fussing over him. "You remember Mister Glover."

"Tom!" the boy shouted, bold, then he hid behind her, shy again, peeked out.

"Hello again, Jamie!" said Glover.

"He's quite taken with you, Tom."

"As I am with him."

He took a gold coin from his pocket, flipped it spinning in the air, caught it, slapped it face down on the back of his hand. Keeping it covered, he bent down to Jamie. "Heads or tails?"

The boy looked at his mother, who shrugged. He had to choose.

"Heads!" he said. "No, tails!"

"Sure?" said Glover.

The boy nodded, changed his mind again. "Heads!"

Glover made a great show of raising his hand, squinting underneath at the coin, not letting the boy see.

"Heads it is!" he said, and gave the coin to the boy, who laughed, pocketed it.

And suddenly there was something in the boy's eyes that made him think the unthinkable.

"He's a fine boy," he said.

"He's a rascal," she said.

"Not like his father then?"

"Or too like him."

She realised what she had said, bit her lip.

"How old would he be then?"

"Old enough."

"I'm guessing he'd be about six."

"You know he is." She looked at him, her eyes fiercely calm. "Don't do this, Tom."

The silence hung between them, the river flowing beneath the bridge, the cry of an oystercatcher, piercing.

"Andy always did carry a torch for you," he said, breaking it at last.

"You've made a life for yourself, Tom. Now, leave us to get on with ours."

She took Jamie by the hand, led him over the bridge. The boy looked back once, startled, called out a shrill goodbye.

He walked into town after that, two miles, not noticing, not aware of his surroundings. The certainty burned in him. He had a son. All these years he hadn't known. Now there was nothing he could do, without causing damage, destruction.

He walked on, found himself before he knew it down by the docks, in the dark backstreets, searching for comfort, oblivion.

The carriageway of the slipdock was over 200 yards long. Constructing it was a major feat of engineering; transporting it to Japan would be a feat verging on the miraculous. Glover had explained to Russell, the yard owner, that the site for the dock, at Kosuge, was already being excavated. The Satsuma clan which owned the land had already invested $10,000. They were building more than a dock, they were constructing a new, industrial Japan. They had to succeed.

Russell's solution was both simple and complex. They would build the dock in the yard, then dismantle it, transport it in sections to be reassembled on site, in Nagasaki.

"It's mad!" said Glover. "It's magnificent!"

Russell was showing him round the yard, at Footdee. The building of the dock was well under way, and work had begun on a ship to transport the separate sections out to Nagasaki. The ship was a five-masted clipper to be named the *Helen Black*, its hold specially reinforced to take the sections of dock and its accompanying machinery, transport it halfway round the world. The whole project was a massive undertaking, provided work for squads of skilled tradesmen, gangs of navvies and stevedores. The air rang with the constant noise of construction, from first light till dusk.

Russell himself had pioneered the yard's production of boilers and steam engines. Now it was paying off. And Glover was holding out the prospect of even more work. The Choshu wanted a warship, this was the place to build it.

"They're serious," said Glover. "They have the money and they've already paid me a commission to get the job done. Until now they've made do with worn-out hulks they've bought from the Americans and the Dutch, sometimes reconditioned merchant ships with a few light cannon. They've had a few disasters, trying to use cannon that were too big and wrecked the ships with their recoil!"

Russell laughed. His eyes twinkled at the implications, but his enthusiasm was tempered by genuine concern.

"These friends of yours, Tom — the Choshu is it?"

"Aye."

"Are they not the rebels you were talking about?"

"They are that. They're changing the face of Japan, for good."

"Be that as it may, I have no wish to incur the wrath of the Admiralty for breaking British neutrality, effectively arming one side in another country's civil war."

"But you'd be arming the right side!" said Glover. "Mark my words, the so-called rebels will be running the country before long. Then they'll be building a navy, commissioning an entire fleet."

Russell took in the enormity of the idea. "I'm inclined to trust your judgement," he said.

"I have the specifications," said Glover. "They've even named the ship, in anticipation. *Ho Sho Maru*. And they're quite clear about what they want. An iron-plated corvette, three-masted, operable by sail or steam; four guns on deck — two 110-pounders and two 60-pounders."

Russell's excitement showed in his eyes. "It's the way we've been going with the yard," he said, "from wood and canvas to iron and steam."

"It's the way forward," said Glover. "Who better to build this ship, and all the rest to follow?"

"I think we can do business," said Russell, and they shook hands on it, the grip Masonic, reassuring.

★　★　★

The boy Nagasawa had struggled. The language had made things difficult, not just English but peppered with the local speak, the doric, that had its own strange music, hard for him to pick up. They said *fan* for *when*. *Fit like?* was *How are you?* He worked at it, listened. Then there was the place itself and its weather, the grey rain, the damp haar, the cutting north-east winds off the sea. He wore warm clothes, clenched against the cold, survived a winter. He was samurai. He was strong. He would thole it. That was the word they used. *Thole.* Endure.

The hardest thing was being so far, so very far from home, from his family. He dreamed sometimes of Kagoshima, woke thinking himself back there and everything as it was, expected to look out his window at Mount Sakurajima with its plume of white smoke. He could almost smell it, the faint hint of ash in the warm air. There were times too when he dreamed of the bombardment, saw buildings flattened, whole neighbourhoods razed. Then the smell was destruction, cordite and burning and churned earth.

At school they made allowances for his English. The dominie said once, "You speak as well as some of these gormless loons." He hadn't understood, till someone explained.

He had always been good at mathematics, and that hadn't changed. The language of that was universal. He excelled, and some of the gormless loons hated him for it. They were the ones who baited him, yelled insults.

He ignored them. He tholed it. Then one day it went further.

Glover saw it from the upstairs window at Braehead, on the side looking over the street. He'd been poring over some plans for the slipdock, heard a commotion, looked out.

Nagasawa was still some way off, heading up the brae on his way home. Behind him four boys were laughing at him, shouting. Then one of them picked up a stone, threw it, and it hit Nagasawa on the back.

Glover was about to rush out, was surprised to see Nagasawa run into the house. He hadn't taken him for a coward, but perhaps the odds were just too great; with his mathematical bent, he would have worked it out, settled for discretion.

He heard the front door open, bang shut, Nagasawa's footsteps on the stairs, heard him take something from his room, clatter downstairs again. The boys who had taunted him were at the gate, still laughing, enjoying their triumph. Glover looked in disbelief as Nagasawa strode towards them, carrying his samurai sword, unsheathed.

The boys must have seen it at the same moment and they froze, all bravado and bluster gone, a gang of scared wee boys. Nagasawa raised the sword above his head, charged at them, roaring out a battle-cry.

"*Kaaaa!*"

"Jesus Christ!" said Glover out loud, and he was down the stairs and out the door.

At the gate he called out to the boy. "Nagasawa-san!"

301

He had chased his tormentors fifty yards down the street, terror making them spring-heeled. At Glover's call he stopped, turned back.

Glover was fierce with him, as he had to be, made him hand over the sword, ordered him inside.

"This won't do," he said.

The boy stood rigid, chastened. "They insulted me. Is a matter of honour."

"I know fine. It's *bushido*, the samurai code."

The boy snapped to attention. "*Hai, so desu.*"

"But we're not in Nagasaki. We're in Bridge of Don!"

"I am sorry if I dishonour you."

"No!" he said. "It's not that. It's just that we do things differently here. And beheading someone for chucking a wee stone is seen as a mite excessive."

"I understand."

"Now," he said, "I'm taking this back, in the meantime, just for safekeeping. Now, if you give me the sheath, we'll put it away."

The boy fetched the scabbard, handed it over. Glover held the sword out towards him, let him nick the tip of his thumb, just a scratch, on the blade, enough to draw blood, satisfy honour. Then he slid the blade home in its sheath.

The boy turned to go, looked so crestfallen that Glover called him back.

"I gave you this as a gift," he said, "and in time I'll return it to you. But for now I want you to have something else as a sign of respect and friendship."

He laid down the sword, took from his top drawer a heavy pocket-watch on a chain.

The boy took it, bowed in gratitude. His eyes shone.

Nagasawa told Glover the story himself.

The same four boys he'd chased with the sword were waiting for him on his way home from school, just before the bridge where a path led up from the river. They'd blocked his way, moved to surround him, started their taunts.

"Hey, chinkie!"

"Yellow-face!"

"Slantie-eyes!"

"You're not so brave without your muckle big sword."

As they'd closed on him, he'd put his schoolbooks at his feet, reached into his jacket pocket, brought out the watch Glover had given him, felt the weight of it in his hand. Then he'd held it by the chain, spun it above his head like a weapon, lashed out at the nearest boy, the ringleader, caught him on the shoulder, a sharp blow. Shocked, the boy had stumbled, lost his footing, fallen to the ground. The others had moved as if to rush Nagasawa, but he'd turned to face them, still spinning the watch, roared out his war-cry and drove them away. The first boy had stood up, terrified now, but Nagasawa had stopped, checked that the watch was still ticking, put it away in his pocket. The boy had moved away, a few tentative steps, then quickening his pace, then pelting after his friends.

Glover listened to the story, nodded. "Thank you for telling me, Nagasawa-san."

Nagasawa handed him the watch. "Now you will take this back also, keep it with the sword. For safekeeping."

Glover laughed. "I don't think that will be necessary. And I don't think those boys will be bothering you again."

Nagasawa looked confused.

"My friend Ito-san," said Glover, "once told me a story, about standing up for yourself."

The boy flinched. Of course. Ito was Choshu, still the enemy.

Glover continued.

"There was once a snake which lived in a small village, and it used to frighten people and bite them. Then one day a Zen master passed through the village, and he gave a talk about non-violence. The snake happened to be passing by, and he stopped to listen. He was so inspired by the talk he saw the error of his ways, and he vowed to be a good snake from that day on. He slithered up to the master and asked his advice. Of course, animals can always talk in these stories. Or perhaps the master could read his thoughts and speak to him in silence."

Nagasawa looked more confused.

"In any case," Glover went on, "the master gave him simple advice. Meditate every day, and stop biting!"

The boy nodded, intent.

"Now, time passed, the way time does, and after some months the master was once again passing through the village. He had a look round, said, Where's my friend the snake? But nobody could tell him. Then just as he was leaving the village, he happened to look down at the side of the road, and there was the snake, all battered and bruised, half dead. What happened? said the master. You told me not to bite, said the snake. And the boys in the village realised I wasn't a danger, and they lost all their fear of me. When they realised I wouldn't even fight back, they took revenge for all the years of biting. They gave me a thrashing and threw me in the ditch. The master gave a wee smile, shook his head, said, I told you not to bite. I didn't tell you not to hiss!"

Nagasawa was still concentrating hard, forehead furrowed, eyebrows meeting.

Glover handed back the watch, said, "Sometimes you have to hiss."

And suddenly there was light; the boy understood; the point hit home, the itzibu dropped. And a huge boyish grin spread across his face, and he threw back his head, for the first time in Glover's hearing laughed out loud.

"*Hissu!*" he hissed, gleeful.

He laughed so much he had tears in his eyes. Glover handed him a hanky and he wiped his face, blurted out another chuckle, then consciously, deliberately, regained his appearance of calm formality, his composure. He handed back the hanky, thanked Glover, bowed and turned to go.

Glover thought a moment, called him back and formally, with understated ceremony, returned the sword to him.

"Don't bite!" he said.

Again the boy grinned, then held it in check, overcome with a deeper emotion, reverence for the sword, pure gratitude at having it restored to him.

He bowed low, said "*Arigato, Guraba-san. Arigato gosaimasu*," his voice hoarse, choked.

It began again with the handshake, the secret sign they were on the level, could trust each other. Hele, conceal, never reveal. Glover was a guest at the Lodge meeting, sat through the formalities, then Russell took him aside, said he wanted a word.

The room was comfortably furnished with a polished oak table, capacious leather armchairs. The walls were lined with books, Masonic texts, and in between the bookcases hung scrolls bearing the secret symbols, the square and compasses, a configuration of stars, a single eye blazing at the heart of a pyramid.

The whisky was poured, cigars lit. Fragrant smoke filled the room, curled in the shadows under the high ceiling. The atmosphere was safe, male. Mackenzie was there, and Robertson, and young John Grant, Martha's lad. He worked for Russell, was an engineer. In this company he was very much the junior, the prentice, but he seemed at ease, affable. Glover had taken a liking to him, thought him a good match for Martha.

Robertson still worked for old George, was a step away from his father-in-law's job. His father-in-law. Christ. When the old man retired, in a year or so, Robertson would step up, run the business. Mellowed by the drink, the good smoke, Glover looked at Robertson with something like warmth. He had plodded away, had everything he'd ever wanted in life. Not enough for Glover, he'd been too restless. And yet. There was the pang again, twisting. This dullard had Annie, and the boy. Christ, the boy. Another sip of whisky, another dram. Don't mind if I do, an excellent malt if I may say so. Ach. They made choices, lived by them. Enough.

Russell was addressing him.

"Scotland has need of men like you, Tom, men of vision. If you should ever be of a mind to come home, there would be no shortage of offers."

"Such as?"

"I don't think it would be unreasonable to talk about a directorship, a seat on the board, perhaps a safe parliamentary constituency."

"T. B. Glover, MP. It has a ring to it. My mother would fair burst with pride!"

"I'm serious, Tom."

"Oh, I know you are, believe me. I know fine, and it's tempting."

"You could buy yourself some land, an estate."

"You're taking me to the top of the mountain. Get thee behind me!"

Russell let the suggestion of blasphemy pass, looked at Glover hard. "Give it some thought."

"I will," said Glover. "I will."

Glancing across, he saw Robertson's face was grim.

Russell changed his tone, was suddenly hearty, proposed they all play golf next morning. "I take it you play, Tom."

"Och, I'm willing to give it a go."

★   ★   ★

The green at the eighteenth hole was right at the edge of the cliff-top, ten yards from a sheer drop, a hundred feet into the North Sea. A fierce wind whipped in from offshore, directly from Norway, made any kind of judgement impossible. Glover's ball landed in a bunker, down a slope from the green.

"Ha!" he shouted, into the wind. "A challenge!" He shielded his eyes, squinted at the flag. "*Another* challenge!"

He had no great skill, played with gusto and energy and no little luck.

He checked the lie of the green, the direction of the gusting wind, took the club his caddie handed him, a wedge. He held it a moment in front of him, raised like a samurai sword, chuckled, shouted again. "Ha!"

Not hesitating, not stopping to think, he hacked with the wedge, chucked the ball in a flurry of sand up out of the bunker, watched it buck at the edge of the green, roll to within a few feet of the hole.

"Yes!" he shouted. "Yes!"

They had come out early, after breakfast, Glover and Russell, Andy Robertson and John Grant. Only Mackenzie had declined, said he had no intention of dragging his old carcass round a golf course at some ungodly hour.

Russell had clearly set up the game as a continuation of last night's meeting, said nothing obvious or crass to mar the play, beyond the odd remark, say, about the freshness of the air, the amenity of the city; and the remarks lent themselves to tangential musings about the future of the Northeast, the planned improvement in road and rail links over the next ten years.

"Imagine it, Tom," said Russell, lining up a drive. "Iron rail bridges over the Forth and Tay. The journey time to Edinburgh will be cut to two or three hours." He whacked his ball, straight down the fairway. "Imagine!"

As a dance round the subject matter, discussing it without discussing it, it was worthy of the Japanese.

"Aye," said Glover. "I know what you're saying."

Russell was easily the best player among them, played a canny game, hit safety shots for the most part, took the odd calculated risk. He was well in the lead. Behind him young Grant had the makings of a decent player; he hit the ball sweetly enough, but lost focus if he mis-hit, skewed off-course, got bogged down in rough. Robertson was cautious, methodical, looked affronted if his shots went agley. On the last green he was only two shots ahead of Glover, who had whacked and sclaffed his way round.

Russell tapped in for a par on the hole and to win the game. The others applauded politely. Grant two-putted, tapped in for second place. Glover strode across the green, gave a moment's thought to the rub of it, pocked his shot maybe too hard. It ran straight at the hole, might completely overshoot, might hit the flag and bounce out, might catch the rim and slingshot past. Grant took two strides, light on his feet, took out the flag at the last second. The ball did hit the rim, spun round it, orbited the hole twice and dropped in with a satisfying clunk.

"*Hai!*" shouted Glover, lapsing. "And again, Yes!"

Robertson still had his last shot to take; just five feet from the hole, it looked easy, but conditions were less than perfect, the slope awkward, the wind tricky, the green itself patchy. He walked round the ball, addressed it from every angle, checked the direction of the wind, got down and smoothed the grass with his hand.

"Come on, lad!" said Russell. "It's gey snell to stand around up here freezing our arses off when we could be sipping a tipple at the nineteenth!"

Robertson smiled, a tense grimace, said, "Right."

He steadied himself, bent over the ball, knees slightly bent, straightened up again, shifted his feet slightly, tried again, drew back the head of the putter and smacked the ball with a dull clack, and they all watched as it trundled past the hole, and off the green, accelerated down the slope and disappeared over the cliff, into the abyss.

The other three were restrained a moment, holding it in, then they all roared with laughter.

"Bad luck!" said Grant.

"You could scramble down and play the ball!" said Russell.

"You'd probably find some poor gannet sitting on the thing," said Glover, "trying to hatch it!"

The others laughed again, but Robertson was downcast.

"Your face is tripping you!" said Russell. "Come on and I'll buy you a drink."

"God!" said Glover as they headed for the clubhouse. "What a great bloody game!" He stopped, a thought forming. "Maybe I could introduce it to Japan."

"Surely it would never catch on," said Russell.

"Ach," said Glover, "you're probably right."

As they walked, Russell asked him, casually, if he'd given any thought to his proposals. And suddenly, as he looked at the flags snapping sharp in the wind, he found himself thinking of Nagasaki with great longing. Up ahead he saw Robertson, head down, crestfallen. Glover could stay, be all Russell had suggested and more, he could prosper, increase his fortune, live off the fat of the land. And if he did, he would be near his son, could watch him grow up. But looking at Robertson, slumped and hangdog, he knew how it had to be. Right now, in this moment, he knew he would have to go back, and it would be sooner rather than later.

The flags flapping in the wind off the sea. Ito and the others would be scheming their schemes.

"I'm truly flattered," he said to Russell. "But I have unfinished business, in Japan."

Flags, flapping in the wind.

CHAPTER
ELEVEN

Daimyo

Nagasaki, 1867–68

Coming back to Nagasaki felt like a return home. He felt no strangeness here, the hills, the bay, so familiar, his own house, Ipponmatsu, so welcoming; the very air was balm to his soul. Now it was Aberdeen that seemed a dream, so far away.

In the house he walked from room to room, touching things, *his* things, reacquainting himself: a Daruma doll that had been Sono's, Matsuo's samurai sword. He heard a movement behind him and Tsuru was standing in the doorway, smiling at him, unsure.

"Tsuru, lassie! It's good to see you!"

She bowed, said *"Irasshaimase!"*, then she covered her face with her hands and burst into tears. He went to her, held her to him.

"Och!"

The visits began that very evening, a steady stream of folk, beating a path to his door.

Walsh was the first, looked excited to see him.

"Damn it, Tom, it's good to have you back!" He shook his hand, clapped him, hearty, on the shoulder,

312

laughed. "The place has been kind of dull without you."

"Now that I don't believe!"

"Well, maybe not! Things have been bubbling away nicely in your absence. But you do add a certain spice to the mix, and that's been sadly lacking."

"I'll see what I can do!"

Walsh's first thought was to drag him out to the pleasure quarter, but Glover was reluctant.

"Bring me the smelling salts!" said Walsh. "I never thought I'd see the day!"

"Did Maki ever reappear?" asked Glover.

"You know, she never did. Darnedest thing. Just vanished off the face of the earth."

"Queer."

"Mind you," said Walsh, "from the rosy glow on Miss Tsuru's countenance, I'd say maybe you have all you need right here!"

"Maybe," said Glover, noncommittal.

"Dog!" said Walsh.

Glover opened a bottle of fine malt he'd brought back from Aberdeen, poured two generous measures. "Now," he said. "I want *all* the news."

Over the next hour, and two or three glasses more, Walsh brought him up to date on everything, from the price of tea to the strength of the new alliances being formed, unholy or otherwise.

"Your old pal, Montblanc, he of the *pince-nez* and the strange predilections, has been muscling in on your territory, trading with the Satsuma."

"Has he now?"

"He brokered the sale of a couple of ships to them, steamers. But I heard he'd made a real *faux-pas* with one of them. He wanted to pull out all the stops, impress these guys. So he had their clan crest incorporated in all the furnishings and decorations."

"Cheap," said Glover. "Just what I'd expect."

"But he made the mistake of having it woven into the carpets, so the Daimyo and the other dignitaries from the clan were practically falling on their faces trying not to step on it!"

"Serves the bastard right."

"Didn't do his reputation much good."

"Well, let's see if we can blacken it even further."

"He's had his knuckles rapped by his own Consul, new guy by the name of Roches, bit of a swashbuckler by all accounts."

"The French stance is still resolutely pro-Shogunate?"

"Exactly. I believe this Roches character had quite a set-to with Sir Harry Parkes last week, real sabre-rattling on both sides. Roches accused the British of being lukewarm in their support for the Shogun and the Bakufu."

"I wish I'd been there."

"I'm sure the sabres will be rattled in your direction before long!"

"What did Sir Harry have to say for himself?"

"Just repeated the party line about Her Majesty's Government being committed to a policy of absolute neutrality and non-intervention."

"That was quite a piece of non-intervention in Kagoshima!"

"But things are changing, Tom. You can feel it, a groundswell. Your old friend Satow seems to have swung over completely to your way of thinking. He's written a few pieces in the *Japan Times*, heavily criticising the Shogun. I've brought copies for you to read when you have a minute."

He took the newspaper reports from his valise, handed them to Glover, who flicked through them, scanned the headlines. *The present situation in Japan. The Shogun's Treachery.*

"So," he said. "Maybe it really is time."

"Meanwhile," said Walsh, "back in my neck of the woods, our little local skirmish has finally come to an end."

"A very un-civil war."

"With a satisfactory outcome."

"I met a Southerner on the way out here," said Glover. "Gentleman from Louisiana. He begged to disagree. He argued the issue of slavery was a pretext only, an excuse by the North to wage the war, break up the plantations, take over the land."

"That's exactly how a gentleman from Louisiana *would* see it. You might as readily argue that your little revolution here is at the behest of the British, with the French waiting in the wings to step in if it all goes wrong."

"I definitely owe Montblanc a bloody nose."

"Whatever the politics of the situation, whatever the ideology, the fact is the war is over, and that means there's going to be a huge amount of redundant weaponry on the market, worldwide: rifles, cannon, Gatling guns, you name it. No better time to arm your rebel army."

Glover raised his glass. "To revolution, and unholy alliances!"

Walsh had no sooner gone than Harrison and Groom arrived, with Shibata and Nakajimo following deferentially behind. Another bottle of malt was opened, a round poured, another toast proposed.

"To Glover and Company!"

"*Kanpai!*"

He had kept in touch the whole time he was away, but communication was slow, he needed to catch up. He poured more whisky, heard what amounted to a company report, enthusiastically delivered.

The traffic in ships continued apace; they had brokered the sale of half a dozen vessels and were currently awaiting delivery of the gunboat *Nankai* to the Tosa clan for $75,000. Jardine's still owed them $20,000 towards the building of three steamers. Glover would write, demanding the transfer of funds forthwith. Harrison had continued to invest in property; Groom's adventures in foreign exchange, playing on currency fluctuations between Nagasaki and Yokohama, still turned a profit and managed to stay, if only just, within the confines of the law. The tea business now employed over a thousand people, and Glover had designed a steam-driven machine for sifting the tea, rendered the whole process more efficient. An improved version of the machine was even now being developed in England

316

and would be shipped out as soon as it was complete. Meanwhile the company's agency work had expanded, and they now acted for Lloyd's as well as a number of Chinese banks.

"All in all," said Harrison, "business is booming."

"And these two fellows here," said Groom, indicating the two Japanese clerks, "have kept everything absolutely ship-shape in the office."

The two men beamed, bowed.

"Another toast," said Glover. "Shibata-san! Nakajimo-san!"

"*Kanpai!*"

When the four men had gone, he sat and read the newspaper articles Walsh had left, Satow's diatribe against the Shogun.

The Tycoon, or Shogun as he styles himself, has arrogated the title of overall ruler, a title to which he has no legitimate claim, and assumed a dignity which does not belong to him, a piece of extraordinary assumption on the part of one whose treachery was apparent in the affair of Shimonoseki.

If criticism like this was being widely circulated, the wind had indeed shifted.

He yawned, stretched. The long journey from Aberdeen was beginning to make itself felt, in a general weariness, an ache in the bones. He would ask Tsuru to draw him a bath. But the thought had barely formed when, for the third time in the one night, there was a tapping at the door. This time it was Ito, accompanied by Godai.

"Dear God!" said Glover. "Unholy alliances right enough!"

Once more a bottle was opened, drink taken. Glover shook himself awake, prepared to talk into the night.

Ito grinned at him, gave a nod to Tsuru, grinned even more. It was Ito who had sent her to him in the first place, after Kagoshima. He shook Glover's hand, looked delighted to see him.

"Guraba-san! Welcome back!"

"Ito-san! You rogue! It's good to see you!"

Godai was more circumspect, formal. He bowed.

"Guraba-san."

"Godai-san. I hope you learned much from your sojourn in the West."

Godai bowed deeper. "*Hai! So desu.* Whole Satsuma clan most grateful."

Godai said in London they had been treated like dignitaries, like ambassadors from a foreign state. Laurence Oliphant, with the perspective of distance, and with his wounds quite literally healed by time, had championed the rebel cause, argued that the Shogun must be deposed if Japan were to progress. Glover saw him a moment, face livid, arm cut to the bone by a samurai sword. Now he had used his influence at Westminster to arrange for Godai to meet the Foreign Secretary, Lord Clarendon, who had shown great interest in what he had to say about the possibility of political change in Japan, the forging of stronger trade links.

"This is all good news, Godai-san," said Glover. "*Very* good." Then he paused. "But I have a bone to pick with you!"

Godai looked alarmed. "Bone?"

"Satsuma have been dealing with this stupid Frenchman Montblanc. He even sold you a ship!"

"Ah," said Godai. "*So desu.*" And he smiled, mouth tight, a hideous rictus, the way Japanese men always did to cover embarrassment. "*Furansujin, hai. Monburo.*"

"The very man," said Glover, terse.

"We learn from you," said Godai. "Make competition. Good business!"

"Oh, did you now?"

"We buy one ship from him, but he is not good man, not honourable."

"Tell me more, and I'll blacken the bastard's name. Then his eye!"

"Sorry?"

"I heard about the clan crest on the floor!" said Glover.

"Bad," said Godai. "Then he want to sell us more ships, but his Government say no. They support Shogun and Bakufu."

"Don't I know it!"

"So we don't pay him full amount."

"Ha!" Glover laughed. "The biter bit!"

Again Godai looked confused.

"Don't worry," said Glover. "He's getting what he deserves."

"But now Daimyo want to meet you."

"Ah."

He minded that ferocious intransigent face, hard set. Kagoshima in flames. Rubble and smoke.

"He want to talk to your Government also, make deal. Want you to bring Sir Harry Parkes to Kagoshima."

"Is that all?" said Glover.

"Is important," said Ito. "It has to happen. Satsuma have made strong alliance with Choshu. Kido-san has made Choshu a real fighting force; *Kiheitai* well trained, well armed. With Satsuma can easily beat Shogun."

Glover breathed out a long slow sigh. "Christ!" he said. "Welcome back to Nagasaki!"

They talked, planned, schemed, through the small hours, and when Glover walked with them to the gate, the first faint light, a red glow, was starting to streak the sky. Ito and Godai still moved with a kind of furtiveness, a habitual stealth, looking about them, always half expecting figures to step from the shadows, the Shogun's agents, French spies. Glover walked to the end of his garden, looked out across the sleeping town with a few lamps lit here and there, the harbour, the vague shapes of the hills. He would have to post guards again, install cannon on the hillside. He rubbed his face, exhausted, breathed in the night air, fragrant and mild.

Back inside, Tsuru was curled in a chair, woke when he closed the door. She looked up at him, sleepy.

"Now then, Tsuru lass," he said. "Where were we?"

★ ★ ★

It was the first time he'd been back to Kagoshima since the bombardment. So much had changed, so much was the same; there was the volcano, *Sakurajima*, the familiar contours of the bay; the air still smelled faintly of ash; there were the docks, rebuilt, and suddenly in the air was the sound of cannonfire. But this time it was a salute, four guns, and it was for him, the honoured guest, and the ship that carried him was the Satsuma's own steamer, the *Otento Sama*. For a moment he was shaken, thought he might give away his emotions but managed to hold them in check, stood to attention and saluted. Godai, beside him on deck, did the same.

Shimada was waiting to meet him at the quay. The old man bowed, greeted him, his manner still formal and gruff, but in the crinkling of the eyes was a glint of recognition and acceptance, familiarity and warmth. Half a dozen guards lined the quayside, and Shimada led Glover to a norimon which would convey him to the Daimyo's residence. It was the first time he'd travelled in one and he felt awkward as he clambered in, sat on the cushion, his knees jutting, angular as the carriage was lifted by two men front and back and he was bumped and jostled on the short journey.

The Daimyo wasted no time, had Glover led to an anteroom where he took off his boots, and from there into the inner chamber where the Daimyo himself sat, cross-legged on a raised platform.

Glover bowed low, but not so low as to undermine his own dignity. The Satsuma Daimyo, Shimazu Saburo, Prince and Regent of the clan, acknowledged him with a nod of the head. The last time he'd come

321

here, Glover hadn't been allowed past the anteroom, and the Daimyo had refused his gift of a pocketwatch, had magnanimously allowed him to leave the place with his head still attached to his shoulders.

This time Glover had again come bearing gifts, entrusted to Shimada on his arrival. Glover brought them forward, two packages, elegantly wrapped in the finest paper, tied with silk. This was important, showed respect, concern for the formalities, the aesthetics of the situation. He placed the packages in front of the Daimyo, spoke with precisely the right degree of respect. He glanced at Godai, who had coached him in precisely what to say. Godai gave a fleeting half-smile, yes, he had got it just right.

"*Dozo*," said Glover, pushing the packages forward. "Please."

The Daimyo nodded to Shimada to open the packages. The first contained another pocketwatch, on a gold chain. The Daimyo shook the watch, held it to his ear, grunted his acknowledgement. His mouth was still turned down, set, but in the eyes that met Glover's gaze there was a flicker, the suggestion of acceptance.

Shimada opened the second package, took out the gift, a pistol, the handle inlaid with ivory. This time the reaction was unmistakable; the eyes were animated, the corners of the mouth twitched, the noise he made was one of approval. He weighed the pistol in his hand, squinted along the barrel. Then, as Shimada had done so long ago, a scene replaying itself, he raised the gun, pointed it straight at Glover's head. And although Glover knew he had not loaded the gun, there was something in the act itself, the intent, that made the sweat prickle on the hands, on the back of the neck, some primal instinct that kicked in under threat.

The Daimyo asked for bullets. Glover said he had more, had brought a box of them, but there was a small pouch here, with half a dozen. The Daimyo asked him to load it, which he did, before handing it back. Now the threat was real, and they both knew it. The look in the eyes was predatory, and mocking. This was a test. Again he raised the gun, pointed it at Glover. This was one of the most ruthless men in the country. He had a long-standing feud with the West. His men had butchered Richardson over a matter of protocol, etiquette. He had precipitated the bombardment of his home town rather than back down and lose face. He was holding a gun to Glover's head.

Glover didn't flinch, knew he couldn't. He bowed, said "*Dozo*," reached forward and pushed the barrel to one side so it faced the wall.

The Daimyo actually laughed, a harsh dry bark, then he put the gun down, nodded again to Shimada, who placed two small boxes in front of Glover. The Daimyo was reciprocating, had gifts for him. Glover bowed, opened the boxes. Each contained a small porcelain vase, one black, one white, each with its characteristic glaze, a subtle lustre.

"*Shiromon*," said the Daimyo, indicating the white vase. "*Kuromon*." He pointed to the black.

"*Kiwamete usukushii desu*," said Glover. And they were indeed exquisitely beautiful. And Glover was caught by surprise once more, in this land that

323

endlessly surprised him, at the combination of refinement and barbarism, delicacy and brutality.

The Daimyo motioned to Shimada to clear away the gifts, stood up and led the way through to another chamber. He was tall, even by western reckoning, as tall as Glover, a good six feet. By Japanese standards he was a giant, broad and powerfully built, an imposing presence, rendered more so by his flowing silk garments, his tunic with wide stiff shoulders.

The room they entered had a table prepared where they would dine, a civilised way of discussing business.

The feast was lavish, ran to some dozen courses, spread over three hours. The discussion, through Godai as interpreter, was at first circuitous, but grew more and more direct as the evening unfolded and the sake and whisky flowed. The Daimyo made it clear to Glover that the situation had changed, and would continue to change rapidly. He was anxious to impress on him, and on the British Government, that the Satsuma clan were no longer hostile to the West, even though it was only three short years since the reprisals against Kagoshima. In fact, he was anxious to expand trade with the British, and that could only come about if new alliances continued to be forged between Japanese clans, led by Satsuma and Choshu, combining to remove the Tokugawa Shogun and replace him with the country's rightful hereditary ruler, the young Emperor, the Son of Heaven. The Daimyo would be most grateful if Glover would relay his message to the Consul, Parkes. They had once been at war, but now must establish friendship. To this end, the Satsuma would be

honoured if the Consul himself would visit Kagoshima
where he would be most royally welcomed. Glover said
on departing here he would go directly to Edo and
deliver the message in person. The Daimyo roared his
approval, said Glover had the spirit of a warrior, a true
samurai. They laughed, drank to each other's health.

Next morning Glover was wakened abruptly by an
attendant, ordering him politely to get up and get
ready, the Daimyo wanted him to go out riding in one
hour. The blood was thudding in his head from too
much rich food, strong drink.

"Bloody hell!"

The attendant backed out. Two young women
appeared, led him to the bathhouse, scrubbed and
rinsed him, giggling. Godai was already in the hot tub,
and Glover eased down into it, the water scalding. The
heat made his head throb even more, thud in his skull;
he felt faint, made a rueful face at Godai, who himself
looked washed out.

"The things we do for Japan, Godai-san!"

The answer came, weak. "*Hai*."

He took the heat for ten minutes, dragged himself
out, shocked himself awake with a dousing of ice-cold
water from a tub, poured over his head. The thudding
ache reached a peak then started to subside.

"Now!"

He dried himself, dressed. The women brought food
and he made himself eat a little rice-porridge, to settle
his gut. Godai couldn't face it, still looked wan. Glover

laughed, clapped him on the back. "Bit of horse-riding will set you straight!"

Outside, the horses were saddled and ready. The Daimyo kept them waiting another twenty minutes then made his appearance, mounted up by placing his foot on the shoulder of a retainer, kneeling beside the horse. He gestured to Glover and Godai to ride alongside him and the little procession made its way out through the gates, an outrider up ahead, carrying the clan banner, half a dozen armed samurai following behind.

All the way along the road out of town, people would stop, get down on their knees as the procession passed, every one of them — women, children, old men — pressing their heads in the dust. Glover was unsettled to be up here, seeing this from the inside. It felt plain wrong to have folk kowtow to him. A few of them met his gaze, curious, before bowing their heads. The Daimyo looked straight ahead, rode on.

Further out the settlement thinned till there were only a few straggled houses, then they were in the open countryside, lush and green, surrounded by terraced hillsides, paddyfields. The Daimyo spurred his horse to a gallop, forced the others to keep up; then he slowed to a trot, stopped altogether in a clearing sheltered by cycad trees.

As they dismounted, Godai said to Glover, "This is a great honour, for the Daimyo to go riding like this with gaijin, he is paying you great respect."

"Let him know I appreciate it," said Glover.

The Daimyo had walked to the edge of the clearing, was looking out over an uninterrupted vista, the city far behind, bright sunlight shimmering on the bay, the bluegreen slopes of *Sakurajima*. He wanted to show Glover the extent of his domain, spoke of how quickly Kagoshima had risen again, been rebuilt. He said Satsuma were a powerful clan, the most powerful in the country. Allied with Choshu they would be formidable, unbeatable, would make Japan a strong ally for the West. He repeated his request for a meeting with the Consul, and Glover said he would not rest till it came about.

The Daimyo gave a grunt of approval. This was the right answer, the only answer. He spoke then of further opportunities for Glover. Out there, he pointed, stretched Ryukyu, a chain of islands under Satsuma control, reaching as far as Okinawa, halfway to China. The silk trade flowed through here, and concessions could be made to Glover instead of to Chinese brokers. There were interests too in sugar — they had built their own factories to process, refine it. Western expertise would be welcome. And of course, there would be a continuing demand for ships and machinery. Glover heard, understood.

On their return to the residence, the Daimyo gave Glover another gift, a small cycad tree to remind him of their conversation in the shade, in the clearing, the view from Kagoshima, the open vista, the future.

Back in Nagasaki, Glover paused only long enough to sign some papers, took time to plant the cycad tree in the garden at Ipponmatsu; he dug the hole himself, took satisfaction in it, eased in the seedling, felt the warmth of the earth between his fingers as he trowelled it back in, patted it in place. Good. Then, true to his word, he headed directly to Edo, by steamer and horseback, went straight to the Legation, rode in along the same winding pathways, over the same bridge, past the same lake, the same grove of pine and bamboo. The defences had been strengthened, there were more guards around the perimeter, but he thought they still looked indolent, could still be cut to shreds by the ferocity of a ronin attack.

Five years since the bloodbath. Takashi's sword coming at him out of the dark. Now Richardson was dead, butchered, and Matsuo slain by his own hand. Alcock and Oliphant were long gone, driven out. Now here he was, back to plead the same case all over again. Time passed. Things changed and stayed the same. The wind still blew in the pines.

He waited in the reception room while news of his arrival was relayed to Sir Harry Parkes. A heavy oak clock ticked the time away and Her Majesty the Queen, Empress of India, Defender of the Faith, looked down from her formal portrait, stern and regal, overseeing this furthest flung outpost of her domain, this little patch of British soil. He sensed for a moment the enormity, the sheer weight of power and responsibilty to which she was heir. It must be overwhelming, especially for a woman, and it was no wonder she appeared dyspeptic, even melancholic.

Parkes came bustling into the room. As Glover had anticipated, he was intrigued at the message he had sent.

"Glover!" he said, shaking hands. "Still meddling in affairs that don't concern you?"

"But they do concern me, Sir Harry. More than that, they consume me."

"You're a battler, Glover, I'll say that for you."

Glover took it as a compliment, nodded.

"But tell me," said Parkes, "have I got this straight? Are you telling me the Satsuma Daimyo wants to receive me in Kagoshima, with full honours?"

"He's most anxious to meet you," said Glover. "I've just come from there, and he treated me like royalty." He glanced at the portrait of the Queen, gazing down at them. "With all due respect!"

"The man who had Richardson slaughtered on a whim, who brought retribution on his own city rather than back down, this ruthless warlord now wants to negotiate?"

Glover noticed, on the lintel above the door, a deep gouge in the woodwork, probably hacked there on the night of the attack by a flashing samurai blade.

"They live by their own code," he said, "and it's a code we don't always understand. But it's grounded in ideas of honour, and duty, and that much we *can* understand. They're also nothing if not resilient. They adapt readily to change, and this is a time of tremendous change. We have to seize the moment."

Parkes left a silence as he pondered. The clock ticked. Her Majesty looked down. Cicada and uguisu chirped and croaked in the gardens.

Parkes rang a little brass bell.

"Let us discuss this further," he said, "over tea. And let's make it proper tea, with milk and white sugar, not the bitter green muck they serve here."

"I admit it's an acquired taste," said Glover, "and I'm happy to say I've acquired it in my time here. But I'll be glad to sup some of your best Darjeeling."

"Excellent," said Parkes, and he rang the bell again.

Next morning Glover rose early, remonstrated with the guards who tried to dissuade him from heading into the city alone. He insisted, said he had his wits about him and knew fine what he was doing. They stood back to let him past and he rode straight to the Satsuma *yashiki*, the clan's residence in Edo. At one point he thought he was being followed by someone on foot, hurrying to keep up; he fancied he caught sight of a figure darting into an alleyway when he turned his head. He dug his heels into his horse's flanks, urged it forward through the narrow streets, folk glancing at him, curious, getting out of his way.

At the residence he talked his way in, saying he was here at the express command of the Daimyo himself, Prince Shimazu Saburo, who had received him in Kagoshima this very week and entrusted him with a special mission in Edo.

The Daimyo's representative, Kinsaburo-san, came hurrying out to meet him, in spite of the early hour, welcomed him with green tea and sweet *mochi* beancakes. Glover told him of his meeting with the Daimyo, the pressing need to arrange for Parkes to go to Kagoshima.

Kinsaburo said with great earnestness, and a certain self-importance, that he would visit the Consul as soon as possible, the next day, and deliver an official invitation on behalf of the Daimyo. He thanked Glover for his visit, warned him, as the Legation guards had done, that he should not travel through the city alone and he would delegate a bodyguard to escort him.

Glover thanked him, said once more he would be fine, could look out for himself, and he took his leave. But again, on his way back to the Legation, he had a sense of being followed, observed, sensed that figure, half glimpsed out the corner of his eye.

Kinsaburo arrived at the Legation the following afternoon, borne in a norimon, with four guards in attendance. He wore a yellow silk robe, an elaborate winged headpiece, carried a scroll. Parkes had been alerted by Glover and was expecting the visit, dressed formally in his gold-embroidered ambassadorial coat. Seemingly by chance, an agent of the Shogun arrived at the same time and was curtly instructed to wait in the reception area while the Consul was engaged in official business. To complicate matters further, the French Consul Roches also, miraculously, by chance, made an appearance, accompanied by another man, clearly a French agent. Something in the agent's appearance, the furtive way he moved, seemed familiar to Glover; then he realised, this must be the man who had shadowed him the day before. So both the Shogunate and the French were spying on him; he was flattered and outraged in equal measure. Roches and his henchman, under protest, were also instructed to wait.

In the drawing room, Parkes took his time, had tea and cakes served to Kinsaburo, who then read out the formal invitation inscribed on the scroll, offering the full unstinting hospitality of the Daimyo if the Consul would do him the honour of paying an official visit to Kagoshima.

The Consul replied graciously that the honour would be all his, he would be delighted, indeed he would have visited Kagoshima sooner had he not been obstructed by protocol and procedure — what the Japanese termed *yaku-bio*, or "official sickness". Further, in the light of current changes in the political situation, he now deemed such a visit essential.

It was a masterly piece of diplomacy and tact, and impressed Glover greatly. He saw the Consul in a new light, heightened by his treatment of Roches and the Shogun's agent after Kinsaburo had gone. He addressed them both, told them the diplomatic negotiations of Her Majesty's Government were none of their business, that Satsuma, as well as Choshu, had a right to be heard, that there was a strong move towards recognising the young Mikado, regarded by many as the rightful hereditary ruler of Japan, and including him in any further negotiations concerning the country's future. If they did not take cognizance of the new situation, the loss would be theirs and history would pass them by.

Roches listened to the tirade, gave Parkes a weary smile, a look full of *ennui* and condescension, but not without a certain sympathy for someone whose ideas he clearly regarded as simply, unfortunately, wrong-headed. He told Sir Harry that history would indeed have the final say. Then he turned to Glover, addressed him directly.

"Monsieur Glover." It was a statement, not a query. He knew who Glover was.

"Monsieur Roches," said Glover.

"I have reports of you from my countryman, Charles de Montblanc."

"Give him my regards," said Glover. "Although I hope to pass them on in person before too long. And no doubt you've had reports of me from your lackey." He indicated the other man, the figure in black. "I'm honoured at the French Government's concern for my welfare, but your man here should be aware of the danger to himself in wandering these streets unaccompanied."

Roches chuckled, said he would pass on the advice. Then he drew himself up, bowed to Glover and Parkes before excusing himself with a wave of the hand that was almost languid, turned and swept out the door with the other in tow.

The next visit to Kagoshima was a triumph. Parkes had accepted the Daimyo's invitation, was accompanied by his wife. They stood on the deck of the battleship

Princess Royal, Glover by their side; two more warships, *Serpent* and *Salamis*, made up the convoy steaming into port past *Sakurajima*. This time the salute was fifteen guns, each report booming over the harbour, leaving a plume of smoke in the air. One of the officers on deck, who had been on the *Euryalus* during the bombardment, spoke to Parkes.

"Last time we were here, those guns were fired in anger. And by God, we gave them what for!"

"I mind it fine," said Glover. "I had an excellent vantage point at the top of yon hill."

"It was regrettable," said Parkes. "But the incident is history."

The guns boomed their salute. Flags lined the waterfront. Crowds had gathered to greet them.

History.

The Daimyo himself, Shimazu Saburo, a magnificent presence in full ceremonial robes, standing even taller in thick-soled wooden geta, was at the quayside waiting to meet the party as they stepped ashore, and they were led in procession, carried in norimon, preceded by banners, thudding drums, shrill flutes, all the way to the residence, the streets lined with people.

At the palace they were received by servants assigned to them, settled in their quarters, served tea and sweetmeats; then the Daimyo walked with them in the surrounding gardens, which even Glover hadn't seen on his previous visit. There were miles of shady walkways, stone paths covered with moss, trees and ferns all around. A clear stream ran through it, at one point cascading down to a little lake, from there into tributaries and fish-ponds brimming with openmouthed carp. Here and there wooden bridges crossed the stream, leading to pavilions, pagodas, shrines, and the air was filled with birdsong, the cries of insects.

Lady Parkes was quite overwhelmed, said she had never seen anything quite so beautiful, and the place was very Heaven.

"*Jodo*," said the Daimyo.

"Pure Land," said Glover.

"One can see," said Parkes, quietly to his wife, "why they regard *us* as unrefined barbarians."

If Glover thought he had been fêted on his previous visit, it paled by comparison with the evening feast, an extravagant lavishness. This time the dinner ran to forty courses and lasted for five hours. They ate entire spit-roasted hogs, stuffed quails, endless variations on vegetables and fish, everything pickled and spiced. They drank not only sake and whisky, but English beer and French champagne. The women retired and the menfolk talked on into the night. Sir Harry explained, through his interpreter, that he had been eager for some time to speak to the esteemed leadership of the Satsuma clan, and would have done so had it not been for the intransigence, prevarication and downright obstructiveness of the Tokugawa Shogunate. The Daimyo proposed a toast to the Great British Empress, the Queen across the ocean. Sir Harry reciprocated, drinking the health of His Majesty the Mikado, the Emperor. They pledged closer relations between their two countries, said let the past be dust.

"To the future!" said Sir Harry. "The past is dust!"

Once again Glover was wakened in what seemed like the small hours of the morning, a dull drumbeat thudding in his skull. Once again the Daimyo wanted to take his guests to the countryside. Once again Glover shocked himself awake with a dousing of cold water after soaking in a hot tub. This time he couldn't even face the rice gruel, made do with a flask of water to slake his drouth.

The morning was fresh, bright. Parkes looked bleary, stunned, his face drawn and wan. The Daimyo was wide awake, eager, ready for more than a canter in the hills. They would go hunting.

Deep in the forest a gang of beaters waded through the undergrowth, kept up a rhythmic chant; some banged clappers, some swept the area ahead of them with bamboo staffs, drove the wild boar in a panic into a clearing. The Daimyo, on horseback, felled the first beast with a blast from a musket. The horse reared, an attendant held its reins, restrained it. Parkes was next, dismounted, took steady aim as a boar was driven straight towards him, squealing and snorting in panic. He held his rifle steady, fired, stopped it dead. Glover did the same, shot from a standing position, brought down his prey. The Daimyo laughed, motioned to them to remount, nudged his horse forward along a path, deeper into the woods. Parkes still looked queasy, rueful, asked Glover if this was their idea of a cure for a hangover. Glover said perhaps they were hunting down breakfast. Parkes quailed, wiped his forehead with a handkerchief.

Up ahead the Daimyo called something out to his attendants. One of them ran to him, handed him a hunting bow, a quiver full of arrows.

He sat upright in the saddle, bent the bow to get the measure of it, the tension. The quiver was at his hip, ready.

He called out a command, urged the horse on at a trot.

Two dogs, mongrel gundogs, had been held in check, nervous and twitching, halters at their necks, straining; now they were set loose, ran straight into the undergrowth, yelping, frisky. They'd be scared of the boar, and that was good, meant they wouldn't be gored on those vicious tusks.

The Daimyo bent the bow, flexed it.

The beaters started up their cacophony again, banged clappers and drums, shouted, swept the cover with their bamboo staffs; the dogs barked, scurried.

Then they heard it, crashing after the dogs, and the dogs turning tail and scampering, and the beast running after them, chasing them down, bursting into the clearing, charging towards the group of onlookers.

The Daimyo bent the bow.

The boar was still some distance away, but picking up speed, getting closer. Glover and Parkes had reloaded their weapons, stood braced. The guards assigned to them stepped forward, their own rifles at the ready.

The Daimyo goaded his horse to a canter, then a gallop, pursued his quarry.

The dogs were in a panic, tongues out, panting. The boar was getting closer.

Glover's eyes were on the Daimyo, and it was as if time itself had slowed. The horse's hooves thundered on the path, its nostrils flared, mane streaming back, flanks in a lather of sweat. The Daimyo drove him on, bent his bow, reached to pull an arrow from the quiver, fitted it to the string, drew back. And every action was fit, right, sure; there was no hesitation, no thought; each movement flowed into the next. He had all the time in the world, levelled the arrow, let fly, and time accelerated again, the arrow whooshed through the air, struck the boar at the back of the neck, made it stumble, and before it had rolled over, tumbled to the ground, the Daimyo had shot another arrow, pierced the hide, and a third, hit the throat, then he pulled up, dismounted, pulled out his dagger and finished the beast off, stabbed it hard in the chest, deep into the heart, watched the lifeblood gush out of it, stain the forest floor dark red.

Glover had never seen the like, spontaneously applauded the Daimyo, who stood grinning, blood on his hands and spattered on the front of his tunic. Some of the retainers also clapped, in unison and looking uncomfortable, those tight smiles not quite masking the awkwardness. Then the Daimyo gave a roar, releasing them, and they cheered, and two of them moved forward to pull out the arrows from the dead animal, drag it to the side of the path.

The Daimyo remounted his horse, led the way to the residence; the day's kill was gathered up, carcasses hogtied, slung on poles and carried back.

"Remind me," said Parkes quietly, an aside, "not to cross this fellow!"

"Or at least," said Glover, "not until you're out of range!"

Roches had been in Nagasaki while they were away.

"He was spitting fire!" said Walsh. "Wanted to know what was going on with you and Sir Harry making overtures to the Satsuma."

"They approached us," said Glover. "I'm afraid Monsieur Roches has burned his boats there. If anyone was making overtures it was his man — I use the term loosely — Montblanc. And for that, I believe, he was in danger of being guillotined!"

"I assume he's redeemed himself," said Walsh. "He was scurrying around after Roches like a little poodle."

The same evening, Glover saw Montblanc at the Foreigners' Club. The Frenchman was holding court about his dealings with the Satsuma, explaining how he had used his good offices to help them establish contact with the forthcoming International Exhibition in Paris, where he promised they would be treated as a separate nation state. His plans had been scuppered by Roches's intervention, and the Satsuma had turned on Montblanc, accused him of behaving dishonourably, reneging on his word. "They behaved like vicious little dogs," he said to his coterie of listeners, "like the savages they really are." He swirled the wine in his glass, sipped it. "Worst of all are the ones who went to the West. They want to become European gentlemen, and even ape the way we dress. And I do mean ape! They look like little monkeys! Some of them even tried to wear these." He indicated the eyeglasses perched on his nose. "But where can they put them? They have these little flat faces and no noses! How can they wear *pince-nez*?"

The group around him laughed appreciatively. Montblanc basked in the laughter, saw Glover glaring at him, waved a hand in the air.

"Monsieur Glover! We were just discussing your little friends!"

"I heard," said Glover.

"In fact," said Montblanc, "since you are their agent, I must ask you to address their disgraceful refusal to pay me what I am owed."

"This is neither the time nor the place," said Glover.

The man had clearly imbibed a little too much wine, was flushed in the face, preposterously confrontational. Otherwise Glover would have invited him to step outside and settle the matter. A straight left to the jaw should suffice.

"So," said Montblanc, slurring a little, "you too have no honour. I insist on receiving my payment!"

Glover met his gaze. "You, sir, can stick your payment up your arse."

Montblanc spat abuse at him in French, in some crude argot he didn't understand, so the insult was wasted.

340

"As far as the Satsuma are concerned," said Glover, "you have been paid exactly what you deserve and are lucky you still have a head on your shoulders. Now, I bid you goodnight."

Parkes wasted no time, began negotiating with the Mikado's advisers in Kyoto. Glover found himself summoned, because of his good relations with the clans in question, to a meeting in Osaka. Ito would be there with Kido, representing Choshu, and Godai would speak for Satsuma. Ryomo Sakamoto would also attend, from the Tosa clan. Glover remembered his calm presence when he'd visited Ipponmatsu, spoken words of moderation to Ito. Glover knew he had worked quietly to persuade Satsuma and Choshu to reconcile their differences.

On the due date a squadron of western gunships, British, French, American, Dutch, steamed into Osaka harbour and dropped anchor. Delegates of the four nations, Parkes for Britain, Roches for France among them, came ashore and were met by dignitaries from the Mikado's court and representatives of the Shogun.

Satow was there, fell in with Glover as they walked up from the harbour to the residence where negotiations would take place.

"A more disparate group it's hard to imagine," he said.

"You think some good will come of this?" asked Glover.

"If not," said Satow, "it won't be for want of trying. Those ships out there are laden down with vast

341

quantities of foolscap paper, silk tape, quill pens and bottles of ink, more than sufficient for the purpose. I feel Sir Harry intends to see this through, no matter how long it takes!"

In effect, Parkes wanted to renegotiate the conditions governing the treaties established between Japan and the various foreign powers, the terms of the trading links with the West. Hitherto the treaties had been ratified by the Shogun, and that had been sufficient to make them law. Now Sir Harry was insisting that the foreign powers had to take cognizance of the Mikado, who must also ratify the treaties.

The Shogunate, backed by the French, were hostile to the proposal. The Emperor's faction were wary, noncommittal. The Dutch were interested observers, happy to take advantage of the situation, however it developed. The Americans were there under protest, and their Consul, Townsend Harris, did nothing to disguise his disgust at European machinations.

"We thrashed all this out six, seven years ago. I sweated blood over that damned treaty. And for what? So that these British freebooters and French fops could move in and bleed the place dry."

Parkes protested that the situation had changed dramatically in the intervening years and they had to take account of the changes.

"Manipulate the situation for your own ends," said Harris. "Legitimate your plundering. Extend your Empire."

"We want what is right for Japan!" said Parkes, exasperated.

"Ah, yes, of course!" said Harris. "I come from good Puritan stock, sir, and my grandmother was a fine, upstanding woman by the name of Thankful Townsend. She gave me three of the soundest pieces of advice I ever had: Tell the truth, love God, and hate the British. And I shall endeavour to follow her advice to my dying day."

Roches laughed out loud. "I shall remember this!"

Parkes glowered at them both, turned and led the way into the meeting room.

Glover, as a mere trader, had no part to play in the official discussions, but Parkes had thought his presence behind the scenes might oil the wheels of discourse. Satow, as interpreter, had a seat at the table, and reported to Glover in full at the end of each session.

They had all known it would be difficult. Finding a form of agreement that would satisfy each of the factions was an impossibility. But even Glover, with his years of dealing with the Japanese, was taken aback by their capacity to niggle, quibble, nitpick over the slightest detail. Satow too was well versed in the degrees of prevarication, formulaic evasiveness, at which they were expert. But even he was exhausted by the extent of it. A week passed with little sign of progress. Satow remarked that they might have to send to Edo for more ships carrying more foolscap, more quills, more ink.

Glover, for his part, took the opportunity of initiating his own discussions. Ito and Godai also kept him informed, and Parkes took him into his confidence. He sensed the historic importance of the outcome, knew if Sir Harry could forge an agreement it would have enormous symbolic significance, send a clear signal to the rebel clans and the embattled Shogunate.

The negotiations continued. If both the Shogun and the Mikado had to ratify the treaty, and any subsequent agreements, which ratification took precedence? It was a matter of honour, and hierarchy, and protocol. Was one ratification contingent on the other? Did one depend on the other for its validity? Who ratified the ratification?

Another week passed. Tempers became short, nerves frayed. Every night the foreign delegates returned to their ships, every morning they came ashore and began the long tedious process anew. The foreigners grew impatient with the convoluted haggling over minutiae. Why couldn't they just sign the damned documents and be done with it? The Shogunate argued the impossibility of frank discussions with a squadron of western warships at anchor in the harbour, said they implied a clear threat. Ito said they were indeed a threat, one that the Shogun should heed. Godai said they had all had to learn this hard lesson, the lesson of Kagoshima, of Shimonoseki. Complete co-operation with the West was now the only way forward. Parkes was at pains to point out there was no bellicose intention in the present circumstances, the ships were for the purposes of transport only and carried nothing even approaching their full contingent of troops and armoury. Satow interjected another reference to the sheer bulk of paper, pens and ink on board, said it left room for little else. Parkes and one or two others chuckled, grateful for the attempt at levity, but it seemed to push the Japanese further into stonefaced intransigence.

The way Satow described it, Sakamoto glared at him along the length of the table, grumbled something to Godai in his sonorous rumble of a voice, and Godai reluctantly translated. Sakamoto had said that the ships were indeed a reminder of how things stood, they had no choice but to co-operate with the barbarians, it was the official policy of his clan, the only way forward for his country, even if his own natural inclination might be to separate a few barbarian heads from barbarian bodies. Then he'd stood up from the table, walked out of the room.

Parkes had sighed. "And these are our allies!"

The haggling continued. Then clearly some agreement was reached amongst the Japanese, some formula which could be interpreted as favouring the Mikado and recognising his preeminence, but allowing the Shogun to retain a measure of dignity so honour was not lost. After almost three weeks of negotiation, representatives of the Emperor brought forth the Book of Irrevocable Wills and a new agreement was signed, to the delight of Parkes, the chagrin of Roches.

Later, as the foreign delegates prepared to depart, Glover found himself next to Harris. It was late evening, growing dark, the lights of the foreign ships bobbing out in the harbour.

"You're Tom Glover," said the American.

"The very same," said Glover.

"I've heard of you from Jack Walsh. He speaks highly of you. Ordinarily that would make me suspicious."

"Jack's a bit of a rogue right enough."

"But he's shrewd, and he knows a good man when he sees one."

"Even if that man happens to be British?"

"Well, you're Scotch aren't you? Different beast altogether."

"Your grandmother sounds as if she might have had Scotch blood in her!"

Harris allowed himself a chuckle, then spoke with an earnestness, an intensity. "What do you young fellows think about the situation?"

"It's hellish complicated," said Glover, "made more so by the Japanese talent for obfuscation. But if I were a gambling man — which I am! — I'd put my money on the Southern clans, the Choshu and Satsuma, to take over, drive Japan forward."

Harris was silent a moment, took a pipe from his jacket pocket, filled it, lit it, puffed at it, contemplative, filled the air with its fragrant smoke.

He spoke again. "I've kept a journal of my time here, thinking it may be of some interest to posterity. And just recently I re-read the entry I made on the successful negotiation of the previous treaty. And when I told that stuffed shirt Parkes that I'd sweated blood over this, it was no exaggeration. So the ratification was in some sense a moment of personal triumph. But what was the entry in my journal? *Grim reflections —*

ominous of change. Query whether this for the real good of Japan. In a sense the beginning of the end. He puffed on his pipe again. "If anything, I feel it even more strongly today. This new treaty is clearly an important development. It represents a beginning. But it's also, I fear, an ending."

CHAPTER
TWELVE

Meiji

Nagasaki–Edo, 1868–69

Like an eggshell held in the hand. That was how Satow had described the situation, and the sheer complexity of it rendered the utimate outcome impossible to predict.

The rebels, it seemed, represented the future, openness to the West. But they rallied under the banner of the Mikado, who was mired in tradition, upheld the old feudal ways, resented foreign intrusion. The Shogun, on the other hand, had signed the initial treaty with the West but had since been obstructive, used the situation for his own ends.

"To be fair," said Walsh, setting down the *Japan Times* which carried reports on the impending hostilities, "he's caught between a rock and a hard place. Damned if he do, damned if he don't!"

"He's damned, all right," said Glover. "His time is over. This revolution is inevitable. Then the country can move forward."

"And the Mikado?"

"He's a figurehead only. He wields no real power."

"You sound very sure."

"I'm sure," said Glover. "I feel it in my bones."

But whatever Glover felt in his bones, uncertainty spread and with it a tension, unease. The Choshu engineered a confrontation, issued demands that the Shogun resign and his Bakufu advisers step down, that the Emperor be restored to full, unalloyed power. The demands were backed up by a Choshu army, marching on Edo. The Shogun's forces came out to meet them and there were initial skirmishes followed by a stand-off. Meanwhile Satsuma troops gathered in the streets of Kyoto, reinforcing the threat.

Now the country was undeniably on a war footing. Rumour and counter-rumour spread. The Shogun had resigned from office. He had been executed. He had not resigned and his troops were marching on the Mikado's palace. They had already sacked it, put it to the torch. The Mikado was dead. The Mikado was back in power and would show his true colours by purging the country of all foreigners.

In the foreign settlements at Edo, Yokohama, Nagasaki, defences were strengthened, women and children sent to the relative safety of Shanghai. For all Glover's confidence, he was canny, took no chances, installed more cannon on the hillside below Ipponmatsu, laid in supplies of guns and ammunition, posted armed guards around his property.

"Still feel it in your bones?" asked Walsh.

"Aye, well," said Glover. "You never know."

The skirmishes escalated into a full-blown battle. The Choshu were outnumbered, but armed by Glover, drilled and marshalled by Kido, they overran the Shogun's army, routed them, drove them back to Osaka.

Again, the country was rife with rumour. The Shogun had committed seppuku. His followers had taken to the hills and would continue to fight until every last man of them was wiped out. No, he was alive and had rallied his troops. Reinforced by the French, they had beaten back the Choshu, taken on the Satsuma for good measure. The intervention of the French had led to retaliation by the British. Now the country was riven, not only by civil war, but by a colonial struggle between two great imperial powers.

"Who fabricates this nonsense?" said Glover. "If we were at war with the French, I'm sure we would have been informed!"

Eventually the more extreme rumours died down, were discounted. What became clear was that the Choshu had indeed won a famous victory, that the Shogun was unharmed but battered and humiliated by his defeat. Further, the Shogun's navy had entered the battle, had also been defeated by the Choshu's Aberdeen-built battleships.

Then in true Japanese fashion, time passed and nothing seemed to be happening. Whatever had to unfold would do so with due convoluted process, in its own good time. The foreigners waited.

Glover had other things on his mind. Tsuru came and told him one morning, there was no doubt, she was pregnant. She also told him directly she had been married before — something she had referred to obliquely, mentioned in passing — and that she had a daughter by the marriage.

"Marriage not good," she said. "Husband divorce. Child adopt. I come here."

She kneeled in front of him, hands on her knees, head bowed, waiting for his judgement, ready to accept it. Like Maki she knew most foreigners disowned the children they fathered here, abandoned their musume as soon as there was complication, responsibility. She also knew he had married Sono, stood by her. Ito had told her the whole story, said he was a good man, honourable. But she did not dare expect.

If he told her to go, she would go. She couldn't face bearing another child to give away. She couldn't bring up a child on her own. If he said No, she would pray to Jizo, visit the doctor at Naminohira.

Glover took her by the hand, raised her to her feet, looked right into her eyes, smiled.

"Tsuru."

He kissed her forehead, her hair, held her to him.

Ito and Kido came to Ipponmatsu. As always they came late at night, for safety. But now there was nothing fugitive about them. They carried themselves with a new swagger, a confidence borne of success. The battle had been a triumph. Kido spoke of the enemy's greater numbers, their own tactics, the western formation, the deployment of artillery. He thanked Glover for his indispensable part in the victory, took full credit for his own military strategy.

Ito spoke like a poet or a preacher. The very spareness of his language, the detail, brought the scene to life.

"Two great armies. Four borders war. Decide fate of Japan. One side Tokugawa Shogun, fourteenth in line, go back 200 years. Other side Mikado, Son of Heaven, born to rule country. Only one side can be victorious.

"Tokugawa army very large, very strong. Cavalry lead attack, ride out of mist. Cold morning. Thunder of hooves on ground. Foot soldiers follow, running in formation. Carry Shogun's banner and flags of clans loyal to him. Some infantry have rifles but most have spear and sword, bow and arrow. Wear old-time armour, leather and iron. Helmet with crest, mask on face. Thunder of hooves. Mist start to clear, sun flash on swords and armour. Other army Choshu clan, led by Kido-san. Also Tora clan led by Sakamoto-san. Clan banners flying. All wear kingire, streamer of yellow silk, show loyalty to Emperor. Thunder of hooves. Rebel infantry hold firm. Wait. Front row fire volley, fusillade. While they reload, second row step forward, fire. Horses and riders crash to ground. From back, cannon open fire over heads, hit enemy infantry. More gunfire then hand to hand fight with sword and bayonet. All fight with courage and honour. Long battle. At end Choshu victorious, drive Shogun's army back. Smoke from cannon and gunfire hang over battlefield. Sun streak through.

"I walk across field. Many dead and dying. Men and horses. Some blown apart, only bodies, no arms or legs, or only arms and legs, or head hacked from body, face still look fierce. Is noble death. Samurai death."

Ito paused for the first time since he'd started to speak, became even more sombre. "Sakamoto-san also fall, die in battle."

"A great loss," said Glover, remembering Sakamoto's calm presence, his insistence that the clans unite.

"But good death," said Ito.

"Yes," said Glover. "Of course."

"I bow to all warriors on field," said Ito. "Make tanka poem.

> Brave warriors lie slain —
> Choshu, Tosa, Tokugawa —
> for the sake of Japan.
> The smoke of battle clears.
> Above, the red sun."

The rumours continued, fabrications that had the ring of myth. One particularly persistent story was that the Shogun, Iemochi, had died, and this time it proved true. He had contracted beri-beri, died a miserable death in Osaka, the first Tokugawa Shogun in two centuries to die outside Edo. While plans were made for the succession — a poisoned chalice to be passed on — hostilities against the Choshu were ceased for the time being.

Less than six months later the Emperor also died. His death was announced as festivities were about to commence for the coming of the new year. Festive decorations of paper and silk which festooned the city streets were hastily removed and a fifty-day period of mourning commenced.

"First the Shogun, now the Mikado," said Glover, looking out from the Foreigners' Club at winter streets now suddenly bereft of these splashes of colour. "One might almost think the whole thing had been orchestrated."

"It certainly thickens the plot very nicely," said Walsh.

It had been hoped the new Shogun, Yoshinobu, a young man, unskilled in the ways of the world, would simply hand over power, make a dignified surrender. But his advisers were adamant, he must not do so.

The new Mikado, Mutsuhito, was even younger, at fifteen not much more than a child. The hope for him was that he would not display his predecessor's truculent dislike of foreigners, would embrace the rebel cause with enthusiasm rather than reluctance.

Again there was a cessation in open hostilities, a moratorium on acts of war. The foreign community waited, apprehensive.

Glover made a trip to Edo, leaving Tsuru in the care of a nurse, a doctor on call. Her time was close.

In Edo he attended to a few small business matters, met up again with Parkes and Satow at the Legation.

"Straws in the wind," said Parkes. "There's talk of more treaty ports being opened up, beginning with Hyogo."

"I'd heard as much," said Glover. "So the new Shogun's been advised to forge ahead, strengthen links with the West."

"It would seem so," said Parkes. "To which end I've been invited to Osaka Castle to meet him in person."

"The Shogun?" asked Glover, surprised.

"None other," said Parkes.

"Now that *is* a new departure."

"Indeed," said Parkes, "though I fear it's a last desperate throw of the dice. He's become an anachronism. His time is at an end."

"The *Japan Times* carried an article about him," said Satow, "based on an account by one of his attendants. It's quite beyond belief. The fellow has been in preparation for this all his life. He spends his days in lavish indolence. He rises late, takes an inordinate amount of time having his hair elaborately dressed before eating an extravagant breakfast of delicacies imported from every corner of his domain. His every garment is of silk, and he never wears anything twice. During the day he may grant audience to one or two of his advisers, then he simply follows his fancy, playing polo, practising his calligraphy, engaging in an archery contest — which he always wins! — drifting in a boat on the lake. Evenings are given over to various diversions in the Palace of Ladies, where said ladies entertain him most royally. All in all, a most taxing round of duties!"

"Mister Satow is most anxious to observe this way of life at first hand," said Parkes. "And I must confess to a certain curiosity myself!"

"I'm sure it'll be enlightening."

"Roches will be there of course. The man is clearly unable to recognise a lost cause."

"I hear Harris has been recalled to Washington."

"And good riddance to him!"

Glover laughed. "I rather warmed to him."

"A thoroughly disagreeable fellow," said Parkes. "Pigheaded and downright rude. Oh, granted, he did good work in forcing through the initial treaty, but his attitude to the rest of us was most ungracious."

"A true barbarian," said Glover.

"Indeed."

Satow proposed a toast. "To British diplomacy, and tact."

"Diplomacy and tact."

Before leaving Edo, he had one more visit to pay. Late in the afternoon, the sky grey, the air cold, he hired a *jinrikisha* to take him to the edge of the entertainment district. He had torn the notice from the *Japan Times*, glanced at it once more as the rickshaw bumped and trundled through narrow rutted backstreets.

One week only! Risley's International Circus!! The Greatest Show in Edo, if not on Earth!!! Marvel at astonishing, nay, breathtaking performances! Thrill to the equestrian skills of real American cowboys as they re-enact a bloodcurdling Wild West skirmish with savage Red Indian tribesmen!! See our troupe of Chinese acrobats defy gravity as they take flight and fly through the air!!! Hold your breath as Professor Risley himself, the Circus Owner and Ringmaster, late of Covent Garden in London, enters a cage with a savage Malay Tiger!!!! Will he survive the encounter? Come along and find out!

Risley was delighted to see him, roared out his name. "Glover!"

"Professor!" said Glover, shaking him by the hand.

In his tent, over tea brewed thick and black and sweetened with sugar, Risley brought Glover up to date with his various extravagant madcap schemes.

"Real milk, this," he said, indicating the tea. "Brought in half a dozen dairy cattle from Frisco, cows and their calves. Damn near didn't make it — the voyage took two months and the poor beasts were dying of thirst. Couldn't bear to see them suffer and thought I'd have to slaughter them. Then there was a miracle, a downpour of rain. Managed to collect enough water for all of us — man and beast! But then to top everything, it whipped up into a full-blown tropical storm, a typhoon. The schooner was blown off course and we were damn near shipwrecked north of Yokohama. But somehow we managed to ride it out, make landfall, and each and every cow and calf safe and sound."

"Remarkable!" said Glover. "The hand of providence is clearly still beneficent!"

"Set up a little dairy business and it's flourishing. Had to deal with the problem of keeping things cool in the dreadful summer heat, so I built me an ice-house!

Set it up near the harbour, brought in hundreds of tons of ice from Tientsin. Turned a tidy profit!"

Glover laughed. "You're indefatigable, and no mistake!"

"Good word that," said Risley. "I shall use it on my handbills." He placed the words in the air. "*The Indefatigable Professor Risley!*"

"It certainly has a ring to it!"

"And what about you, Glover? I hear you're involved in all manner of intrigue."

"These are what the Chinese call Interesting Times!"

"And what about those charming little women of yours, those lovely butterflies?"

"Maki just disappeared. Was gone when I came back from Scotland." As always when he thought of her he felt a curious pang, a stab of melancholy. "Tsuru is expecting my child, in fact the arrival is imminent."

"I take it congratulations are in order?"

"Indeed. I've grown fond of her. We'll marry."

"Do the decent thing. Good for you!"

"Now," said Glover. "How's Yaban?"

Risley led him out past the main tent, to a smaller covered area, guarded by two Japanese warriors, armed with pikes. They stepped back to let Risley pass, he lifted back the tentflap and he entered, Glover following behind. The light in the place was dim, the smell unmistakable, raw meat and blood-soaked sawdust, the rank animal odour of the beast itself. It was curled in the corner of an iron-barred cage, rose slowly as if to greet them, imperious, admit them to its lair, its domain. It sniffed the air, glanced at Risley, fixed its gaze on Glover. Once more he felt its immense power, the mystery of its sheer otherness. Its look was predatory, a threat; he sensed himself weighed up as so much meat, flesh and sinew on the bone.

Risley held up a lantern and the light flashed in the animal's eyes, glinted, demonic. It bared its great fangs, rumbled a deep muted growl in its belly.

"Aye, big fella," said Glover. "It's good to see you."

The animal growled again, glared at him, implacable.

Still holding the tiger's gaze, Glover spoke to Risley. "The notice said you'll go in the cage with him."

"I've rehearsed it. We still have to resort to laudanum, though not enough to make him groggy. And we make sure he's well fed — a hog or two usually do the trick! But if he should decide he fancies a roly-poly Englishman for pudding, these stout fellows are on hand with their spears!"

The show drew a reasonable audience, given that all forms of entertainment had been so recently discouraged during the period of national mourning for the Emperor. There was an equal mix of Japanese, eager to see the spectacle, and bored foreigners desperate for a little stimulation. A crowd of young bucks roistered and swaggered through the place, took over a whole section of seating, rollicked and hollered, cursed up a storm, swigged liquor from their own flasks, jeered and catcalled at the performers.

The lights were dimmed then there was a sudden flash, a magnesium flare, and a troupe of Chinese acrobats leapt and bounded into a dragon dance, drums and cymbals banging and clashing. The rowdies howled, cheered, stamped their feet. The acrobats climbed thin bamboo poles, swung and spun and launched into the air, seemed indeed to fly, landing so lightly they hardly touched the ground before leaping again, almost running up the poles and soaring once more. Risley's publicity was right. It defied all physical laws, was breathtaking.

The acrobats were chased out of the ring by another troupe, half a dozen men in light samurai armour. Again they spun, dizzying, clashed flashing blades in a choreographed sword fight, balletic and graceful and military in its precision. Glover wavered a moment, lightheaded, remembered the attack on the Legation, the swordblade an inch from his tingling scalp. The young bucks yelled and stamped their feet, all pigheaded bravado.

The Wild West scene caught their fancy. The redskins were clearly Chinese in long wigs, their faces daubed with war paint. They whooped and yelped as they urged their ponies in a circle round the beleaguered pioneers in their covered wagon. The groundlings whooped and yelped along with them, howled like wolves. When the cowboys came charging to the rescue, chasing the Indians down and firing at them from horseback, the bucks roared and cheered, quite beyond themselves with drunken excitement. One stood and fired a pistol in the air, to the huge amusement of his friends. Glover saw Risley step from the shadows, size up the situation. The young fool sat down again and one of his friends took the gun from him, for safekeeping. Risley stepped back.

An oompah band struck up, raucous, between acts; the Wild West extravaganza was followed by a gang of jugglers and acrobats, fire-eaters, tumbling midgets; they all exited to a drunken fanfare, rasping brass; the groundlings howled their derisive approval, laughed.

Then, with a dramatic drumroll, the thunder of timpani, the mood changed. A huge cube, draped in shimmering velvet, was carried by a squad of workmen and placed in the centre of the ring. Risley spoke through a megaphone, stilled the audience by the intensity, the sheer drama, of his delivery. "Ladies and gentlemen! I crave your indulgence for the final act of the evening! For this, I am putting my very life at risk!"

The drapes were removed revealing the iron cage, the tiger, suddenly uncovered, pacing back and forth, restless, snarling. There was an audible gasp from the audience, and even the young bucks had the decency to be impressed.

"This magnificent beast has been brought at considerable expense from the Malay Straits where until recently he roamed the jungles, the lord of all he surveyed. He is the finest specimen you're ever likely to see of *Panthera Tigris Malayensis*, the great Malay tiger, the embodiment of strength, power and mystery. I bring you Yaban!"

The audience applauded, the Japanese laughing behind their hands at the appropriateness of the name.

"It has been argued that such beasts cannot be tamed. They are man-eaters, fearsomely strong, capable of tearing a man in two with one snap of those mighty jaws."

As he spoke, Risley moved towards the gate of the cage, stopped.

The realisation spread through the audience that this man was indeed about to enter the cage. There was a sudden hush, broken only by a cough, an inappropriate laugh that was instantly stilled. Risley put down his megaphone, held up a key; he opened the lock, entered the cage, locked the door behind him. The tiger turned to face him and he picked up a whip, a wooden chair.

For the next ten or fifteen minutes he cracked his whip, goaded the tiger to walk round the cage, climb on an upturned wooden tub, leap through a hoop. By sheer force of will he kept the beast at bay, bade it perform, turn tricks.

He ended with a flourish, turned his back on the tiger and bowed, walked calmly to the door, unlocked it and stepped out. The crowd roared.

"Impressive," said Glover afterwards.

"I don't mind admitting," said Risley, "I was in a sweat. Something was telling me I shouldn't presume on the beast's patience with me. Just something in his eyes. A few more minutes and I fear he might have mauled me."

Glover took a last look at the tiger, saw exactly what Risley meant. There was no containing this power, except by sheer brute force. As he stared at the beast he felt it stare right back at him, defiant. And there was something more he couldn't define, a sense of the beast's awareness, its consciousness; it was utterly alive, self-existent, other; and he felt something akin to recognition, identification; for a moment he *was* the tiger, looking back at himself.

He minded the last line of the poem young Mitchell had told him.

Did he who made the lamb make thee?

He bowed to the tiger.

"*Yaban-san. Sayonara.*"

The beast bared its teeth.

The tiger's face appeared before him in a dream. He had to hold its gaze, not blink or flicker. If he looked away it would swipe him with its great paw, rampage through his home. Sono was next door, giving birth, but that was impossible, the tiger had already destroyed her. It was Tsuru, and at the same time Maki, and he had to protect them both, hold steady, face the tiger down. But he was consumed with foreboding, knew the tiger's power was great and if it broke free there would be no end to the havoc it would wreak. He woke in a sweat, shouting out. Maki calmed him. No, Tsuru.

Tsuru.

She gave birth a week later. A message was brought to him at his office and he ran all the way back, along the Bund, folk stepping aside, startled, to let him pass, up Minami Yamate, in at the gate of Ipponmatsu and through the front door.

The Japanese doctor stood in the hallway, stonefaced. The bedroom door was closed.

God.

No.

The doctor smiled.

"Guraba-san. You father. Baby girl."

Yes.

Yes!

A squall of a cry. He pushed open the door, saw Tsuru with the baby held to her, wrapped in a shawl. She looked exhausted but calm, smiled out at him from a deep quiet place. The baby was a wee red puckered thing, like the son he'd lost. But somehow he knew the life was there, the will to survive. She held her up, the tiny hands grasping, tiny eyes screwed shut.

"Bonny wee thing," he said, taking the baby, overwhelmed for the second time in his life by the sheer miraculousness of this. He heard what he'd said, line from an old song, from back home in that other life. Burns again. *Bonny wee thing, lovely wee thing, canty wee thing.*

Tsuru spoke, quiet but strong, from that place he'd never go.

"We call her Hana."

They'd already discussed it. Tomu for a boy, Hana for a girl. It meant Blossom. Was good. And it sounded like Anna, or Hannah.

"Hana," he said. "*Hai!*"

Hana.

Later the doctor asked to speak to him. He had given Tsuru something to make her sleep; the baby was being looked after by the nurse.

"Baby girl very strong," said the doctor. "Very healthy. Be very well."

364

"I thought as much," said Glover. The baby cried, lusty, on the other side of the door. "She has a fine set of lungs in her!"

The doctor looked serious again. "Sorry to say is complication for Tsuru-san."

Glover tensed, a feeling like cold stone in his belly. "What kind of complication?"

"She have baby before?"

"Aye. She was married very young."

"Maybe was difficult birth."

"She didn't say."

"I think is almost sure. Make complication this time. And maybe she not be able to have more children."

The baby cried again, was shooshed to calm.

"What are the chances?"

"Not good."

"But otherwise she'll be fine?"

"I think so. Just no more children."

Glover was quiet for a while, thanked the doctor, bowed, paid him handsomely for his time and trouble.

"*Domo arigato gosaimasu.*"

"*Do itashimashite.*"

The simple everyday formality of the words, the little politenesses in the face of events, imposing order. Thank you. It's nothing.

He went quietly into the bedroom. Tsuru was in a deep sleep. He smoothed her hair back from her face, kissed her cheek.

They held a simple ceremony in the garden at Ipponmatsu on a cool spring morning, the sky washed a pure clear duck-egg blue, a few high clouds scudding. There was traffic out in the bay, junks and cargo boats, ominous warships. The *Ho Sho Maru* was somewhere at sea, on its way from Aberdeen. The slip-dock had arrived, was under construction, would change the whole face of the port, the whole face of Japan. The bay would be lined with shipyards; this was just the beginning.

Ito was in Kagoshima, planning strategy, the next phase of the rebellion. Walsh was in Shanghai, securing another deal. Mackenzie was in retirement, in Edinburgh. They had been the witnesses when he'd married Sono; such a short time ago but it seemed a lifetime. Two more years and he'd be thirty. It was true what they said, time accelerated with every year that passed.

The constants from that first ceremony were the minister, Cameron, and the Buddhist priest. The witnesses were the doctor and Tsuru's nurse along with Harrison and Groom.

"So there are two Grooms today!" said Harrison.

The ceremony might have little or no legal validity. For Glover it was simple acknowledgement of Tsuru, of Hana, conferring on them the status of wife and daughter, at least in the eyes of the community here.

The minister read the vows, Glover and Tsuru repeated them.

Forsaking all others.

As long as ye both shall live.

The priest chanted his invocation, sonorous and resonant, bowed as always to Amida, the Buddha of the Pure Land.

Namu Amida Butsu.

He lit incense, wafted its fragrant smoke over them, clanged a handbell.

Glover held Tsuru's hand, said it again, "Forsaking all others." And she bowed to him, smiled, her eyes brimming.

The change, when it came, came quickly. The combined rebel army, under the banner of the Mikado, marched on Osaka Castle. There were skirmishes, a last desperate resistance from the Shogun's troops, but again the rebels, better organised, better armed, were victorious. The Choshu fleet, with the recently delivered *Ho Sho Maru* as its flagship, and styling itself the Imperial Japanese Navy, won a decisive final battle at sea.

The Shogun fled from the city, dressed in monk's robes, took refuge in the sanctuary of a Buddhist monastery in the hills to the north. He sent a messenger bearing a scroll, impressed with his official seal, signed in his elegant, fluid calligraphy, renouncing all power and pledging his allegiance to the Emperor in whose divine hands he now placed his fate. The Tokugawa era was at an end.

There were factions calling for the Shogun to be hunted down and executed.

The French Consul, Roches, paid for his misreading of the oracle, his faith in the Shogun; he was summoned home to Paris in some disgrace. That left Parkes in the prime position of authority and power among the western diplomats, and he used his influence with the Daimyo to dissuade him from ordering the Shogun's disembowelment, the removal of his head.

In spite of the Daimyo's reassurances, and Glover's faith in Ito and the rest of the rebels, there was still widespread fear among the foreign community. One of the Shogun's last official acts had been to convey a message to Parkes expressing his regret that he could no longer guarantee the safety of any foreign resident. Roches, on his departure, fired a parting shot, declared with Gallic insouciance that the Mikado's armies would set fire to every foreign settlement in the land, butcher every man, woman and child who survived the conflagration.

The Shogun's desperate strategy of opening further ports to the West was extended to Kobe, and a delegation of diplomats and traders, among them Glover and Satow, went there for the inauguration of the new Customs House. They were wandering aimlessly around the area when a rag-tag gang of samurai warriors rode out of the town towards them.

Glover realised something was wrong when the men stopped and dismounted, lined up in straggled ranks and started loading their rifles. Then he realised there was something familiar about the commander marshalling them, something in his demeanour, his bearing. Glover looked again, saw it was Takashi, and in the same moment Takashi saw him, knew him.

"Jesus Christ!" said Glover, and he dived for cover as a volley of shots flew high in the air, ripped into the front of the building, damaged the roof tiles, tore the British flag to shreds. Glover peered out through a window, saw the samurai in disarray, some of them jolted backwards by the recoil from their weapons, the use of which they clearly hadn't mastered. Takashi was screaming at them and time itself seemed to slow as they began laboriously to reload. But before they could regroup and fire again there was the clatter of hooves and a detachment of British cavalry, summoned from the quayside by the sound of gunfire, were riding towards them. The samurai were swift to remount and they rode off, break-neck, followed by the marines, sabres drawn, ready for battle.

Glover stepped outside, where the rest of the foreigners, Satow among them, picked themselves up and dusted themselves off, looking around, dazed and unbelieving, at the damage to the building.

"Fucking hell!" said Glover.

Satow was already scribbling in his notebook.

He recorded the incident in yet another piece for the *Japan Times*, which appeared a week later.

The troop of samurai, he wrote, were a motley disaffected crew from a number of clans, but predominantly, it seemed, from the local Bizen. They were pro-Mikado, had been part of the rebel alliance, but were also staunchly anti-barbarian. Their commander, incensed at the sight of the foreign devils casually taking charge of the town, had ordered his troops to open fire on them. Only the fact that the samurai had just recently been armed with their American rifles prevented a massacre. They hadn't mastered the use of the weapons, didn't understand how to line up a target in the sight, fired wildly in the air. They had been driven off, pursued by the marines.

But the Bizen were better horsemen than they were riflemen, and they knew the twists and turns of the roads and pathways, made good their escape into woodland at the edge of town.

Satow's tone, as ever, was detached, amused. The British horsemen, he wrote, executed a brilliant cavalry charge down an empty road, returning empty-handed except for a few trophies. These spoils of war included sandals, straw *kasa* rain-hats and a bundle of papers, tied with twine, which Satow was handed to translate and which proved to be highly charged love letters from a young woman. Satow concluded the piece by appealing for calm, repeated his own conviction that this was a random and isolated incident, in no way indicative of a threat from the new regime. But once more, throughout Japan, foreign residences were barricaded and sandbagged, protected by armed guards. Glover, like Satow, still had faith, but the presence of baby Hana made him mindful of any threat, and he doubled the defences at Ipponmatsu.

★ ★ ★

Ito arrived one evening, unannounced, gave Glover absolute reassurance that there was no danger. Rogue elements, renegades from any clan, would be rooted out. In fact Takashi had already been apprehended and would commit seppuku in front of witnesses from the foreign community. He would be punished for his crime, but as a samurai warrior loyal to his clan and his Emperor, he would be allowed to die with honour.

Ito stood, straightbacked and dignified as he said this, and Glover could already see a change in him. This was his old drinking companion, his *ancient trusty drouthy crony*, carouser and reveller and singer of lusty songs about pillowing his head in some beauty's lap. But that particular song had continued with the line about seizing power and leading the nation. Now he was in the process of doing exactly that. Ito the revolutionary, the rebel, was transforming himself into Ito the statesman.

He even displayed respect for his fallen enemy, the Shogun, telling of his fall with that same resonance as he had used to describe the Four Borders Battle, the speak of myth, turning the hard, spare facts into legend.

"Tokugawa time over. Osaka Castle fall. Choshu, Satsuma victorious once more. Shogun go, sit at feet of Buddha. Now Mikado make new Japan. We build."

Again he had composed a tanka poem for the occasion.

Cold rain falls.
Defeated, he lays aside
his fine clothes,
flees to the Buddha
for refuge.

"Now," he said. "Let's drink!"

A month later Glover, for his part in the rebellion, was invited to join a deputation visiting Osaka Castle to see it for themselves. Parkes was there, and Satow, and they rode slowly in procession led by the Choshu and Satsuma Daimyo, Ito and Godai, a contingent of samurai from both clans.

Again it rained, a cold needling downpour that reminded Glover of home. They rode in through the gates, entered the castle keep, and the scene that met them was one of destruction, desolation; the place had been battered by artillery fire, bombarded by cannonshot, then sacked and looted and put to the torch. Great gaps had been blasted in the walls and where the palace had stood was a burned-out ruin, jagged blocks of masonry jutting above what had been a tiled floor. Abandoned weapons, damaged armour, scorched and seared by the heat of the flames, lay scattered here and there, some of it warped and tangled, melted in the fire.

Glover felt none of the triumph he might have expected. Instead there was an emptiness, a kind of melancholy, shared also by Satow and Parkes.

"Depressing," said Satow.

"It's not so long since I sat in that very palace," said Parkes, "being fêted by the Shogun. And I found him the handsomest and most refined of men."

"Albeit one unfitted for life in the present age," said Satow.

"It makes one wonder what we may have unleashed in the land," said Parkes.

The rain drove harder, advanced in squalls across the courtyard. The Emperor's banner flapped above the ruins. If Glover had any misgivings he kept them to himself, said nothing.

The three men were invited to attend, as witnesses, the execution, the ritual suicide, of Takashi. The Satsuma had now set up their headquarters in the town, in a spacious temple in its own grounds, and this was where the execution was to take place.

"Vile business," said Parkes, uncomfortable at having to be there.

Satow on the other hand seemed almost to relish the prospect of observing the proceedings at first hand.

Glover, like Parkes, had no wish to attend, but felt it would be an insult to his Japanese hosts to turn down the invitation. He tholed being there, endured it, but he felt his guts clench, his palms sweat, as the prisoner was brought into the temple hall.

Takashi was dressed in robes of rough, dark-blue cotton, walked with the dignity befitting a samurai, in no way cowed or fearful. He was flanked by armed guards in helmets and breastplates, and a few paces behind him, respectful like a retainer, walked a man in grey.

Ito whispered to Glover. "He is *kaishaku*."

"Executioner?" said Glover.

"No," said Ito. "Friend."

Takashi stepped up onto a low dais draped with pure white cloth on which had been spread a bright red thick felt rug. He stared ahead, kneeled down on the rug, the man in grey, the kaishaku, kneeling beside the platform.

Takashi bowed, not victim but supplicant. He looked each of the witnesses straight in the eye, bowed to them individually. He held Glover's gaze only a moment but in that moment Glover felt Takashi was already somewhere else, beyond this place, beyond even hate or disdain. The look was piercing, cold, detached.

An official in white robes stood in front of Takashi, bowed and presented him with a black lacquer tray on which lay a short wakizashi dagger, unsheathed. Takashi bowed in return, took the knife, held it before him with a kind of reverence, placed it down in front of him. Then he slipped the robe off his shoulders, let it fall about him, sat naked to the waist. Careful and unhurried, he gathered the sleeves and tucked them under his knees, to prevent him falling backward.

The cold in the hall deepened. Every sound was magnified in the tense silence, the sudden muffled bark of a cough, awkward, a scuff, a shuffle as one of the observers, uncomfortable, shifted position, then the studied movements of Takashi himself as he readied himself for the last act of his life.

374

He took the dagger in his right hand, held it again before his eyes, seemed almost to caress it. Then he drew in a quick sharp intake of breath, and without flinching, drove the blade hard and true, pierced the left side of his belly. The sound that followed was a faint, collective gasp from the witnesses; no matter that they had known what was to happen, had prepared themselves, the harsh actuality was shocking, brutal, took them aback.

Slowly, inch by inch and still unflinching, Takashi drew the blade across from left to right, cut through his own flesh. Parkes looked away. Satow took in every detail, the sound of the knife, the red wound opening, would commit it later to his journal. Glover fixed his gaze on the man's face, stoic, impassive, focused inward.

When the blade reached the right of the abdomen, Takashi gave it a final twist, a last cut upward, withdrew it, bloodied, and placed it once more in front of him. Then he leaned forward, stretching out his neck. His face for the first time contorted in a grimace of pain, but still he made no sound. The kaishaku leapt to his feet, in one movement drew his sword, raised it and brought it down, beheaded Takashi with a single swift stroke.

The severed head thudded to the floor; the blood flowed, seeped into the felt rug, deepened the red.

Glover took a last look at the face, suddenly lifeless, eyes shut, the corners of the mouth clenched, turned down in that mask of pain.

Outside in the cold, Parkes had to steady himself, gagged and retched, ready to vomit. Satow was chattering. "I didn't find it at all disgusting." He was already scribbling in a pocket notebook. "In fact, I thought it a decent and decorous ceremony, rather more respectable than what is produced for public entertainment outside Newgate Prison!"

Glover closed his eyes, could not erase the image of the man's face, that death mask. And this was how Matsuo had died, brutally, painfully, for the crime of breaking an obscure vow. This code was too harsh, too barbarous. And yet.

Ito approached him, bowed.

"Emperor's justice seen to be done."

"But with honour."

"So."

A clear signal was being sent out. The regime of the Emperor was hospitable to the West and no further attacks on foreigners would be condoned or even tolerated.

The Emperor himself moved to Edo, the former stronghold of the Tokugawa clan, which would now be renamed Tokyo, the Eastern Capital. There he occupied the former Shogun's palace, and he too assumed a new name; from now he would be known as Meiji, the Enlightened Ruler, and the year would be designated *Meiji Gan Nen*, the first year of his reign.

CHAPTER
THIRTEEN

Maki

Nagasaki, 1869–70

Walsh was leaving, getting out, heading home. He came round to Ipponmatsu for a last drink. "Here's to the new Japan!" said Glover.

"Good luck to them!" said Walsh.

"And what do you mean by that?"

"You know me, Tom. Quit while I'm ahead." He looked at Glover over his glass of whisky. "Maybe you should do the same."

"Quit?"

Walsh laughed. "I guess it's true. You really *don't* know the meaning of the word!"

"Why should I quit? We still have so much to do."

"We?"

"I'm part of this, Jack."

"I know you've invested heavily in this place, Tom. Hell, you bankrolled their goddamn revolution! But financially the situation's unstable."

"That's to be expected, after a revolution!"

"They've overreached themselves. They can't pay back their debts."

"Not for a while, no."

"And if they do pay you back, their currency's so devalued you'll lose heavily."

"I'm in this for more than the money."

Walsh chuckled. "You *have* come a long way!"

"I belong here. We'll make this work."

"*We* again."

"Aye. That's the way I see it."

Tsuru was putting Hana to bed, brought her in to say goodnight to him. The child was barely awake, bleary with sleep, clutched a doll made of coloured cloth. He kissed the top of her wee head, noticed Walsh smiling to himself.

"Quite the family man!"

Walsh said goodnight to Tsuru, who nodded a polite "*Oyasumi nasai.*" Glover knew she didn't approve of him, understood why.

The two men stepped outside, into the cool night, and walked together as far as the gate. Walsh was heading down to the Sakura for one last visit, across *Shian Bashi* and *Omoikiri Bashi.*

"There are *some* things I'll miss about this place!" He chuckled. "Don't suppose I can tempt you to join me? I mean, a family man can still have a fling!"

"I'm fine," said Glover. And he meant it.

Walsh was right. The delay, the devaluation meant his debts had accumulated to an alarming degree. Jardine's alone were pressing him for payment of $100,000 he owed them, money he had borrowed on behalf of the clans. With the fighting effectively over, the arms trade had declined. Glover's tea business had over-expanded and was failing to turn a profit, his trading in silk had run its course, as had his dealing in opium.

Groom, Harrison and Ringer decided to go their separate ways. They bore Glover no illwill; there was simply a sense that they were no longer able to follow his lead, an implied, if understated, criticism of his headlong rush to support the revolution at all costs.

He argued the revolution was just the beginning; what was required now was industrialisation on a grand scale; the Japanese must mine their own coal, forge their own steel, build their own ships.

They respected his vision, but were no longer committed to it. Instead of expansion, they argued for diversification, specialisation. Ringer would take over the tea factories in his own name. Harrison would set up his own company, returning to property investment as his principal activity. Groom would move to Shanghai, specialise once more in currency exchange.

It took a whole day of argument, negotiation, to thrash out a broad agreement. There were harsh words, accusations, claims and counter-claims. The discussion grew heated, but was grounded in their common respect for one another. The sums the three men would advance him would go some way towards clearing his debts, but it was not enough, not by a long way.

At the end of it, Glover shook hands with all of them, thanked them, wished them well. When they'd left his office he slumped at his desk, exhausted. The air was thick with the fug of tobacco smoke. His head ached.

On the desk was his little collection of mementos, reminders, good luck charms: the bamboo token, the paper butterfly, the silver dollar, the itzibu coin. He had added to these a length of yellow-coloured silk, Ito's kingire, badge of allegiance to the Emperor. Behind these sat the little Daruma doll, child's toy, its painted face fierce. He cuffed its head, knocked it over, just to see it right itself, bounce back. Eight times up.

He pulled on his coat, went out into the street, and instead of heading straight home he walked along the waterfront, breathed the evening air, tried to clear his head. He liked this time of day, the sky beginning to darken but still streaked with light, the yellow lamps lit in shops and houses, on the boats at anchor in the bay. He passed the market, on a whim turned in and walked through its narrow passageways, its clutter of stalls, lost himself in it, surrendered to the cries of traders, the smells that assailed him, of incense and kerosene and hot smoky oil, musky spices and dried fish. It was the end of the day, some of the traders already packing up, and it made him feel a kind of melancholy, an emptiness, a nostalgia for something he couldn't name. So many lives being lived. So few he would ever know. This place he moved through. This, here, now. The warmth and the sadness of it. The evening light.

A few yards ahead a young woman, her back to him, a shawl round her shoulders, was paying for her few purchases and for some reason the stallholder seemed to be speaking to her roughly. He couldn't make out the words — even after all these years much of the language was still impenetrable to him — but the tone was unmistakably harsh. The man threw down her purchases, she picked them up and moved on. Glover still couldn't see her face, but there was something so familiar in the way she moved, the turn of her head, the line of her neck: she reminded him of someone.

Then he saw she had a child with her, a small boy; she took the boy by the hand and hurried away. Glover turned to go then stopped. He knew who it was she had brought to mind. He started walking again. It was just coincidence, a passing resemblance. Then he stopped again, caught. He had to follow her, see for himself. But she had disappeared down one of the aisles, could have turned in any direction, might be deeper into the market or out in the street. Which way to turn? The walkways were crowded, people blocking his way at every turn. Now the smells and the noise were an annoyance, the calls of *Irrashaimase* an irritating litany, the dried fish stink sickening.

The whole business was ridiculous. He would never find her. And in any case, the resemblance was probably imagined, sheer fancy born of his tiredness, his state of mind. He stopped again, turned to retrace his steps, head home, and she stepped out in front of him, distracted. She was suddenly, undeniably, irrevocably there. Maki.

Dear God.

Maki.

She saw him, let go of the boy's hand a moment, put her own hand to her throat, and her eyes widened as she recognised him, and the sound that came from her was part gasp, part choked sob, a cry from deep. And the hand went to her mouth, to stifle the sound, then as if remembering the boy again she took his hand once more, pulled him close to her.

"Maki," he said, felt the surge of emotion in his chest. Once as a boy, in Banchory at the falls, he'd seen the salmon in their upstream rush leap out of the water, flip in the air. That was the feeling.

Or a flurry of birds startled from cover.

"Maki!"

She looked bewildered, in a dream, as she carefully set down the basket she was carrying, held the boy even tighter, bowed.

"Guraba-san."

"Christ, Maki, it's me! Tom! Your gaijin. The hairy barbarian. Yaban!"

"I thought you go home," she said. "To Sucoturando. Not come back to Japan in this life."

"I did," he said. "Go home, I mean. But I've been back three, four years."

"So long time?" she said.

"A lot's happened," he said. "A hell of a lot. We say, a lot of water under the bridge."

"*Hai*," she said. "*So desu.* Water."

"So much has changed."

"Much change," she said. "Everything."

"Upheaval," he said, gesturing with his arms, trying to encompass it all.

"Water under bridge."

"Aye."

She'd spoken quietly, now fell silent, pushed back a stray hair that had fallen across her face. She looked tired, a deep weariness in her eyes. She wore no jewellery and her clothes were simple, a dark cotton robe tied with an obi sash at the waist. The boy was burying his face in the robe, hiding there, clinging to her. He peered out, stared up, awed and fearful, at Glover, who looked back, saw him for the first time, this wee frightened creature, eyes wide. There was something in the features, the skin paler than his mother's, the hair not jet black but light brown, and something too in the eyes that looked out at him. And in the moment Glover knew, beyond all doubt, the way he'd known with Annie and her lad Jamie, at Brig o' Balgownie in that other life.

He crouched down, spoke quietly to the boy. "*O namae wa?*"

The boy buried his face again, hid.

"His name is Shinsaburo," said Maki.

Glover bowed to the boy. "Shinsaburo-san. *Yoroshiko onegai shimasu.*"

The boy peered out again, squinted at him with one eye. Glover covered his own face with his hands, peeked out. The boy was still unsure, moved round behind his mother for safety.

Glover stood up.

"His father is gaijin?"

"Yaban," she said with the faintest hint of a smile, sad and tired, ironic. "You know."

He asked the question. "My son?"

She nodded. "*Hai. So desu.*"

He drew in a deep breath. "You're sure?"

She looked right at him, right into him. "All that time, was nobody else. You only one."

He reached out a hand to the boy. The boy turned away, his again.

His son. Shinsaburo. Flesh of his flesh.

"God," he said. "Maki. Why didn't you tell me?"

"I try," she said. "You not there. Woman at house tell me you gone, maybe not come back."

"Tsuru?"

"*So desu.*"

"That's why you left?"

She nodded. "Happen all the time. Gaijin go away. Not want to know. Then not easy for me. I pray to Jizo, go to doctor to lose child. But not do it. No hard heart." She held the boy close again, tight. "So, have to go. Not work at Sakura. Go to home village."

"Christ, Maki, if I'd known!"

Her shoulders hunched, her head sagged forward. "I also not know. Not know you. Not know what you do."

He tried to take it in, adjust.

"Christ!"

"Bad time for me," said Maki. "After baby born, people see he is gaijin child. Many not kind to me. Shout at me. Sometime throw things at me in street."

"Just now," he said, suddenly making sense of what he'd seen. The stallholder had been angry with her, brusque. "That man just now, he said something?"

"*Hai,*" she said. "But not matter. Happen all the time. Is nothing."

"No," he said, "it's *not* nothing! It's bloody insufferable!"

The anger welled up in him. He moved as if to double back and find the stallholder. He would make him apologise, beat the bastard black and blue if he refused. But Maki put a hand on his arm, restrained him with the lightness of her touch, familiar after all this time.

"No," she said. "It not help."

He knew she was right. He unclenched his fists, tried to quell the useless rage. Her hand still rested on his arm; he took it a moment in his own.

They walked, along by the waterfront, spoke little in between the silences.

"It's cruel," he said. "Now Tsuru is my wife. We have a daughter, Hana."

"*So desu.*"

It was uncanny that he'd stayed late at his office, hammering out the agreement with the others, that he'd left at that time, taken the detour, wandered through the market, something he never did. And she had come in from the village to shop there, had also been later than usual. She would stay the night with her friend Yumi. Yumi too had left the Sakura, married one of her clients, a wealthy merchant from Kobe. When the husband was in Osaka or Edo on business, Maki could stay overnight.

"Yumi understand," she said. "She is kind to me."

The boy was tired, was starting to whimper. She picked him up, held and shooshed him.

The darkening night. The resignation in Maki's eyes. The boy's crying. The starkness, the sheer complexity of it all.

"I need time," said Glover. "I need to think what to do."

"What to do," she echoed, and she smiled at him, wry and sad. "Maybe is nothing to do."

He hailed a *jinrikisha* driver to take her to her friend's house, gave her the little money he had in his wallet.

"More tomorow," he said. "You come to my office. Same time."

"*Hai*," she said. "*So desu*. Tomorrow."

He watched the rickshaw trundle into the night, turned home towards Ipponmatsu, to Tsuru and Hana.

Tsuru was calm, showed no emotion, said nothing as he explained the situation, just gave the slightest nod of the head.

"I just want to do what's best," he said.

"*Hai*," she said. "Best."

The day had been long. He was tired. He soaked in a hot tub, dried off, lay down. But his sleep was restless, fitful, twitching between waking and dream. He was in some kind of temple, looking for Maki, and everyone was giving him advice. Walsh was laughing. *Got yourself the mother of a dilemma here, Tom, with real big horns!* He mimed being a pantomime devil, forefingers to the sides of his head, sticking out like horns, then they metamorphosed into real horns, sharp enough to gore and wound. Mackenzie was shaking his head. *Ach, Tom, daft loon! I told ye, I told ye, to mind where ye dipped yer wick. And did ye listen? Did ye hell!* Then Ito was offering him a drink. *Drunk, I lie, head pillowed in some beauty's lap.* He leered. *Great man have many women! Ha!* Then the mask of his face changed, became serious. *But you marry Tsuru, have duty.* He withdrew the drink he was offering, swigged it himself, laughed again as it slobbered down his chin, wiped his mouth with the back of his hand. *Is koan, Guraba-san. Question to answer. What to do?* And he clanged an iron bell that rang in Glover's skull as he woke and sat up.

The bed beside him was empty.

"Tsuru?"

He got up, lit the lamp and went through to the next door room where Hana slept. Tsuru was sitting there in the dark, in her nightgown, her hair undone, beside the child's bed. She looked up, startled, as he shone the lamp, and in its flicker he saw she was crying.

"Tsuru," he said.

She hung her head, sobbed.

"What is it, lassie?"

He moved closer to her, put a hand on her arm, let the crying subside.

She sniffed, wiped her face.

"Now you have son," she said. This was difficult for her. "Tsuru not have son, ever. Maybe you want marry other one, bring son here. Send Tsuru and Hana away."

"Tsuru," he said. "For God's sake! You're my wife! Hana's my daughter! Do you think I'd just throw you out?"

"I not know," she said. "How I know? Not know gaijin way."

"Christ Almighty! Or should that be, In the name of Buddha? Amida Almighty!"

He could see she didn't understand what he was saying, but his manner, the cajoling reassurance, seemed to reach her, and she laugh-cried. He put an arm round her shoulder, took her back through to the bedroom, blew out the lamp and lay down beside her, held her in his arms till she fell asleep. But he still lay awake, staring into the dark.

Jardine's were still pressing him for payment and the currency fluctuations continued. He was in the process of selling his slipdock to the new government for $130,000, a profit of $60,000 — a bargain for them and it would buy him time, breathing space. A second battleship, the *Jho Sho Maru*, was on its way from Aberdeen. It was larger than its predecessor, more powerful, more heavily armed. The Japanese would learn to build on that scale themselves. With Scottish expertise they would build bigger and better docks, develop their own industry, mine their own coal, forge their own iron and steel. He would be part of that, would ride out this storm. He had already invested in a coal mine, on Takashima island in Nagasaki Bay. When the operation was up and running, it would produce coal at a cost of $2 a ton; that would sell in Nagasaki at $4.50. If it produced 300 tons a day, working 20 days a month, that would make a profit of what?

He was tired. Tsuru moaned in her sleep. He saw Maki's face, the boy, his son. $2.50 a ton. Pure profit.

The price of coal. Work it out. 300 tons. The *Jho Sho Maru* cleaving through the waves. He couldn't concentrate. It kept slipsliding away. Like trying to hold water cupped in your hands. Like trying to thread a needle. Ito laughing. Fluctuations. Profit and loss. Those stupid unanswerable questions. One hand clapping. The wee small hours.

Maki didn't come the next day. He waited in his office into the evening, paced the floor, peered out the window, watched the sky darken, the lamps flicker in the shops and stalls, but there was no sign of her. It began to rain. He locked up and headed home, took a detour through the market again, just in case. He found the place even more irritating, the noises and the smells. He saw the stallholder who'd been rude to Maki swiftly filleting fish with a razorsharp chopping knife, his movements practised, deft. The man caught his eye, smiled, a twitch of the lip, half-obsequious half-ironic, and Glover was overwhelmed with the urge to punch him in the face. He imagined himself going further, grabbing the knife from the man's grasp, slicing his throat, gutting him. The ferocity of the thought, its sheer violence, shocked him. His hands were clammy, damp. He turned away, headed for home, felt the night air cool the sweat on his face.

He was curt with Tsuru when she asked if he was all right, told her brusquely that Maki hadn't showed up and he hadn't taken her address, had no way of contacting her right away. Tsuru nodded, looked relieved, and that annoyed him even more. He said he would track down Maki through the madame at the Sakura; she would lead him to Yumi and he would take it from there. But it would all have to wait a few days; he had to go to Tokyo for a meeting with Ito.

Tsuru bowed low, kept her head down. He saw she was sobbing and it tore at him.

"Och, lassie," he said. "The boy's my son."

"I know," she said, her voice bleak. "I know."

Prince Ito Hirobumi of the Choshu clan, Prime Minister designate of the Meiji government, was waiting to receive him, in a spacious office furnished with heavy European chairs, an oak table.

"Guraba-san! It is good to see you!"

"Ito-san! It is an honour to be ushered into your magisterial presence!"

"You rascal!"

"You rogue!"

A painting of the Emperor hung on the wall behind him, further along a smaller portrait of Ito himself looking massively dignified, a row of medals on the jacket of his well-cut English suit.

"Impressive," said Glover.

"Thank you," said Ito, offering him a cigar, motioning him to sit in one of the chairs, upholstered in dark leather.

They discussed again the devaluation of the currency. Ito expressed his regret that Glover had suffered losses.

"That was the chance I took."

"Situation should calm down," said Ito. "Get on even keel."

"I hope so," said Glover. He told Ito about his debts, his investment in the mine, his other plans. And he told him about Maki and the boy.

"Son make it complicated," said Ito.

"Like one of your damn riddles," said Glover. "Those bloody infuriating conundrums."

"Koan," said Ito. "*Hai*."

"Insoluble."

"My favourite is one about master Nansen," said Ito. "He come into meditation hall one day and two monks are fighting over a cat, both say it belong to them. He take up the cat in one hand, take sword in the other. He say if one of them can say good word they can save the cat. They tonguetied, say nothing. He cut the cat in two."

"Good God!"

Ito mimed slashing with a swordblade. "Ha!"

The story was still troubling Glover when Ito said there was someone he wanted him to meet. He struck a little brass bell that sat on his desk and a young man came hurrying in to the room, bowed low. Ito barked a command at him, and the young man backed out, returned with the visitor, a middle-aged Japanese businessman, dressed, like Ito, in a western suit, a collar and tie.

"Guraba-san," said Ito. "This is Iwasaki-san. He is anxious to meet you."

"*Hajimemashite*," said Glover. "*Dozo yoroshiku*."

"An honour," said Iwasaki.

They bowed, each to each, equally.

"I admire what you do for Japan," said Iwasaki. "For Japanese industry."

"Thank you."

"Slip-dock. Now coalmining."

"Not to mention the battleships!"

"*Hai, so desu!*"

"Iwasaki-san also has big plans," said Ito.

"Indeed?"

"Japan need to build these things here, make for ourselves."

"Exactly! Develop heavy industry. Compete with the West."

"I form company, for shipbuilding, engineering."

"Wonderful."

"I would be honoured if you would be adviser to company."

Glover was silent a moment, puffed at his cigar. "I am honoured that you should ask me," he said at last. "Of course I have other commitments."

"I am sure we can make agreement," said Iwasaki. "Make worthwhile."

"I shall give it serious consideration," said Glover.

"Company named after clan crest. Call it Three Diamond. *Mitsu-bishi.*"

"I like the sound of that. It has a ring to it."

They bowed again, shook hands.

"*Mitsubishi.*"

Glover had taken a battering and his creditors were closing in. There was a further communication from

Jardine's, regretfully requesting payment in full. The letter angered him. After all these years, the work he had done for them, the commitment he had shown, to be treated as just one more bad debt was intolerable. He crumpled up the letter, threw it across the room.

There was a letter also from the City of Glasgow Bank, demanding repayment of a loan he'd taken to help finance the building of the *Jho Sho Maru*. Even if the clans paid him in full for the ship, the devalued currency meant he would lose on the deal.

He had gone, cap in hand, to the agent of the Netherlands Trading Company, who had themselves invested heavily in Japan. He'd asked them to invest in him as part of the country's future. Now they had written, agreeing to underwrite his debts, but only on condition that he sign over the coalmine as security. He had no alternative but to accept. He was effectively sunk, bankrupt.

The Daruma doll sat on his desk, stared at him with its fierce-comic face. He cuffed it, knocked it over, watched it roll and right itself, bounce back up.

He crossed the two bridges, Hesitation and Decision, into the pleasure quarter, went straight to the Sakura. It looked different during the day, somehow smaller and shabbier, unprepossessing. By night it had always held a magic, an allure: glow of lantern-light, shadows on the shoji screens, sweet scent of incense. This daylight was too harsh for it, rendered it ordinary.

He stepped onto the porch, slid open the screen, and in a moment it all came back to him; he breathed in the smell, the very atmosphere, remembered the boy he had been, an acolyte entering the temple. The sliding of the screen. Sono's face. The intensity of those nights with Maki that had restored him to some kind of life.

Maki.

A figure moved in the dimness inside, the madame, recognising him, clapping her hands, welcoming him in, calling two of the young girls through to attend to him. It was good to have him back, and at this time of day he must be keen, she had somebody special for him, would take years off his life.

He laughed, explained he couldn't stay, had only come to ask her a favour. He had to find Maki. The madame looked disappointed. He told her the story and her face was all exaggerated sympathy. She was sorry, she had heard that Maki had a child, but she didn't know where she lived. But Yumi, perhaps she knew where Yumi lived? Yes, she knew, she could write down the address, it wasn't too far, he could go in a jinrikisha. And he must come back soon, she missed them all: Ito-san, the American Walsh, but especially Guraba-san, it was good time and they could make good time again.

He thanked her, sincerely, bowed and backed out, retraced his steps over the two bridges, hailed a rickshaw and showed the driver the piece of paper with the address in the madame's scribbled, effortlessly graceful calligraphy. The driver nodded, indicated Glover should climb aboard. Glover looked apologetic, mimed being big and heavy, cumbersome. The driver laughed, held up his skinny arms, flexing them. But he was wiry.

"*Tsuyoi!*" he said.

"Strong!" said Glover.

"*Hai!*"

He spat on his hands, rubbed them together, set off at a trot, dragging the rickshaw laden with Glover's bulk.

They crossed *Motokago-machi*, a busy road lined with shops and market stalls, cut down quieter side streets, rutted lanes, eventually came to a stop outside a compact wooden house on two floors.

"This is it?"

The man nodded.

"You wait?" Glover took out his pocket-watch, traced the passage of the hands, time passing. The man nodded, hunkered down on the ground beside his rickshaw.

Glover approached the house, called out.

"*Yumi-san! Gomen kudasai!*"

There was no reply. The wind ruffled a pine tree behind the house. He tried the shoji screen door and it slid open easily. He called in.

"Hello! Yumi! Are you there?"

There was a rustling inside the house, the sliding of another screen, and Yumi was shuffling towards the door, the look on her face wary, apprehensive.

"Yumi!" he said again, and her eyes widened in startled recognition.

"Guraba-san!"

She fluttered, seemed to be trying, at the same time, to bow, to step forward to welcome him and to turn and step back inside, no doubt anxious to tidy some imagined clutter before receiving a guest.

"It's all right!" he said.

She bowed and bowed, ushered him inside. "*Dozo!*"

He took off his boots, left them in the entranceway, followed her in. She flustered round him, plumped up cushions for him to sit on, went through to the kitchen area and filled a small iron kettle, set it to heat on the stove.

She came back through, tidying her hair, smoothing her blue kimono. He noticed for the first time she was pregnant.

"Congratulations," he said.

"Thank you!" she said, delighted, embarrassed, then as if remembering herself, put her hand to her mouth. "You want Maki. So sorry, she not here today. She come tomorrow, no, yesterday."

"I need to find her," he said.

"*Hai,*" she said. "I show you where."

She fetched the kettle, brought it through, made tea for him as a matter of course, without giving it a moment's thought. She whisked it in the bowl, frothed the bright green bitter mix, turned the bowl and handed it to him.

"*Dozo.*"

"*Arigato,* Yumi-san." He took a sip. "*Itadakimasu.*"

She nodded, pleased. Normally they would make ritual, formalised small talk about the weather, the quality of the tea, the glaze of the bowl. Instead he said again he had to find Maki.

"I met her. I know about the boy."

"She tell me," said Yumi.

"She said she would come next day, to talk."

"She not want. Too sad."

"I understand. But . . ."

"Your son," she said.

"*Hai.*"

She explained where Maki lived, further out this same road.

"Far?" he asked.

"Past temple," she said. "Long way."

She offered him more tea and he was about to refuse, then remembered the formalities, thanked her, accepted another cup, drank it.

"Your husband is a very lucky man," he said.

"No," she said. "I lucky one. Now, you go find Maki."

Outside the driver was dozing beside his rickshaw. He woke and jumped up as they approached. Yumi brought him a cup of water, explained where he should go next. He caught Glover's eye, flexed his muscles again, gave a wee half-smile, conspiratorial.

They passed the Suwa Shinto shrine with its red torii gate, the Buddhist temple at Teramachi; the road grew narrower, more rutted; space opened up between houses. Glover began to wonder if they had missed a turning, come too far, then they reached the settlement, not much more than a village, a cluster of shacks and godowns. At the last of them the driver stopped, his back running sweat.

"*Are wa*," he said, breathless.

That one.

Glover thanked him, walked towards the house. It looked fragile, temporary, as if the first storm, a strong wind, might blow it away. The shoji screen door was not completely closed, and as he approached, the door slid open and she was kneeling there, looking out at him.

Maki.

She showed no emotion, stayed calm, bowed low, almost as if she had been expecting him, that it was inevitable. There was a movement behind her and the boy, Shinsaburo, was peering over her shoulder. She stood up and reassured the boy, put a hand on his shoulder. Then she invited Glover to come in, stepped back into the room.

The interior was dim, a little smoky from the stove against the far wall, the bittersweet reek of woodsmoke mixed with cooking smells, a faint trace of incense, not quite overriding the dull stink of a dry privy in the corner behind a screen. In the other corner a wooden bathtub was propped against the wall. In the centre of the floor was a low table, and beside it, rolled up, were two futon mattresses. So they did all their living in this one room. But for all it was cramped, Maki had made space for a little shrine with a hanging scroll, a little clay Buddha, a single spray of flowers in a plain unglazed vase. Beside it lay her samisen, draped with a silk cloth.

"How you find me?" she asked.

"Yumi."

She nodded, gave a tired smile. "I knew you come one day."

"Why didn't you come to see me?" he asked. "After we met that last time. Next day I waited."

She took in a long deep breath, let out a slow weary sigh. "Is not simple. You have wife, daughter, other life."

"But the boy is my son. I'm responsible for him."

"No," she said. "I the one responsible. I decide to have him, not offer to Jizo, kill him before born. I give him life. Is my karma."

He felt a familiar discomfort, a kind of mounting panic, the way he did when Ito settled an argument with reference to bushido, his ferocious unbending code, or asked one of his unanswerable questions, his koan. No answer, except in action. But what action? It didn't matter, as long as it was right action! And how to know what was right? Only by acting.

He found himself telling Maki about his last visit to Ito, his story about the master cutting the cat in half.

"It made me feel uncomfortable," he said. "Not understanding."

"Is difficult," she said. "Take whole life to understand. This one about the cat very hard."

"Brutal."

"*Hai*."

"Ito used to shout these things at the Sakura, these questions, in between songs!"

She smiled. "I think maybe *he* not understand."

"Maybe not."

She spoke to the boy, sent him outside to play.

"You used to tell me stories," said Glover.

"Maybe *I* not understand," she said.

"I remember the one about the man running from the tiger, and hanging from the vine with the other tiger waiting."

"And tasting the strawberries."

"Yes."

She was quiet a moment. "I have favourite story, for now. In small village, young girl become pregnant, young man the father, she not want to tell. Family ask, she blame Zen monk who live alone outside village. They go to him very angry, say he is the father. He say, Is that so? Then baby born, they go to him, say, This is your child, you have to look after. He say, Is that so? And he take child into his home. Some time pass, and girl feel very bad. She tell truth. Family feel terrible. They go to monk, say, We are so sorry, is not your child, we take him back. Monk say, Is that so?"

In the silence they could hear the bark of a dog, the boy running and playing, chanting something to himself.

"This is no place for the boy," he said. "You can't bring him up here."

Maki had grown up here, in this place, been sold into Maruyama when she wasn't much more that a child herself. But the floating world would have seemed an escape, into freedom.

She looked straight at him. Her hair was tied back, her face bare of make-up, but still her beauty roused him, those eyes, the line of her neck. She wore a simple cotton robe and she pulled it closer around her.

She smiled at him from far away inside herself; there was a sadness in it and something like compassion.

"Is that so?"

He said there was room for them at Ipponmatsu, they could move in.

She laughed, said Tsuru-san would not be happy.

He said it was his house, he could do what he liked.

"House may be big," she said. "But not big enough for two women!"

He knew she was right, had known all along.

He gave her an envelope he had brought, with money to help her look after the boy. It would help a little, in the meantime.

She took the envelope graciously, thanked him, put it, unopened, in front of her shrine.

His creditors held a meeting in his office. He had employed a young Scottish accountant, Simpson, to go over everything meticulously, set it down in black and white, and he read out the figures sonorously, unemotionally, like a judge pronouncing sentence.

"You should have donned a black cap." said Glover.

His debts in total were $500,000. His assets, apart from the mine, were $200,000.

There was no other recourse but to cease trading on his own account and put himself in the hands of the Netherlands Trading Society, whose offer was still on the table. Their representative, a man named Baudian who had been in Nagasaki for years and knew Glover well, had already drawn up the paperwork.

The company would clear his existing debts in exchange for his share in the mine, in which he had invested heavily. They would employ him to continue running the mine, at a salary of $200 a month.

Glover read over the document, took up a pen.

"Where's the clause that mentions the devil coming to collect my soul?"

He signed with a flourish, shook hands with Baudian and everyone else in the room, went to supervise the removal of the sign that read *Glover & Co.*, its replacement with one reading *NTS*.

He threw himself into the work, even more eagerly than when the mine was his own. Working on the company's behalf seemed to liberate him. He invested in better machinery, sunk another shaft; a steam engine was brought in to pump out the tunnels; the existing galleries were widened so the coal could be brought out in trucks which were raised in cages to the surface, unloaded directly onto barges waiting at the pier.

The company praised his energy and perseverance. The Japanese Government expressed regret that Japan had not embraced this technology, developed its own mining industry years ago. Nevertheless, Mister Glover had shown the way, and as always others would follow.

He even set up a telegraph link — the first — between the pithead on Takashima and his office in the Bund. The *Nagasaki Advertiser* called this a remarkable innovation, and also an act of bravado reminiscent of Mister Glover's opening of the country's first railway line some years before. He was firing, the article read, on all cylinders and showing once more his indomitable spirit.

The work served, for hours at a stretch, to take his mind off Maki and the boy.

Months had passed. He had sent more money, by messenger, to Yumi, who passed it on. He hadn't been back to visit Maki. He had been too busy with the mine, with his other commitments. But in his heart he knew it was more than that. The situation was impossible. Cutting the cat in half. A decision had to be made.

He sat down to discuss it with Tsuru. She kneeled, silent, her face a mask, as he talked about adopting the boy.

"You know I want a son," he said. "Every man does."

She bowed her head, looked crestfallen. "So sorry, I not give you son."

"No!" He held his head. "Christ, this is difficult enough! That's not what I'm saying."

It had been the same with Sono, the sense that she'd failed, was to blame.

"No blame," he said. "We *both* want a son, and we can't have one."

She nodded. "*Hai.*"

"Then it turns out I do have a son, and he doesn't have a real home, and Maki can't look after him. We have all this space, and we're not poor. All right, the Dutch are paying me a pittance, but the debts are being cleared and things will pick up again."

The offer from Ito's friend Iwasaki still stood, to help with his new company, this Mitsu-bishi. It would mean spending time in Tokyo, perhaps eventually moving there. The *Jho Sho Maru* was on its way, he would be payed something for that, if not its full worth.

"We'll be all right when my ship comes in!" he said.

She didn't understand the joke, nodded and smiled anyway, and he felt a sudden tenderness towards her.

"Och, Tsuru! What I'm saying is that we can manage. We can bring the boy here, take him in, adopt him."

She bowed her head again, meek. "*Hai, so desu.*"

"He'll be a brother for Hana."

"*Hai.*"

She was silent again, let the silence sit there a while.

"What about woman?" she asked at last. This was painful for her. "She not come here?"

"No," he said, quiet but definite. "That wouldn't work."

"Work?"

"It would be impossible."

Another silence.

"So what she do?"

Unerring as one of Ito's unanswerable questions. A punch to the stomach.

"I don't know," he said. "Maybe she'll move on, find work."

"Maybe go back to work at Sakura."

"No!"

His own vehemence took him by surprise.

"So what else she do?"

He really didn't know, had no idea. It wasn't his problem, but it was.

★　★　★

404

This time he decided against the jinrikisha, hired a horse from an Englishman who kept stables near Dejima, rode out past the Suwa shrine, the temple at Teramachi. Maki had told him once that the priests at the shrine kept a pure white horse that was only to be ridden by one of the gods. He had no idea what that might mean. The horse he'd hired lolloped and trotted along, iron-shod. He minded Ken Mackenzie telling him with such enthusiasm about the Japanese seeing iron horseshoes for the first time, copying them, changing things overnight. He missed Ken, his straightforwardness, his dour wisdom. And he missed Walsh with his cynicism, his ironic wit. Ten years Glover had been here. A long time.

He nudged his horse forward along the narrowing roads, the dirt tracks. Above the village a blue kite tugged and scudded in the wind. It fell beside Maki's house and Shinsaburo was chasing it down; he saw Glover on the horse, gathered up the kite and ran pellmell inside, calling out to his mother.

She came out to meet him, trying to tidy her hair, fasten it back with a clasp. She looked up at him, bowed and smiled, unsure, and Glover was undone again, felt that surge, that salmon-leap of the heart.

The boy stared and stared at the horse, scurried away when it flared its nostrils, snorted. Glover dismounted, tied the horse to a post.

Inside, Maki had lit an incense stick to bless the place, fumigate it. She thanked him for the money he had sent, said it made a difference.

"It's nothing," he said.

"Not nothing," she said. "Is a lot."

"Ach!"

The room smelled the same, with maybe a hint of damp, mildew, added to the pungent mix. She twirled the incense stick in her fingers, wafted its fragrance.

"You still play?" he asked, indicating the samisen under its silk cloth. He could almost hear the sound of it, remembered nights at the Sakura.

"Not so much," she said. "Not now."

"No."

The sadness, the emptiness hung there.

"*Chotto monoganashii*," he said.

"Not *chotto*," she said. "Not little. *Motto*. Is much."

"*Motto monoganashii*."

"*Hai*." She stood up. "I make tea."

She busied herself, boiled water, rinsed and wiped the bowls, mixed the tea and let it stand, poured and frothed it with the bamboo whisk, all the time losing herself, escaping into the formality, the studied repetition of the actions, absolved from having to talk or think.

For his part, he sat still and watched, smiled and nodded once or twice at the boy, who had positioned himself close to the door, ready for flight.

In her own time, Maki poured the tea.

"*Dozo*."

And he sipped it, expressed his appreciation.

"*Itadakimasu*."

She poured a second cup, he drank it, put down the empty bowl.

"Maki," he said, "we have to talk about the boy."

406

She put the teapot on its tray, turned the bamboo strainer upside down to drain. He continued.

"I can give him a better life."

She looked right at him, that way, right into him.

"Is that so?"

And he felt a moment the emptiness open up, deepen.

She made no argument, listened, then said, simply, "Not today."

"No," he said. "You say when."

"Two weeks," she said.

"Two weeks it is."

She came with him to the door and he turned and held her, pressed her to him. The boy tugged at her sleeve, started to cry, and she disengaged, picked him up.

Outside, Glover mounted the horse. The boy looked up, again awed by it. Glover held his arms out, offering to take the boy, let him try sitting in the saddle. Maki looked hesitant, nodded, uncertain, her brow furrowed. She said something softly to the boy, reassuring, held him up. Glover reached down, took the boy by the arms to lift him, and for a moment he hung there, dangling, between them. Then he started to squirm, wriggle, let out a cry, and Glover handed him back to Maki, who held him, shooshed and calmed him. Glover gave them a wave, turned the horse and nudged it forward along the track. He looked back and they were still standing there, mother and son, watching him go.

★ ★ ★

The moment, distorted, came back to him in a dream. Maki was handing the boy to him and the boy was reluctant, struggled, kicked his legs. Glover had climbed down from the horse and had the boy by the left arm, Maki holding the right, not handing him over but pulling him back towards her. They tugged him, one way, the other. Then there was a figure standing between them, dressed in black robes, a monk or a priest, and Glover knew he was the master from Ito's story, was asking his question, insisting they respond.

"What do you say?" the master asked, producing a sword. And Glover was dumbstruck, could not say one word, choked and gagged on it, stuck in his throat. Not one word. And he couldn't move as the master took the boy by the scruff of the neck, like lifting a scraggy cat.

"One word."

Nothing.

And the master set the boy down and with one stroke of the blade cleaved him in two, split him in half and the two halves fell apart.

And Glover woke up screaming it out.

"No!"

Tsuru seemed reconciled to the idea of bringing the boy in to the house. She too had wanted a son, a brother for Hana. She had prepared a space for him, divided Hana's room with a screen, put down a small futon on a wooden base. She had even bought him clothes from the market, a few toys. She was ready.

The dream had unsettled Glover, but he'd pushed it aside, was preoccupied with the running of the mine and the imminent arrival of the *Jho Sho Maru* from Aberdeen.

The mine was thriving. The second shaft was operational and drainage and ventilation had been improved. The shaft was sunk 160 feet, opened onto a seam of coal eight feet high, worked day and night by shifts of labourers. He visited the island every day, marvelled at the swift efficiency of the workforce as the coal was dug, brought to the surface, transported by a human chain, men black with coaldust, passing buckets hand to hand and down into the bunkers of waiting junks and barges.

Glover stood at the dock, watching the operation, amazed at the speed of it all, the briskness and lack of fuss, amazed too at their seeming good humour. All day they kept up a stream of chatter, laughing and joking. He understood very little of it, barked out in their harsh argot, but he guessed most of it was ribald, obscene, caught the odd lewd gesture and let it pass, laughed it off. The next time Ito was in town he would bring him here, get him to translate. He imagined Ito roaring with laughter.

Ito would be here for the arrival of the battleship, and Iwasaki would come with him. Already, with Glover's help, they had bought land on the far side of the bay, started building a bigger slip-dock, laying out the Mitsubishi shipyard.

It was raining on the appointed day, a thin drizzle at first, getting steadily heavier, the sky darkening as he rode out of town, along the narrow road. He had brought in his saddlebag an oilskin cape to wrap round the boy, keep him dry, and at Tsuru's insistence, a small straw kasa umbrella-hat.

As he neared the village, the track was churned up, muddy. He stopped outside the shack, tethered the horse, called out.

"Maki! *Guraba desu! Gomen kudasai!*"

He waited for the response, the *Hai, dozo!* But there was no reply, no sound from inside. Nothing.

The screen door was on a simple wooden latch. He slid it open, looked in. The place was empty. He stepped inside, conscious of the mud on his boots, stooped and untied them, prised them off. The rain battered on the roof, deepened the sense of emptiness, desolation. The damp seeping into the walls overlaid the other smells, added to their rankness, the incense now faint and stale.

She couldn't be far away, had perhaps just gone to some market, been caught out by the rain, taken shelter somewhere. He would wait.

Tsuru answered the door, saw the woman, Maki, standing there with the child, both of them bedraggled, soaked through by the rain. It made no sense, but composing herself she stepped aside, invited them in. Maki shook her head, said she wouldn't stay, but pushed the boy forward, explained to him everything would be all right.

Tsuru asked why she was here, Guraba-san had gone to her place. Maki said the boy had been afraid of the horse, she thought it might be difficult, so she had brought him.

Tsuru said again she must come in, dry herself, have something to eat. Maki said she couldn't, it was impossible, she had to go.

Tsuru understood. Maki handed her a canvas bag with a few of the boy's things, his clothes, sandals. Tsuru took it, nodded. Maki bowed, turned and went.

Perhaps she had changed her mind, taken the boy and run away. But there was no sense that the place had been abandoned. There were fresh flowers in front of the little shrine; the samisen was there, under its silk cover; cooking pots, tea-bowls had been left upside drown to drain on a wooden rack; the bedding had been rolled up, tidied away.

She could not have gone far. He pulled on his boots again, turned up his coat collar against the rain and stepped out, swung himself up into the saddle. He began by riding round the village, crossed a bridge over a river, running high because of the heavy rain. He asked one or two women, scurrying to get out of the rain, if they'd seen her. They waved him away, kept their heads down.

She might have gone to visit Yumi, and if not, Yumi might know where she was.

But no, Yumi hadn't seen her all week. The last time she'd come she'd been quiet, sad.

He was suddenly fearful. It came to him with awful clarity. She had thrown herself in the river. He saw it, vivid as a dream, saw her floating in the water, face down, the sleeves of her kimono spread out like wings. He shook himself. This was madness. Perhaps she had just been confused about the day, had gone into town to the market, taken the boy with her.

It would serve no purpose riding back and forth along this road, in the rain. He thanked Yumi. He would go home, come back in the morning, early.

Tsuru had peeled off the boy's wet clothes, scrubbed him clean, rinsed him with buckets of warm water poured over his head, wrapped him in a towel while she ran hot water into the bath. Then she'd lifted him up, this little creature, frail and naked, eased him into the tub, let him soak in it. And all the while the boy said nothing, looked around him dazed, in a dream. He stared straight ahead as she lifted him out of the bath, rubbed him dry, dressed him in his new clothes, a navy blue sailor suit she had bought for him. She introduced him to Hana, said she was his sister and this was his new home. She gave him toys, a bright-coloured ball, a carved wooden horse, said they were his to play with, to keep. He looked at them, his eyes dull.

When Glover came home, soaked through, the boy looked up at him, startled, unsure.

"Thank God," said Glover. Then he looked around. "Maki?"

"She leave the boy and go," said Tsuru.

He turned towards the door again, for a moment was about to go back out, into the night. But he stopped himself. He was being ridiculous. Maki could look after

412

herself, would have taken a rickshaw, be back home or at Yumi's. He would go and talk to her in the morning. That was time enough. In the morning. He was weary.

Tsuru filled the tub for him, almost too hot to bear, but he tholed it, lay back, let the blood thud in his head, light flash behind his eyes. He drifted, again saw Maki, kimono-wings spread, flying. No, she was swimming. No, the garment was wet, heavy, pulling her down. She was drowning.

He thrashed, surfaced, again called out, "No!"

His voice boomed, echoed. Coils of steam, condensation, filled the room. He gasped, gulped in warm air. Tsuru hurried in, anxious.

He came to himself; he was here now in this place, his home, soaking in the hot tub.

"I'm fine," he heard himself say. "Just a daft dream."

He climbed out, dripping. Tsuru brought him a towel and he dried himself, put on a yukata and a thicker cotton robe.

The boy still sat, looked lost. But Tsuru had made food and the smell of it filled the room, ginger and sesame, onions and fish, a smoky tang. The boy must be hungry. He stood up and came to the table, stared. The solid oak table, the dining room chairs, were too high. Hana had a little table of her own where she kneeled. Tsuru had put another bowl there for the boy, laid out chopsticks. She dolloped out a serving for him, noodles in broth.

"*Dozo.*"

He set to, shovelling with the chopsticks, his face almost in the broth, slurped it all down, intent and greedy as a young animal. Then with perfect civility he piped in his wee reed of a voice, "*Itadakimasu.*"

Tsuru refilled his bowl. Glover brought his own food and kneeled down at the low table beside the boy and Hana. Tsuru did the same. Hana clapped her hands, laughed; the boy looked at her and smiled, uncertain.

"This is your home now," said Glover. "*Katei desu.* And this is your family."

"*Kazoku desu,*" said Tsuru.

She explained to him he would have a new name for his new life. They would call him Tomisaburo. That would be shortened to Tomi. And his second name would be Guraba. So he would be Tomi Guraba, like his father, Tom Glover.

The boy looked around him, at the faces of these strangers. He asked for his mother. He didn't understand.

Maki got back to her house, such as it was, shivering, miserable. The long walk, both ways, had exhausted her. She had asked a jinrikisha driver to bring her, but the rain was so heavy, the journey so far, he'd refused, even though she'd offered to pay double.

She slid open the door, collapsed inside, lay huddled on the floor. She should heat up some water, fill the tub. She should make herself eat something. But she couldn't, she could do nothing, just lay curled in a ball.

She lay a long time. The light was fading. She sat up, stiff and aching, thought about lighting the lamp, didn't. She couldn't bear to look at the room, see it empty.

414

In the corner was something angular, blue in the half-light. She couldn't get it to take shape, make sense; she stirred herself to look closer, saw it was the boy's paper kite. She picked it up, felt the sharp pang of familiarity, loss. She set it down again, gently, kneeled in front of her shrine, tried to offer a prayer to Amida. But she felt only numbness, the words heavy and meaningless in her mouth, just empty sounds, breaking the silence to no purpose.

Her hand rested on the samisen and she pulled back its silk cover, plucked the taut strings and they jangled, harsh and out of tune, no resonance, no *yo-in*.

By the door was an axe she used for chopping wood. Before she knew it the axe was in her hand and she was hacking, smashing the samisen, splintering the wood, the gut strings giving out a last strangled screech, a dying pang. In a dream, watching herself, she dropped the axe, pulled open the screen door and stumbled outside.

The rain was still heavy. She'd forgotten that. It didn't matter. She had come out barefoot. She didn't care. Her clothes were still heavy and wet from before. She felt the chill as they stuck to her. The rain battered her bare head. Her bare feet slid in the mud. She half staggered to the edge of the village, onto the wooden bridge over the river. She stopped halfway across, looked down.

The river was high because of the rain, flowed in full spate. The water was cloudy, discoloured, thick with mud and silt. She'd thought she would see her own reflection in it, one last time, but she didn't.

Guraba-san, Tom, had said it in English, a gaijin expression. Water under the bridge.

So.

She climbed onto the wooden handrail, let herself fall.

Namu Amida Butsu.

The cold was pain. The weight of her clothes dragged her under. She gulped and choked as her lungs filled up. The water closed over her head.

The *Jho Sho Maru* had made an arduous journey since its launch in Aberdeen. News of its progress had been sent by telegraph as far as Shanghai and conveyed by steamer to Glover in Nagasaki. Its launch from the Hall Russell yard had been a triumph, confounding critics who thought at 1500 tons and 200 feet long it was simply too big, would plough into the opposite bank of the Dee. But the massive chains had held, the ship had stayed afloat. Glover could picture it, massive bulk righting itself in the grey waters. Now those same critics would see; Aberdeen could compete with the bigger yards further south, on the Clyde and the Tyne.

After fitting out at Victoria Dock, testing its 1000-horse-power engines, the ship left the harbour, watched by cheering crowds. It sailed first to Ireland to pick up some of the ninety-strong crew and a handful of skilled engineers. From there it headed south to the Cape where it narrowly missed being wrecked in thick fog. Loading up with coal at Cape Town, it continued to Shanghai, surviving storms in the Indian Ocean. Now, five months after setting out, it was steaming into

Nagasaki harbour, and half the town had turned out to see it. They cheered, waved banners, and a brass band struck up a march.

Glover was at the front of the crowd, in a section cordoned off for guests of honour, among them Ito and Iwasaki. Beside him was the boy, dressed in his sailor suit. Glover introduced him formally to both men. His son, Tomisaburo.

His son.

It had been a month since the boy had moved in and he was still confused, awed, still asked for his mother, asked when he would be going home. There were times when he would forget, lose himself in playing, making his own world, completing some small task. Then he would suddenly look round again, lost, waking from a dream.

After the upheaval of the boy's arrival, a week had passed before Glover had gone to find Maki again, talk to her. Again her house was empty, but this time it felt abandoned, uninhabited. The screen door was bolted shut. Two women from the village passed by, perhaps the ones he'd seen before. He called out to them, asked if they knew where Maki had gone, but they hurried away as if fleeing from the evil eye. He went round behind the house, saw where a paper screen window was torn. He peered in, could see little in the dimness, but the overriding smell was damp — mildew and rot; no cooking smells, no incense. Further back was an overgrown gully where household rubbish had been tipped, and in amongst it he saw what looked like the smashed fragments of a samisen.

The band were playing another march and Ito straightened up, asked if he recognised it. To his ear it was just a cacophony, a din, blared by an out-of-tune oompah band. But Ito stood to attention, said it was their rebel marching song and it was glorious. He saluted to the boy, who looked even more bemused. Glover picked him up to reassure him and to give him a better view. He saw a moment, in the boy's eyes, something of his mother.

He had gone from Maki's desolate shack to Yumi's house. Her husband had been there, all deference and civility, but in behind the formality, hostile, suspicious, smiling with the mouth and not the eyes. Yumi had been uncomfortable, not looking at him, said simply that Maki had gone, she would not be coming back. He knew there was more to the story, something she wasn't telling him. He also knew that asking was useless. He thanked her, bowed to the husband, took his leave, rode back slowly to his home, his life.

The ship pulled into the dock, towered over them. Now they could see how massive it was.

Its bow was decorated with a sunburst, the same rising sun design that flew on the masthead, the Imperial banner.

Ito was grinning. "Emperor himself will come on board. This will be flagship of Imperial Japanese Navy."

The crowd roared. The band played the national anthem. Ito and Iwasaki saluted. Glover lifted his son up higher, let the boy sit on his shoulders.

"Look, Tomisaburo!" he said. "Look and see!"

CHAPTER FOURTEEN

Hot Ginger and Dynamite

Tokyo, 1911

"This old man Glover has nothing to tell you." That was how he had begun the interview, seated in his old leather armchair, in the living room of his spacious house in Tokyo.

The young journalist, Lawrence, had thought at first the old man was serious, that his journey through the cold and snow had been a wasted one. Then he'd caught the twinkle in the old man's eye.

Two hours later he had scribbled down pages of notes, struggling to keep up as Glover told the story of his first ten years in Japan. The old man's style was terse, direct, only occasionally boastful.

"Say what you like, son," he'd told him. "I was the greatest rebel. Without me the new Japan would not exist. It's as simple as that."

And the story he told was indeed remarkable, a ripping yarn, a tale of derring-do. From his arrival as a callow twenty-year-old, in a land intensely hostile to outsiders, he had gained an unparalleled pre-eminence, established himself as one of the most powerful men in the country, and all by the age of thirty. It was the stuff of fiction, romance.

"You certainly burned bright," said the young man.

"Aye," said Glover. "I was a bit of a firebrand right enough. Now, can I offer you some tea?"

The tray was brought by a young Japanese maid. She caught Lawrence's eye, smiled that way, poured the tea into two delicate china cups.

"Miruku?" she asked.

"Milk," he said. "Sure, thanks, *arigato*."

She smiled again, amused at his accent, bowed and took her leave.

"I see you too are susceptible to their charms," said Glover.

"She's exquisite," said Lawrence.

"Indeed," said Glover. "Yuko-san is a treasure." He stirred his tea. "Now, where were we?"

"The rebels triumphant," said Lawrence. "The Shogun overthrown, the Emperor restored, Ito-san established as Prime Minister, the new, industrialised Japan on the march, with the three-diamond banner of Mitsubishi in the vanguard."

"Glorious." Glover seemed to wince a moment, in pain. But it passed and he composed himself, motioned to Lawrence to continue.

"You're sure you're well enough?"

"I'm not in the best of health. Now, what else do you want to know?"

420

Perhaps it was just the effort of talking for two hours that had exhausted the old man. But Lawrence felt it was more than that. In telling his tale, he'd been reliving those ten years, the years when he'd been fully, vividly alive. Now a light had gone out.

"I moved to Tokyo. I grew rich. I grew powerful. I grew comfortable." He paused. "I grew old."

He closed his eyes, breathed deep. Then he sipped at his tea.

Lawrence waited, then tried to draw him out again. "There had been these . . . setbacks, immediately after the rebellion."

"It was inevitable," said Glover. "It was a period of great turbulence, upheaval."

"Interesting Times!"

"Aye."

"You were effectively bankrupt."

"I don't like to use the word, but yes."

"And you clawed your way back."

"I'd made a fortune, I lost it, I made another one."

"Then it was Mitsubishi and the move to Tokyo."

"And the rest, as they say, is history."

"But you kept one foot in Nagasaki?"

"I kept the house there."

"Ipponmatsu."

"Couldn't bear to sell it."

"Too many memories?"

"Indeed. But aside from sentiment, it's a matter of practicality. My son Tomisaburo still lives there with his charming wife Waka. I myself return there frequently. My daughter Hana is also happily married, to a decent young fellow, an Englishman by the name of Bennett. They have four children, so I'm a grandfather four times over! Unfortunately her husband works for my old partner Ringer, and the work took him to Korea, so the whole family had to up and move."

"And your son Tomisaburo never followed in your footsteps?"

"In what sense?"

"He wasn't a gung-ho adventurer? He didn't make fortunes and lose them again? Didn't bring about a revolution?"

The old man smiled. "Perhaps Tomi lacked a certain . . . *fire*. But he's made a decent enough life for himself. By nature I suppose he's rather reserved, studious. He visited your country, you know. Studied Biology at the University of Pennsylvania."

"Is that a fact?"

"On his return he went into shipping, so I suppose I influenced him a little. With my help he negotiated the purchase of Japan's first steam trawler — the *Smokey Joe!* — built in Aberdeen. It revolutionised the fishing industry."

"You just can't help yourself, can you?"

"Perhaps not! Tomi's interest was always more academic. He'd be down at the dock every day, checking the catch, but not for commercial reasons. Biology was his first love, and he'd be examining the fish, cataloguing them. He's been working for years on a project to make a kind of atlas of all the fish in the area. He's employed artists to make detailed drawings. It's quite an undertaking."

422

"Do you and your son get along?"

"What kind of question is that?"

"I just thought you must have been, as they say in vaudeville, a hard act to follow!"

Glover grunted.

Lawrence changed tack. "Speaking of vaudeville, there's a litle ditty doing the rounds of the bars in San Francisco. You might like it."

He cleared his throat, sang in an exaggerated, nasal twang, beating time on the arm of the chair.

> Hot ginger and dynamite,
> There's nothing but that at night,
> Back in Nagasaki
> Where the fellers chew tabacky
> And the women wicky wacky woo!

Glover's eyes opened wide, then he roared with laughter. "Wicky wacky woo!" But the laughing made him cough, splutter, red-faced, gasp for breath, clutch his hand to his side as if in pain.

Yuko hurried in, brought a glass of water, watched him sip it, saw him calm as the spasm passed.

"It's a bugger," he said.

"I should go," said Lawrence. "You're tired."

"I'll be fine," said Glover. "Just don't make me laugh, that's all!" He handed his glass to Yuko. "*Biiru, kudasai. Uisukii. Arigato.*"

She looked uncertain, almost reluctant, then bowed, threw a look at Lawrence, left the room.

"I just asked her to bring something a bit stronger," said Glover. "Now, where were we?"

"Hot ginger and dynamite!"

"Indeed!"

Yuko returned carrying a lacquer tray, set it down on the table. On it were two bottles of beer and two pint-glasses, a decanter of whisky and two cut-glass tumblers. With the same grace and adeptness she had brought to serving the tea, she unscrewed the bottletops and poured the beer, angling each glass so the froth was just right. Then she poured a measure of whisky into each of the tumblers, added a little more at Glover's unspoken command, his finger and thumb held an inch apart. He nodded, smiled. Again she bowed, backed out of the room.

"The beer is from my own brewery," said Glover, holding up his glass.

"Kirin," said Lawrence. "I've sampled it. It's a fine brew."

"The *kirin* is a mythical creature," said Glover, "half horse, half dragon, a symbol of good luck."

"An appropriate choice then," said Lawrence.

"So it proved," said Glover, taking a sip. "It was the Dutch who introduced beer to Japan, and the Japanese quickly developed a taste for it! Initially, of course, it was all imported. Then an American opened a small brewery in Yokohama, Spring Barley it was called."

"Another fine name."

"Not as fine as Kirin," said Glover. "It failed for various reasons. But the idea was sound."

"There was a market for the product."

"Indeed. I saw the possibilities, took over the company, scaled up the operation, made it work."

"Impressive."

"It's always the same story," said Glover. "It's a case of getting the Japanese to manufacture their own products, here." He drained his glass, set it down, picked up the tumbler of whisky. "The Scotch, however, is from home. There are some things even the Japanese shouldn't be trusted to copy!"

Lawrence laughed, raised his glass. "Your health!"

"I'm afraid that's long gone," said Glover. "*Kanpai!*"

They swigged their whisky. Glover grimaced, poured more, knocked it back in one go, stood and excused himself.

"Nature calls."

He was away an inordinately long time. Lawrence took the opportunity to look round the room, at the framed photographs on the wall.

The battleship *Jho Sho Maru*; a family group, Glover and Tsuru with Tomisaburo and Hana. Glover at his daughter's wedding reception in the garden at Ipponmatsu; Glover as he was now, a distinguished old man, surrounded by Japanese naval officers, among them Admiral Togo; and on his own, in full formal dress with a medal pinned to his chest; Ito Hirobumi in an elaborate military tunic covered with medals, the photograph signed to Glover; Glover as a young man, standing with hands on hips, looking out at the world.

"A whole life there," said Glover, coming back into the room. "Now it's come to this. Aching, puffed-up, pissing blood."

"I'm sorry."

"So am I, laddie. So am I." He sat down in his armchair again. "The doctors reckon it's Bright's disease. Steady failure of the kidneys. It's not pleasant."

"No."

"They said I shouldn't be drinking or smoking, should be careful what I eat. I said For God's sake why?"

Lawrence chuckled in spite of himself.

"I mean," said Glover, "they're all dead." A sweep of the arm took them all in, all his contemporaries. "All gone, all buggered off." He poured more whisky, for himself and Lawrence. "Tsuru passed away more than ten years ago. She's buried in Nagasaki, at Sakamoto Cemetery. When I breathe my last I'll join her there." He raised his glass again. "Cheers."

"*Kanpai*," said Lawrence, more subdued.

"When Tsuru died, my sister Martha moved out here. Bless her. She'd lost her own husband, and a daughter. Our parents were long gone. I suggested the move to her, she said Why not?"

"And did she like it here, did she settle to the life?"

"Like a fish to water. She was always of a spiritual disposition and she converted to Catholicism, busied herself with good works. She was much loved. She too is buried in Sakamoto."

Outside the day was growing dark. Yuko came in and lit the lamps, drew the curtains, stoked the fire in the grate.

Glover looked at the photographs on the wall, firelight glinting on the glass. "Ito's gone too, of course. Killed by an assassin's bullet. Some fanatical young Korean nationalist. Who would have believed it? Ito the great rebel, the great reformer, executed in the name of rebellion."

"It's often the way of it," said Lawrence. "Each generation has to break in order to build anew."

"Ito kept in touch with me right to the end," said Glover. "He still wrote poems, and he sent me what may well have been his last verse. I can quote it from memory:

> Nothing changes in the universe.
> Past and present are as one.
> Fish swim in deep waters.
> Seagulls soar across the sky."

"Very profound," said Lawrence. "Rather more so than *Hot ginger and dynamite*!"

"But Ito would have enjoyed that too!" said Glover. "Most definitely!"

"I see you're something of a music aficionado yourself." Lawrence nodded towards a gramophone resting on a small table, firelight giving a glow to the polished mahogany box, glinting on the brass horn.

"A miracle of modern technology," said Glover. "Yesterday evening you would have sworn Count John McCormack was singing in this very room! But listen to this." He picked up a record in a brown paper sleeve.

"Are you familiar with Mister Gilbert and Mister Sullivan?"

"I'm not much of a one for opera."

"Nor am I. To sit through an entire evening of the stuff would leave me with my brain aching and my arse numb! But these fellows are wonderfully entertaining. This is from *The Mikado*, and I doubt if it would go down well in Japan! Someone at the Consulate bought it for me in London, thought I would be amused by it. Listen, this is what I want you to hear."

He lifted the needle-arm, placed the record on the turntable, cranked the handle, set the arm down on the Bakelite disc, the stylus resting in the groove. There was a crackling and hissing, then the unmistakable sound of a band striking up.

"There! That song being played — it's the marching song of the kingire, the rebel troops who overthrew the Shogun. It was played at the launch of the *Jho Sho Maru*. The Japanese have a reputation for being stoical, unemotional. But I swear to God, old Ito had a tear in his eye."

The song came to an end, the stylus clicked and hissed on the disc, stuck. Glover lifted the arm, looked quite moved himself.

"If I may make so bold," said Lawrence. "Ito and his government have themselves been criticised."

Glover met his gaze. "As you said yourself a moment ago, it is often the way of it."

"In particular they have been accused of being belligerent, warlike."

"You refer to the wars with China, with Russia."

"Both of which were initiated by the Japanese."

"They have learned from their erstwhile superiors. Like any developing nation they have to protect their borders."

"By seeking to expand them."

"The war with China was over disputed territory."

"Manchuria, and by implication Korea."

"Japan is a very small country surrounded by large predatory neighbours. It saw Korea as a buffer."

"And by subjugating that nation brought about the very hostility that resulted in Ito's assassination."

"You're discussing a friend of mine, sir. You're stepping out of line."

Glover was irked, Lawrence could see it, still cantankerous and fiery enough to be riled. Lawrence saw for a moment the young man he had once been.

Yuko had come into the room, anxious at Glover's raised voice.

Lawrence took a step back. "I apologise, Mister Glover. I meant no offence."

"Aye, well," said Glover. "Just mind you're in my house."

"Indeed." Lawrence looked at Yuko, shrugged and smiled. She didn't respond, cleared away the tray, the empty glasses.

Glover waited till she'd gone, levelled his gaze again at Lawrence.

"I don't recall the British and American press being anything less than enthusiastic about the outcome of these skirmishes. In fact, there was general rejoicing, especially over the Russian Bear having its nose bloodied."

"By the Japanese Monkey!" said Lawrence.

"Quite," said Glover. "Ito was incensed by that particular caricature of his people."

"That's journalists for you!"

The young man was trying to restore a measure of jocularity, amiability. But Glover remained serious.

"I did hear other reports," he said, "after the fighting with China, but I tended to discount them."

"Tales of barbarism, brutality, excessive cruelty."

Glover nodded. "Those were the rumours."

"It was documented by one of my countrymen who chanced to be present," said Lawrence, "a vagabond and gunrunner by the name of James Allan. He wrote a rather lurid account of the whole business, and it's not for the squeamish. What he describes is nothing less than carnage, the Japanese army running amok with a savagery that beggared belief — wanton killing, beheaded corpses piled up in the street, severed heads impaled on spikes."

"You describe the imagined scene with some relish, Mister Lawrence. Perhaps you should turn your hand to the writing of penny dreadfuls. I am sure your Mister Allan could do the same."

"To my knowledge," said Lawrence, "he has written nothing other than his account of this atrocity and what he deemed his miraculous escape."

"You called him a vagabond," said Glover. "Perhaps he embellished his story somewhat."

"Perhaps."

They were silent a while, Glover staring into the fire, then they both spoke at once.

"I . . ."

"It . . ."

"Pray continue," said Lawrence, deferring.

"I was going to say it may have been that the Japanese soldiers grew drunk on the ease of their success. This was Japan's first military engagement outside its own borders for two hundred years."

"Well then," said Lawrence. "They are making up for lost time. Their defeat of Russia was as swift as it was unexpected."

"Russia had been belligerent ever since the Chinese affair. They have had their own designs on the region, of course, backed up by the persuasive power of their navy, and they forced the return of the disputed territories. For the Japanese it became a matter of honour."

"Isn't it always?"

"They live by a code," said Glover. "And that is not something to be dismissed so lightly."

Mounted on the wall, in its sheath, was Matsuo's sword.

Lawrence was looking at the photographs, indicated the one of Glover with the naval officers.

"I see you have made the acquaintance of Admiral Togo."

"On more than one occasion," said Glover. "I know him well."

"His handling of the Russian campaign was described by one observer as bushido in action, his attacks like the swift stroke of a samurai sword."

"I am sure the Admiral would be proud of such a description. You know, as a young boy he manned a gun emplacement at the bombardment of Kagoshima."

"Indeed?"

"And instead of making him angry, it filled him with admiration, the desire to match and emulate that British and American sea power."

"I would say he's well on the way to fulfilling that desire," said Lawrence. "With no little assistance from you." He looked at the portrait of Glover, wearing his medal. "I take it that's the decoration you received from the Emperor."

"Just a year ago," said Glover, straightening his back. "The Order of the Rising Sun. I was greatly honoured."

Again he took a sharp intake of breath, as if in pain.

"Forgive me," said Lawrence. "I've taken up a great deal of your time."

"It's been a pleasure," said Glover, recovering. "For the most part!" He shook the young man's hand, his grip still firm, his gaze still clear, direct.

"Thank you," said Lawrence. "You're part of the history of this country, these times."

"An ancient monument!"

"You changed things," said Lawrence. "How many of us can say that?"

Glover looked again at the photographs on the wall. His life.

"I don't think any of us realised how quick the changes would be. Japan's gone from the Middle Ages to the twentieth century in forty years. And of course it's been messy. But what we have here is a dynamic, forward-looking nation. I think Ito and the others have worked wonders. They not only got rid of the Shogun and the all-controlling Bakufu, they took power away from the Daimyo, stopped the samurai strutting the streets with their overweening arrogance, expecting everyone to kowtow. You know there were whole strata of society, the poorest working folk, the *eta*, lower down the social scale than the peasants, in fact right off the scale altogether. They had no rights whatsoever."

"Like the untouchables in India."

"Exactly so. Legally they did not exist at all, and were completely ignored. Except, of course, when it came to the dirty work that nobody else would touch. Slaughtering animals and butchering the carcasses, burying the dead, assisting at executions."

"And their situation has changed?"

"The Emperor has decreed it. The eta are human beings, have rights and freedoms. They can live and work where they choose, and like the peasants they are now known as *heimin*, the common people."

"Progress!" said Lawrence.

"It is," said Glover, narrowing his eyes, staring Lawrence down. "Not democracy yet, but a step in that direction."

"A democracy presided over by the Emperor, the Son of Heaven."

"He is a figurehead. He leads by example in embracing the new ways. When he cut off his top-knot, half the nation's menfolk copied him!"

"Have you met Mister Rudyard Kipling?" asked Lawrence.

"*If you can keep your head when all about you are losing theirs and blaming it on you.* Now that's great poetry!"

"It is."

"Yes, he visited Nagasaki some years ago. I met him at a reception in the Foreigners' Club. Why do you ask?"

"It's just that I met him too. In fact, I interviewed him. And he was complaining about some of the changes, what he thought the *too* rapid modernisation."

"I seem to recall he hated the sight of Japanese men in western suits! He said perhaps their forebears had the right idea in turning the first Christian missionaries into beefsteak!"

"A character indeed!"

Without being summoned, Yuko had appeared, brought Lawrence's hat and overcoat.

"*Arigato gosaimasu.*" He bowed.

"*Do itashimashite.*" She bowed lower.

He turned to Glover again. "Did you also meet another writer, a Frenchman by the name of Pierre Loti?"

"Once, I think, in passing. Why, did you meet him too?"

"No, his sojourn in Nagasaki was before my time. I just wondered if your paths had crossed, that's all. He

434

wrote a rather successful novel called *Madame Chrysanthème*."

"I'd heard some talk of it. But I'm afraid I haven't read novels since I was a boy. Adventure tales. *Treasure Island. Robinson Crusoe*."

"Fine books. I read them too! No, this Loti fellow was none too enamoured of the Japanese, and it shows in his writing. Yet it's spawned a fashion for *japonisme, japonaiserie*. An American named Long has written a rather more sympathetic tale entitled *Madame Butterfly*, and that's been dramatised and turned into an opera by Signor Puccini."

"As I said, I'm not a devotee of the opera."

"No, of course." Lawrence buttoned up his coat. "Forgive me. I'm just making small talk. Idle curiosity. But if I may, I'll track down copies of these novels and send them to you with a recording from *Madame Butterfly*."

"You're too kind," said Glover.

"I'd be interested in what you make of them," said Lawrence. He was about to say more, changed his mind, made a comment instead about the house, how fine it was, what an excellent location.

"Smalltalk indeed!" said Glover. "But, yes, it's a fine house, effectively bought and paid for by Mitsubishi, with a little help from Ito-san."

"The district is called Azabu?"

"It is. We're really in the country, Shiba Park. The only drawback is that we're three miles from the Mitsubishi office at Marunouchi. Until recently I was still going there most days, but it was a devil of a

435

journey by jinrikisha along these wretched rutted roads. Of course in this weather it would be out of the question."

"Six inches of snow on some of the roads."

"And in any case, I am no longer fit for the journey."

"Perhaps come the spring."

"Perhaps."

Lawrence was suddenly awkward, felt an almost unbearable weight in the words and in the silences between. They were discussing mortality, not discussing it.

"My carriage should be waiting at the road-end," he said.

"Godspeed on your own journey," said Glover, and they shook hands again.

Yuko opened the door and the wind blew in a flurry of snow. She slammed it quick shut when the visitor had gone, then she ushered the old man into the living room, stoked the fire in the grate, and he sat staring into it, watching it flicker and glow.

It was still cold, though the snow had begun to clear, a few weeks later when Tomisaburo came to visit. Glover was fond of his son, was always glad to see him, but he regretted the stiffness and formality that seemed to characterise their dealings.

Hana was her father's daughter through and through, had inherited his feistiness and fire, knew how to banter with him, placate him, make him laugh. But with Tomi there was always that distance, a reserve.

436

That damned journalist had touched on it, hit a raw nerve. He'd been happy to talk to the man, bask in the memory of it all. But the interview had tired him, left him irritated in ways he didn't quite understand.

Yuko had taken Tomisaburo's coat and hat and he'd bowed to her, slightly awkward as he always was with young women. Now he sat in the armchair by the fire, facing his father, sipping his tea as the old man told him of the journalist's visit, how it had unsettled him.

"You probably told him too much," said Tomisaburo.

"Aye," said Glover. "Right enough. He'll likely be turning it into a lurid article for some scandal sheet!" He laughed and it set him coughing, brought the jab of pain stabbing at his side. "Christ!" he said. "If I can't even have a laugh, there's not much left."

"You should rest more," said Tomisaburo, anxious.

"Ach!" said his father. "I've an eternity of that ahead of me, one way or another. Now, what brings you to Tokyo?"

Tomisaburo's eyes brightened. "I wanted to see you, of course. But I also wanted to check a consignment of hand-made paper, for the book."

"Ah!" said Glover. "Your atlas."

"I have commissioned a few more artists, and the work is well under way. By my reckoning there are 558 species of fish in the waters around Kyushu, and the book will contain in excess of 800 illustrations, including drawings of shellfish and whales."

"Impressive!" said Glover, meaning it. Then he couldn't help adding, wry, "And of course you have Admiral Togo to thank for the progress of your project."

437

Tomisaburo looked bemused. "How so?"

"It was his victory over the Russians that extended Japanese fishing grounds."

"Ah," said Tomisaburo, seriously. "Yes."

"And how goes the fishing industry? How fares the *Smokey Joe*?"

"Very well," said Tomisaburo, back on safer ground. "Another steam trawler is on its way from Aberdeen, and two more are being built in the Mitsubishi yard."

"Excellent."

"And we are planning, as an experiment, to send shipments of fish to the markets in Osaka by the new railroad."

"If folk had listened to me," said Glover, "the railroad would have been built forty years ago!"

The railtrack laid along the Bund, the engine roaring along in clouds of steam, the crowds waving, Glover sounding the whistle, firing his pistol in the air.

"Perhaps the country was not ready, the time not right."

"Ach!" said Glover. "You always did err on the side of caution!"

Tomisaburo was tightlipped. "I am who I am, and what my life has made me."

"Have more tea, for God's sake!" said Glover. "And tell me what else is happening in Nagasaki."

Tomisaburo unclenched a little. "I am hoping to be elected Chairman of the Nagasaki Golf Association," he said. "There are plans to open a public course at Unzen."

438

Glover laughed. "I mind hacking my way round the course on the clifftop at Stonehaven! I believe there was a suggestion made that the game might catch on in Japan. But that was one development I didn't foresee!"

Flags in the wind off the North Sea. Unfinished business.

"The International Club is flourishing," said Tomisaburo, with a kind of hesitant pride. "I am on the committee."

"You are a busy lad," said Glover.

"We recently held a meeting to inaugurate our new meeting rooms. And you'll never guess where they're located."

"In Maruyama," said Glover, "in the flower quarter."

"No," said Tomisaburo, patient. "In Dejima."

"Dejima!" said Glover. "Now that *is* appropriate!"

His younger self, all gauche and eager. The mob across the bridge, smashed windows. The hot night. That first young girl.

"It is indeed," said Tomisaburo. "Singularly so! There were seventy-six members at the meeting, Japanese alongside Americans and Europeans, even Russians and Chinese."

"You do surprise me. Perhaps there really is hope for the future."

"That's why the club exists," said Tomisaburo, serious again, "to foster that hope through the bonds of friendship and understanding."

"A noble goal."

"It really was a splendid evening." Tomisaburo warmed to the telling. "The Mayor was presiding, and the Governor was present, as was the American Consul. And yet there was no undue formality to the proceedings, and an excellent meal progressed in an atmosphere of conviviality throughout."

Glover laughed again. "There are times, Tomi, when you sound like the perfect English gentleman!"

Tomisaburo looked confused by the remark. "Indeed," he said, and fell silent.

Glover knew it had not been easy for the boy. His years at school, *Gakushuin*, had been troubled. The other boys, sons of the aristocracy, had shunned him, called him a half-caste. More than once he'd come home battered and bloodied, but he'd borne it, stoical, retreated into that carapace, that hard protective shell, withdrawn to somewhere inside himself.

I am who I am, and what my life has made me.

"The irony is," continued Tomisaburo after some time, "many of the English gentleman with whom I've had dealings regard me as a little Jap upstart with ideas above his station."

"Worst of both worlds," said Glover, suddenly feeling the weight of it all.

Again they sat in silence. The fire sputtered in the grate.

"You know," said Tomisaburo, "I am *ujiko*, parishioner of Suwa Shrine. This is a status not granted to outsiders, foreigners. So at least in that one respect I am wholly Japanese."

"I know Suwa Shrine," said Glover. "Do they still have the white horse, for the gods to ride on?"

"They do."

Riding out past the shrine, on his way to see Maki. The boy awed, terrified by the horse, by the terrible gaijin, come to change his world.

"What do you think of such things?" asked Tomisaburo, tentative.

"What things?"

"Shrines. White horses. The gods."

"Religion?"

"Religion, philosophy, superstition, call it what you will. We never discussed such matters."

"No." He gave it some thought. "I suppose I inherited a certain reticence from my own father, God rest him."

"And you also inherited his faith?"

"I suppose I did. A grim northern fatalism! I may have spent my life defying it or ignoring it, but it's there nevertheless, a bedrock."

"Was it never shaken by the theories of Mister Darwin?"

"I never troubled to give them a great deal of thought."

"I find his ideas interesting."

"The biologist speaks!"

"And you know, from a Shinto point of view, or Buddhist for that matter, there is no conflict with these ideas. Shinto has an inherent animism, a sense that everything has a soul, and the soul transmigrates. Buddhism already recognises the idea of evolution, through reincarnation. It's only the Judaeo-Christian tradition that has a problem."

"So you believe in this . . . reincarnation, that we live many lives?"

"I try to keep an open mind, and live from moment to moment as best I can."

"You're right," said Glover, "we've never discussed such things."

"No."

"Or much else, for that matter."

"You were a busy man."

"And now I'm an old man, a sick man, and soon I'll be a dead man."

"It comes to us all, father."

"Too damn soon." He coughed and the spasm shook him, the pain so sharp a stab he cried out, choked, gulped in air. Tomisaburo called for Yuko, who was already on her way, bringing water, a whole jug of it; she poured a glass and Glover swigged it, held it out for a refill, his hand shaking; he was red-faced and sweating, Yuko dabbed his forehead with a cloth, said to Tomisaburo in Japanese that his father was tired and needed to rest, that he was grateful for the visit, but perhaps she could humbly and respectfully suggest it was time to leave.

He nodded, bowed. Glover waved a hand, struggled to speak.

"Bloody hell!" he said. "The attacks get worse." He drew breath. "They come quicker."

Tomisaburo was anxious. "Maybe you should go to hospital." He darted a glance at Yuko for confirmation, support. She looked away.

Again Glover waved a hand, grimaced, managed to speak. "Nothing they can do." He concentrated hard. The worst of it passed. "When the time comes I want it to be here, tended by this ministering angel."

Yuko didn't understand completely, but she got the gist of it. She put a hand on Glover's arm, turned and left the room, quickly.

Glover got to his feet, shaky but taking charge again.

"It was good to see you, Tomi. Good to talk to you." He reached across and they shook hands.

"I'll come again," said Tomisaburo. "Next month."

Glover nodded but the look in his eyes held a certainty, a foreknowledge. "Give my love to Waka, and to Hana and the children when you see them." He squeezed his son's hand, said "Ach!" and hugged him, something he hadn't done since Tomi was a child. And Tomisaburo the man looked startled, dumbfounded.

"We should have talked more," said Glover.

"*Hai*," said Tomisaburo. "Yes."

Glover crossed the room, took down the short samurai sword in its sheath, turned and held it out, in both hands.

"I'd like you to have this."

"But this . . ." said Tomisaburo. "This is . . . It's . . ."

"I know," said Glover. "Please." And he bowed, stepped forward, held out the sword again. And Tomisaburo, caught in the ritual formality of the moment, could do nothing other than respond, bow, take the sword.

In his eyes Glover saw for an instant something of the boy's mother, just a glimmer, then gone.

"Ach, son," he said. "I'm sorry."

"Why?"

"I just am."

Tomisaburo bowed again, touched the sword to his forehead.

He was burning up. The pain seared through him, racked and tore, beyond bearing. He sweated and shook, smelled rank, his nightshirt stuck to him, drenched. Was this it? Had he died and gone to hell? The minister had ranted about it in the dank grey kirk, in the cold north, a lifetime ago. Lead us not into temptation. Deliver us from evil. Hellfire and damnation. The wages of sin. He was on fire, fevered, he writhed and kicked off the bedclothes, tugged at his throat. Needed to cool down, douse the flames. He imagined diving into cool water, saw himself a wee skinny boy near naked diving off the bridge, arms flailing legs pedalling the air to splash and plunge into the cold Don, go under and come up gasping, exhilarated, shake the water off like a mongrel tike, run and clamber back up the bridge to dive in again for the sheer joy of it, the sensation. And himself as a young lad, about the town with his cronies, drunk and climbing onto the parapet, balanced there, and the young fellow Robertson keeling over, falling in, himself not thinking, jumping in to drag him out. And win the keystane o' the brig. Dripping wet his clothes soaked boots the lot waterlogged. Robertson. Was he still alive? An old man with grown-up family, grandchildren. Dear God, Annie. Those blonde curls, the bonnet, a summer night at Brig o' Balgownie. Bonnie lassie O. Down among the dunes, a long spurt into nothing, Houghmagandie. Fuck. Annie's white hanky smeared with red. Fuck. No. Ah, Tam. Ah, Tam. Thou'll get thy fairin. In hell they'll roast thee like a herrin. Burning turned on a spit. No not this.

He sat up in bed, he was here, it was night, the wee small hours. Yes. There was water in a jug at his bedside. Yuko, God bless her, a treasure. His hands trembled as he picked up the jug, slugged straight from the lip of it, spilled as much as he swigged, but the drouth was killing him, he had to swallow it down, drank and drank to slake this thirst, slopped and swilled, wet his face his shirt the bedclothes, drank. He was here in his own home, his house. Azabu. Shiba Park. Tokyo. Japan. As a boy at school, the solid granite Gymnasium in the Chanonry, he'd written his name and address in his exercise book, inside the front cover. Thomas Blake Glover. The Coastguard Station. Bridge of Don. Aberdeen. Scotland. Britain. Europe. The Northern Hemisphere. The Earth. The Solar System. The Universe. Spinning the globe in the shipbroker's office, putting his finger on Japan. Here be dragons. A land that floweth with milk and honey. A bit far, is it no?

Now he shivered, the water he'd spilled started to chill him. And the cold feared him more than the fire, the thought of it, descending into endless dark, buried in the cold hard ground. The earth. Without form and void. Nothing. A tiger, he'd burned bright. Now the fire would be doused, extinguished. Tomi had said we

445

continued. As long as the red earth rolls. To end for good, be finished, be nothing. To go forever to heaven or hell, a dream or a nightmare everlasting. To keep coming back again and again. He would find out soon enough. He would ken.

Now he was really shivering. It was winter. Out there the earth was frozen, the trees were bare. Azabu. Shiba Park. Tokyo. Kyushu. Japan. Asia. The Northern Hemisphere. The Earth. The Solar System. The Universe. The Void. His nightshirt was wet. He curled under the covers, cooried down to get warm again. He wanted to sleep, feared if he did he might not wake up. He lay still, huddled, felt the warmth come back to his core. Atsuka! Old Ken Mackenzie had laughed at that. And Ken too was long gone, dead and buried, and Walsh, in some accident after he'd gone home. A rogue. The pleasure quarter, soaking in the hot tub. The screen doors opening.

Sono.

Och, lassie, so young so young, and the wee bairn that never lived at all. He didn't want to think about this, about any of it, he just wanted to sleep, but it came at him, battered him. Kagoshima, the town bombarded, laid waste, fire raging along the waterfront, the smell of burning, the dead bodies so much meat. Sono. A wisp of smoke as he looked back. The pain tore at him again, again, now there was a steady throb that wouldn't stop, an ache that was constant, and at intervals the jab and jab of real deep pain, sharp point of a blade twisting. He had given Matsuo's sword to Tomisaburo, seen the look in his eyes, the look that had minded Glover of

Maki, gone these long years but still there, like that, in the memory. Maki. Sound of the samisen. Nights at the Sakura, the sheer intensity of it, fire of the flesh, never so fully alive before or since. Lying in her arms, sated utterly, breathing in the smell of her, hearing her laugh. The stories she'd told him, haltingly. One hand clapping. Cutting the cat in half. The cliff-edge and the tiger chasing, the tiger waiting, the sweet taste of the strawberry. The tiger roared. Burning bright. Hot ginger and dynamite. Nothing but that at night. Back in Nagasaki where the fellers chew tabacky and the women, the women. He felt another pang, saw Tsuru his goodwife all these years, the young woman she was, grown old with him and gone. Turned to dust in Sakamoto. He would join her there when his time came, soon. Drifting into sleep, just letting go.

He was on his way home to Ipponmatsu where they were all waiting for him, were throwing a party in his honour. But every step was effort, hurt, and he moved so slow so painfully slow. Someone gave him a white hanky and he wiped his brow with it, so hot, *atsuka*, then the pain racked again and he coughed and hacked, spat into it, saw the spatter of bright red blood, opened it out and it was the Japanese flag and he didn't dare to drop it on the ground. Another step on and up, another, in pain. Just to rest was all. He stopped and leaned against the tree. They were waiting for him, were all inside. Then someone was striding straight towards him, a dark hostile figure he knew, a threat, and he couldn't move, couldn't get out of the way. And Takashi had drawn his sword, was coming at him, blade raised, and all he could do was bend his head, and the blade cut and cut, stuck in the overhanging branch so the blow never fell. This had happened before. And so had this, Takashi kneeling and falling forward onto the blade. Glover was the witness and Ito was the kaishaku, the friend ready to behead him. It was swift, a single stroke and the head rolled on the ground, face grimacing. But then the face was Glover's own, looking up at him, resting on the flag now placed there. He couldn't move, he had to, he gathered all his strength and dragged himself up out of sleep, a dream, all of it.

This was real. This. The constant pain deeper, the gaps between the sharp jabs less. This. His bare feet on the floor, sweat-damp nightshirt clinging to him. This. Bedside candle lit, its flicker. The porcelain pisspot under the bed. The effort to bend and pick it up. Fuck. Leave it on the floor stand over it, piss a red trickle, sear of the pain, the gaps between would close altogether be one long pain. He needed laudanum. The bottle was in the cabinet across the room, a distance. His feet swollen and hot. On impulse open the curtains and look out. Frost on the ground. The faintest suggestion of grey light in the sky. Bare forms of the trees and through them the stars, high far and cold. He opened the drawer took out the bottle of tincture, the little glass dropper with the rubber bulb, filled it, squeezed the drops into his mouth. Got back to the bed, shoved the chamberpot under again with his foot, felt it slop. Lay down, head back on the pillow. This.

That last poem of Ito's. Nothing changes in the universe. Past and present are as one. But it did

448

change, everything did, nothing stayed the same. Then something about swimming in deep waters. Water under the bridge. Time passed. Everything aged and died.

He'd arrived in autumn, felt the warmth, breathed the air. The hillside opposite the harbour had been a swathe of bright red, maple. He'd come off the boat down the gangplank, unsteady. He'd seen the young girl, keeping the paper butterfly in the air with the updraft from a fan, he'd been enchanted.

He closed his eyes, saw water and dived in, it was cold and dark, he surfaced, went under again and the water closed over him.

Yuko found him in the morning, already stiff and cold, face clenched in a last grimace. She stood a moment in silence, bowed, pulled up the sheet to cover him.

CHAPTER
FIFTEEN

Form is Emptiness

Nagasaki, 1945

The sergeant flicked his Zippo lighter, the flame flared in the darkening room. He lit his cigarette, shook another from the pack for the corporal, who took it, put it behind his ear for later. As an afterthought, the sergeant offered one to Tomisaburo. The old man shook his head, said, "No. Thank you. I don't."

The sergeant blew out smoke; its sweet acrid haze filled the room. He said they should be going, and Tomisaburo would be hearing from them.

"Indeed," he said, and made no effort to fill the silence.

When he'd smoked the cigarette down to the tip, the sergeant stood up, dropped the butt on the floor, ground it with his heel.

"OK," he said. "I guess you won't be going anywhere in the meantime."

"There is nowhere to go," said Tomisaburo.

"Right," said the sergeant.

The two GIs fastened the chinstraps on their helmets, shouldered their guns. Tomisaburo showed

450

them to the door, splintered now where they'd kicked it in. It didn't matter. Nothing did.

He went back to the drawing room and sat in his armchair, trying to think. Cigarette smoke still hung in the air, clung.

He was tired.

At length he came to some kind of decision, got to his feet and lit a stub of candle, made his way to the bathroom, set down the candle on the edge of the tub. He knew the water was almost gone; at best there would be enough in the tank to fill the bucket he used to rinse himself. He placed it under the spout, cranked; a gobbet of dirty brown-black water coughed out, spurted into the bucket, enough to fill it a few inches.

Fine. It was better than nothing.

He took off the clothes he had worn for days, ever since the blast, the black jacket and trousers, the waistcoat, the shirt and tie, the socks and underwear; he left them in a heap on the floor, stood naked; and suddenly he saw his mother's face.

Not Tsuru. His real mother, turning away, letting him go.

She had called him Shinsaburo.

Her face, now, so clear.

Tsuru had peeled off his clothes, burned them; she'd cut his hair, scrubbed him clean, dressed him in a new white sailor suit, harsh cotton that chafed.

He climbed into the cold tub, hunkered down, wet a clean cloth and washed himself as best he could, poured the last of the grimy water over his head, stood up, shivering, towelled himself dry.

Now.

The candle guttered as he walked through, still naked, to his bedroom.

He opened his wardrobe, pushed aside the sober black business suits, the wing-collared shirts, took out instead his Japanese robes. With a solemn formality he put them on, the white tunic and wide trousers, the wide-sleeved grey robe tied with a sash, the white cotton socks. He saw his reflection in the mirror, wavering in the candlelight. He bowed to it, as if to someone else.

In the drawing room he set the candle down again, on his desk. It was burning down, but would last long enough.

His gramophone was covered in dust; he had no idea if it would still function. He lifted the lid, cranked the handle. The turntable rotated. The mechanism seemed unharmed. His records were stacked in a wooden box. He sifted through, found what he was looking for, the aria from *Butterfly*, eased it from its brown paper sleeve. The Bakelite disc was scratched from much use, but not cracked, in spite of the upheaval. Miraculous. He wiped it with his cuff, placed it on the turntable, cranked the handle again, turned the brass horn so it was facing into the room. He lifted the arm, swung it over, placed the needle in the groove. The familiar introduction crackled into life, filled the room.

He took his father's sword, the wakizashi, kneeled on the floor and placed it in front of him. Then he touched it to his forehead, slid it out of its sheath, the candlelight glinting on the steel blade. There were

452

Hindu texts that described the soul leaving the body as akin to a sword being drawn from its sheath, the sheath cast aside, the soul shining, free. Others talked of casting off an old worn-out garment.

That old suit of clothes he'd left on the floor.

He glanced up at the portrait of his father, the face stern, admonishing. But strangely he felt something like compassion. His father too had lived and striven and suffered. His life too had been a tale told by an idiot, full of sound and fury, signifying what?

Nothing.

Form is emptiness.

Now his own time was ending. The barbarians at the gate; the Americans or the kenpeitai, it didn't matter which. A rock and a hard place. Devil and the deep. He was in no-man's-land. Nowhere to go.

He put the sword down again, untied the sash round his waist, removed his robe. Then he opened the tunic, felt the old slack skin of his belly; picked up the sword and placed the tip of the blade there, below the navel, a little to the left. Even this, the slightest pressure, pierced the skin, made him flinch, breathe deep. The music built to its glorious climax, heartbreaking. *Un bel di . . .* Then the needle stuck and stuck and stuck. He took one sharp intake of breath, leaned forward with his whole weight onto the blade.

453

CHAPTER
SIXTEEN

One Fine Day

Nagasaki, 2005

The young couple, Andrew and Michiko, queued at the gate to the grounds. The August heat was sweltering, muggy. Andrew bought a plastic fan from a vendor, gave it to Michiko to cool her down. She laughed, did a stylised dance, part *geisha* part *harajuku* girl, gave him an exaggerated flutter of her thick dark eyelashes.

She switched off her iPod — she'd been fastforwarding through the quirky mix she'd downloaded, Joy Division, White Stripes, Miles Davis, Megadeth — and looked at the illustrations on the fan. On one side was a cartoon version of Glover House, Ipponmatsu, with a little four-piece jazz band playing in front of it. Up above, on a yellow moon, sat a round-eyed cherub; yellow stars filled the night sky, twinkling as they fell to earth; one of them had landed in the garden, lay embedded in the ground, and on it sat a little couple, gazing into each other's eyes, the man in a dark blue suit, the woman in a short pink dress. The musicians were Japanese, the couple western, round-eyed.

"Ha!" Michiko loved kitsch, was delighted.

On the other side of the fan it read, in English, *Glover Gardens*, above a cartoon-Glover, a caricature of his portrait as an old man; the figure was squat, blacksuited, standing to attention, right hand raised in greeting. In a speech-balloon, coming from his mouth, he was saying, *Yo!!*

"Yo!!" Michiko laughed again. "Guraba-san! Yo!" And she fanned herself, took Andrew's arm.

They'd met in Kyoto — she was a student, he was teaching English on a JET course; they'd been seeing each other for a month, and his time in Japan was almost over.

It had been his idea to come to Nagasaki, a place he'd always wanted to see.

It was sixty years since the bombing, to the day. They'd stood in silence with the crowds at the memorial, a simple black monolith. Moved, they'd held hands, walked slowly through the town, still in silence. Then they'd stopped for coffee and doughnuts, and Michiko had texted her friend Yuko in Kyoto, then she'd asked if they could come and see the Gardens.

"Any special reason?" he'd asked.

"No," she'd said. "Just read about the place, is all."

So they'd come here, and queued, and she'd listened to her music. *Same boy you've always known. Love will tear us apart again.*

Now they moved in through the gate and on up a moving, motorised, walkway through the gardens while piped Puccini filled the air. *Un bel di vedremo . . .*

In the house they wandered from room to room, not bothering with a guide. It was unlikely the furnishings were original, but they were of the period — old, heavy, dark polished wood, atmospheric. In the drawing room were mannequin figures of a young Glover plotting with two of the rebel samurai. The figures had the artificial, slightly shabby look of seaside waxworks, Glover looking startled, the samurai apprehensive. Again Michiko laughed, took a picture on her mobile phone to text to Yuko later.

Outside they walked through the garden, read the inscription on the statue of Glover, a bronze, grim-faced bust. Andrew flicked through a leaflet he'd picked up. He knew the bare bones of the Glover story, the myth. The statue faced the house, had its back to the city below, the bay beyond. Andrew half closed his eyes, tried to imagine what the view would have looked like in the 1860s. Much the same, except for the miles of shipyards.

"Fucking ironic," he said, looking out.

"I like when you swear like that," she said. "Very sexy. Very Scottish!"

"Fuck!" he said.

"Ha!"

"But it is. Ironic." He indicated the shipyards opposite. "Fucking Mitsubishi. Glover helped found the company, set all this up. And why did the Americans drop the bomb here? To take out these fucking yards!"

"Bad," she said.

"You're not fucking kidding."

"But doesn't mean he was bad man," she said.

"No?"

"He has nice face. Strong face. Like you."

"It's a statue!"

"But still must look like him," she said. "Is something there."

She handed him the mobile, said, "Take picture."

"I know," he said. "Text it to Yuko!"

She climbed up on the wall beside the statue, smoothed down her miniskirt, kicked her legs in the stripey kneesocks, the red Doc Martens; put one arm round Glover's neck, grinned, gave the peace sign, a two-finger V.

"Yo!!"

He got her in the frame, laughed at her sparky energy, her vibrant irreverence, the cheeky grin a total contrast to the dour bronze features of the statue with its lowering brow. She looked right at him, right into him, in that instant turned him inside out. He took the shot, caught the moment.

She jumped down from the wall, wanted to see the photo, clapped her hands, happy with it.

He kissed her, hard and intense, held her.

"Hey!" she said, laughing again, stroking his cheek, weighing up this new mood, the new thing that was there. She kissed him back, lightly, took his hand and led him on to the other statue, the one she had wanted to see, the figure of the woman, Cho Cho San, Madame Butterfly, with her child, the young boy.

From somewhere came the sound of women's voices, singing, and he thought at first it was another tape, but as the music swelled he realised it was live, a choir of Japanese women. They were lined up in front of the house, all in long skirts and tartan shawls, singing *My bonny lies over the ocean*. Again it was kitsch, bizarre, sentimental, but he found himself absurdly moved by it.

Michiko took a picture of the women, skipped ahead to the statue, stopped and looked up at it. Cho Cho San was in a kimono, hair caught up in traditional style. Her left hand pointed into the distance, across the bay, her right arm was round the boy, protecting him.

Andrew was expecting Michiko to start clowning again, but she was suddenly subdued, serious.

"Photo?" he said, and she looked at him, distracted, from a long way off. Then she brought him into focus, handed him the mobile.

"*Hai*," she said, quietly.

Again he framed her in the tiny screen, but this time there was no smile, no sassy peace sign, no in-your-face harajuku look. Instead she stood, unselfconscious, almost wistful, her head slightly tilted. When he showed her the picture, she glanced at it, looked back at the statue. He saw there were tears in her eyes.

"Hey!" he said. "What's up?"

She waved her hands in front of her face, tried to laugh. "I don't know," she said. "Is very strange."

She fished a packet of tissues from her purse, dabbed her eyes dry, blew her nose hard.

"*Chotto monoganashii*," she said.

She couldn't translate exactly, perhaps because the words had no equivalent.

"Little bit sad," she said. "Don't know. I want to know what happened to her, the woman in the story.

And it give me kind of *déjà vu*, you know, familiar feeling."

And as he looked at her, he suddenly felt it too, the sense of familiarity. He touched her face, recognised her in a way he hadn't before, *knew* her.

Chotto monoganashii. He understood that too, intuited it. A little bit sad, bittersweet. Everything passes, is fleeting. He looked up at the statue, heard the women's voices, the nasal singsong of it not quite in tune. *Bring back my bonny to me.*

What happened to her? The woman in the story.

A good question.

Chotto monoganashii.

He kissed Michiko's soft warm living mouth.

CHAPTER
SEVENTEEN

The Pure Land

Nagasaki, 1912

Sometimes the fire of it came back to her, even in old age, and she remembered her previous life, who she had once been. This too, she realised, must be necessary, to see it clear then let it go. She had written a tanka poem — one of many — about the journey of her life, inscribed it on a scroll with a few deft strokes of the brush.

> Crossed hesitation-bridge
> and decision-bridge,
> passed through
> the floating world
> to the pure land.

Even now, though her hands sometimes shook, the brush-strokes were still firm, strong. Her calligraphy had been praised by master Shinkan himself for its effortless elegance, its fluidity, tempered by a certain roughness that rendered it real, not artificial, not over-refined by intellect. Of course the master had no

460

sooner praised her than he thought it might go to her head, make her arrogant, so he had withdrawn the praise, criticised her brushwork as clumsy and crude, clearly the work of a weak-willed woman.

This too. Let it go.

The floating world.

Her life as Maki Kaga was long past, another incarnation, a dream. And this life too, as the nun Ryonen, would soon be over. She knew it.

This too.

Guraba-san. She thought of him fondly, with compassion. He had even taken to the Japanese version of his name, had it rendered in *kanji* script. Even though the characters meant *empty room*, or *empty store*, he liked the look of it, the sound of the words. It was endearing, and for all his fieriness, his warrior-spirit, he had something of the boy about him.

She remembered it, smiled. He had caught her in his arms, spun her round, laughing.

She bore him a child, Shinsaburo. Her son.

A dream. Let it go.

Existence is suffering. Its cause is desire.

The night she had gone to his house to tell him she was pregnant. The other one had been there, the one he married, Tsuru. She had guessed the whole story, let her believe he was gone for good, sent her packing.

Like an ancient tale, from Kabuki or Noh. One of those moments when her whole life changed, by fate, or karma or pure brute chance. If she had gone a week earlier. If the other had told the truth. Would she still

461

have led this life? Would she have followed the Buddha-way?

Namu Amida Butsu.

The full moon had been red. She had stopped at the end of the garden, bent double and vomited. She had gone to the teahouse and packed her things, moved out of town that very night.

The birth was difficult. *Existence is suffering. Its cause is desire.* She had almost died from loss of blood, had somehow survived. The village women had helped her, nursed her till she was strong enough to look after the boy.

She couldn't return to the teahouse. That life was over. She worked when she could, sewed garments for women from the town, wrote letters for those who could not write. She managed, made do, eked out a living. Not good, not bad. Then she saw him in the street, a ghost, a figure from a dream but so real; and he saw her, and that life too was over.

She would hang the scroll with the tanka poem on the bare wall of her room, leave it as her epitaph, the way the haiku poets made their *jisei*, their death-verse, when they knew their time had come. She would make another copy of it, now, take it with her to the hillside, leave it as an offering.

She sat straightbacked in *zazen*, silent meditation, the way she did every morning, before first light. Cold, old bones aching but mind clear, heart pure, she chanted, as she always did, to Amida Buddha, the Buddha of Compassion, Buddha of the Pure Land, heard her own voice as if not her own, deep and powerful, resonant.

Namu Amida Butsu.

Namu Amida Butsu.

She recited a verse from the Diamond Sutra. *Shiki soku ze ku.* Form is emptiness. She inhabited it, sat in this bare place, a stone garden of the mind.

Perhaps an hour passed, outer time. The first thin rays of watery sunlight came through the shoji screen, across the wooden floor, touched her feet with a faint promise of warmth. She bowed, picked up the small iron bell and struck it once, listened as the sound swelled and died in its own time away into silence once more.

Form is emptiness.

She unfolded her old limbs, joints stiff and cracking, gone beyond ache, become numb.

There was a faint sound on the verandah ouside, the lightest of footsteps shuffling across the boards. She smiled. A tray was set down. The screen opened and Gisho, the young nun, was bowing, had brought her tea. Ryonan nodded, welcomed her in.

She said one morning Gisho would find her like the Bodhidharma, Daruma, who sat so long in meditation his legs withered and fell off. *That* was discipline!

Gisho smiled, her eyes twinkling, said she'd had a Daruma doll at home.

Round at the bottom, said Ryonan, so he rolls. If you knock him over he bounces back up. There's a children's rhyme about it. *Seven times down. Eight times up. So!*

A good lesson.

Gisho boiled the little kettle of water, placed the powdered green leaves in Ryonan's favourite bowl, poured in the water, let the mix settle and brew. Then briskly, with the bamboo whisk, she whipped it to a froth, turned the bowl round one and a half times and offered it to Ryonan, who bowed and thanked her, took a first sip. It was perfect, the bitterness a sharp jolt awake.

This too we owe to Bodhidharma, she said. He once fell asleep in meditation and was so angry at himself he cut off his own eyelids, so his eyes would always stay wide open. He cast the lids to one side, and where they fell, the first tea-plant grew. So, ever after the monks could drink tea, to keep themselves awake!

Again Gisho smiled. She had heard the stories many times, but never tired of them.

Ryonan took another sip, savoured it. In the outside world Gisho had trained in *cha-no-yu*, the art of tea, was in preparation to be a geisha. But there had been complications. Ryonan hadn't wanted to know the details. They probably involved a man. Most stories did.

It was hardest for the pretty ones. They had most to give up. And Gisho reminded her of herself at that age, had the same fire, the same love of life, the same spirit. That might just sustain her. The way was not for the weak. She would be broken and broken again, that spirit crushed. But she might survive, break through. Eight times up.

Ryonan's bowl was empty. She handed it to Gisho, who wiped it, deftly, with a small cloth — this too was part of her training, the formality of the ceremony — refilled it and passed it back once more, commenting on its beauty.

This old thing, said Ryonan. It's nothing special. The glaze is cracked, the surface is chipped and worn.

That's why I like it, said Gisho.

It serves me well, said Ryonan, then she drank the last drops. The tea is perfect. It warms this old heart.

Gisho bowed, pleased.

Since you like this so much, said Ryonan, handing the bowl to her, I would like you to have it. Keep it.

Gisho was caught off-guard, looked genuinely surprised, moved.

Now, said Ryonan. You have other tasks. Go.

She prepared the inkstone, unrolled the scroll of paper, pleased at the simple roughness of its texture, weighed it down with wooden blocks to hold it in place. She took up the bamboo brush, bit the tip and wet it with spittle to soften the bristles. Her teeth ached a little, but no more than the rest of her. These days life was one long ache. Existence was suffering, indeed!

But it was good to be born human, good to be here this autumn morning, good to be following the Buddha-way. Good the autumn breeze coming in through the open screen; good its chill, not yet the stark cold of winter. That would come soon enough.

She could savour a faint aftertaste of Gisho's tea, its bright bitterness, and this too tasted of autumn. She had lit a single incense stick, its fragrance not cloying or sweet, but mellow, resinous, like autumn woodsmoke, like the deep dark scent of the old beams in the meditation hall.

She straightened her back, loaded the brush with ink and made the first stroke.

So.

The opening of the poem was about crossing hesitation-bridge. She let her hand shake a little, imbued the characters with some of the uncertainty the words implied. Hesitation-bridge. *Shian Bashi*.

She took in a sharp breath as the shapes of the words brought it back to her, the actual, physical bridge, her former self, the young Maki Kaga, reluctantly crossing it. So young. *So* young. She felt a stab of pity for her, her heedlessness, her beauty.

She dipped the brush in the ink once more.

On to the next line, the next bridge. Decision-bridge. Certainty. Mind made up. *Omoikiri Bashi*. She rendered it briskly, confidently. And again the very shape of the letters affected her deeply, took her back, and for a moment she *was* that young woman, hurrying across the second bridge, into the pleasure quarter, buoyed up and hopeful that he might visit.

That storm of the flesh, the sheer excitement, the intensity and brightness of it. Even at the time she had known it was fleeting, a dream; but how vivid, how real!

She took more ink, wrote the next line in fluid, eloquent curves. The floating world. *Ukiyo*.

The pleasure quarter as dream of heaven, all fragrance and elegance, the swishing of silks, music and laughter, sheer elegance and refinement, intoxication.

All faded, gone.

She put down her brush as a sudden pain stabbed her gut. She breathed deep, tried to go beyond it. This too would pass.

Namu Amida Butsu.

As young Maki, she had passed through hell. The *gaki*, the hungry ghosts, had howled in her brain, driven out all thought, all hope.

He had gone and taken her son. They'd agreed it was the right thing, a better life for the boy, security, a good home. A life she couldn't give him. It was for the best. But it left her desolate, facing the emptiness, nothing to live for. Nothing.

The voices howled and all she wanted was release, an end of it. The waters closed over her, filled her lungs and she started to move out, beyond the shock of cold, even beyond the struggle for breath, the inrush of the darkness. Then she was back in herself, back in this sack of bones as hands grabbed, dragged her clear into the other element, beat and pressed and pummelled her, back to this life that was all harshness and pain and gasping for air that seared the lungs as she retched and gagged and lay on the riverbank twitching and shivering, spent and half dead.

Then other hands were lifting, carrying her, wrapping her in blankets, keeping her warm. The women of the village, taking over from the men, bore her to the bathhouse, peeled off the wet clothes that clung to her. They soaped and washed her, eased her down into the hot tub. Again she was immersed in water, but this time the warmth of it was healing, restorative, brought her back from the other shore.

She was overwhelmed by the simple human kindness of these women, the sheer functional goodness of it. She cried and felt purged, empty.

The spasm had passed but still she didn't pick up the brush again, sat calm and still, looking at the unfinished poem. The last line was the most important, the final statement, answer to the mystery; journey's end. The calligraphy had to be perfect.

The women had looked out for her, brought her small amounts of food, rice gruel, vegetables in broth. She survived, got through it day by day. She couldn't call it living; she existed, mind numb, body weak. She shook sometimes, shivered. She had half-drowned; she was still racked by coughing as if trying to expel the water that had filled her lungs to bursting. Cold mornings were the worst, and waking in the night, panicked and trying to gulp in air. Sometimes she thought perhaps she really had drowned, was dead, and this state was some grey afterlife, a realm of ghosts, and she herself one of them.

One morning, early, in the grey halflight, she dressed and set out walking, mindless, no idea where. She found herself on a bridge over the river, stared down at water flowing past. At moments she could see her own reflection, not clear, broken over and over by the ripples on the surface, but there, definitely there, even if only glimpsed. Ghosts cast no reflection. So she was no ghost. Then came another sensation, eerie, as if what she looked down at was her old self, Maki, still struggling under the water, still drowning, looking up to her for help.

She stumbled off the bridge, onto the other side, continued walking down a narrow road out of town. The sky was beginning to lighten, the birds were starting their sharp cacophony, shrieking their need. She had not eaten, still had no idea where she was going. Then she tensed as she saw a dark figure approaching, a man, walking slowly. She thought of turning and running away, finding somewhere to hide. But she was too tired, her legs suddenly heavy, leaden. She stopped, waited, and as she stood there she saw the man was a monk, in black robes, his head shaved.

The monk also stopped, bowed to her, held out his begging bowl.

I have nothing, she said.

Well then, he said, give me your nothing, and he turned and walked on.

She felt as if she had been struck, a sharp blow that knocked the wind out of her.

He stopped and called back to her. Well? Are you coming or going?

Without thinking, mind empty, she dragged herself, stumbled and ran to catch him up.

★ ★ ★

The whole way to the temple, the monk spoke no word to her, just walked ahead, expected her to follow. Only in the way the other monks greeted him, their deference verging on fear, did she realise he was the master, Shinkan.

He gave her no instruction, handed her over to a young nun who showed her the room where she would stay. It was tiny and dusty and draughty, tatami mats worn and frayed, shoji screens ripped. There were cobwebs in the corners, birdshit and mouse-droppings on the floor. She turned to leave but found she couldn't move, couldn't force herself to take one single step. The young nun had left her alone, now she reappeared with brooms and dusters, cleaning cloths and a bucket of water, nodded and rolled up her sleeves. At least this much she understood. When they'd cleaned up the room, the nun disappeared again, came back with scraps of tatami matting, odd pieces of shoji paper, a few simple tools.

They broke for food, a few minutes only, ate rice and pickles, a thin watery soup. By mid-afternoon they had done running repairs to the room, made it at least habitable. She felt a ridiculous sense of satisfaction, smiled at the nun and stepped outside.

The master was passing and she wanted to tell him how hard she had worked, cleaning and patching up the room, how she didn't really know why she was here but was willing to stay and work for her keep.

He listened, nodded, said the first meditation session was at 3 a.m.

There were four nuns, who lived in a separate corner of the compound, and twenty monks. They did not mix, except in the meditation sessions, zazen, the long hours of sitting, and at mealtimes when they all sat in silence, ate their meagre rations, stared straight ahead. But right from the first day she noticed one or two of the monks glancing in her direction in that way she recognised, that grubby, furtive longing that was all the worse for being hidden.

Again she tried to speak to the master, asked him why she was here.

That is for you to ask yourself, he said. And the way to ask it is by sitting, and the way to answer it is by sitting some more, until there are no questions and nobody asking them, no striving after non-answers. It is hard work. Now, get on with it.

She blazed with irritation at that, and the anger carried her through most of a session, made her almost forget the pain in her back, her knees and ankles, her very bones. Then, when the pain demanded attention and she shifted her position, the master was standing behind her with a long flat wooden lath in his hand. She had seen this, knew what to expect. She bent forward, tensed, and the master struck her across the back, eight times, *whack*, each blow sharp and quick but stinging. Then the master bowed and she bowed in return, ostensibly to show her gratitude for his concern, though in reality to keep her rage in check. The master's faint half-smile showed he saw this, then he nodded, grimfaced again, told her to continue.

Every nerve in her was screaming to leave, to run out. Nothing was stopping her. The gate was open. She sat on.

The second week she shaved her head. Her thick locks, lacquer-black, lay coiled in clumps on the floor. Her pate was bald, stubbly to the touch when she ran her hand over it. Her scalp stung here and there, nicked by the razor. She was glad she had no mirror to see how she looked. But the morning breeze felt cool.

Now at least the monks would stop looking at her in that way, burning her with their eyes.

No.

One night a note was slipped under her door. It was from one of the monks, declared his love for her, asked her to give him a sign and he would come to her the next night. It was unsigned, ended with a tanka poem.

> Shifting and turning
> the long cold night,
> thinking, thinking
> of nothing
> but you.

At the end of the early morning zazen, she bowed to the master, asked if she could read something out. He looked surprised, but nodded permission. She uncrumpled the piece of paper, read the whole note, the poem, then she ran her gaze along the row of monks, said if the author of the note really did love her, he should step forward and embrace her now.

472

For a moment the silence deepened, then there was a gruff clearing of throats. One of the younger monks stifled a laugh, composed himself immediately.

She crunched the piece of paper once more into a ball, recited a tanka poem she had made herself, in response.

> The long cold night,
> thinking of nothing,
> nothing at all.
> My shaved head is rough
> and stubbly to the touch.

The master grunted, told her to pour the tea for the monks. None of them looked her in the eye.

It continued. In spite of her shaved head, her drab robes, her intensity, every new monk who arrived at the temple seemed to fall in love with her, as if she still carried the fragrance and allure of the floating world. Even one or two of the older monks, toothless ascetics, looked at her with longing, made her uncomfortable. A visiting abbot from a temple in Kyoto was delivering a sermon on impermanence, the transience and illusoriness of the world. He caught her eye, stuttered, hesitated, lost his thread; then he blustered through with references to the sutra of Hui Neng, concluded with a commentary on the fleeting nature of beauty and hurried from the hall.

She asked for an audience with the master. He made her wait a week then granted her request.

473

When she entered his room he was seated with his back to her, intent on the scripture he was reading. He ignored her, made her wait. She sat, in silence. At last he spoke, still without turning round.

Why did Bodhidharma come from the West?

She said nothing. She was flummoxed. This was not what she had expected.

Don't worry, he said. I'm not expecting an answer. But you know of Bodhidharma?

Yes, she said, I know some of the stories.

There are many stories, he said. Children's tales for the most part. But they do embody some teaching.

I'm sure, she said.

You know he is supposed to have cut off his own eyelids?

And tea-plants grew from them.

Yes.

He turned for the first time since she'd come into the room. He held in his hand an open razor, its blade glinting in the light from the candle on his shrine. He placed the razor in front of her.

There is a saying that the way of truth is narrower than the razor's edge.

She kept silent, looked at the blade, imagined its sharpness.

Have you heard the story of the nun Ryonan?

No, she said.

She was a rare beauty, he said. She was descended from a famous warrior, Shingen, and inherited some of his spirit. With her beauty and refinement she was a favourite at the court of the Empress. But when the

474

Empress died, she saw how fleeting was human life. Her youth and beauty would fade; she resolved to turn her back on the world and study Zen. Unfortunately her family had other ideas. They forced her into marriage, but agreed that she could become a nun after she had borne three children. She did their bidding, bore the children; then she shaved her head and went to a Zen temple. However, the master would not accept her. He said she was too beautiful, even with her head shaved and in her nun's garb.

She went to another master, the story was the same. She travelled the country and everywhere met with the same rejection. Her beauty was a curse.

Maki felt a coldness like stone chill her belly. The master continued his story.

At last she came to the master Hakuo, in Edo. Like all the rest, he turned her away. She was far too beautiful. Her good looks would only cause trouble. So she went to the kitchen, got a red-hot poker, and held it to her face.

Maki flinched.

The master waited a moment, went on.

She burned herself badly. The scars would mar her looks forever. She went back to Hakuo, who took one look and said, Fine, you can stay.

Maki was shaking. She felt tears choke her, felt misery and hopelessness and rage.

The master said, She took on the name Ryonan, which means Clear Realisation. She wrote of her experience in a poem, in the tanka form which you yourself favour.

475

> In the Empress's palace
> I burned incense
> to perfume my clothes.
> Now I burn my face
> to enter the Zen temple.

The master left a silence, then he pushed the open razor closer to Maki.

Well? he said.

Time passed. She heard the wind in the trees, felt a thin trickle of sweat down her back. The shaking stopped. Her mind was clear and cold, awareness centred on her own breath, her heartbeat. She could still leave at any time. The gate was still open. Nothing was forcing her to stay.

She reached forward and picked up the razor, held it out. One sharp gash should be enough to slice the flesh, leave a scar. She braced herself.

Namu Amida Butsu.

She closed her eyes, struck. But before the blade could reach her face, she felt her wrist gripped hard.

The master had grabbed it, eased the razor from her grasp.

You are strong, he said. With this kind of determination you can succeed. You must not be deflected from your purpose by these foolish men and their unwelcome attentions. The problem is theirs, not yours.

And he gave her the name Ryonan, said, May your realisation be clear.

★   ★   ★

476

It all seemed so long ago, a lifetime. But the memory of it was vivid, intense. She remembered exactly how it felt, the panic, then the detachment, the actual feel of the razor in her hand.

She had once asked the master, years later, What if you had not caught my hand? What if I had slashed myself, even cut my own throat?

He had answered roughly, There is no *What if?* There is only what happens, what *is*.

But from that day on, the day she became Ryonan, it had changed. It was as if she *had* scarred herself, carried the mark. Her gaze turned inward. The look on her face was calmness and strength. In itself it was protection from the monks, withered their ardour, made them think twice.

The thought of it now made her smile. Poor foolish men, trying to douse that fire, or channel it into their meditation.

Existence is suffering. Its cause is desire.

Right up till the last moment, before liberation, before realisation, the dragon could still rear up, still roar.

Her smile became a chuckle. Even this morning, when she'd thought with compassion about Guraba-san, she had seen him clearly, the golden young man he had been. And that tenderness, that fondness, had allowed a faint memory, a stirring, even in this old flesh. She might tell young Gisho, if she thought it would not be discouraging!

It was as well she had no mirror to look at. The face that looked back at her would be the face of an old crone, wrinkled and gaunt, a leathery old lizard. It was years since she had seen her reflection, except for the odd glimpse in passing, crossing the river and glancing down, seeing it there, still broken and broken, unclear.

The last time she had seen an actual mirror, she had been in middle age. At the master's suggestion, she had gone beyond the village to the town, to beg from door to door, chanting as she went.

I go to the Buddha for refuge. I go to the order for refuge. I go to the dharma for refuge.

At one house an old woman had bowed, invited her in. She had left her geta, her wooden sandals, at the door, stepped inside and stood waiting in the cool hall.

The sounds and scents of domesticity came to her. The smoky sesame and ginger smell of noodles cooking in hot oil; the shrill singsong voices of children playing. The old woman's grandchildren, life continuing, living itself, from generation to generation.

She took off her old straw kasa that was hat and umbrella to her, shelter and shade, protected her whatever the season.

Basho had written a haiku.

> When I think it is my own
> snow on my kasa
> it feels light.

She smiled at that, looked up and saw another nun, older than herself, face weathered, smiling back at her. She was startled, hadn't noticed her. She bowed, and the other did the same. She put a hand to her face, and so did the other. Then she realised, it was a looking-glass. This was her face as the world saw it, the face of a stranger, and yet . . .

The struggle was there, the years of hardship, in the lines around the mouth, on the forehead. But something shone in the eyes, an inner light, a clarity; it had more beauty in its way than young Maki's easy charm, though it had even been part of that. In behind the young woman's mask, it had been there all along.

She bowed to this other, this reflection, herself.

Namu Amida Butsu.

The old woman of the house came out, gave her some rice, a few coins.

She bowed, offered gratitude, put on her kasa and her sandals, walked on.

It was later that same day that she saw him, tall, unmistakable, walking on the other side of the road. His hair, his whiskers, had started to grey, but he still looked handsome, had grown distinguished. The woman walking behind him must be Tsuru, older, heavier, and behind her was the boy. She felt a sharp little intake of breath, a sudden stab to the heart.

Guraba-san glanced across at her. Was there something, a moment in the eyes? A flicker? Recognition? Remembrance? He doffed his hat with a touching politeness, a gentlemanliness, that tugged at her. Tsuru looked right through her, saw nothing and nobody, an ageing nun, a shabby mendicant. The boy stopped, crossed the road towards her. A young man almost, in a school uniform, dark military tunic buttoned up to the neck. He peered through round-framed glasses, looked at her, looked into her. His hair was darker than it had been, but still light brown, halfway to fair. She almost broke as he reached out his hand, and she realised he was offering alms. Her own hand shook as she held out the begging bowl and he dropped in a single silver coin, bowed.

She bowed deeply, thanked him, invoked the blessings of Buddha Amitaba on his head.

Tsuru called out to him. Tomisaburo. The name they had given him to sound like his father's. Tom Glover. Tomi Guraba.

Her son, Shinsaburo. But no longer hers. In reality, never had been. Not Guraba's either, or Tsuru's. How could anyone own another? This young man was living the life he had to, following his karma, as they all followed theirs.

The family group headed on up Minami Yamate to their home. Ryonan took the coin from her bowl, kissed it. For the first time since she'd taken her vows, there were tears in her eyes.

She had kept the coin, turned it now in her wrinkled hand. She would give it to Gisho, along with her few other meagre possessions. She would take nothing with her.

She had already given Gisho her tea-bowl, seen the momentary flutter of alarm in the girl's eyes, the apprehension, the half-knowing fear of what the gift might mean.

She had said often enough she would be like the nun Eshun. When it's my time, she said to Gisho, I'll tell you, and I'll go.

Eshun had reached the age of sixty, announced she was leaving the world. She had a funeral pyre built, then sat crosslegged in the middle of it, had it set alight.

As the flames rose, a monk shouted in to her, Is it hot in there?

She shouted back, What a stupid question! And she died, and burned.

When it's my time, I'll tell you, and I'll go.

The look in Gisho's eyes.

It was time.

She turned her attention once more to the scroll with her unfinished calligraphy, the tanka poem.

The great master Genshin had described the Pure Land as absolute perfection, said the way to attain its bliss was by chanting the name of Amida, the Buddha of compassion.

Namu Amida Butsu.

Once again she loaded the tip of the brush with ink, wrote the character with a single, confident flourish.

Jodo. Pure Land.

There.

It was done, complete.

She laid down the brush, rang the iron bell to summon Gisho, tell her.

The two headstones stood side by side, a few feet apart, in the Sakamoto Cemetery. The one on the left was taller, narrower, carved with Japanese script. *Tsuru*

481

Glover. 1850–1899. Ryonan knew enough of English notation, its alphabet, to read the inscription on the other stone. *Thomas Blake Glover.* 1838–1911.

A visitor to the monastery had told her the year before, had read an account in the newspaper. Guraba-san, the visitor said, had been a great man, one of the founders of modern Japan. He had died in Tokyo after a long illness, been cremated, the ashes brought back to Nagasaki and buried here. The casket had been carried in procession through the town, led by his son, Tomisaburo. Many dignitaries had attended, including some who had travelled all the way from Tokyo.

Ryonan had thanked the visitor, vowed to come here and pay her last respects when the time came.

She bowed to Glover's gravestone, asked the blessings of Amida Buddha to guide him on his continuing journey. Then she bowed to Tsuru's grave, wished the same for her, that she too in her turn might receive the Buddha's blessings.

Acceptance. Forgiveness. May all sentient beings become enlightened.

Namu Amida Butsu.

She took the rolled-up scroll from her sleeve, read once more her final tanka poem, her *jisei*, nodded approval at the calligraphy.

> Crossed hesitation-bridge
> and decision-bridge,
> passed through
> the floating world
> to the pure land.

A few simple offerings had been left in front of the graves; a sake flask, a holder for sticks of incense, a handful of flowers in an earthenware jar. She placed the scroll beside them, bowed, moved on.

According to Genshin, she had read, all the pleasures and glory of the world are as nothing, a drop in the ocean, compared to the beauty and delight of the Pure Land. The Land itself is made of emerald, and in each of its precincts are millions of temples, pagodas of silver and gold. In the gardens are silver ponds, covered with lotus blossoms that sparkle in myriad colours. Birds of every description hover in the air, singing, and above them soar the sweet-voiced *Kalavinka*, winged beings with the faces of beautiful women. Crystal streams and rivers flow sparkling across the landscape, bordered by sacred trees. The trees have silver stems and golden branches and blossoms of coral and pearl. From the trees hang jewelled cords, each attached to a sacred bell, ringing out the message of the Supreme Law. The air is filled with intoxicating fragrance, the sweetness of flowers, the richness of incense. The sky never darkens, shines with endless light, and petals eternally rain down. Sweet music constantly flows, from nameless musical instruments that play themselves, without being touched, and celestial beings endlessly sing in praise of Tathagata Buddha.

She stopped for breath halfway up the hill, near Ipponmatsu where her son might still be living. She wished him well. May he one day attain enlightenment. She carried on up the slope.

483

The going was hard, and she sweated in spite of the autumn cool. The old shrine at the top of the hill had fallen into disuse, lay abandoned, a ruin. A good place for her to sit and rest her old bones.

She leaned against a stone wall, sheltered, warmed a little by the late afternoon sun. From here she could see the city spread out below. Near Ipponmatsu were a few other western houses, a settlement. She looked beyond them, past the pleasure quarter, down to the harbour, Dejima Island. She had looked out at this with Guraba-san, a lifetime ago.

Things changed, did not change. Now there were the docks and the factories, the shipyards, but beyond all that, the hills across the bay, swathed in the rich red of the maple trees in their full autumn glory.

This.

Somewhere in the distance, hidden from view, was the temple where she'd lived through all these years of struggle, striving to be true to the Buddha-way.

This too.

A dream.

Carrying on the air she heard the harsh rasping cry of a cicada. Soon its day would be done, just its dried-up husk remain. Cutting across it came the cry of a shrike, piercing and melancholy, and beating across the sky came a flight of wild geese, a straggled line, rehearsing their departure.

She caught the scent of woodsmoke, and she breathed it in, bittersweet incense, sat up and focused her gaze.

484

Genshin had written that the power of concentration, awakened imagination, can lead directly to the Pure Land. Focus on a single lotus flower can open out to infinity, beyond all horizons. He spoke of meditation on the lotus seat in which the Buddha sits, the lotus of the heart.

Up here there were no lotuses blooming, only a scraggy chrysanthemum hugging the wall, a scatter of morning-glories.

She smiled at them and they nodded, acknowledging her gaze.

She slowed her breathing, felt it come and go of itself.

The lotus of the heart. She felt it open, petal by petal.

The jewel in the lotus.

Om.

The city sparkled beneath her. This place. This time. The Pure Land.

One day it would all be dust again. Civilisations came and went, rose and fell. Tathagata breathed in, breathed out.

Form is emptiness.

She sat as the light began to fade and the evening grew chill. But nothing touched her. She had gone beyond it all.